P9-EFJ-027

Outstanding praise for the novels of Roz Bailey!

RETAIL THERAPY

"If readers thought Becky Bloomwood of *Shopaholic* fame was bad, wait until they meet Alana Marshall-Hughs . . . The author of *Party Girls* and *Girls' Night Out* again delivers a lighthearted, entertaining comedy."—*Booklist*

"A pleasant, easy read, enlivened by fast-paced storytelling."
—*Romantic Times*

GIRLS' NIGHT OUT

"Even better than her first outing, Bailey's second novel is delightful and impossible to put down."—*Booklist*

PARTY GIRLS

"Roz Bailey's trio of fabulous 30-something Manhattanites are still the eponymous party girls in this *Sex and the City*-style urban romp."—*Publishers Weekly*

"Bailey's tale is snazzy, fun, and filled with likable characters worth rooting for."—*Booklist*

"An invigorating story, filled with dynamic, appealing characters . . . Highly recommended, *Party Girls* is a thoroughly satisfying read."—*Romantic Times*

Books by Roz Bailey

Party Girls

Girls' Night Out

Retail Therapy

Postcards From Last Summer

Published by Kensington Publishing Corp.

Postcards From Last Summer

ROZ BAILEY

KENSINGTON BOOKS
www.kensingtonbooks.com

KENSINGTON BOOKS are published by

Kensington Publishing Corp.
850 Third Avenue
New York, NY 10022

Copyright © 2006 by Roz Bailey

All rights reserved. No part of this book may be reproduced in any form or by any means without the prior written consent of the Publisher, excepting brief quotes used in reviews.

All Kensington titles, imprints and distributed lines are available at special quantity discounts for bulk purchases for sales promotion, premiums, fund raising, educational or institutional use.

Special book excerpts or customized printings can also be created to fit specific needs. For details write or phone the office of the Kensington Special Sales Manager: Kensington Publishing Corp., 850 Third Avenue, New York, NY 10022. Attn. Special Sales Department. Phone: 1-800-221-2647.

Kensington and the K logo Reg. U.S. Pat. & TM Off.

ISBN 0-7582-0567-8

First Kensington Trade Paperback Printing: August 2006
10 9 8 7 6 5 4 3 2 1

Printed in the United States of America

This one is for my beachcombing family,
distant stars that converge each summer on sandy shores.
Whether on the ever-changing shoreline
of Cannon Beach, Torch Lake, Bethany Beach,
Rodanthe, Deep Creek Lake or St. Thomas,
the old songs are still the same
and the company just keeps getting better.

Acknowledgments

Many thanks to my brother, Jack Noonan, the windsurfing engineer, for his accurate and comical surfing tips. Special thanks to Nancy Bush for reading over trouble spots and to Lisa Jackson for her guidance on all things promotional, and to both sisters for their constant support. My editor, John Scognamiglio, is the most patient, savvy man in the publishing industry and I thank my lucky stars for him every day. And finally, a shout to my kids who succumbed to way too many meals of peanut-butter toast and yogurt while I was finishing this manuscript.

Prologue

An August afternoon in Southampton, 2006

Why am I here?

I press my hands to my cheeks, feeling very much like the psycho man in that Edvard Munch painting *The Scream*. Really, what the hell am I doing here in the middle of all these acutely fashion-conscious people in designer heels and Botox-enhanced faces and skinny camisole tops with skinnier straps over their air-brushed tans? Handsome young waiters, their bronze skin a stark contrast to their crisp white shirts, circulate through the crowd dispensing trays of lemon drops and smiles. This is the Hamptons I'd spent my childhood competing with: the other side of the dunes, where the rich kids crash their parents' Jags and down fifths of Dewar's on the beach as they lament over piddly problems.

Certainly not what my grandparents envisioned when they settled here, my grandfather serving as town doc to the local shopkeepers and hunters, farmers, clammers, and fishermen. They came to love the isolation of the east end of Long Island, its substantial distance from New York City, beyond the reach of expressways. Feeling more simpatico with New England to the north, Grammy and Grandad lobbied for this area to secede from Suffolk County and form their own Peconic County.

What would Grammy think of this McMansion of a building set on a bluff overlooking the beach, its neat green-and-white striped awnings and etched glass windows shrieking "look at me!"?

How Grandad would crow over the expanse of green lawn, the "unnatural" appearance of grass in an ocean setting, the conspicuous consumption of it all. And Ma . . . she'd really sink her teeth into all this juicy "hoopla" over her daughter. My mother would have been quite at ease here, but I am freaking quietly inside.

What am I doing here?

I am sitting at a table stacked with dozens of copies of my book, ready for purchase and personalized autograph, as if any of these people care. The lemon yellow cover tugs at my heartstrings, as I've poured so much of myself into this piece and hate to see it so on display, so vulnerable and neglected. It's titled *Greetings from Bikini Beach*, and the cover features a simple black string bikini, an image I have always loved until this moment when I look down and see it taking the shape of a face, the bikini bottom smiling back at me.

God help me, it's alive. If one strap slipped, the damned cover would be winking at me.

"Could you sign this for Carole with an *e*?" A woman hands me a book. Her blond hair is pulled back in a twist, emphasizing her cheekbones. Huge cheekbones. She could be hiding golf balls in there.

"Sure," I say effusively, worried about my cover. "Are you Carole?"

"No, it's for my friend. She likes this kind of book."

Liar. I wonder what kind of book that might be . . . perhaps novels with winking bikinis on the cover?

"Where's the guest of honor?" a cranky female voice demands. "I'm looking for the guest of honor!"

Oh, God, that's me, but she sounds so imperious I don't dare look up from the book I am signing for Carole, with an *e*. Not that I'd be able to get away from Carole, the crystal-eyed woman murmuring under her breath as she waits for an autograph. Her eyes are so blue, I wonder if it's those colored contacts or worse . . . transplants. Are they doing eye transplants yet? Pick your eye color; choose classic baby blues or rare, exotic purple. "Do I have stories to tell you," she prattles. "My boyfriend is the bouncer in a private club, and the things that go on there . . . You could write another book, maybe two."

"I'll bet."

"Really, I'll have to take you there sometime. It's a sex club."

"Really?" I try to keep that squeaky squirrel quality out of my voice. About to hit my thirties and having published a book, I shouldn't sound like a five-year-old anymore, but I do. And I'm sure the big, round belly of baby bumping into the table isn't helping me look like a worldly, sexy sophisticate. As I try to sign the book, the pen seems to be running out of ink, and this is a woman who'd probably be a complainer if the signature is too light or not loopy enough. "We'll have to catch up on stories someday." I say this hoping it will never happen, of course. Although the woman looks familiar—one of Elle's neighbors? A clerk in a Hamptons store?—I don't think we'll ever get together and chat, but I don't know how to tell her that I've got a bazillion stories swirling in my inadequate brain and a significant lack of organization and time to write them all down.

"Where's the guest of honor?" the woman with the cranky voice demands, and I see her pausing beside a giant bin of pansies, a remarkably petite little thing for such a big voice. A waiter points her over to me as the next person in line slides her book over.

"You're not at all what I expected," Carole tells me, her eyes mysterious marbles behind a thicket of moussed bangs. "I mean, you're so much older than I thought. And, well, look at you . . ."

We both look down at me, at the bulk I had thought the table hid fairly well. "I'm not thirty yet," I tell her. "Not quite." My upcoming birthday would slam me into that new decade.

Mrs. Cranky pushes ahead, shouldering the woman out of her way with a linen suit so crisp it could cut the brie on the cheese platter. "Are you Lindsay McCorkle, the guest of honor?" She tips her head down so that she can spy me over the wide lenses of her sunglasses. "I just had to introduce myself—Esther Lefkowitz, lifetime Hamptons resident. When I heard about your book I knew you'd want to meet me, since I know everyone and everything in the Hamptons."

"How wonderful for you," I say, confused. The book is written, and since it's fiction I didn't exactly interview people for research.

"Yes, I'm fourth-generation Southamptonite. My grandfather was a trapper, back in the days when folks knew the only good beaver was a dead one." She folds her arms across her black and red print smock. "So go on, ask me anything about the Hamptons . . . I know it all."

"Um . . . actually, I'm working on my next book, which is set in Seattle, and I've already switched gears."

"Did you know Tony Curtis used to vacation here? Marilyn Monroe and Arthur Miller honeymooned in Amagansett. And let me tell you, I've met all the big ones. Donna Karan, the famous fashion designer. JFK Jr.—such a pity about that boy, and thank God Jackie didn't live to see it! I've rubbed elbows with Bianca Jagger and Andy Warhol. And Lorne Michaels and that Chevy Chase fella. I know which house belongs to Jerry Seinfeld and which one used to belong to Billy and Christie. Oh, and Sarah Jessica . . . such a doll, and the manners on that girl!"

"That's quite a gallery of celebrities." I nod, realizing there's no one else in line and I'm stuck with Esther, at least for the moment. Unless of course one of my friends arrives and saves me. What are the chances of that? My husband is here, but I doubt that he'll make any rescue attempts—my best friend is known for choosing the path of least resistance. "Esther, would you like me to sign a book?"

"No, thank you, dear. I'll pick up a copy at the library." She knocks on the cover with her tiny fist. "I've already got you on order."

"Thanks. I'm flattered."

"And such a fancy-pants party. You must be very important to your publisher."

I am tempted to tell her that my publisher isn't even here and the party is being paid for by one of my old friends who's been hung up in Paris and can't even be here, but I'm feeling deflated enough as it is.

"Thank you, young man," Esther says, stealing a V-shaped lemon drop from a passing waiter's tray. She slugs back the drink, blinking. "I'd offer you one, toots, but I see you're in no condition. So . . . did you ever think you'd become a big, hotshot writer, getting paid for your autograph?"

"The autographs are free; it's the book that'll cost you."

"Very good." She finishes her drink and nods like a bobblehead. "So go on, don't be shy. Ask me about anyone. If they've come to the Hamptons, I've met them."

I mention a television star, and Esther rolls her eyes. "Couldn't come up with anyone more challenging? Let me tell you about Penny . . ."

As she begins to recollect the many times she'd met Penny, my eyes wander to the near horizon, the beach below our grassy bluff, where a handful of kids kneel in the sand. The skinny girls bent over, digging in the sand, probably for sand crabs or seashells, remind me so much of my friends and myself, some twenty years ago. Most of us were eight when we met—goofy third graders who enjoyed riding bikes, having bubblegum bubble-blowing contests, and staying up late to watch *Saturday Night Live*. Even at age eight, our personalities were well formed. There was Darcy the Queen Bee; Tara, the noble voice of jurisprudence; Elle, the brilliant eccentric. And me? I guess I was always the sucking-up peacemaker, the great facilitator.

As I watch, one of the scrawny girls slings a bucket of water on her friend, who shrieks and leaps to her feet to chase her friend and wrestle her to the ground.

I smile, recalling the first year the four of us were together . . .

We have been digging in the sand all afternoon, answering to Darcy's orders to build an elegant sand castle with perfect, conical towers, a moat, and a precise trim of uniform shells. The castle is nearly finished when Elle argues with the design, deciding that the seashell trim is overdone. She begins to remove clamshells, which sends Darcy into a rage.

"No, no, no!" Darcy stomps around the castle and gets right into Elle's face. "Don't touch those shells. Are you crazy?"

Elle's green eyes flame, her nostrils flare. In one quick move she hoists a bucket of water and slaps it onto Darcy.

Darcy whirls around, her blue eyes snapping with fury. "Fuck!"

Tara freezes as Darcy mouths the forbidden word. I shoot a nervous look at the sunbathers around us, wondering if any of the adults have noticed, especially nosey Ms. Janice Olsen, who loves to catch us doing something wrong.

Fortunately, Ms. Olsen is walking Nipsy down the beach by the jetty.

Only Elle is unscathed, laughter bubbling out of her as she rolls back in the sand, unable to contain her joy at having dissed Darcy, who is now on her feet and crossing to Elle's towel, which she uses to blot off most of the water and sand. When Darcy pulls the towel away from her shoulders, she is model perfect once again. You'd never know she was wet, except that the material covering her boobs (perfect ones, that grew last winter) is a slightly darker shade of hot pink. Only eleven and already she's on her way to having all the stuff the boys want.

"Don't you ever, ever do that again!" Darcy shrieks in a voice so stern I sense the sand crabs burrowing deeper in the sand . . .

Now, watching as one of the skinny girls stomps off the beach, I sigh. It's a wonder that Tara, Darcy, Elle, and I are still friends. Then again . . . here I am at my big pompous book signing in the Hamptons—the party Darcy insisted on—and where are they?

"Who else?" Esther prods, tinkling her fingers at a waiter with a tray of drinks. "Who else would you like to know about?"

I tap my chin, wondering if the number 15 sunblock will be enough to keep my skin from burning. It's supposed to be particularly bad to get a sunburn when you're pregnant, though I cannot remember the details on why that is so in my Esther-induced glaze. "How about Darcy Love. Have you ever met her?"

She accepts another lemon drop and holds it high with flair, as if to say: Ole! "Do you mean Darcy Love the actress?"

Is there more than one? "That's the one," I say, opening my eyes wide. "What do you hear about her?"

"She's a hot one now, isn't she?" Esther puts her drink down on one of my books and makes a show of adjusting the rings on her fingers—sapphires and amethysts, like jewels from the sea. Cocktail rings, my ma used to call them. "I happen to have attended a party here, when this place was the Love Mansion." She nods toward the house looming behind me. "Of course, back then Darcy Love's parents were players in the Hamptons. The money they threw around! It was appalling, but not so bad if it was getting thrown on you."

"Esther," I say, intrigued. "Were you a player, too?"

She presses her palm to her cleavage, her rings sparkling in the sun. "Esther Lefkowitz. I write the Beach Buzz column for the *Hamptons Register*."

I blink. "A reporter?"

"A gossip columnist," she says. "And over the years, I must admit, my columns have gotten a few boosts from the activities of the Love family. But now Darcy . . ." She sighs. "She's become quite the phoenix, hasn't she? From the ashes rising? We all love a good redemption story."

"Esther," I pretend to be dumbfounded, "it sounds like you've read my book already!"

Esther snorts. "No, dear, but I can tell you a thing or two about Darcy Love. The girl spent every summer here. Let me tell you . . ."

PART ONE

One Big Sorority Bash

Summer 1997

1

Lindsay

My friends tell me I'm always the narrator of their lives, the person who helps them decipher their feelings and attach meaning to life events. If that's true, I guess I have to start with Darcy Love in the summer of 1997, a hot day for May, and it was shaping up to be the last day of our friendship.

The minute she emerged from the path between the dunes, her golden hair blowing in the offshore breeze, I knew there was going to be trouble. Darcy was twenty-one, slim, wealthy, and gorgeous, and she knew it. I had decided to be her friend years ago, when she was eight and I was seven. Back then, we'd both been slim. Even last year, I was passably fit. Now, unfortunately, I wasn't, but I was working on that. So what if I didn't have the kind of svelte body that Darcy owned with such entitlement? I'd spent the winter working on my mind, dammit. If I had to spend the summer surfing in these swim trunks borrowed from my brother and this old Billabong surf shirt, it was still okay, right?

The scowl that pinched Darcy's face immediately let me know that it wasn't okay with her. Strike one.

I solemnly wished that I could fast-forward a year or two. A sad thing, to want to skip the year of your twentieth summer, but I had a strong suspicion my big fat self wasn't going to make it into Darcy's posse this year. Darcy had always warned us that she'd "divorce" anyone who blimped out, and during a rather intense junior year at college, aliens from the planet Chunky Monkey had kidnapped me, Lindsay McCorkle, and dropped my slender surfer's body into a hideous fat suit. Somehow, while I was exercising my mind, pursuing Jungian theory and the juicy atrocities of abnormal psych, my body had fallen into disrepair.

"Holy crap!" Darcy cursed, good Catholic girl that she was. "What happened to you?"

I pulled the wet surf shirt away from my tummy, trying to distort my overall shape. This was the reason I hadn't called Darcy or Tara when I arrived last week. I'd decided to play it under the radar, but necessity had forced me into her sights this morning.

"I mean, I heard you put on a few pounds but, whoa, girl," Darcy pushed on. "Time to drive past the drive-thru."

"Thanks for sharing, but I didn't call you in to be my personal trainer," I said, trying not to reveal that she'd stung me anyway. I pointed down the beach, to where Kevin McGowan, the love of Darcy's life, lay in a drunken heap. She nearly yelped when she spotted him there. "The lifeguards are going to call the police if he's not out of here in ten minutes," I told her.

"Oh, poor Kevin!" She pressed a fist to her glossed lips and began marching down the beach toward him. "Is he okay?" she yelled back over her shoulder. "Did anyone even check? Maybe he's sick."

Against my better judgment, I followed her. "He's drunk, Darcy. Or stoned. And he's scaring people away from Bikini Beach."

"Maybe he just fell and hit his head or something," she said hopefully.

"He was here with Fish." Fenwick "Fish" Peters, local pothead, was Kevin's sidekick, supplier, and enabler. "Fish left when the lifeguards mentioned calling the police."

"That is just so wrong," Darcy said. "This is parkland. A free beach. Kevin should be able to take a nap, just like anybody else."

"A nap?" I stopped walking, not wanting to get any closer to Kevin, a nasty drunk. Darcy and I had been down the road of denial before. She refused to accept that the boy she had some twisted attraction to had an addictive personality. "What's wrong is that your boyfriend, who's so blown out of his shorts he can't even stand, is freaking out little kids and families."

She froze, then turned to glare at me. "Well, isn't that just the voice of compassion from the psych major? How can you talk that way about my boyfriend? You never did like him, did you?"

Strike two—I couldn't stand the love of her life. In my book, Kevin McGowan was a soulless, spineless creature, a scavenger bird, circling until he could swoop down on the next feeding frenzy. Aside from the fact that his father owned Coney's, one of the coolest hangouts in the Hamptons, I didn't understand the attraction at all.

"You know what I think?" she said when I didn't answer. "I think you're just jealous of Kevin. Jealous that he's *my* boyfriend."

In her dreams. Darcy had been sniffing after Kevin McGowan since she was ten years old, the day we came across Kevin in his cutoff denim shorts trying to float down the beach in an apple crate. Not even in a trainer bra yet, and Darcy had begun plotting and scheming ways to win over the smiley, freckle-faced boy and secure her place as Mrs. Kevin McGowan, queen of a small but popular restaurant empire. It was a dream we'd all come to call the Darcy and Kevin Bliss Package, as if it were something you could win on a game show. The big quandary was that Kevin wasn't falling for Darcy. Although she possessed the three girl *B*'s my brother's friends so admired—Blond, Beautiful, and Bodacious in Bed—for reasons none of us could decipher, Kevin remained lukewarm toward her.

But I didn't want to go there, especially since I was already low on her list. This year she was drinking age and I was not, which probably accounted for the fact that I hadn't heard from her at all over the past week. So now my limited summer options were dwindling fast. There'd be no cruising in Darcy's lipstick red convertible, no tanning by the pool, no country club visits or yummy meals cooked up by the Love family's housekeeper, Nessie. It bugged me to miss out on all these summer goodies, but were poolside perks worth sucking up to the Queen of Mean? I had to think not.

"What am I saying?" Darcy let out a bitter laugh. "Now that you're a full-figure gal, you probably don't even have a boyfriend. Certainly not the hillbilly surfer you always moon over."

"Shut up," I said, wishing I'd never told her about my feelings for Bear, one of my older brother's surfer friends. I wrung out the hem of my stretched-out surf shirt, wishing I could wring Darcy's skinny neck. Did she know that Bear was within hearing range in the water behind me, surfing less than a hundred yards away?

Just minutes ago, I'd been on my board, bobbing in the water beside him while I waited for Darcy to arrive. We'd been talking about repairs on his VW camper, and he'd told me about some of the surfing competitions he'd entered over the winter. Bear wanted to give up his part-time jobs and surf for a living but didn't have enough sponsors to do that yet.

"If I had to pick, I'd say the Pipeline tops everything," he said, all the guys in the lineup listening with a far-off glaze. Skeeter and John Fogarty, Napolean and my brother Steve—they all had jobs now. Skeeter and John even had wives with kids on the way. The guys were mired in commitmentland—all except Bear. Most of us had never even been to Hawaii, let alone surfed the Pipeline.

"I hear the reef is deadly there," Skeeter said.

"Scary awesome," Bear answered, swiping a handful of salt water over his board. "You gotta die a few times before you come alive. You need to have nine lives."

I found my eyes following the line of his board to his sturdy legs, his Hawaiian-print Jams, and up to the Billabong shirt stretched over his shoulders and rounded muscles.

"Is it worth it?" I asked. "Surfing the Pipeline?"

"Definitely," he said, his blue eyes flashing, killing me.

That's one death, I thought, feigning interest in a piece of bobbing seaweed. With rare dimples, glimmering blue eyes framed by impossibly dark lashes, and dark hair buzzed short, Bear was heartthrob material. His chipped front teeth gave him a look I thought of as "gritty," though my friends labeled it hillbilly. Still, he was my secret crush, which was an exercise in futility, since it was one of those unwritten rules that a good guy does not go after his best friend's little sister.

Now I swallow hard, wishing that Darcy didn't own any personal information about me. Stupid me, I had spilled my guts over the years. She could be a walking Lindsay encyclopedia.

"You know what?" I said, my voice a little too high pitched to call calm. "I'm sorry I got involved, okay? Next time your boyfriend passes out in the surf from partying his brains out, I'll just let them call the cops."

"You wouldn't. You . . . you'd better not. The next time, why don't you just keep your fat ass out of my business, okay? The lifeguards can call me directly. If there even is a next time."

"Oh, there will be." I knew Kevin's addiction wasn't drying up anytime soon. "You can bet your perfect highlights on it."

"Stop that!" she hissed. "Just stop. You never liked him, and I'm not going to stand here and let you tear him down. So just stop it!" She kicked at the sand, sending fine grains spewing onto my legs.

"Or what?" I put my hands on my well-padded hips. "What are you gonna do, Darcy? Push me off the jetty?"

Strike three—hit on Darcy's weak spot, the one event in her life that still made her awaken in the middle of the night in a cold sweat and a case of the guilts.

Furious, she held her hand out in front of her eyes. "You no longer exist in my world," she said as she repositioned her hand to block her view of me. "I have blotted you out. Not an easy task, at your size. But . . . there. You're gone. That's a relief."

As she turned away and ran over to croon over the lame boyfriend, I lifted my board and tried to talk myself out of feeling any responsibility for the end of this relationship. Darcy had always been a high-maintenance friend, and somehow I was the one making peace between Darcy and Elle, smoothing things over between Darcy and Tara, hiding Darcy's smokes or her diaphragm, tutoring her in math so that she could get out of summer school. I was the great facilitator, and did she thank me?

As I paddled out, I wanted the cool water to wash me clean of any bad feeling. The Darcy years were over. Done.

End of a bitchy era.

2

Lindsay

I had mixed feelings that afternoon as I leaned my board against the shed and ducked into the coolness of the Southampton house, the screen door slamming behind me. Home in the Hamptons was a three-story cedar-shingled house on Rose Lane that over the years had been a boardinghouse to any number of McCorkles and their friends, dogs, cats, two snakes, and a pet hamster named Wiggles who met an unfortunate end in a ride down the laundry chute that was supposed to be all in good six-year-old fun.

I'd left the beach with a vow to skip dinner, but once here in the kitchen, with the savory smell of goulash swirling from the kitchen and Mom smiling expectantly as she stirred, I knew I'd be obligated to fill a bowl and sit down with the crew, as was everyone in the McCorkle house.

"Isn't tonight the night your friend Milo is coming for dinner?" Ma asked.

Milo, of course! I smacked my sunburned forehead. "I forgot."

"Forgot?" Ma rapped the wooden spoon against the kettle. "Well, then, I suppose you were serious when you said he was just a friend."

"You gotta meet Milo, Ma," I said. Milo Barry was a friend from college, my lab partner in bio who'd become a great sounding board and confidant. This year he was sharing a house with a bunch of guys in Sag Harbor, parking cars at Hamptons clubs to make summer money. I hadn't met any of the summer shares in Milo's house, but I sensed they would not be wild and crazy frat boys. I was fairly sure Milo was gay, though not sure he knew that just yet. So for the time being we avoided the topics of sex and romance, except to make our usual disparaging remarks.

As I stole a celery stick from the cutting board and headed up the back stairs to shower, it struck me that I had a lot more in common with Milo than with any of my Hamptons friends, or former friends, in Darcy's case. Milo and I shared a similar socioeconomic background—working our way through college, patching together scholarships, scrambling from one on-campus job to the next. I worked in the library and dormitory, he worked for the registrar and the theater box office. Our parents didn't hand us cars and clothes and spending money. No silver spoon for me, unlike Darcy and Tara, whose fathers were high-profile, high-salaried professionals. My father had been a New York City cop when he died, my mother a homemaker and a crossing guard in Brooklyn.

Basically, we McCorkles were a Hamptons novelty. Years ago working-class fishermen, trappers, and farmers resided in the Hamptons, but as the years went by it was changing as rocketing real estate prices made it more lucrative to build condos than work the land. Although my family had possessed the good fortune to buy this house on Rose Lane years ago, we would never have been able to afford it today. "Thank God your grandparents had such foresight," Ma always said. So while we enjoyed the house and the beach and the beautiful town of picket fences, tidy gardens, and majestic beaches, the McCorkles were not among the wealthy Hamptons elite, the social whirl that Darcy's parents enjoyed and Tara's parents skirted. Don't get me wrong, I don't resent the fact that their families are loaded. I just didn't like the way Darcy was so obtuse about it, so insensitive to the fact that we all couldn't shop at Saks or party in Fort Lauderdale for spring break.

So as I stepped into the shower, part of me felt good about washing my hands of Darcy. If I had a nickel for every time that girl had gotten me into trouble, I'd be the one driving the lipstick red Saab convertible.

On the other hand, the jetty comment was a low blow. Not that she hadn't deserved it, but I felt kind of rotten about adding to her nightmares.

The jetty incident was one of those freakish childhood events that unfolds like a surreal movie in my memory. Years ago, Darcy had been accused of pushing our friend Elle off the rocks into the deep, churning waters of the Atlantic Ocean. Elle was only eleven at the time, and when the current swept her body away, most adults assumed the worst. And so thirteen-year-old Darcy was immediately blamed, which wasn't a stretch since she and Elle had always competed and argued, a relationship more tempestuous than the sloshing ocean that day. The miracle of it was that a Coast Guard ship found Elle and plucked her out of the ocean alive and surprisingly copacetic. But the consequences were harsh, as Elle's parents, these bookish, doctoral doctor types, had whisked her away from the Hamptons, taking her out of the country and vowing that there'd be no more summering in the Hamptons with Elle's pistol of a grandmother and those bad-influence girls. Which probably included me.

In the end, our circle of friends was left with a hole. Darcy reveled in the new dynamic; suddenly she was top dog, or, more appropriately, top bitch. But Tara and I missed Elle and kept in touch, through letters, postcards, and the occasional phone call.

I remembered the jetty incident as if it were yesterday, and yet Darcy didn't recall it. She had repressed the memory, which might account for some of that bitchy anger she loved to toss around. Repression definitely fit Darcy's take on the jetty incident. She'd pushed it so far back that it had to seep out in vicious nightmares.

Then again, I'd have to say she also displaced her anger, blaming me and anyone else who crossed her path for things that went wrong in her life.

Here's the thing about majoring in psychology: it's way too tempting to go through your abnormal psych textbook and find deviant behaviors to explain all the bizarre traits of your friends and family members.

In my opinion as a junior in college, my brother and his friends all suffered from the Peter Pan complex. I even called them the Lost Boys, and they were sick enough to like it.

I diagnosed Sonia, one of my roommates at school, with hydrophobia; she was afraid to put her head underwater, and consequently couldn't shower or go swimming (and I guess surfing was out!).

Were it up to me, I would have diagnosed my sister-in-law Ashley with multiple personality disorder years ago and called it a day. I mean, anyone who could insist on those low-cut, harlot crimson bridesmaid gowns and then have a Catholic wedding? Believe me, if you met her—or one or two of her personalities—you'd concur with my diagnosis.

I worried that Tara's mother had narcissistic tendencies. I avoided the head librarian at school, convinced that he suffered from schizoid personality disorder.

And yet, despite my zeal for deviant behavior, I really didn't aspire to be Dr. Lindsay. I just didn't possess the patience a good therapist needs, the fortitude to listen as Ralphie droned on about why he couldn't get his life together or Tiffany complained that men were so mean to her. Ten minutes with one of these losers and I'd be snapping my fingers and doing a Z-wave with my hand. Yo, Ralphie! Get your feet off my couch, get your butt out of your mommy's basement, and get a job already! Hello? Tiff? Stop playing the doormat, and when you get home, throw out all those magazines you've saved with profiles of your perfect man. Maybe in a perfect world, chump girl!

Somehow, I don't think the licensing board would appreciate my direct approach, but really, it doesn't seem fair that I can't forgo the passive standard treatment of patients and just fix their fucked-up lives.

Wrapped in two fluffy pink towels, I left the billowing steam of the shower and sat at the old vanity table, a piece of princess furniture that I'd covered with pristine white linen when I hit the teen years. My attic room had lemon yellow walls that were like a big smiley daisy on a summer day. The woodwork was painted stark white, as was the old mantel of the fireplace, which, of course, didn't work but looked charming. I pulled the turban off my head and crimped brown hair tumbled onto my shoulders. Among my fabulous friends, I was the boring brunette with chocolate hair and chocolate eyes, skin that loves to freckle and that black Irish tendency to grow so much hair that I had to begin plucking my eyebrows and shaving long before junior high. Not that I'm complaining, but Darcy was born with pure vanilla blond dazzle, and Tara, with her mocha skin, amber eyes, and straight silky hair that could take a curl or wrap like a sophisticate, possessed an exotic quality that eluded me.

As I tossed the towel onto the vanity, a postcard that I kept forgetting to mail slipped to the floor.

Dear Elle:

Having a great time with the boys on the flip side! Kidding. How's London in the summer? Are you freaking them out at Cambridge with your secret genius? Darcy's a bitch this year—no friend of mine—but then you always saw that coming. God, I wish you were here.

xxxoo, Lindsay

The postcard photo was this year's crop of Southampton lifeguards, looking buff in their red suits and bronze tans. Just a little something for Elle to drool over. I propped the postcard against the lamp, vowing to mail it tomorrow. In fact, maybe I'd write Elle a long letter or call her. That would piss Darcy off, big-time, if, of course, she ever found out. Which she wouldn't. Because I was never speaking to her again.

As I finger-combed my hair I skimmed the collage of postcards tacked onto the wall over my bed, postcards from far-reaching locales like Thailand and Algiers, Paris and Vancouver and the Great Wall of China. Although the DuBois family had lived in some exotic places in the past eight years, Elle wasn't into it. I knew she missed having a home, missed her grandmother who never left the Hamptons, missed me.

Tucked among the postcards were snapshots that I took with a camera that last summer Elle was a part of our group. There we were, perched on a red-and-white striped blanket on Bikini Beach, Elle and Tara still looking boyish and flat-chested while Darcy and I smiled proudly over our expanding A-cups. Other photos showed us struggling with dripping ice cream cones on Southampton's main street, arm in arm in front of the windmill, and leaning off plaster horses on the Montauk carousel the night Elle got the golden ring. Elle's bright red ringlets curled around a face far too adorable for her own good. How many times had I studied these photos carefully, looking for some hint of sadness in Elle's green eyes, some forecast of the disturbance that would rock her world and cause her parents to spirit her away from the Hamptons and out of the States?

"You were always so skinny," I said to the Elle in the photos.

Unfortunately, her photo didn't return the compliment.

By the time I got downstairs, Milo had arrived, met my mother, and been recruited to set the table. "And here I thought this was my night off!" he joked as he dropped place mats around the table. Since Milo Barry was one of those people wired with natural energy, it was probably best to keep him busy. High-strung and goofy, he'd gotten me through a handful of all-nighters during finals week at school on his caffeine-free charm.

"I'll help you," I said, grabbing the silverware bin from the kitchen. "How many are we?"

"Seven!" Ma called from the kitchen. "Stephen and his friends are going to join us."

"Hold on to your hat." I handed Milo a stack of napkins. "The surfer dudes can be a real workout."

"Linds, after six straight nights of parking cars for people who don't even look me in the eye, I can take on the dudes."

"You know, your work schedule would actually be very surfable," I said. "Why don't you come down to Bikini Beach one morning and I'll give you some lessons? If the surf is right, you'll be standing the first day."

"No can do." He folded his arms with a sigh. "I just got a job working at the Bridgehampton bakery in the mornings. Six to two."

I flicked his shoulder. "You're insane! When are you going to sleep?"

"Between shifts. It's very good money."

I groaned, knowing I'd been putting off job hunting, half hoping the whole dilemma would just go away. "So when am I going to see you this summer? Is this your last free night?"

"We'll work something out," he said. "Or else you can come down to the bakery. I'll sneak you a cinnamon roll."

"Like I need it," I said as Ma carried in a crock of steaming goulash.

"Sounds like you're going to be working your fingers to the bone, Milo," Ma said.

"Please!" Milo adjusted his glasses—very cool rectangular frames, a new acquisition this year. "I'm just happy to have escaped Brooklyn for the summer. Last year I had to play slave to my father on job sites, and believe me, it's no fun running around fetching hammers and nails and sweeping sawdust when it's ninety degrees and humid as Hades." I hadn't met Milo's father, but got the picture when Milo called him Brooklyn's answer to Archie Bunker.

"See, Lindsay? He's happy to be in the Hamptons, something we take for granted. And did I mention that I ran into Mr. Marino yesterday and he's looking for someone to work the counter at Old Towne Pizza? I told him you were looking for employment and I'd have you stop in right away."

"Pizza?" I felt a wave of disappointment at the thought of hot ovens and baking dough. "Don't you think I'm a little overqualified for that?"After my work experience at school, I'd been hoping to work with people, not food. Even a gig as a counselor at a sweaty day camp would beat that.

"It's honest work," Ma said, the gleam in her soft brown eyes warning me not to argue with the creed that had seen the McCorkle family through hard times over the years. Honest work, and lots of it.

"I'll go see him tomorrow." I knew there was no arguing with my mother—one of the downsides of being a McCorkle.

Steve and his friends filed in, and I silently willed the other guys to the opposite side of the table so I could sit between Milo and Bear, who was cool and crisp in khaki shorts and an orange and blue Hawaiian shirt. Tonight he had that sweet, limey smell that lingers around guys just out of the shower—probably just deodorant, but better than any cologne, in my book. I tucked in my chair, melting as our bare knees brushed under the table. Cheap thrill, I know, but I'd take it.

As the noodles and goulash were passed, I made quick introductions. "The blond guys are Skeeter and Johnny Fogarty. Johnny's the one with the moon-shaped scar over one eye."

Johnny tipped his head to the side, showing off the scar. "Got that from a shark attack," he said.

"You did not!" I snapped. Although the Fogarty twins were pushing thirty, they'd never grown out of the Lost Boy thing. Hard to believe they were holding down jobs, but then the family business had been handed to them—a chain of Christmas stores, where business conveniently slowed during the surf season. Perfect surf mojo.

"The big ugly one is my brother Steve"—Steve reached over to give me a noogie, but I ducked—"and that's Bear."

"Where does the name Bear come from?" Milo asked, focusing on my crush.

"My real name's Barrett," Bear admitted, all dimples and flashing blue eyes. "Which means 'mighty as a bear.' "

"He says that," Steve said, "but the truth is, he still sleeps with a stuffed animal named Huggy Bear."

"Get a life!" Bear snarled, which made me wonder if it was true; was there really a worn stuffed animal in the van parked at the edge of Bikini Beach?

As we ate, the guys talked surf. Everyone was jazzed because, after years of lugging packages for a delivery service, Steve was going to put his engineering degree to use at a real job with a company that specialized in sports equipment. A real job, with an office and a salary and paid travel expenses.

"You should get Victory to start a line of surfboards," Bear told Steve.

"I'd love to do it, man," Steve said. "First, I need to dig in, get the lay of the land."

"And we could help you try them out," Bear went on. "Test them for endurance . . ."

"Bang 'em on rocks," John said, his gray eyes popping against his sunburned skin.

"That'd be cool," Skeeter agreed. "I spent a fortune on that board I lost down in the Keys. That hurt."

Johnny laughed. "You were crying, man."

"Ginny was crying." Ginny was Johnny's wife. "She was calculating how much it cost. I was just pissed."

"Now, we'll have no cursing at the table," Ma warned, glaring at Johnny until he apologized and hung his head over his stew. Go Ma—the only woman who could tame Steve's motley group. My brother and his crew respected my mother. If only Steve could muster a scintilla of respect for his little sister.

"Gidget," Steve started on me, "you might want to reel in the blond pop-tart. We saw her rip through Southampton at warp speed this afternoon," he said, waving his fork. "She's gonna take out half of the antiques shops on Winthrop Lane."

I shrugged. "If you're referring to Darcy, we are no longer on speaking terms."

"What's that?" Ma's dark eyes went wide. "Did you two have a fight?"

"You might say that." I filled Milo and my mother in on the morning's incident at the beach, which the other guys had witnessed. "I don't think Darcy wanted to hear what I had to say. She's in denial about Kevin's addictions. Honestly, right now I have no desire to be around her." Except for the cool car and lux house, of course.

"And here I thought this summer would be my chance to meet the notorious Darcy Love," Milo teased.

"Believe me," Steve said, "you're not missing anything."

"Stephen . . ." There was warning in Ma's eyes as she added pepper to the goulash. "I don't know what her parents were thinking, handing a young person a car like that," she said. "There's something wrong with that. Poor Darcy will never have a chance to learn true responsibility."

"Yeah, poor Darcy," Steve mused, "crying all the way to the ATM."

"Ma, the money's not the problem," I said, feeling this developing into a McCorkle debate. "It's her sense of entitlement." That and the fact that she'd nearly compared me to a beached whale. "Darcy has become this insensitive, selfish, beautiful monster. I feel like I don't know her anymore." I pushed the noodles around on my plate. "I'm not sure I want to know her, and that's a very bad feeling."

"Well, you can put that feeling on hold and think about what Darcy's been through," Ma said sternly. "The Loves may have more money than God, but that girl has been neglected since she was ten, raised by a housekeeper now and again. All that money couldn't buy her the love and nurturing she needed. The girl has no family, she never has, and if you ask me it's a crying shame."

"Who needs a family when you've got a million bucks?" Steve asked.

I felt some sick need to defend my friend, but fortunately Ma intervened as she passed the rolls down the table. "No need to be flippant, Stephen. Now put your napkin on your lap and pass the carrots, please."

And though the topic of dinner conversation moved on, I was stuck with an unbidden image of thirteen-year-old Darcy, her blond hair stringy and sticking to her tear-stained face as she waited at the police precinct for parents who never arrived. Finally, when the police released her to my mother's care, even more tears had welled up in Darcy's periwinkle blue eyes as she sobbed a thank-you and collapsed in Ma's arms. That was my first glimpse of the importance of family . . . and the despair of having no one.

3

Darcy

"Anybody here?" The sun was low in the sky as Darcy hugged the container of take-out sushi to her chest, hoping that one of the cleaning ladies or the day maid, Nessie, might still be around.

She hated coming home alone. Next time she was going to drive Kevin straight over and dump him on the overstuffed sofa. Even passed out, he'd be more reassuring than the hollow darkness.

Damn Kevin. Damn Nessie, too.

When there was no answer she braced herself and stepped into the grand foyer, hardwood floors gleaming up at her, the new tapestry print runner zigzagging up the stairs looking more welcoming than last year's cream Berber carpeting. Mother had swept through here with Miguel, her design consultant, last month and ordered a few decorating changes, but no amount of renovation or redesign could bring the life that was lacking to this house—people.

Darcy hated being alone in the house in particular. She was often the only one living here, and some nights, when she was alone in bed and listening to the scrape of tree branches against the side of the house, she felt like the last person on earth.

Lowering the thermostat, she wished Kevin had come home with her. Even if he wanted to sleep, it would have been better just having him in the house, but somehow he didn't get that. No one understood how lonely Darcy's perfect life was inside this architectural gem.

The Love Mansion was the envy of anyone who dared to trespass down the private Mockingbird Lane. Darcy saw them sometimes from her bedroom window—faces looming in the open windows of Mercedes and Audis, twentysomethings in big, bruising SUVs soaking up eyefuls of the lush, luxurious estate. But Darcy wanted to yell at them that it wasn't all it seemed. Despite the family name, this gorgeous house had never become the warm, familial home she'd dreamed of when her parents had purchased it from a famous actress. Dad rarely spent more than a weekend here. He was CEO of a giant corporation, and his job always demanded his presence in the office, in the boardroom, in the convention center. On the rare weekend when he did make it out to the Hamptons, Bud Love spent his time barking on the phone by the pool or golfing with business associates. And while Darcy's mother, Melanie Love, had plenty of time on her hands, she'd always found it difficult to extract herself from the social whirl of their home in Great Neck, the Garden Society, and the girls at the country club and, of late, the young tennis pro at the club who Darcy suspected was fooling around with her mother. Disgusting. Not that Mother hadn't kept herself in good shape, but really, what did a young, okay guy like Jean-Michelle see in her mother, a woman as chiseled as a cathedral spire and cool as cucumber gazpacho?

No, the Love Mansion had never fulfilled its name. Couldn't feel the love in this place. "It's all crap!" she once shouted down from her window to a bald man with the nerve to drive by in a Porsche convertible. "It's *crap!*" He'd turned that dick-mobile around pretty fast.

"Hello?" Darcy called out again, but Nessie was long gone. Damn. Although Ness had done a good job cooking and corralling Darcy and her friends for many years, Darcy didn't really need her anymore. Twenty-one and going into her last year of college, she didn't need a nanny. And now, each afternoon, Nessie seemed eager to get back to her own family in Riverhead, Long Island, much to Darcy's regret. She didn't blame Nessie, and she didn't know how to ask her if she could occasionally stick around to keep her company, to make some normal household noises and ward off the evening shadows.

If only she could have a big, noisy houseful of people, the way it was at the McCorkle house. Darcy used to love staying over with Lindsay, listening to Granny McCorkle's stories and sitting at the dinner table with all the cousins. She'd been planning to wrangle a few invitations out of Lindsay this summer, but those prospects were shot now that Lindsay had said all those mean things about Kevin. Besides, Darcy didn't think she'd want to be seen hanging around with someone that chunky. Darcy couldn't understand how her friend could let herself go that way. For chrissakes, why didn't she just stop eating?

Darcy wandered down the hall, stopping to stare into the darkness that loomed there. The living room, or parlor, as Mother called it, was way too grand for anyone to ever relax or want to spend any amount of time there. A large stained-glass piece set into the center window always reminded Darcy of a medieval chapel, and the silk upholstered furniture, including authenticated pieces from one of those King Poopy-pants dynasties, made the room feel like a museum. Darcy paused in the doorway, wondering for a moment if she'd ever in fact sat in that room.

She padded barefoot over the Chinese rug and chose the red silk chair, sitting like a queen on her throne. The chair creaked, and a faintly musty scent mixed with the mango-coconut smell of her suntan lotion. Wouldn't Mother freak to know she was getting Coppertone on the antiques.

Whatever.

Popping open the container, she bit into a slice of California roll, not worrying about the grains of rice that fell to the floor. That's what the cleaning people were for, right? Gotta give Nessie and the girls something to do.

The cozier den in the back of the house, with its brown suede chairs, entertainment center, and gray stone fireplace, was more her style. She snapped open a Diet Pepsi, turned on the VCR, and sank into a chair to devour sushi and catch up on the soaps she'd missed that day. The characters of daytime dramas were Darcy's year-round friends, and they never failed to appear with a new scandal or heartbreak, a thorny, submerged problem that made the issues swirling beneath the surface of Darcy's life seem simple and harmless. Soaps broke through the hollow aloneness. So what if her mother was sleeping with a tennis pro? Affairs were a daily occurrence in soaps. And all the accusations swirling around Dad's investment firm were petty grievances compared to the serial murders, switched-at-birth babies, and vindictive lovers of the daytime soaps.

Watching as two lovers shared a kiss on a moonlit balcony, Darcy glimpsed her own future, and it was good. No more putting up a happy front and knocking around in empty houses. No more being alone. No more Darcy . . . just Darcy and Kevin. The McGowans. Mrs. Kevin McGowan . . . God, that sounded good. Together, Darcy and Kevin were going to make a life right here on America's Riviera, where Kevin's father already owned Coney's on the Beach, a buzzing hotspot, a small gold mine. She and Kevin would have money, lux houses and sleek cars, great bodies, and lots of good sex.

Really, when you got down to it, what more could a person want?

4

Tara

If Tara had to hear one more word of debate from her mother regarding the merits of microblinds versus sheers she was going to rip the window dressing aside and jump out onto the sand.

"I don't know . . ." Serena Washington stepped back from the window and lowered her reading glasses. The cat's-eye rhinestone glasses fell to her chest, dangling on their chain as she reassessed the design crisis. "The microblinds are better for privacy, but then the sage drapes go so well with this armoire. Very seventeenth-century French provincial."

But we're in a twenty-first-century Southampton beach house, Tara wanted to tell her mother. *The era of microwaves and VCRs.* "Whatever you think," she said dutifully.

"Though I worry that this armoire might be too big for this room." Tara's mother paced around the bed in Wayne's room, her Dolce and Gabanna sandals leaving footprints in the deep carpeting. "I wouldn't mind getting rid of the armoire altogether, but your brother is so attached to those video games and he'd pitch a fit if I got rid of them."

Tara just nodded and stared down at the carpet, thinking how the family had always catered to Wayne while Tara and her older sister, Denise, were the ones moving the armoires and cleaning the blinds and vacuuming footprints of designer shoes out of the carpeting. In some ways she envied Denise, having a life in Baltimore, a house of her own where she could fill each room with five armoires and not worry. Denise had hit the jackpot, landing on freedom and a guy her parents approved of, an African American architect with a steady business and a rambling, warm, loving family in Baltimore.

Serena Washington had moved from the furnishings to the wall treatments when the phone rang.

"I'll get it," Tara answered, running for her life down the stairs of the starkly geometric beach home.

"You have got to meet me tonight," Darcy ordered, bossy as ever. "I'll be at Coney's."

"Somehow that doesn't surprise me," Tara said, familiar with Darcy's quest for Kevin McGowan. "But I'm incarcerated in spring-cleaning boot camp," Tara said under her breath.

"Hire a maid service," Darcy said.

"Have you learned nothing about my mother over all these summers?" Tara said. "Serena Washington has two maids, Tara and Denise, only Denise wised up and got the hell out of here."

Darcy laughed. "You're so funny. Meet me in half an hour."

"What about Lindsay?" Tara asked. "Is she coming?"

"Big groan. I'll explain when I see you," Darcy said, then clicked off.

Promising to return the sage curtains to the store in Riverhead tomorrow, Tara managed to escape Design 101. Soon she was cruising down Southampton's Main Street, a charming stretch strung with tiny white lights—small cafés, upscale boutiques, galleries, bed and breakfast inns, and outdoor markets that had a New England feel.

Waiting at a red light as a flock of pedestrians—all white—passed in their summer whites, Tara got to wondering why her parents, two educated, hardworking individuals, had chosen Southampton as their summer residence twelve years ago.

Tara was just nine when her parents bought the oceanfront house in the Hamptons, a sleek contemporary box on the beach that an architect had designed for his beloved wife, then put on the market when she left him for an artist she'd hooked up with at a cocktail party. Typical Hamptons story. Although Tara and her older siblings Wayne and Denise were not consulted about the purchase, Tara recalled the thrill of thinking her parents had purchased this house with its turquoise swimming pool and Jacuzzi tub, this land with its stubbly dunes and front-row view of the crashing ocean. That they owned a second house on the beach, well, surely this must mean they were rich and were simply feigning poverty when Tara pleaded for a television in her room and a VCR and a complete collection of Louisa May Alcott's books.

It wasn't long until Tara realized the Washingtons were not the average Hamptons summer residents. Though she was only nine she'd already developed a keen sense of the world around her, the awareness that African Americans were still a minority race but a significant part of New York City's ethnically diverse population. In Brooklyn, people didn't stare. *I belong here*, she used to tell herself as she walked down along a cobbled Park Slope sidewalk to the park with Denise or went down to the pizza place with a quarter for an Italian ice. Brooklyn was her home, and it welcomed her as readily as it embraced the Chinese, Latvian, and Pakistani children in her class.

But somehow, walking along the white picket-fenced gardens of their Hamptons neighbors, nine-year-old Tara didn't feel the safety in telling herself she belonged here. When all the faces around her were white, the bone structure and gazes as generically smooth as vanilla pudding, her mantra lost its power, becoming just a sequence of words. Especially when the murmuring started.

Murmured questions and curious looks. The staring waitress behind the counter in the diner. Patrons in the hardware store whispering about "passing." Ladies who chose not to look beyond the brim of their floppy hats while strolling past the colorful awnings of Main Street.

The probing eyes and dull whispers were unsettling, but never menacing or threatening. Whenever Tara had feared someone would swoop closer and prey upon them, her mother would lift her menu and announce, "Laurence, let's order an appetizer for the family." Or Serena Washington would pull a twisted brass concoction out of a bin in the hardware store with a hearty laugh and ask: "Now what in heaven's name would you use this for?" Or she would pause at a shop window, wondering about the price of a suit and whether the color would be flattering for her skin tone.

Skin tone . . . the bane of Tara's existence. Although she was African American, people often assumed that she was Caucasian because her skin was light, a creamy mocha shade. Their mistaken perception was a constant source of discomfort for her. Throughout her four years of private high school, she'd overheard murmurings from the other students, speculation over whether she was black or white, mixed race, Caribbean, or a descendant of Sally Hemmings.

Skin color was not discussed at home. Once, back in nursery school days, she had teased Wayne that she and Denise were better because their skin was lighter. They had even dumped out the bin of art supplies to search for crayons or markers that matched their skin tones—until Mama shut down the activity with a stern reminder that "we are all African American and we do not differentiate based on skin color."

It was the same wherever she went, high school or college or summer camp; dark-skinned girls eyed her with suspicion, Latina girls snapped at her in Spanish, and during lecture halls she noticed other students staring at her curiously, as if a closer look at her hands or hair or feet would reveal the key to Tara Washington's ethnic identity. It made Tara want to turn inward, to remind everyone that race was just one part of a person's identity. As a teenager she'd felt freakish, until she glommed onto individuals who'd struggled to make their own way, their own identities. Princess Di, and Stephanie and Caroline of Monaco. Gypsy Rose Lee. Ellen DeGeneres. Elton John. Halle Berry. Sometimes she studied their bios, wishing for clues, searching for the key, the way to make it work.

Here in the Hamptons, Tara wondered if the fact that she hung out with white girls confused people all the more. But could she help it if her two best friends at the beach were Irish-Catholic and WASP wannabe?

Every year, as summer shimmered over the city, Tara wondered if this would be the last year she'd leave Park Slope to hook up with her Hamptons peeps. She had gone through a lot with Darcy and Lindsay, but sometimes, as she packed up for the summer, she felt like these girls were way too much work and fantasized about spending a quiet summer in the half-empty city, wandering in the coolness of museums and taking in matinees in dark cinemas.

Coney's was hopping with patrons when Tara arrived, but it wasn't hard to find Darcy. Like the sun, she was the center of the bar, half the guys in the room caught in her gravitational pull.

From head to toe, Darcy was model sleek—gold on blond high-lights in waist-length hair, periwinkle blue eyes that sparkled with confidence, sheer white blouse that revealed the electric blue camisole underneath. Looking down at her own black tank and jean skirt, Tara felt like she was slumming.

Darcy greeted her with a lift of the chin. "Tara! Thank God." She gave her a bony shoulder hug. "I was worried that you'd porked out, too."

"Excuse me?" Tara squinted.

"Haven't you seen Lindsay?" Darcy's eyes closed to slivers. "I guess not. She's enormous. She'd make Carnie Wilson look svelte."

"I haven't seen her," she said haltingly, thinking that Darcy looked unattractive when she was being catty. "But I'm sorry to hear that." Poor Lindsay. "So why isn't she here?"

"Are you kidding me?" Darcy shot a glance over her shoulder at two guys who seemed to be waiting for an audience. "She wasn't invited. I'm not going to be seen with a girlfriend like that. I mean, what'll people think?"

"They'll think you're her friend," Tara said pointedly. "Which I thought you were. What's going on with you, Darcy?"

"Listen to me," Darcy said, stepping up beside Tara so she didn't have to shout over the music. "I'm just not comfortable hanging out with someone like that. It's gross, okay?"

"She's your friend!" Tara shot back. "Our friend, since we were little kids."

"Well, those days are gone," Darcy said, raking back a strand of blond hair with crimson nails. "So why don't you move on, honey? Kevin is going to be here any minute, and if you mellow out and have a drink, we can have a few laughs, okay?"

But Tara was shaking her head fiercely. "I don't think so. Right now, I'm not liking you so much, *honey*."

Darcy cocked her head to the side, a strand of hair falling se-ductively over one eye. "Oh, don't be that way. Come on, I'll buy you a drink. Want a margarita? A cosmo?"

But Tara backed away, shaking her head. "I don't think so. I've suddenly lost my appetite." And with rage thrumming in her head, Tara pushed past Darcy, leaving the bar.

What an incredible bitch, Tara thought as she closed the door of her mother's Mercedes and gripped the steering wheel. She still couldn't believe Darcy was that shallow, that catty.

As she started the car, Tara felt doubly guilty for not calling Lindsay in these past two weeks. She'd wanted to, but she had been under her mother's thumb, cleaning and redecorating. That would change this week, as soon as the guys got here from Korea, where Tara's older brother was stationed in the armed forces. Although Tara didn't feel a strong bond with her older brother Wayne, it would be a relief to have him finally arrive and put an end to the neurotic preparations. Besides, Wayne would provide enough distraction for Tara to get some of her life back.

Whatever was left of it.

Years ago they'd lost Elle in a near-tragic incident. Thank God Elle had survived, but when her parents whisked her away, never to return again, Tara felt as if Elle had taken a piece of them with her. And now this. Damn it, at the rate Darcy was cutting people off, there'd be nothing left of the Hamptons friends.

This was unacceptable. Time to take a stand.

Tara stopped at a pay phone and, surprised that she remembered it, dialed Lindsay's number. "Hey, girl," she said when Lindsay got on the line, "I'm headed over your way and I won't take no for an answer. How about we catch a movie or something?"

That would show Darcy that she didn't have the power to decimate Tara's relationships. Granted, she could destroy her own, but while Darcy crashed and burned, her friends would be getting their groove on.

5

Darcy

They all love me.

Putting Tara's angry exit out of her mind, Darcy focused on what she had going for her tonight. The guy thing. She moved her slender body between two guys lined up at the bar, feeling a subtle thrill as one of them slid his hand down her firm backside and the other teased a glance at the tan line along her cleavage. All the guys liked the way she looked and responded to her easy way of moving a conversation along. A feeling of power burned bright inside her at the realization that she could probably have her pick of any guy in Coney's tonight. Any of these tan beach boys with six-pack abs would be happy to be her boyfriend.

But she was holding out for Kevin. And where the hell was he? His father, currently backing up the bartender, had told her he'd be here soon. She suspected that he was with his loser friends, Fish and David, but she didn't want to ask Mr. McGowan too many questions, didn't want to appear too desperate.

Licking the sugared rim of her red martini, she made her way down the bar in search of Kevin's gold-tinged, spiky hair, the shaggy beach-boy look that had won him a place in her heart years ago, her fourteenth summer. Somehow, even back then, she'd known that Kevin was the one. Although she'd started sexual experimentation at an early age, kissing boys and letting them feel her up in the darkness of movie theaters or the cover of the dunes, she knew enough to save the best for Kevin.

She still remembered that night when she was just fourteen, the party at the McCorkle house, the perfume she wore, and the packets of condoms she'd tucked into her bag for the right opportunity with Kevin. He'd been playing quarters on the screened-in porch and the smell of beer was heavy on his lips as she caught him leaving the bathroom.

"There's something up here I want to show you," she'd told him, nodding her head toward the stairs. He'd followed her up, his mouth agape in curiosity as she led him into the master bedroom, once the sacred ground of Lindsay's grandparents, the current bedroom of her mother.

"Are we supposed to be in here?" Kevin had asked, looking up at the crucifix on the wall.

Darcy pushed the door closed behind her. "I just wanted to show you this." The snaps of her blouse opened with a row of pops, and Kevin stared down at her lacy bra.

"Wow," he'd said, sampling the mound of one breast as if he'd discovered gold.

She'd moved into his arms and kissed him hard, rubbing against him to feel the hard lump under his jeans. She'd never done this, not all the way, but she figured it was about time she became a woman, and doing it with Kevin would serve the double purpose of getting rid of the virginity badge and wrapping him up as her boyfriend.

When he pressed into her, it seemed like it couldn't happen. It hurt too much, the stinging pressure between her legs, and Darcy let out a yelp and pushed him away. They had to be doing something wrong for it to hurt this much.

"It's okay," he whispered into her ear as he looked down at their joined crotches and pressed, hard.

"Ow!" She squeezed back tears, but he didn't seem to notice.

"It's smooth going from here," he said. He started moving slowly then, in and out, in a rhythm that made Darcy wonder how many times he'd done this before. The thought of Kevin doing this with other girls brought on a pang of anger, but that quickly faded as he drove into her in easy rhythm, the gentle stroke of his body against hers reminding her that this was it—she and Kevin were finally together.

In the warmth that washed over her after that, she told him how she felt about him, how she'd always wanted to be his girlfriend. He'd seemed surprised that she'd given him her virginity, surprised that she was interested in him. When she mentioned being his girlfriend he told her he was "cool with that," that he really liked her but couldn't really get tied down right now.

Not the response she'd anticipated, but she figured it was a start.

Since that summer seven years ago they had dated off and on, always over the summer, always at the whim of Kevin and his male buddies who, as far as Darcy was concerned, spent way too much time smoking pot and waiting for killer waves to roll in. One summer Darcy gave him an ultimatum: be a good boyfriend or lose her forever. Kevin had failed, and Darcy had tried to move on. But she found herself back in Kevin's arms, more specifically rocking in the back of his van, the first day of the very next summer. She knew her parents kept hoping she'd meet a more worthy man—a son of one of Dad's investors, a Great Egg millionaire's son, a Bennington boy with a strong moral code and a financially secure future. But that hadn't happened, and though she'd dated other guys and had good sex with enough of them to form some basis of comparison, Kevin was the one she always returned to, the boy who brought that electrical charge into the room, the guy she wanted to be connected with, the only guy who could save her from her family, and from herself.

Taking a sip of her drink, she checked the landing, where three guys paused on their way to the bar.

Fish, David, and Kevin.

Darcy felt sparks fly as his eyes met hers. Trite, yes, but undeniably true. There was a potent chemistry between them. She was glad he'd made it, glad he'd recovered from this morning so that he could get out and party on this important night, the sendoff into summer.

He swaggered over, his jeans low on his hips, his Billabong T-shirt torn at the shoulder. "Darcy . . ." He leaned over her, his curly gold-tipped bangs in his eyes as he pressed his tongue to his lower lip.

That adorable lick-smacking thing, as if he couldn't wait to kiss her. "Hey, how's it going?"

She shrugged, trying to appear casual. "Okay, I guess. Another Hamptons summer."

"I hear you." He leaned closer, teetering a bit, and she smelled the burnt smoke of weed on him. "You look fucking great," he whispered with a sly smile.

She grinned, loving his giddiness. "I know. And you look a lot better than you did this morning."

"Yeah." He swiped his hands over his face, as if rubbing away the memory. "You were there, right?"

"I drove you home."

"Right, yeah. That was weird."

Did he really not remember that she drove him home, or was that just part of his smooth cover-up? "Feel better now?"

"Definitely. And you look great, Darcy. Really." His pink tongue peeked out, teasing his bottom lip.

"Yeah, I know," she said, though his comment warmed her like a hot-stone massage. She leaned back, pleased at the way her hip-bones jutted out in her DK linen skirt.

"Tell me, Darce. Are Mommy and Daddy home tonight?"

She smoothed the pencil-thin linen skirt over one hip, leaning away coyly. "Actually, I've got the whole house to myself tonight."

"All alone in the Love Shack?" He leaned forward and cupped her butt, his hazel eyes sparkling. "Maybe I'd better keep you company."

Darcy swallowed hard as feelings of love and desire tugged deep inside her. She nuzzled his ear, leaning into the strong line of his body. Although she hadn't seen him in months, she didn't mind that he cut through the formalities, pushing their relationship along. She reached around his waist, loving the lean feel of him as she sidled into his arms, her lips veering close to his. "So . . . let's get the hell out of here."

6

Lindsay

With one phone call Tara and I reconnected, catching up on events over the school year and sharing our various experiences with Darcy. That first night at the movies, Tara could barely contain her anger toward our former friend, but a few days later she sort of forgot about Darcy's bad karma. Tara's brother Wayne, a soldier stationed in Korea, flew home with a friend, a guy named Charlie Migglesteen, and the idea of lusting for a guy under the same roof had delicious possibilities. Tara choked over his last name the first time she told me as we biked past an open market on Main Street.

"Migglesteen. I can't believe I like a guy named Migglesteen."

"And what's wrong with that?" I asked.

"It just makes me smile. He's Jewish, and very cute. Not too tall, but with chocolatey eyes and a really strong sense of himself. You should see him handle my parents. Manners that shut my mother right down."

"Mr. Migglesteen sounds nice," I said as we turned off Main Street onto a tree-lined avenue. "Are you thinking of changing your name to Mrs. Migglesteen?"

"Get outta town." Tara leaned over the handlebars and coasted, looking trim and sporty in her hot pink shorts, black tank, and black helmet with matching pink stripes. "I'm not even sure he likes me."

"I'll bet he does," I told her. "But what about the parents? How are they handling it?" Although Tara had gotten involved with white boys before, nothing had ever developed to a level that her parents learned of the relationship, but this was right under their noses.

"I'm not sure how my parents would handle it," Tara said thoughtfully. We were quiet as we passed tidy green lawns lined with flower beds of tall yellow tulips and lush red, purple, and orange impatiens with blossoms so thick they reached over the sidewalk. It was a sunny June afternoon, and the sleepy shingled colonial cottages of Southampton seemed not quite awake to the potential of full-blown summer yet.

"I'm not going to worry about it now," Tara said. "If something develops, then I'll deal with it, but as it is, Wayne keeps pulling Charlie into these stupid Xbox competitions that go on all day long. And when Charlie manages to extract himself from my brother, there's Mama watching us like a hawk." She sighed. "I gotta tell you, it's not easy falling for your big brother's friend."

"Oh, please." I tucked a clump of dark hair into my bike helmet. "Now you're preaching to the choir."

Although I managed to stall for another week, by the beginning of June I was walking down Southampton's Main Street, past the quaint blue striped awnings of exclusive boutiques and gourmet shops, for my first day as a pizza girl. The smell of baking pizza, sweet tomato sauce, and melted cheese brought tears to my eyes as Sal Marino welcomed me to his shop.

"Come in, come in. You gotta duck behind the counter here." Sal wore a tired smile, but his warmth seemed genuine as he wiped his hands on a white towel, telling me I looked just like my mother and grandmother. "So, Lindsay . . . grab an apron, wash your hands, and I'll show you how to use the register."

Scrubbing my hands with astringent pink soap, I observed that the back room of Old Towne Pizza was surprisingly clean for a small hole-in-the-wall take-out joint—the only pizza parlor in Southampton, where a monopoly could mean a fortune during the short summer months. It was four-thirty, the lull between lunch and dinner, and the dining area was empty. But by dinnertime on a Friday like this, the place would be packed with people grabbing a slice or waiting to pick up pies.

Back in the kitchen, Sal was stacking round silver platters of un-cooked dough into shelves of the fridge and calling out things like "Three cases of whole tomatoes" and "Ten pounds of semolina." Biting his lip, Mickey nodded and scratched out a list.

Ironic that both pizza guys were thin. Skinny, even. Did it have anything to do with being near the ovens and sweating it off? Maybe I should have tried for a job in a Laundromat. As a red car flashed past the shop window, I imagined Darcy driving by and spotting me inside. Brakes squealing, she'd pop out and square off with me, hands on her skinny hips. "Whoa, girl! Don't you know pizza puts on the pounds?"

The bitch. Part of me hated her and part of me missed her like crazy. Schizoid, I know, but the summer was not going to be the same without her, even if I did manage to trim down on my fabu-lous new weight-loss plan. So far today I'd only eaten a peach, two boiled eggs and a slice of special fat-free toast—inspired by a celebrity diet I'd seen in *Glamour* magazine. Between the diet and the surfing, I figured that the pounds would eventually melt, right?

Smoothing a red and white checked apron over my khaki shorts, I stepped up to the register and found someone sitting at the counter, facing away. Okay, time to be a waitress. "May I help you?" I asked, aglow with professionalism.

Bear turned to face me. "Hey, squirt. I'm just waiting for the calls to start."

Calls? I nodded as if I got it, though I didn't.

"Duh. I'm the delivery guy."

"Oh." So this was the night job that kept Bear on the beach all day this summer. "Does Sal pay enough to keep you in Sex Wax?"

He shrugged. "I'm working on getting something going. Real sponsors, so I can focus on the surfing, maybe get to the coast."

"The West Coast?" This was news to me. "Did you like it out there?"

"It's different, but yeah. I'm talking to a guy who manufactures his own boards in Hawaii. If he comes through with the deal, I'll be surfing in the islands this winter."

"Professional." Bear was good enough; I just never thought he had the confidence to pursue his obsession.

"Lindsay?" Sal called from the back. "You want me to heat you a slice before the rush starts?"

A slice, hot from the oven. Crisp crust and bubbling cheese . . . My mouth watered profusely, but I swallowed it back, thinking: *Carbs are evil. Carbs are not your friend.* "No, thanks." I choked on the words.

"I'll take one," Bear called to the back.

"You?" Sal waved him off dramatically. "You, I know. Always. You'll eat me out of business one day. I should take it outta your salary."

Bear stepped behind the counter for a cup, then filled it at the Coke dispenser as if he owned the place. "You'd better grab something now, squirt. Soon it'll be so busy in here, you won't have a chance."

"I'm trying to cut down." I tried to sound positive, keep the desperation out of my voice. "You know . . . the freshman five. Sophomore seven. Jumbo junior."

He let out a short laugh, then his eyes moved over me as he took a sip. "Don't go anorexic on us. You look good to me." As he spoke, he leaned around me, as if trying to get a better look at my butt.

With a squeal, I swatted him and ducked back behind the register.

"Hey, you two," Sal called. "No roughhousing near the pizza ovens. Lindsay, if you will, the red pepper and oregano need to be refilled and put back on the tables."

"I'm on it!" I called, gathering up a tray of glass shaker bottles.

I pretended to be all business as Sal came out and served Bear his slice. I acted like filling the green flecks of oregano to the top was of utmost importance, but my thoughts were on what Bear had said.

He didn't think I looked so bad. In fact, he thought I looked good, and it wasn't that dismissive "Oh, you look fine so stop complaining" crap.

My heart did a happy dance as I shook the red pepper shaker like a maraca.

Bear thought I looked good, and the sun just rose over my summer.

7

Lindsay

"Here's a quandary," my brother Steve announced to his buddies bobbing in the lineup. I paddled beyond him, suspecting I didn't want to be a part of this. "If you had a choice, which would you rather grow—a second dick, or fins?"

The Fogarty twins let out a roar of laughter, as if it were the first time they'd ever heard that old nugget. I ran my fingertips over the tacky wax on my board, thinking how there were advantages and disadvantages to being accepted as "one of the guys." I liked being able to float in the lineup and pop up on my board without feeling that the boys were eyeballing me. The downside was that now that I was in, they had no qualms about acting like big beef jerkies in front of me.

"That's not a tough choice. Who could resist a second one?" Johnny said, swiping his wet hair back. "Imagine the possibilities. Double dipping!"

More laughter, but I noticed Bear wasn't going for it. "You guys are full of it," he said. "You can't even handle the one you got."

Staring down into the sea, I was glad Bear didn't go for it. The water was clean today. With crisp waves coming from an offshore breeze, the undertow was quiet, and I enjoyed peering through the blue-green water to the bits of seaweed and shell gently lolling on the sandbar. The water rose, a swell rolling in. Most of the surfers turned their boards quickly, moved onto their stomachs, and started paddling.

I paddled, pushed ahead of the wave, and popped up to a crouch. Water surged beneath my board as I got lifted and pushed ahead. Picking up speed. Angling in, my arms out for balance. This was it! The water rushed beneath me, a free thrill ride.

Then, suddenly, the board dropped down and came to a halt in the shallows, where I swerved and dropped into the water beside it. "Woo-hoo!" I shouted, slapping the water with my hand.

As I lingered in the shallows, I caught sight of two figures heading over the dunes. Dressed in a sleek turquoise and black wet suit, Tara walked alongside a short, solid guy who was carrying a surfboard under one arm. This had to be Officer Migglesteen, the soldier Tara couldn't stop talking about. They seemed like a couple, quietly exchanging conversation. I floated my board into the beach and flopped it onto the sand.

"You picked the right time," I called to them. "The waves are just starting to get interesting."

"Would that be good or bad?" the dark-eyed guy asked, lowering the board.

"Lindsay . . . Charlie." Tara introduced. "He's never surfed before. I promised to give him a lesson."

"Brave soul," I said. "Tara will be a good teacher, but watch out for those ballbusters in the surf. They're ruthless."

"I'll take that under advisement when I'm flailing in a riptide and they're surfing wheelies around me," Charlie said as he placed the board on the sand.

"That's a little extreme," Tara said.

"What? They won't let me drown?"

"No. They can't surf wheelies."

"Very reassuring." He spread his arms out wide. "Okay, Tara, have at me. You're the great Kahuna and I'm Gidget, just grabbing a board for the first time."

I smiled. Charlie Migglesteen was a little nerdier than I'd expected, but he seemed to like Tara, and she obviously enjoyed moving beside him as she demonstrated how to stand on the board, how to pop up and balance.

"You think *I'm* a goofy foot?" he said with a deadpan expression. "You should see my cousin Leo."

Tara and Charlie waded into waist-deep water to watch as I demonstrated how to maintain trim and stand at the same time. Then I loaned them an extra board so Tara could paddle out with Charlie.

"Not bad," Bear said, watching with me on the beach as Charlie wiped out. "At least he got on his feet." Leave it to Bear to see the good.

I nodded, thinking that Charlie was built right for surfing—solid and short, a compact body with a lower center of balance. "He could do well with some practice. Though I guess you don't see many waves in North Korea. He's stationed there with Tara's brother."

Bear scratched his chin. "Aw, man, I envy him. He could surf Fiji!"

By noon the tide was high, slamming onto the beach in sick, unsurfable waves. Tara and Charlie followed me home, where Charlie, Steve, and Bear went through Steve's collection of boards in the yard, looking for something to loan Charlie for the next few weeks.

In the kitchen, Tara and I reached into the cupboards, searching for some spices and condiments to zing up a big batch of tuna fish for sandwiches to feed the crew.

Tara called out the inventory. "We've got onion flakes, Italian seasoning, dried mustard, paprika . . ." The top of her suit was unzipped and peeled down to her waist, revealing a chocolate bikini top. In contrast, I felt doughy, with sand caught in the seam of my swimsuit, a sheen of salt caked on my legs. "How do you feel about capers?"

"Bring on the crazy capers." I was opening a large can of tuna when Ma came in the porch door with a bag of groceries.

"Tara, hello! Will you sit for a cup of tea?" my mother asked. Although born and raised in Brooklyn, Mary Grace had picked up the lilting cadences of her parents, Irish immigrants. My maternal grandfather, James Noonan, a carpenter, had come to New York with a sack of bedding and the clothes on his back—or so went the family lore. A quick-footed dancer and scotch drinker, James had worked long hours as apprentice to a cabinetmaker to perfect his craft—work that ultimately paid off when he fast-talked his way onto the crew of a Park Avenue apartment renovation, where he convinced the designer to upgrade the wood and proceeded to craft a masterpiece.

From then on, whenever a "Park Avenue swell" was renovating an apartment, James Noonan was hired to do the cabinetry. Now, as Ma opened a dark walnut cabinet to stow two boxes of tea, I was reminded of the history in this house. Her grandfather used to see weekend patients in the dining room. My parents were married here, a slew of children baptized here. And James Noonan had been hired by Dr. McCorkle to renovate this very kitchen. In an age where so many kitchens were prefabricated pressboard, I felt a deep, timeless connection to family every time I swung open the dark walnut cabinets that had been built by my grandfather.

"You're getting way too skinny there, Tara," Ma said, taking a box of Hostess cupcakes out of the brown bag. "These will do you good."

"You always did try to fatten me up." Tara's amber eyes were lit with defiance. "All the moms and aunts give it their best shot, but it never works."

"So tell me what you're up to." Mary Grace filled the kettle at the sink—no microwaved water for her tea; that would be a travesty. "One more year you've got at college, then to work with the both of you."

"We don't mind hard work, Ma." I peered out the kitchen window at the guys around the shed as I rinsed my hands in the sink. "It's those guys you need to worry about."

Cocking one eyebrow, my mother agreed. "That's for sure. Your brother hired to play with toys. Whoever heard of such a thing? And those Fogarty brothers, getting the family business dumped in their laps. It's a shame, but they've got too much time on their hands. It's a wonder they've not been incarcerated, but don't get me started. How are your parents?"

"They're fine. My brother's visiting on leave, and Mama's still floating on a cloud."

"The prodigal son. Of course, we love the one who ran away." Mary Grace squinted out the window. "Is that your man with my Stevie?"

Tara's pale brown skin flushed pink. "He's a friend. One of Wayne's friends."

"Of course he is." Mary Grace placed a wrapped chocolate cupcake on a plate and handed it to Tara.

"Ma . . . don't make her eat it." I jabbed at the tuna with a vengeance. "You don't have to," I told Tara.

"It's okay." She tore open the clear wrapping and pulled off a curlicued edge of frosting. "I'd be a junk-food freak, except my mother banned it from the house."

Twenty minutes later, the guys filed in, along with Skeeter and Johnny, and everyone was sitting around the McCorkle table eating sandwiches along with juicy peaches and tomatoes Mary Grace had brought from the farm stand down the road.

Spooning peaches into a bowl, I marveled at how my mother managed to get half a dozen people settled and fed while tossing off questions that elicited participation from the more reserved and pointed up things everyone had in common. Ma was awesome at the social thing. She suggested Charlie give Steve tips on traveling to China, where sporting goods were manufactured for Victory Sports, and Steve seemed open to it all, not jealous at all. Which surprised me, considering the attraction that had once burned between him and Tara. They'd crushed on each other, back when we were in junior high. Not that they'd gone anywhere with it or even been an official couple. But watching them now, it all seemed so civil and grown-up.

Ma coaxed Tara to describe the needs of kids in a Trenton neighborhood association where Tara had been volunteering time while at Princeton. She started Bear talking about his week in Maui, sharing a shack with another surfer in the land of wild hibiscus, blue crush waves, and residents who could barely afford the gas to drive to the other side of the island for a surf competition.

At times like this, I could fool myself into believing there was a very real connection between Bear and me. *Close your eyes and pretend you're a girlfriend.* Of course, I'd never even been inside his VW camper, never visited the inner sanctum, but then I'd never heard of a girl who had.

"You should write some of those things down," I told Bear. "Such vivid images." I had always found his surfing adventures fascinating.

"Yeah, maybe he could make it into a limerick or something." Steve grinned maliciously, then bit into a hunk of sandwich.

Skeeter snorted, that pig snort he'd perfected at the age of ten. "There once was a loser from Brooklyn, who surfed Maui and . . . wait. What rhymes with Brooklyn?"

"Nothing, dirtbag," Steve said.

Charlie held the relish tray while Tara took some pickles. "Finding a rhyme for Brooklyn, I believe, would be a challenge for an experienced lyricist."

"Oh, you're just jealous that you don't have the gift, Stephen," Ma chastised. "Now Lindsay here, there's a talent. Though we haven't seen your writing lately, have we? Weren't you working on some short stories for one of your classes?"

"It's just a hobby, Ma," I said, quickly changing the subject back to surfing, something everyone would pick up on. "Did you hear, Ma? Charlie rode his first wave today."

And my mother gasped and made a fuss over Charlie's feat as Steve mentioned a surfing competition down the coast, and the conversation took off once again.

Biting into a juicy slice of peach, I felt a twinge of longing for the way things used to be, back when Elle and Darcy nearly lived in this house. Funny, the things you remember. Elle used to jump on my brother's back and hold on until he rolled onto the ground. Darcy once played a whole game of Life with her swimsuit stuffed with a roll of wadded toilet paper, not caring when Steve and his friends walked through the room gaping. With my girlfriends around, I never had to worry about being outnumbered by Steve and his friends. Most of all, I didn't have time to worry about anything.

I missed them both.

8

Elle

Stuck in Connecticut, Elle DuBois sat at the edge of the turquoise pool, kicking her legs to break the monotonous surface of the water. She loved swimming and had already done thirty laps, which was not the easiest feat in a pool shaped like a warped Frisbee.

"Do you guys ever swim?" she asked her cousins.

"Sure we do. I do all the time." Liam looked up from the filter, which he'd been reaching into, showing off in that eight-year-old boy show-offy way by pulling out insects and leaves and gunk with his bare hands. He slammed the filter cover on, stood at the edge of the pool, and called, "See?" as he cannonballed into the water.

"Ach!" his sister Gabby scoffed from the lounge chair behind Elle. "You little freak! Jump from the other side."

"I don't get it," Elle said. "Everyone on this street has their own pool. And right now, it's almost eighty degrees, and no one but Liam is using it." She squeezed water out of her hair, pondering the mysteries of suburban Connecticut. "What's that about?"

"People have other things to do," Gabriella said with an air of importance that made Elle want to flick her on the shoulder. Then again, most things Gabby said made Elle want to inflict some form of torture. Like the first night Elle arrived and Gabby asked if she had to share her room with Elle. And if she could still go to her friend's house for a sleepover. And if she needed to include Elle at the birthday party she'd been planning for so long "with only my best friends." A pool party, this Saturday. A stupid idea, as far as Elle was concerned, since neither Gabby nor her "very best friends" were going to go near the water.

This suburbia thing was worse than she'd expected.

Her cousins were complete strangers, little power brokers embedded in television shows and electronic games Elle had never even heard of. Aunt Deanna couldn't have cared less that Elle was there, as long as she had a chance to do her "thing," which was daily workout sessions at a gym where the women idolized emaciated models and talked about the evils of carbs and alcohol. Uncle Thomas was the sort of guy you could talk to, a lot like his brother, who used to be Elle's confidant before he'd decided that having a teenaged daughter made him feel too old. Unfortunately, Uncle Thomas was gone from the house most of the day and evening, absorbed in the business of lawyering for Keller and Steinberg.

"It's just for the summer," her mother had stressed, back in the safety of their close but cozy London flat. "In September, as soon as the dorms open, you'll have your own room in New Haven."

"I don't understand why I can't stay here," Elle had insisted, causing her parents to exchange that look again: the pale, stone-faced panic that their daughter was going to unearth a boulder they'd hoped was safely embedded. "Or I could go to Africa. Wouldn't Africa be a fabulous life experience?"

"Nigeria is no place for a young woman these days," her mother said candidly. An immunologist, Genevieve DuBois was employed by the World Health Organization, and at this point in her career a move to their offices in Nigeria was the key to advancement. Elle got that, and though she would miss her mother, she could live with the distance if it would keep her near her chums in London. "Right now, your education is of utmost importance."

"And your mother and I agree that it's time you returned Stateside. Time for some cultural exposure, too."

"I have all the culture I need here in London," Elle argued. "I don't see why I can't stay here with Dad."

At that point she'd caught her mother scowling at her father, a quick facial barb before she turned away, pretending to study the flower box of petunias outside the kitchen window. Elle felt the moment like an earthquake along a major fault; the earth was rumbling and two geographic plates were rumbling, rubbing against each other, pushing for power even as they shifted away from each other.

"What?" Elle pressed. "What is it?"

"You can't stay here," her mother hissed. "Dad is giving up the flat."

"Genevieve! I thought we agreed—"

"I never agreed to anything," Elle said. "Why didn't anyone ask me what I wanted? Why didn't you tell me, Dad?"

"There's nothing to tell," he snapped. "Your mother's off to her new job in Africa and you're to return to the States to finish university."

"But why aren't you keeping the flat?" Tears were welling in her eyes, damned tears over this unexpected ambush. She swiped at her face with one hand, then pointed to her small bedroom. "I can stay in my room. Right there . . ." Her voice was quavering.

"It's too late," her mother said. "Dad's decided he needs a new start. Another stab at . . . oh, I don't know, what is it you're looking for, Jasper?"

Never before had Elle seen her father gripped by horror. "This is not the appropriate time or place," he growled.

The strain was obvious on Genevieve DuBois's stricken face as she turned back to Elle. "Pardon me for being inappropriate, but I really don't know the proper way to tell our daughter that you're shacking up with your twentysomething girlfriend."

That had been the moment when Elle's life rumbled out of control.

Suddenly, her father wouldn't talk to her, not in the honest, open way they'd always maintained. After Dad packed a suitcase and slipped out of the apartment with a guilty kiss to her forehead, Mom had apologized halfheartedly, her voice cracking with emotion as she said that Dad was "in crisis" and that it was best for Elle to head back to the States, where she could set herself on solid ground, make some friends, embrace her own culture.

"Shopping malls and baseball and McDonald's?" Elle thought as her mother locked herself into the bathroom for a shower. "I think I can live without those displays of conspicuous consumption."

Her mother didn't answer. But a minute later, when Elle pressed her ear to the door, she could hear the shrill mew of sobs only slightly muffled by running water.

And that was the worst part—worse than banishment back to the States. The fact that her parents had lost control of their lives—that they had lost momentum and security after having traveled the world as best friends—that part frightened Elle most. Because if their lives were spinning out of control, how was Elle supposed to find solid ground?

Liam was singing a song, trying to goad his sister. "Chuck, Chuck, bo Buck. Banana-fana . . ." The name game, with an interesting choice of names. Elle had to admire his adventurous spirit.

She cupped a handful of water and let it trickle down her neck as she floundered for a way out of this cage. Yesterday she'd walked for an hour, cutting across people's lawns and gardens because there were no sidewalks or paths. All that walking, and she'd arrived nowhere, since there was nowhere to go. She'd asked Aunt Deanna about buses or mass transit, which made the poor woman seem perplexed and horrified. "Not in this neighborhood," her aunt had said, "but Gabby will be happy to drive you anywhere you want to go."

"But Mom!" Gabby had shrieked in a barrage of whiney complaints that had sent Elle scurrying from the family room with its slippery leather sofas facing a big-screen TV that seemed to be running 24/7. Unfortunately, having fled the family room, Elle had nowhere to run to. The room she shared with Gabby was so Gabby-inspired, with its canopied bed, tiny tulip wallpaper, and red microblinds, that it provided no refuge for Elle. With no spare, quiet room in the house, nowhere to walk, and her only mode of transport the grim prospect of a car ride with her sulking cousin to the mall, Elle felt trapped.

That was when she'd discovered the pool, the shimmering turquoise retreat that the family had seemingly abandoned . . . until today. Now that Elle had staked her claim on the great outdoors, Gabby and Liam had risen in protest, dusting off the lounge chairs and pretending to care about the pH balance and the filter system.

Liam was out of the pool now, creeping behind Elle.

"What are you doing?" she asked.

He giggled.

"Trying to drip on me?"

"And it's working," he said.

Elle reached behind her and grabbed hold of something—his ankle. She gave a tug and he fell onto her, sopping wet. Laughing, she leaned forward and they fell into the pool together in a burst of bubbles.

"Gross!" Liam gasped when his head popped above the surface. "She touched me! My own cousin! Ew!"

"Get over it," Elle said, bringing a leg to the surface to kick water in his direction. "You'll survive."

"Let's play a game," Liam said. "We can dive for pennies in twelve feet."

"Burn!" Gabby shouted. "Dad said no more coins. They're clogging the filter."

"That is not a burn, and how can a penny get in the filter? Eh-eh-eh-eh-eh! It doesn't float, you penis-head."

"Dad said," Gabby insisted.

"Penis-head." Elle wiggled her toes in the water. "And I thought I'd heard them all."

"Okay," Liam went on, now peeking into the side of the pool's filter. "How about Marco Polo. Or races. No, wait. Let's do a diving competition. Elle, did you know I can do a double backflip?"

"Really? I can't do a single backflip."

"You're not allowed to do flips off the side," Gabby squawked. "God, don't you know anything?"

"More than you," Liam taunted his sister as he climbed out of the pool. He positioned himself on the edge, facing away from the water.

"Don't you dare," Gabby threatened. "Stop it now."

Although Elle realized a backflip probably wasn't the safest maneuver, the goading in Gabby's voice made her wish Liam would do it—just launch himself into the air and bundle into a spinning ball and land in the water with a splash that shot chlorinated water all over her new swimsuit. God, she hated when bullies prodded and dared. More than once, she'd gotten herself in trouble taking up the challenge. Usually, she got away with it, but not that day on Bikini Beach, that stormy day when they'd all been warned to stay out of the water because of the riptides that had been reported . . .

"Don't you dare," Darcy had warned. "Don't be an idiot, Elle."

"I just want to go for a swim," Elle had said, edging out along the rocks of the jetty. Jagged, black chunky rocks. She'd expected the wet part to be slippery, but it wasn't hard to gain footing. Stepping from one to another, her arms outstretched like a graceful gymnast on the balance beam.

That day on the rocks had been a turning point, one of those moments she would later point to and think, that was it, that was the moment it all started to go wrong. Mom, being a doctor, began to ask herself how she missed all the warning signs. Her father insisted on selling Gram's house and whisked Elle away from "negative influences." That was the beginning of many visits to a coven of therapists who, at the time, seemed very nosy about Elle's personal business.

Those jagged rocks, hundreds of them dumped there by the Army Corps of Engineers to prevent another hurricane from wiping away the beach and tearing a bay into the coastline . . . there was something mesmerizing about the rocks that day: a dark whispering spell that seemed to summon her even before Darcy voiced the dare.

"You're full of shit." Darcy stood there, hands on her hips, an indignant princess. "You're not going in the water. And I know why you're doing this, Elle . . ."

Really? Elle thought with a secret smile. *If you know, then I wish you could explain it to me: the cutting, the brushfires in the dunes, the plover eggs stolen from nests and cracked on the sidewalk.* Elle was always getting in trouble, always the one behind small bits of mischief that horrified her parents. She'd been riding a wave of self-destruction, on a highway to hell, but none of the grown-ups had understood what pushed her.

"At the age of ten you should know better," her mother said, sitting upright on the sofa during a family meeting. "Playing with fire? Think of the wildlife at stake in the dunes. And I can't imagine the tragedy if the fire had spread from the dunes to someone's house."

But it was a game, Elle wanted to tell her. *A game of skill, or so Darcy had said. Here's how you play: Whoever can toss a lit match the farthest without the flames going out wins.*

But Elle hadn't mentioned the game. She was the only one caught, and she knew it would be the ultimate betrayal to give up her friends.

So Elle took the rap for the brushfires. And Elle got blamed for the smashed plover eggs, and for a stolen bicycle she knew nothing about. And when her parents grounded her, then found her in her bedroom slicing into her arm with a razor, she didn't have an answer beyond the simple fact that they had sequestered her in her room and she was bored out of her mind and helpless to stop the anger that swirled in the pit of her stomach and lashed over her, reminding her that she was a stupid, moronic idiot whom no one cared about.

All those merciless names Darcy had called her every time she refused to follow her to the ice cream shop or on those fancy picnic lunches packed by the Loves' maid. Triangles of turkey sandwiches with the crusts cut off. Mandarin oranges packed in delicate Tupperware cups. And for dessert, Twizzlers and pixie sticks and nonpareils that Nessie had frozen to keep the chocolate from melting during the picnic.

Elle hated those lunches, the evidence that so many people cared about Darcy Love. She had them all wrapped around the tendrils of her flaxen hair.

"Don't you dare jump, you moron!" Gabby snarled at her brother, jarring Elle back into the present.

Why do bullies have so much power? She stood up at the edge of the pool, wondering why she ever let Darcy get to her.

Whatever had happened to Darcy, anyway? She'd just run into Tara, and over the years she'd gotten a few postcards from Lindsay, her only real friend in the group, but Lindsay had never mentioned Darcy.

Why am I even wondering? Why don't I go there and check it out? She could stay with Lindsay; the McCorkles always managed to squeeze one more into their rambling house with its screened porches, window seats, and attic cubbies. Of course, there was the sticky matter of getting clearance from the relatives. Not that she couldn't just leave, but she didn't have a U.S. dollar to her name, and she sensed that hitchhiking was not the thing to do in the States these days.

Damn, but her parents had cut her off at the knees. Didn't trust her. Pissed her off to no end.

Did she have Lindsay's number in her cell?

"Elle . . ." She was jarred from her plan by Liam, who leaned into the pool, bored as usual. "Do you want to have a race?"

"Just as long as you don't splash me," Gabby carped.

"I have an idea," Elle told Liam, feeling brighter as she curled her toes over the edge of the pool and flexed her knees like a racer on the starting block. "Let's jump together. Why don't you come to this side of the pool." She motioned him over, secretly pointing a finger toward Gabby lounging in the chair behind them.

Glancing over one skinny shoulder, Liam shot her a look of annoyance. But he came around the pool, water slapping on the pavement under his flame-print swim trunks.

"Right here." She showed him where to line up for maximum effect. Then, on the count of three, Elle and Liam cannonballed into the water. When Elle surfaced, Gabby was on her feet, shrieking.

"I hate you both!" She dabbed at her face with a towel, then headed into the house. "I'm telling Mom!"

"I think we're in trouble," Liam said, grinning.

"It's not the first time, and it won't be the last." Elle floated onto her back, loving the silky feel of warm water around her body and the satisfaction of having annoyed Gabriella. Nothing like bullying the bully. Gabby would be relieved to have her cousin drop out of her life again. No love lost there, though Elle would sort of miss Liam. It wasn't often Elle met an eight-year-old who could beat her in a game of spades.

9

Darcy

"Another night at the mansion of Love!" Kevin stepped into the pristine living room and touched the hooves of a sculpted horse adorning the mantel. "Don't you ever feel like you live in a museum?"

Moving the candles to the center of the Louis XIV table, Darcy tried not to notice the dirtprints his shoes had left on the carpet of the "parlor." What the hell, Nessie would whisk it all up in the morning, and she doubted that Mother or Dad were going to make the trip out here anytime soon. Dad was embroiled in the accounting fiasco at the firm, and Mother was embroiled in the tennis pro's embrace. "To be honest, I think this house is way overdone. Tacky, really."

"No way! It's the Love Mansion. It's famous. People cruise down this road just to have a look." He crossed back to Darcy, strung his arms behind her, and ground his hips into hers. "Everybody wants to feel the love."

"Our house is going to be different," she asserted. "Gorgeous but cozy. Full of real love."

"Really? You mean, a place where I can fuck you every day? Like, three times a day?"

"Mm-hmm." She smiled, relieved to see Kevin in a good mood and fairly sober. The past few times they'd been together, often heading over here after he helped close up Coney's, he'd been too drunk to really talk, and the sex had been hurried and halfhearted, all about dousing the fire so Kevin could pass out and get to sleep.

Not tonight, Darcy thought, rocking against him. The bulge in his pants hit her bare tummy, and as she pressed against him she felt herself grow wet with wanting him.

"Let's get naked," he growled.

At first Darcy felt hesitant to do it here, in mother's cold cathedral parlor. But when Kevin dipped his hands inside her halter top and brushed over her hard nipples so abruptly that it took her breath away, a new desire to defile streaked through her. She tugged off her top, then unbuckled her tight combat pants. "You want naked? You're going to have to work for it tonight."

"Ooh." He pursed his lips, dropping to his knees to unzip, then scrape her pants down over her shapely thighs. "Nice." He ran his fingers over the scalloped edge of her lace thong, slipped his fingers under the edge, then dipped them into her, into the warm, creamy wetness. "Ooh." His fingers swirled, gently at first, then with more pressure as they danced over her.

That motion always drove her to climax, and he knew it. She closed her eyes, letting herself go until a tiny gasp escaped her. Thank God for Kevin and his fingertip dance. She pushed her pelvis into him, wanting him in the worst way.

"You are hot. Hot and ready." He pulled down her panties, cupped one hand over the mound of her pelvis, and rested his cheek against her thigh for a close-up view.

"Kevin . . ." She laughed. "Don't weird me out."

"I just love to look at your pussy."

Such a boy. He seemed to like talking dirty when all she wanted was to hear him say that he loved her, that he couldn't live without her, that he wanted to spend the rest of his life with her and no one else. "Well, you can look all night." She reached down and peeled the rest of her clothes off her ankles. "Or you can see how it feels."

"Aw, man." He stepped out of his jeans, his cock pink and upright.

Darcy tried to open her legs and pull him in between, but she was too short to take him standing. Thinking fast, he quickly lifted her and sat her on the fat, rolled arm of the velvet settee. Balanced there, she spread her legs, ready to take him in.

He thrust his hips forward and speared her. "Nice and deep. How's that feel? Huh? Huh?"

She didn't answer, too preoccupied in sensation. In truth, it was just the right angle for moist, deep probing, and she needed all her concentration to keep herself propped there, meeting his slamming thrusts.

Heat rose inside her, sensation mounting, pushing her steadily toward orgasm. It was fast, but she didn't care. They had all night for more . . . hell, they had the rest of their lives. She heard a little gasp escape her throat as she came, and he plunged harder, pausing deep inside with a heaving groan.

She pressed her eyes closed, hoping he could feel it, the bond between them. The love. Definitely love, or else she wouldn't be able to tolerate the feeling of his sweat, salty and gritty, on her thighs and breasts. Sometimes Kevin didn't appreciate how she kept her body perfect, her skin well hydrated and exfoliated, her nails perfectly shaped, manicured, polished.

With a deep breath, he hunkered over her, resting his sweaty forehead on her shoulder. "That was so awesome!" He pulled out of her and she felt moisture trickle out, spilling onto the arm of the love seat.

Wouldn't Mother be horrified.

Kevin thrust his fists in the air and roared, the lion victorious over the kill. Sometimes he could be an asshole. Crossing her arms over her breasts, Darcy realized that she had a good amount of work ahead of her in trying to turn her diamond in the rough into a faceted, polished stone. Lately she felt more and more discouraged now that she was in this alone. Much as she hated to admit it, Darcy missed her friends. She missed Tara, the voice of reason, and some days she felt that the whole summer had soured without Lindsay narrating her life, building her up and cheering her on.

As Kevin cranked up the CD player and danced naked on the coffee table, Darcy lay down on her side and contemplated the old stones of the mantel. Each one was distinctive, a different size and shape, and yet they fit together perfectly, as if destined to be that way.

Sort of the way she'd fit with Lindsay and Tara. Her friends . . . her only friends.

Not that people weren't nice to her at college, and of course, she had a few girlfriends from high school in Great Egg, but they were all distant. Just because she knew their names and had spent some time playing tennis with them didn't mean she really cared.

Which was the problem here. God help her, she cared about Lindsay and Tara, and it was killing her right now, wondering if they were at Lindsay's house playing Scrabble or out at a club or catching a late movie. How could they have a good time without her? Didn't they feel the loss—the stone missing from the mantel?

The other day she'd seen them on Bikini Beach, surrounded by surfboards and guys. It looked like Tara had scored herself a boyfriend, a compact, Tom Cruise type, and whatever they were doing, telling stories or jokes, it was all punctuated by laughter and comments. They were having so much fun they didn't see Darcy peering at them from the dunes, and she didn't dare head down the path to the beach. Because then it would be incredibly obvious that they were having fun and she was not.

Outside, tires whirred on the circular driveway.

"Whoa." Kevin stopped his naked dance as headlights flashed through the huge arched windows. "Somebody's coming."

Pressing a pillow to her chest, Darcy edged to the window. The wood-sided Jeep creaked to a stop. The passenger door popped open and Fish dropped to his feet.

"It's Fish and David," she said.

"Really?" He reached for his jeans.

"I'll give you two minutes to get rid of them."

"I can't do that." He pulled on his pants and zipped carefully.

"But Kev . . . You don't want to go out now, do you?"

"Fuck, yeah."

"It's almost midnight."

"So? Sometimes we get a late start." He raked his fingers through his hair and pulled on his T-shirt.

She shook her head, flabbergasted. "Doing what? Where are you guys going? All the bars are closed."

"We just drive. Park along the beach and party. Do you want to come?"

The prospect of sitting in a van and listening to David and Fish ramble on in that bizarre nonsense language they'd devised, steaming while they laughed at each other's stupid jokes made her feel weary. "I already came, thanks."

He laughed. "Good one, Darcy. Okay, then." He walked to the wide beveled glass door, pulling it open just as the gong of the doorbell sounded.

"We thought you'd be here."

"Yeah."

And with that, the guys were gone.

Darcy tossed the pillow to the couch and picked up her clothes gingerly. Blowing out the candles, she tried to shake off the bad feeling. She was friendless and her boyfriend was in deep with those guys, who were definitely a bad influence. Neither Fish nor Dave was married, and neither of them had a girlfriend or job waiting in the wings.

Darcy wasn't the most creative or intelligent student at Bennington, but when she wanted the lead part in a show or the favor of a teacher, she won through sheer persistence. She usually knew how to get exactly what she wanted, but then she'd never had to win her friends back before.

Falling into the posh white chair, Darcy pressed her shirt to her face and burst into tears.

10

Lindsay

It sort of happened by accident. One June night when the surf was up late in the afternoon, we ended up riding some impressive waves until the sun began to sink low over the dunes, a sizzling ball of orange laced by purple clouds. Everyone was in a good mood from the awesome surf and we didn't want it to end, so Bear invited us back to his place, just up the path through the dunes.

"I've got some brats," Bear said, "and I'll send McCorkle for beers."

"That's a great offer," Charlie said, wiping his wet hair vigorously with a towel. "Is it far?"

And the rest of us laughed, since Bear's camper was walking distance, just beyond the parking lot. "Just up the path and left after you cross the dunes," Bear said. Although Bear officially lived with his mother in Wading River, the VW was his real home, and the town of Southampton allowed him to stay with the small community of campers on this parkland as long as he purchased a greenkey pass each year.

That evening was an eye-opener for me, sitting on a blanket, Tara and Charlie and the other guys in armchairs clustered around the hibachi. We offered to help, but Bear had it under control, roasting the bratwurst till the skins crisped. He served the wieners with toasted bread, cheddar cheese, and mustard, and I remember thinking the meal was a slice of heaven. Afterward he carved up a fresh pineapple with a minimum of mess and brought the platter around to us, a patient server. That was the thing that surprised me about Bear; he was surprisingly capable, a calm, generous host. As night rolled in around us, he opened his oceanfront home to us, and realizing how he lived here under the stars, humbly and respectfully, made me love him that much more.

"How's that generator been running?" Steve asked Bear, and they talked shop for a while. Steve's engineering degree made people think he was an expert repairman, but in truth he'd always been good with his hands, always very logical.

Beyond the flames of the hibachi, Bear's VW pop-up camper seemed embedded in the sand, the roofline extended by blue awnings. Two fishing rods and a handful of boards were staked in the sand amid a clutter of bicycles. I was dying to know what it was like inside, but today I'd gotten closer. I was even wearing a big, oversized sweatshirt Bear had loaned me when the sun went down. I hugged my arms, loving the feel of it, not caring that my hair was stiff from salt water.

Through the bordering stand of pine trees, the bright lights of a car swerved through the empty parking lot. I didn't think much of it, assuming someone had come for a late walk on the beach.

"It's a cop," Napolean said. "I swear, it's park police. Anybody got anything on them?"

"It's not the police," Bear groaned.

"Looks like a kid," Steve speculated.

"Hey!" Skeeter jumped up, shouting at the stranger. "Who are you?"

We all laughed at that, until the stranger called back, "Darcy Love."

The guys kept laughing, all except Charlie who asked: "Who's that?"

Tara and I shook our heads at each other.

"It must be a joke," I said, knowing Darcy would never come out here.

But as the figure tromped closer in the sand, I recognized the unmistakable swagger and waist-length hair of Darcy Love. She was lugging a shopping bag over one arm, humming something under her breath.

"I heard there was a party," she said, moving into the fire's circle of light. "Is this the party of the first part? Or wait. This ain't no disco?"

"Hey, Darce," my brother said, ignoring the fact that she wasn't making a whole lot of sense. "Have a seat. Join the circle."

"Well, how do I get in?" She pressed her hands together in prayer position and moved them like a fish trying to wriggle in.

"Here you go," Bear said, opening a folding chair for her. "Can I get you a beer? I could throw a few more brats on the fire."

I bit my lip, loving him for being so kind to her, despite the fact that she'd pretty much behaved like a prima donna for as long as he'd known her.

She listed to the side a bit, tilted by the weight of her Bergdorf shopping bag. "I don't need a beer, that's for sure." She dropped the bag into the sand with a dull thunk, then sank down into the lawn chair. "I've already got a head start." She reached into the bag and lugged out a gallon bottle of scotch. The expensive kind—Chivas Regal.

A third of it was gone.

"Darcy, did you drink all that?" Tara asked, sitting up in alarm.

"Did I?" Darcy curled the bottle up, her lean bicep popping. "I don't know."

"Darcy, you're drunk," I said with a mixture of concern and disappointment.

"Am I?" She pointed a manicured finger at her chin, but missed and poked her nose. "I guess I am."

That was when she turned and faced me, really looked me in the eye. Hers were bloodshot. "I'm sorry, Lindsay," she said, suddenly misting over, her face crumpling.

Across the fire circle Skeeter, Napolean, and Steve exchanged awkward looks, probably wishing this "chick stuff" would stop before they got too uncomfortable.

"You know," Steve said, pushing out of a low beach chair, "this would be a good time to look at that generator that's been giving Bear trouble." And the three of them peeled out of their chairs and went around to the back of the camper. With a sad smile, Bear followed them.

"I am just so, incredibly, freaking sorry," Darcy crooned.

I kneeled in the sand beside her, a hand on her shoulder. "I know, Darce," I said, patting her shoulder. It seemed pathetic and sad that the only way she could apologize was in a drunken sway, but what could I do? This was Darcy in all her inebriated imperfection. Besides, wasn't intolerance of imperfection the very thing that had started this whole mess?

"I was so awful," Darcy sobbed, turning tearful eyes toward Tara. "And I want to make it up to you guys. I will. I don't know how, but I will."

"You don't have to make it up to us," I said. "But your apology is accepted."

And she welled up again and just about fell into my arms, her tears falling onto Bear's thick, soft sweatshirt. I hugged her, surprised at how soft and warm she felt—especially for a skinny girl. I guess when it comes to hugs, anatomical structure is secondary when you're swamped with emotion.

That night I was a good friend to Darcy once again, driving her home, tucking her in, even holding her hair back when she shot out of bed and leaned over the commode. It was not the way I'd hoped to spend the evening, especially after finally being invited to hang at Bear's place. But hey, what are friends for?

11

Tara

Tara had never fallen for that stardust-and-flowers notion of love at first sight. She understood intellectual attraction from the way she had clicked on a higher plane with two of her professors at school. She also understood sexual attraction—totally got it—but unfortunately she'd never felt the heart and mind tug at the same time.

So it had been an oddly disarming, even startling sensation when Charlie Migglesteen had filed into the living room of the Hamptons house behind her brother, both guys toting duffel bags and wearing military uniforms that reminded Tara of something her brother had worn back in Boy Scouts. She had never met Charlie before, and so there was no reason for her to feel anything toward him at all. Anything.

And yet she did. When he spoke, he told stories full of imagery that transported her to a country road in Korea or a crowded hut the size of a one-car garage that was shared by a family of eight, stories that revealed social context and compassion, cultural awareness and willingness to connect. From the day he arrived, she found herself wanting to be near him, helping her mother cook in the kitchen or serve drinks on the deck or even drive into town so that she could be near Charlie, basking in his presence.

And then, there was the physical attraction, the surprising curiosity of how it would feel to press her fingertips into the hollow of his neck, to feel his thick lower lip move over her skin, to explore his smooth chest, following the line of feathery hair that dipped past his navel, below the waist of his shorts . . .

"I think I've lost my mind," she told her friends one of the first days of the tentative truce as they cruised down Southampton's Main Street in Darcy's convertible, passing picket fences and gardens, small shops and boutiques, and Darcy's eastern shrine, Saks Fifth Avenue. "My brother used to drive me crazy. Whenever he was home, I had to get out of the house. But now, I don't mind him. I think of reasons to stay home. I don't know what's wrong with me."

"Oh, come on. This is not about your geeky brother," Lindsay squeaked, her freckled nose scrunched in a grin. "Admit it: you're into Charlie. Do you want to stop for ice cream?"

Darcy nodded knowingly as she angled into a parking spot. "Yeah-huh. Yes on the ice cream, yes on the secret attraction. It's so obvious, Tara. So, have you done it yet?"

"You seem to forget, I live with my parents." Tara climbed out of the car and followed them into the shop.

"I take that as a no?" Darcy asked.

"A definite no, and it's not going to happen. There's no way any sex will be had in my parents' house. The Washingtons have a strict rule about that. No opposite-gender visitors in your room or behind closed doors. I don't even think my parents have had sex in the last decade."

"Too much information." Lindsay scanned the chalkboard of flavors. "Raspberry sorbet sounds good."

"Sorbet?" Darcy's eyes flickered with approval. "Good for you, sticking to the diet. It's paying off, right?"

Lindsay lowered her voice, as if on guard for the fat police. "I'm just about into last year's swimsuit. But I figure one cheeseburger and it's all going down the drain."

"Hold tight," Tara said. "You've been doing great." She propped her sunglasses on her head and looked up at the menu, craving a hot fudge sundae but deciding to resist in deference to Lindsay.

"But let's get back to the crisis at hand. Alone time for Tara and Charlie." Darcy licked the edge of her chocolate chip cone and pressed a napkin to her lips. "It seems like such a natural since you're staying under the same roof. No way to sneak away? Pull him into a closet? Lock him into your room at night?"

"Not happening. Mama watches us like a hawk, when she isn't busy cooking up ribs and sweet potato pie for Wayne."

"Of course you can't do it at home," Lindsay said. "That could put you in therapy for years. You guys have to step out, find some other place."

"A summer place," Darcy sighed. "Remember that movie? We must have watched it, like, eight times the first summer we had boyfriends."

Tara remembered. It was the summer after Elle left, the summer they'd wrangled up boyfriends. Darcy had lost a highly manipulated game of Truth or Dare and taken the challenge to go make out in the dunes with Kevin McGowan. That had left Lindsay and Tara back on the blanket with two other boys—Anthony and Brian. Brian Salerno, with shaggy red hair that needed trimming and broad shoulders that seemed too big for the rest of his body. While Anthony and Lindsay wandered down the beach, Brian had leaned back on the blanket and shown Tara the Big Dipper, and though she already knew most of the basics of astronomy she pretended to learn, letting him lead the way. She didn't speak when he kissed her, didn't stop him when he put his hand over her left breast and started tickling it, paying special attention to the nipple. It was her first time being touched that way, and although anything more would have been out of the question, Brian had never pushed her. She'd liked that about him. He seemed to understand her need to feel safe, her limits.

After that night, they started meeting most nights, the six of them, for games like Spin the Bottle and Truth or Dare. Inevitably, they'd split into couples toward the end of the night for more kissing and caressing. At the time it had worried Tara that Brian only liked her because she let him get under her shirt, but the warm, tingling sensations he brought on were sweet, and he was fun to talk with, too.

Her first boyfriend . . . not the most meaningful relationship. On the other hand, she'd suffered huge crushes that never reached a physical level. As a kid she'd always mooned over Lindsay's brother Steve, and one summer the girls tolerated her need to follow him secretly and spy on him, hiding out behind picket fences or privets or dunes. And then there'd been a crush on her dance teacher, who turned out to be gay. And Professor Spencer, Contemporary Poets 101, who could crack open a poem and reveal the still waters that ran so deep.

But looking back, she had to admit that Brian had stirred up sweeter physical sensations than anyone since. Sometimes it bothered Tara that she didn't have the knock-down, screaming orgasms Darcy talked about, the earth-shattering events depicted in movies. When she was in the mood, sex was a ticklish, hungry experience— more an act of compliance than a soul-shaking experience. And there was so much to worry about, running the range from pregnancy to STDs, that she found herself more involved in worrying whether the condom stayed on and intact, and whether her period came on time. She played it ultrasafe with condoms and birth control pills, but all those mechanics outweighed interesting sensations. From what she'd read, she was missing something, but though she'd tried, she was beginning to accept that the big "O" just might not be a part of her sexual alphabet.

Darcy handed over a twenty to pay for their ice creams, then whirled around with a snap. "I know what we can do! A party. A big, crazy sleepover party at my house, with boyfriends invited. Each couple gets their own private, luxurious suite for the night. How's that? Better than any game-show prize, right?"

"Awesome." Lindsay handed out napkins. "I'd do a happy dance if I had a boyfriend to invite."

"Just shut up and ask Bear already." Darcy tilted her head, staring through a spray of gold hair. "You know you like him, and it's about time he stepped up and claimed you as his woman."

"That sounds wonderfully barbaric." Lindsay licked the edge of her sorbet. "Uh-huh. Just as soon as he discovers fire and invents the wheel, I'm sure the next thing on his list will be throwing me over his shoulder and ravishing me."

"You'll never know if you don't try," Darcy told her. "And you, you need to hook up with Colonel Wigglesteen before he's shipping out of here and your summer is wasted."

It wouldn't be a total waste, Tara thought, realizing the value in their emotional connection, but Darcy wouldn't get that. "What are your parents going to think?" Tara asked.

"They're not going to be there. Just like every night. Dad never gets out of his office and Mom's too busy screwing that tight-assed tennis pro back in Manhasset."

Lindsay rolled her eyes. "Again, too much information."

"We'll do it the weekend after July fourth. I'll have Lupe cook us a really nice dinner and we can mix up a big batch of frozen drinks—margaritas or piña coladas. It'll be a real party."

"What'll I tell my parents? Mama's already got her eyes on the two of us. I think she's suspicious."

Darcy lowered her shades to glower at Darcy. "I can't believe I'm hearing this. Get creative! Or tell them you're staying at my place. It's the actual truth, so you don't have to eat yourself up with guilt."

"That's true." Tara let out a laugh. "A deceptive truth . . ."

"But who's counting?" Lindsay said. "Go for it, Tara. You deserve some time with Charlie."

Tara could think of a million reasons to argue, but as she was about to wax prudent she realized this would be her one chance to be with Charlie, who was so tantalizingly close this summer, and yet so out of reach. What would it be like to fall into his arms and have the freedom to spend all night together, just kissing and touching each other?

"Well . . ." Tara felt her cheeks grow warm. "If Mr. Migglesteen goes along with the ruse, I mean, if he's into it—"

"That's not going to be a problem," Darcy said. "That boy's got 'Lust for Tara' written across his forehead."

"Do you think?" Tara squinted. "I mean, I'm really into him. I haven't felt this way about a guy for a long time, and I'm sort of hoping that, if we do connect, I'll finally get to . . ." She looked around to make sure no one was listening in. "I think orgasm is a possibility."

"Again!" Lindsay clapped her hands over her ears. "Way too much information. Just say yes, get the boy in bed, see how he tickles your taco, and then we'll talk."

"Okay." Tara's friends were handing her the one thing she'd been craving this summer: a chance to be with Charlie.

Time to shut up and go for it.

12

Lindsay

Today is the day; you've got to ask him today, I told myself as Bear came into Old Towne Pizza, grabbed a Coke, and took his usual seat at the counter.

"Hey, squirt," he said, all business. "Want a drink?"

"I'll take a Diet Coke." Not that I couldn't have gotten one myself, but I was tickled to let Bear serve me. "You're in early."

"Yeah, the surf sucks." He sat in his usual seat at the counter, huddled in a red hooded sweatshirt with Old Towne Pizza emblazoned across the chest. A cool rain had blown in that morning from the northeast, and everyone was feeling the chill. Of course, Bear didn't abandon summer completely, wearing flip-flops and shorts that suggested a tight, square butt.

Three weeks at this job and I hadn't tired of watching the delivery guy. If I didn't work here I could probably get arrested for stalking, but I looked forward to hanging at the counter and talking with him, laughing over his anecdotes about eccentric customers, who were in bountiful supply in the Hamptons. But most of all, the downtime at the pizzeria had given us a chance to talk about more important things, things that mattered in our lives, like Bear's dream to make it as a pro surfer and my secret wish to be a writer one day. Already our relationship had moved up a few notches from the easy camaraderie of two surfers waiting in the lineup. I was a little worried that asking him to the dinner party at

Darcy's would ruin everything. He'd ask if it was a date, and I'd say, well, yeah, and he'd freak out and read me the "I just want to be friends" speech that every boy was programmed with in seventh grade.

"Any chance this storm will kick up the surf?" I asked.

"Not according to the Weather Channel." He flipped open the *Newsday* that Sal left on the counter each day. "What's Ann Landers got to say today?"

"Ann thinks a mother-in-law should mind her own *beeswax*," I said with a midwestern twang.

"And horoscopes. Let's see. You're supposed to start something new, and what's this mean? Saturn is leaning on your midheaven?"

"I think it means Sal's working me too hard," I said.

"I heard that," Sal called from the kitchen.

As Bear read his horoscope and asked for my help figuring out the Jumble, I thought of how I loved this daily ritual with him. Sharing a Coke, discussing the news. Some nights Bear folded pizza boxes and stacked them to the ceiling in a space beside the pantry while I wiped down tables and vinyl booths, refilled dispensers, and counted out a drawer for the register, the way Sal had taught me. Tonight I needed to get the mop and wipe the floor by the door, where wet footprints stamped the concrete.

"Um, these have the hauntingly familiar shape of large flip-flops," I said.

Bear looked down at his feet. "Guilty. But Sal has a rug in the back for nights like this. Can't have some bony old Hamptons heiress falling on her way to grab a slice."

"How did two poor kids like us end up out here?" I said, realizing that when it came to money I had more in common with Bear than I did with Darcy, corporate heiress from the land of opportunity, and Tara, whose strict parents sometimes made everyone forget that Mr. Washington was a famous trial attorney, known as much for his million-dollar retainers as the celebrity clients he defended. Aside from Hamptons summers, I lived in a modest brownstone in Brooklyn. Bear's mother owned a small bungalow in Wading River, a quiet town on the North Shore that edged into the Long Island Sound, a stone-muddled, still body of water. His father, now remarried, had left New York, moving out to the Midwest.

"Somebody's gotta take care of the tourists." He disappeared into the back room and returned with a nubby gray mat lined in black rubber. It fell into place in front of the door, and he was back on his stool, back where I loved having him watch as I wrote down orders, served slices at the counter, and made change at the register.

"So what are you doing for the Fourth?" he asked.

"Let's see . . . I'll probably sleep in, then kick myself because I can't drive through town because of the parade. When the tourists get tired of monopolizing the streets with their miniature flags and decorated wagons, I'll drive to the beach. But then the surf will be too crowded with all the weekend warriors, so I'll head out to Coney's, where they'll charge a cover to watch the fireworks on the beach. So I'll head home and pull the covers up over my head and hope some jerk kid doesn't blow the roof off the McCorkle house with his M-80 firecracker."

"Feeling cynical today?"

"I hate the rain."

"I'll give you that. But this is more than that. I've seen you laughing in the rain."

The words "laughing in the rain" made me want to jump over the counter and kiss him. I knew what he was talking about, the times when we were surfing and rain started and I hopped up on my board with a hoot because the beach had cleared, leaving us wide-open spaces to surf the splattering waves. I always loved those storms, and I loved him for remembering.

"What?" he prodded. "What's this blue funk about?"

"Nothing." That sounded coy. I had to go on. "There's this thing coming up after the Fourth." Something sagged inside me, pulling at my resolve. *Go on, you big wimp!* "What're you doing on the Fourth, anyway?"

"Steve and I were going to head down to Hatteras Island end of June, check out a competition there. One of the guys I've been talking to about sponsorship will be there."

I nodded, not liking the idea of spending the Fourth without Bear anywhere near the Hamptons. Of course, if I said something like that, I knew he'd feel totally trapped. That whole crew—my brother's friends—they were raised in a culture of no commitments, no tethers, except to your board. I calculated, knowing that most surf competitions lasted a day or two. He'd be back in time for the party.

"The thing is, Darcy's having a party at her place. Just a few friends. Some food and drinks. It's the Saturday after the Fourth, so you should be back." I shrugged, not sure what he was thinking. "She thought I should ask you."

He squinted at me. "Let me get this straight. Darcy wants me to come?"

"Sure."

"Does Kevin know?"

"Oh, no. She . . . I mean, I want you to come. With me. *I'm* asking." How many ways could I trip over myself?

"So the weekend after the Fourth?" He squinted toward the back of the kitchen, as if the answer were printed under the sailboats on Sal's calendar. "Yeah, I could do that."

His simple words sounded like a declaration of love. The edges of the windows were steaming up, but I could see that the sky was darkening early, the streets slick with rain.

But the rain didn't matter. Bear had said yes.

To keep myself from staring at him in glee I filled a Diet Coke for myself. Suddenly I didn't mind the rain that kept me close to Bear inside the pizzeria. There was a certain stillness and peace in the dry quiet under the storm of a long summer day. I sipped my Diet Coke, smothering a laugh. What would Steve think when he figured out his best friend was going to become his brother-in-law? Ha!

13

Darcy

"You're not eating any of that chocolate, are you?" Darcy called out into the dining room, where Lindsay was arranging lavender M&Ms and mini–chocolate bars Darcy had special-ordered from a local candy shop. The overnight mailing had cost more than the candy itself, but Darcy had just smiled at the alarmed clerk and flicked her shiny gold credit card onto the counter. Why these people got so freaked about money, she'd never understand.

"I only polished off the lavender ones," Lindsay called back.

"What?" Darcy's head snapped up as Lindsay appeared in the kitchen doorway, hands behind her back.

"Don't be a pain in the ass. Besides, I'm saving myself for the shrimp cocktail, which is on my diet, Richard Simmons." Lindsay fanned her hand through the air, revealing a crystal dish laden with pearly smooth lavender candies. "Voila! Nice, huh? The little candy bars are cute, too. Should we garnish with a few orchids?"

"Excellent idea, but float them in one of those little lavender bowls," Darcy said, pointing toward the table stacked with soft pale purple candles, bowls, and plates. The lavender color theme had been inspired by a magazine piece she'd read the last time she had her toes done at the salon—"How to turn your get-together into an A-List Party." Part of the appeal in the photos was that the party planners kept to a specific color theme, making the room look like a department store display or a Hollywood set. So Darcy had decided to take her favorite purple to a tropical level, to a bluish, silvery lavender, soothing and relaxing. It seemed appropriate for the "truce" party to be decked in calm, copacetic tones, and although her friends kept joking about it, this party was important to her. She wanted to make things up to her friends. She wanted to do something nice and show them a good time and prove that she was a solid friend after all.

"Uh . . . Darce?" Lindsay leaned over the open box of flowers and stared at the invoice tucked inside. "Did you really spend more than a thousand dollars on flowers?"

"Was that the total?" Darcy crumpled up the invoice and tossed it into the garbage. "Two points! No wonder the wonky florist kept asking me if it was for a wedding."

"That's more than I make in a month."

"Really? You gotta get that pizza man to step it up." *Please, don't play the poverty card again*, she thought, turning away from her friend. Just when they were getting along so well, too. Lindsay had been a great help, shopping with her and dreaming up ideas. It was Lindsay who'd pointed out that people don't like food that's too hard to eat at a party. "Date food is not ribs or chicken wings that can get stuck in your teeth," she'd said. So they'd opted for mini–hot dogs, miniburgers, shrimp cocktail, and a chopped salad that Lupe would serve in the elegant lilac bowls they'd found at the South-ampton gift shop. Working as a team, they'd whipped up a fabu-lous fete; Darcy hoped Lindsay wasn't going to ruin it all now with a pity party for herself.

"Wait till you see the lanai," Darcy said, trying to distract her friend. "Don't look now; I want it to be a surprise. But it's amazing. The florist sent his guys out to do it personally, and I swear it looks like a little bungalow on a Caribbean island. And the lavender was a perfect choice, so calm and romantic. While everyone else is draping their porches in tacky, flaming red, white, and blue, we'll be ultracool in ultraviolet."

"From today's forecast, it looks like we got lucky. It's supposed to be clear and in the eighties."

"Well, I forecast that we're all going to get lucky tonight," Darcy said, peering at her friend over a bouquet of sweet-smelling orchids. "A very high probability of satisfaction."

Lindsay's dark brows shot up. "A warm front blowing in?"

"So warm it's going to be downright hot."

* * *

Why am I the one who has to fix everybody else's life? Darcy thought as she flopped onto her bed and clicked off the phone. She'd just stepped out of the shower when Lindsay called in a blue funk, telling her she wouldn't come to the party because Bear had cancelled. Something about him being stuck in South Carolina.

"Just get your butt over here. I'll get you a date," she'd told Lindsay, who'd argued for a few minutes, then finally agreed to put on a happy face and come to the party "for Tara."

Now, all Darcy had to do was produce a relatively cute guy, within the hour.

She sat up, pumped moisturizer from the bottle on her nightstand, and smoothed it over her long legs, now tanned a honey amber. Kevin was going to get lucky tonight, if he kept his promise to stay conscious. Lately he'd been staggering or passing out before the end of the night, to the point that Darcy was beginning to feel less like a girlfriend and more like a sitter by the time two A.M. rolled around. She'd given him a little pep talk and he'd promised to stay awake and in the game tonight.

Kevin was under control, but who could she lure in for Lindsay?

The gardener's son was hot, but not so good with English.

There were a few bartenders at Coney's who always loved to leer at Darcy, but some of them were married, and last week when she let a couple guys do navel shooters, Kevin had turned bright red in jealous fury.

"The thing is, I'm having a party tonight, and I thought you might like to come."

"Really? A party of two?"

She laughed. "More like six of us, but it's going to be fun. Why don't you come?"

"Are you going to be there? I'll come for you . . . or better yet, *with* you."

"I've got a boyfriend."

"I don't mind if he watches."

"You are outrageous," she said, though secretly she savored the fact that Austin wanted to be with her. It felt good, having that power over him. "So . . . do you want to come?"

"You know it."

"To the party!"

He let out a low, growly laugh. "Yeah, okay. But you're not expecting me to dance or wear a tux or anything."

"Just be nice to Lindsay."

"I'm always nice," he insisted. "Which one is Lindsay?"

Darcy bit her lower lip, wondering if he was thinking about Lindsay's weight. It was hard being friends with someone so out of control, but at least Lindsay had been making an effort this summer, and she'd trimmed down a little. "She's the brunette," she said carefully.

"The buxom brunette." There was a pause. "Yeah, okay. Want me to bring some beer?"

"I got that covered. Just bring your six-pack abs," Darcy said as the image of Austin jogging down the beach flashed through her brain—curved biceps, broad shoulders, tight butt . . . If she didn't have Kevin, she'd be into him, at least for the summer. Everyone knew a lifeguard was not a long-term investment.

"You know, sometimes I think you just like me for my body," he teased her.

She laughed, leaning down to rub moisturizer into the golden skin of her lean calf. "Yeah, I have that problem, too. Beauty is a bitch, isn't it?"

14

Lindsay

Why do I have trouble coping with parties? I wondered as I sat back on the chaise and pulled down my crimson tunic top in a way that minimized my stomach and hips.

Is it me, or has my life been a succession of disappointing parties? I thought of the many parties that had gone awry: the birthday with the velvet cake from the fancy bakery that had turned out to be a yucky brown spice cake when Ma had cut into it; my twelfth birthday when every gift I received was embarrassingly childish, adorned with roses or yellow duckies; the countless Sweet Sixteen parties I'd attended in Brooklyn, mostly catered affairs with deejays and packs of spoiled girls who plotted for boyfriends but didn't have the nerve to sit and talk with a guy; the family barbecue my seventh summer when my father had collapsed in pain to be rushed off to the hospital, where they pronounced him dead from cardiac arrest. One would think that after a traumatic event like that the McCorkles would come to their senses and abandon festive gatherings, but the events rallied on, the bigger and noisier the better.

All week I had helped Darcy with shopping and last-minute planning for the truce party. A week of planning and nervous stomach, and for what? So I could feel like a fifth wheel and pretend I was into Austin Ritter without ruining the party for Tara and Darcy?

All because Bear had ditched me.

As the guys polished off the rest of Lupe's cheesecake and argued about whether Army or Navy had the better football team, I took a deep sip of the purple drink Darcy had whipped up in the blender for all the girls; if I couldn't wash back the bland disappointment, maybe I could numb the pain by freezing it. Sort of like a grape daiquiri, sweet and strong. Drinks like this were probably *not* on my diet, but at the moment I was beyond caring. I'd spent a week's pay on this shirt to make the perfect outfit, my old denim shorts dressed up with a filmy, low-cut red tunic top embossed in sparkly gold filigree. It showed a little cleavage, and the red was so good for my coloring that even Ma had commented on how lovely I looked.

All for Bear, the bastard. How could he do this to me?

He'd said he would be here, and I'd spent the entire week planning the evening in my head, fantasizing about how we would laugh together, walk along the beach, play in the pool and hot tub . . . and probably more. I'd chosen the Caribbean Suite, where I'd lovingly plumped the pillows and discreetly moved the jar of condoms to the bathroom, not wanting to appear too pushy. If Bear wanted to stay and make out and cuddle in the big turquoise bed that reminded me of the warm waters of crystal-clear beach in a travel ad, that would be okay, too. Or, if he wanted more, then . . . okay. After much deliberation I had given myself permission to take it all the way in one of the bedroom suites, as long as Bear felt right about it.

But no . . . the deliberation was all in vain because I'd been stood up, dumped through a circuitous route, a message delivered by my mother, for God's sake, telling me that the guys were going to stay on for a few days in Hatteras. It hurt too much to think about without crying, even if Darcy had saved the day by recruiting Austin Ritter to be my date for the night.

Gorgeous Austin Ritter, perched at my feet on the poolside lounge chair. He wore khaki shorts and an emerald green golf shirt that stretched over his shoulders. The shorts were pleated and loose, but I knew he was built, with a tight butt, muscular thighs, and a flat stomach. I'd seen Austin's bronze-tanned buffo package every day on the beach.

All-American lifeguard. A real catch. But not what I'd been fishing for.

Sucking down another mouthful of Purple Passion, I allowed

myself to wallow in supreme self-pity. It was the middle of my fat-test summer on earth and I'd just been stood up by the love of my life. Didn't I deserve a little self-indulgence?

A moment of silence for the fat girl without a boyfriend.

I leaned back in the chair, staring sadly at the tiny peek of cleav-age meant for Bear. What a waste.

"I'm feeling up for a walk on the beach, or even a swim," Kevin was saying. "What do you think, Darce? It's a gorgeous night." He was talking a mile a minute, so unlike the drowsy Kevin perpetually pickled in alcohol. Maybe Darcy's pep talk had done him some good.

"The beach sounds great." Darcy bounced to her feet, the candle-light glimmering on the Swarovski crystals embedded in the bodice of her camisole top. Way too energetic for me, both of them. "Anyone coming?"

"I want to check out the hot tub," Charlie said. "It's probably the one thing I'll miss the most when my furlough is up and I have to head back to cold, hard reality."

"Hot tubs?" Tara squinted at him. "That's near and dear to your heart?"

"Strange, what you come to value when you're living on a mili-tary base in Korea. Hot tubs and McDonald's fries."

Tara shrugged. "Well, I can understand the fries . . ."

He cocked his head to the side. "Come here, you." And he pulled her to her feet and guided her toward the pool house.

Which left me staring awkwardly at my date, wondering how to tell him the party was over. When he caught me looking I quickly averted my eyes, but he didn't seem rattled or nervous as he took a swig from his bottle, emptying his beer.

"Want to give me a tour of the house?" he said, surprising me as he swung around and smiled enough to show one dimple. "Every-body's always talking about the Love Mansion."

"Sure," I said, trying to pull myself out of the low chair without knocking over a potted palm. Things were a little spinny from the purple drink, but I wasn't drunk. I felt completely aware, sharp and alert, and Austin had been so pleasant at dinner that I didn't want to offend him with the bum's rush.

"Welcome to the Love Mansion," I said, gesturing toward the lanai door like Vanna White pointing to a letter. "It's sort of like Disney World. You need a monorail to get from one end to the other."

He laughed, bolstering my confidence. I pressed on through the museumlike living room, the huge pantry behind the kitchen, the paneled library with shelves of real books that had never been read but were chosen because the color of their spines matched the decor. A large alcove off the dining room held a wet bar, a wine refrigerator and shelves decoratively stocked with liquor bottles lit by recessed spotlights pointed to illuminate colorful blue, amber, and red glass.

"And now we ascend the central staircase." I swung my arms dramatically, cracking myself up. "Mrs. Love makes the staff dip each crystal teardrop of the chandelier in vinegar twice a day for that perfect prism effect, and she has the carpeting replaced every week because she can't bear that musty odor you get at the beach."

Austin's eyebrows arched. "Really?"

"Just about." As if I were conducting a tour for *House and Garden*, I showed him the upstairs bedroom suites, including the master with the stone waterfall shower—set up for Tara and Charlie—and Darcy's bathroom with four showerheads. One of the other guest bedrooms—a beachy room with bleached wood furniture and cool turquoise bedding and a woven straw rug—had been assigned to me tonight, but I wasn't really into Austin and I knew he'd only come to impress Darcy, so I moved past it quickly, dubbing it the "Caribbean Suite" as I tossed an arm in through the threshold and made no mention of the decorative bowl of condoms beside the bed. Condoms? Hadn't I moved the bowl into the armoire once I found out Bear had cancelled?

"Is something wrong?" Austin asked, peeking into the room over my shoulder.

"I just realized I almost forgot the third story," I said, quickly striding down to the door at the end of the hall and nearly falling up the steep stairs. "Our tour culminates in the turret room on the third story of the house, designed as a study for entrepreneur Bud Love, who rarely finds time to use it as his work keeps him in Manhattan." I paused in front of the semicircular window seat, now upholstered in apricot brushed satin. Many summers ago I'd sat at this window with Darcy and Tara and Elle, spying on the gardeners and housekeeping staff, plotting against the local shop owners who didn't appreciate unescorted kids roaming their stores, making lists of the clothes we wanted for school or boys we liked.

This had been our room, a clubhouse of sorts, until Darcy began to have issues with her parents and she didn't want to hang in the Love Mansion. On a whim, I bent down and opened a cabinet in the built-in shelves, hoping to find an old bottle of nail polish, a yo-yo or Eight Ball or list of prospective boyfriends like Don Johnson or Michael J. Fox.

But the fabric swatches and feather duster inside seemed alien, almost an insult to the girls who had once commandeered this room in the first stage of their master plan to take over the world.

"Did you lose something?" Austin seemed annoyed at the delay in the tour.

Had I? Had I lost my connection to Darcy? It bothered me that she'd allowed them to give this room a makeover, but then we hadn't used it in years. And did our friendship rely on preserving the past like a shrine? We were getting a little too old to hang on to the clubhouse. But still, I found it hard to let go, sentimental Irish girl that I am.

"It's nothing," I told Austin as I closed the cabinet. I straightened my crimson red tunic top and led the way back down the hall, ready to continue the tour until I realized we'd seen the entire house. Oops. Amazing to run out of real estate in the Love Mansion.

I stretched my arms wide, Vanna gone wild. "And that concludes our tour of lifestyles of the rich and gorgeous," I said, hamming it up. "Please proceed to clearly marked exits here, here, and here. Enjoy your stay here in Southampton, and tune in next week to see if you, too, can be a millionaire."

I laughed out loud, amused with myself. Okay, I'd had a few glasses of that purple passion, but it was still funny—the game-show tour of Darcy's house. Wouldn't Mrs. Love freak over that.

"We can't let the party end so soon," Austin said, walking slowly behind me.

I turned back, suddenly nervous as he paused in the threshold of the Caribbean Suite. "I don't think you showed me this room," he said.

"Yeah. I did. Yup."

He shook his head. "Come here."

Was that a dare, or a trick? His eyes seemed dark—angry or sexy? Too difficult to decipher as I crossed the hall and faced him. "That's the Caribbean Shh-weet."

He laughed, and suddenly his hands were on my waist, pulling me against him. His jeans were stiff, not the washed-out kind. Or was that stiffness something else?

"This is a great place," he said as his fingertips did ticklish circles up my waist. I sucked in a breath to make my tummy thinner, but already he had worked his way to my breasts. The movement of his hips revealed that his jeans weren't the only thing stiff.

I couldn't believe my body still knew how to do this so well. Heat was rising through me, billowing up from my belly to my face. I felt myself blush but it didn't matter because suddenly he was kissing me, his lips pinching mine lightly, making me lift my head to him as he deftly slid his hands under my shirt and cupped my breasts.

I couldn't believe how good it felt.

It had been so long since I'd had sex, so long I'd stopped counting the days. Maybe two years. In freshman year Milo and I had played around, more like experimentation between friends than a relationship, but we had tried sex in a few different satisfying positions. Since then I'd been involved with a low-energy statistics major named Phil, but we'd stopped crunching numbers months ago, and by college standards a few months of celibacy was cause for canonization. Somehow, not being in love with Austin, not actually liking him, I didn't expect my body to respond to him so rapidly, so wholeheartedly.

It was too confusing!

I let out a giggle when he whirled me around into the suite and kicked the door closed behind us. I was still laughing as he lifted off my shirt, unstrapped my bra, and stripped it away, letting my breasts bounce, free and full.

The lifeguard definitely had speed on his side.

"Very nice," he said, lowering his mouth to cover one nipple.

I yelped in pleasure as he sucked on one breast and squeezed the other with his fingers. Maybe Austin wasn't so bad, after all. Could I really like him?

I glanced down, then cupped his face gently, feeling the stubble on his jaw.

This gorgeous guy was getting me stoked. How could I not like him?

He laid another kiss on me and pushed me toward the bed, where we fell into the pool of turquoise sheets.

"Take these off," he whispered, running a hand over my hips and down to the sensitive inner thigh.

I popped open the snap of my denim shorts and peeled them down, turning away from him to strip them off. I was sober enough to want to hop into bed and hide under the turquoise sheets before he could get a good, long look at me. Beside the bed I noticed the bowl of condoms again. Had Darcy moved them back in here? I blinked in wonder. Was this going to really happen? Was I going to have sex with Austin and take the chance that Bear would find out about it?

Would Bear find out?

Of course he would. No secret went untold in the Hamptons.

But so what? Why would it matter to Bear, the guy who'd stood me up? The guy who was such a good friend to me, but never really *really* my boyfriend.

Fuck Bear. Really. Maybe this would be the kick in the pants he needed.

Make him jealous.

"Whoa. Is that, like, a goody bowl of condoms?" Austin came up from behind and rubbed against me. His taut body pressed into me, accentuated by the thick, dense mass at my butt.

"I'm not sure we should do this," I admitted.

"Come on," he said, sliding a hand down my tummy and sinking it between my legs. Being touched there made me want to sing out on the spot. "Come on," he whispered as he found the sensitive nub. "Doesn't that feel good? We can make each other feel good, Darcy."

I closed my eyes against the tears, pressed them shut tightly and gave in to the intense sensation between my legs. It did feel good, and what did I have to lose?

Nothing.

And maybe, sometime in the morning when we were cuddling in the turquoise sheets or laughing over a joke, I'd remind him that my name wasn't Darcy.

15

Tara

Tara had never felt so on fire for sex, her nipples tingling, her lower body tightening in anticipation. The warm water of the hot tub soothed and tickled as it bubbled over her body, helping her relax enough to look Charlie in the eye. It was silly to feel uptight. This was Charlie, the guy who made her laugh, the storyteller who understood so much about people.

She had made him look the other way when she'd dropped her towel and stepped down into the water, but now, having discussed mosquito repellents and chlorine levels, barometric pressure and green tea, Tara was getting that giddy feeling again. Nothing was off limits for discussion with Charlie, and since he seemed to know a little about a lot of things, he could hold up his end of a conversation.

"Why don't you come over here, where I can touch you?" he asked after they'd basked in the water a few minutes.

In the blue light of the pool with their skin slick and shiny, she didn't feel embarrassed anymore. In fact, she let herself stand in the center, watching his face react as water beaded and dripped down her shoulders, over her small, firm breasts.

"That's it, right beside me," he said, his dark, smoky eyes intent on her.

She felt the hairs on his legs brush against her thigh as she nestled beside him, hip against hip. His hand touched her knee, then slid up along the tender skin of her inner thigh. Moving close, closer, then stopping just at the top of her leg to circle the mound of hair. She sighed with longing, shocked at the sweet sensation.

"Your friend Darcy was a mensch to set this up for us," he whispered as his hand traveled along the inner thigh of the other leg. "Otherwise, we'd be wrestling in the backseat of a car somewhere, dodging the cops."

She let out a breath as he reached the top of her leg again and circled around the most sensitive area, driving her wild. "Without Darcy, it might have never happened."

"Oh, it was going to happen." Suddenly his hand was at her center, gripping her pelvis firmly. "This had to happen for us. From the minute I met you, I knew I was going to have you, Tara."

She sucked in a quick breath, shocked and delighted at his firm grip on her. "Aren't you cocky?" she teased. "You sound like a pirate."

He growled. "Never say pirate to an army man."

Wrapped in fluffy towels, they slipped quickly through the velvet night and into the house, now lit by lavender-scented votive candles. Moving quickly, Tara led the way up the stairs and down the long corridor into their room.

Charlie closed the door and turned to her, his eyes widening with a gasp.

She stood before him naked, the white towel pooled around her feet.

"Wow. Bonus day." He yanked at the towel at his waist, and she let her eyes run down the dark line of hair that fanned out over the erection cradled in his square hips.

In the past, she had always felt awkward about this part, but now she stepped toward him and wrapped her fingers around him, stroking, squeezing with want.

"That feels good." He groaned. "But I gotta warn you, I'm so far along I can't take much. Let me fuck you, please."

She placed a kiss on his lips, then went to the small basket of condoms that Darcy had left beside the bed. Charlie rolled one on, turned to her perched at the edge of the bed, and gently parted her thighs.

Open to him, she let herself watch as he nudged her, teasing the folds of delicate tissue, stroking her with a steady rhythm. The sight of them joined together excited her all the more, and all too quickly that image along with the motion created a fire between her legs—a new sensation for Tara. "Don't stop. Don't stop . . ." she murmured desperately.

But he was already dropping to his knees and pressing his mouth to her, his lips and tongue pressing on in the same, aroused areas. "Oh, Charlie . . ." She let her head fall back on the bed as she gave herself up to sensation, to the sweet rumble of sexuality thundering through her body.

It had never been like this. Not even close.

And even as his mouth brought her to new heights, she knew she had to have him inside her, in the most primal, natural ritual of all.

"I need you now," she gasped, flexing her knees and pushing back on the bed. "I need you to fuck me."

Charlie lifted his head, his eyes gleaming with a very basic hunger as he planted his knees on the bed, aimed, and plunged into her.

With a meteoric scattering of tiny stars in a field of velvet darkness, Tara Washington finally understood what all the buzz was about.

16

Darcy

"You're so beautiful . . ." Hot words whispered in her ear and groping fingers nudged Darcy awake. "Come on, now." She felt bone dry and exhausted, but he was on her again, trying, trying, trying to feel something for himself.

For the first two rounds Darcy had been in the game, shrieking and laughing as Kevin devoured her, but now she was satiated and exhausted and she just wanted to be left alone for some sleep.

"I'm tired," Darcy said, turning her head away from the light filtering in through the plantation blinds. Morning light, and she'd barely slept at all.

She pulled the thin Ralph Lauren summer quilt up to her chin. "Go to sleep, Kevin," she said, with the authority of a stern mother. "Just sleep."

He didn't answer or stir, so she figured he was following orders. And it was about time. He'd been a royal pain in the ass through the whole party. Granted, she had asked him not to be falling-down drunk, but this wild zeal was way over the top.

He'd been unusually animated when they walked down the beach, chattering on about his plans for the bar and how his old man was sitting on a gold mine. Some of it was so rapid-fire, "I said this, then he said that, then I told him no, and he just shakes his head . . ." that Darcy gave up trying to follow it.

Then, just when Darcy felt the urge to stop and take advantage of the expanse of stars overhead and the tropical breeze in their hair, he insisted on chasing her, tagging her. Not a fan of stupid games, Darcy had refused until he'd creeped her out with a story about a body that had floated up onto the beach, not far from the point near Bikini Beach.

"The detectives did all this DNA testing and checked fingerprints and stuff, but they never did identify that stiff. Some old guy. Fish thinks it was Jimmy Hoffa."

"That's awful." The breeze lifted her hair and Darcy tamped it down, searching the velvet darkness of the water's surface for some clue. "You know, Kev, if you're trying to get me in the mood, the dead body thing doesn't work for me."

"It's just a story." He stared ahead, walking with that sexy swagger, his jeans hanging so low on his spare body Darcy always thought it was a wonder they didn't slide right down to his ankles. "Doesn't it scare you at all? Make you just want to snuggle up close so I can protect you from"—he turned to her, one brow lifting in a sinister scowl—"evil stuff."

"Oh, come off it."

"They say it snuck up on him from behind . . . like this!" He lunged toward her, trying to clamp his hands around her waist.

"No! Get off!" She scooted away from him, running backward. "Cut it out!"

"He tried to get away," he said, jogging after her. "He ran, just like you, but it was no use . . ."

"Kevin! Stop!" she shouted.

But he tore after her, leering with wild eyes, chasing her all the way down the beach . . .

God, he'd been in a bizarre mood tonight. All that energy on the beach, and then in bed he'd been insatiable, impossible to please even though he was hard as a rock. She glanced over at his sleeping form, watching as he suddenly twitched, his shoulders seizing.

Edging away from him under the covers, she saw it happen again, the twitch, then a quiver.

Cocaine . . . it had to be. Darcy was a neophyte in the world of drug use, but she'd been around enough of it at parties to know the act. This behavior was not the result of that batch of purple passions she'd stirred up.

In the warming light of the sunrise, she watched him, wondering why he couldn't just be himself and have a good time. Didn't he realize that they were going to have the perfect life together if he would just relax and let things happen? She should have known the only way he could make it through the party without getting drunk would be to get some other kind of boost. But coke . . . so addictive and so expensive.

She hoped it would just be a one-time thing.

Fighting off a shudder of apprehension, she moved to the window, pressed her nose to the screen, and pulled the white sheers in around her naked body. The party hadn't been a total success for Kevin and her. At least Tara and Charlie had gotten some quality time together. The last time she saw them, they were headed off to the hot tub, and she was sure they enjoyed their deluxe accommodations in the Love Mansion.

The great irony of the Love Mansion . . . no love for the Loves.

Outside, birds were chirping now, and the air smelled fresh with a mixture of clover and pine and sweet rose. Years ago her mother had been so captivated by the rose garden here, but now the lush, ripe blooms seemed just another symbol of the Loves' overabundant cache of riches.

Behind her, fabric swished and his feet hit the floor.

"Hey, you." He came up behind her and nudged her with his hips. He slid his hands up along her rib cage and cupped her bare breasts. "Just one more time."

"Sun's rising, Kev." *And apparently, so are you.*

"Do you want to go down to the pool, maybe watch the sun come up?" she suggested, not turning away from the window.

"I've got something better in mind."

"Look, can you give it a rest, Kev? I'm beat."

"You can sleep later," he whispered, then pressed his lips to her ear to make wet, smacking noises.

Like a dog, she thought, wanting to swat him away as another sound penetrated the aura of annoyance. The purr of a car engine. "Who is that?"

Probably some gawking tourist again. She went to the window and flipped down the blinds, peering through the slats at the shiny slate gray BMW in the driveway. Kevin stood behind her, rubbing up against her, pinching her nipples so hard it was painful. Two doors were flung open, and on this side she noticed a young woman with blond hair pulled back in a ponytail. A nosy little bitch.

Pulling away from Kevin, Darcy yanked the window open and yelled down. "You're trespassing!"

The woman pointed up at her. The driver turned and glanced up, shielding his eyes with one hand. She recognized the gesture, the way he moved. It was her father.

"Shit!" Darcy slammed the blinds shut.

"Don't worry about them." Kevin pressed against her. "We've got something more important to do."

"Tell that to my father," Darcy said, stomping across the room to find some clothes and stop Daddy dearest before he trotted upstairs and found Tara and Charlie in his bedroom.

"Good morning, Daddy." Darcy leaned up on tiptoes to kiss him, knowing that she smelled of booze and sex, not an image Bud Love would want to associate with his only daughter. As she hugged him, she glanced over his shoulder to the patio, wondering if Lupe and the other housekeepers had been outside to pick up the beer bottles—dead soldiers, as Kevin called them—that lined the poolside. Not that she wasn't allowed to entertain here, but it wouldn't help Dad's disposition when he found a few empty bottles from his wine cellar littering the lanai.

"Hey, pumpkin. You know Stephanie, from the office." Bud Love's voice was smooth and breezy, but Darcy could smell the guilt on him, guilt mixed with self-righteousness. Stephanie from the office was obviously his new squeeze, and although Darcy wasn't surprised that Dad was fooling around, it was unusual for him to be so brazen.

Mom would have a fit when she found out he'd brought a girl to the Hamptons house, and Darcy would make sure she found out. In her opinion, this was not the time for her father to be fooling around. The media kept reporting about charges swirling around Bud Love—corporate fraud and embezzlement and conspiracy. Darcy didn't even try to follow all the finger-pointing, but right now, Dad's first priority should have been straightening out the facts and clearing himself of the charges.

Instead, he was dicking around with a secretary at the beach?

"We thought that, since we have to work through the Fourth, we might as well work at the beach," her father offered.

Darcy eyed the blonde through sly, lowered lids. Steph was young, not much older than Darcy, and she wore a yellow and orange sundress—an Oscar de la Renta, Darcy suspected—with tight spaghetti straps and a low-cut bodice that showed off ample cleavage. Not exactly office attire. "By my calendar, the Fourth was last week," Darcy said, staring pointedly at Stephanie's cleavage. "But I bet it was getting *really* hot in that office."

"Who's this?" her father asked, nodding over her shoulder.

Steph's lips curled in a naughty smile. "The boy in the window?"

Darcy turned, relieved to see that Kevin had pulled on his jeans. "You remember Kevin McGowan, Dad? His father owns Coney's on the Beach."

"Is that so?" The sour pucker didn't leave her father's lips as he took in Kevin, bare chested, worn jeans, and scruffy blond hair in need of a trim. At least he shook hands with Kevin. "Coney's is one of our favorite places," Dad said.

Darcy could hear the lie in his voice; he'd never liked the restaurant, and he didn't like Kevin. He'd delivered that verdict years ago, telling her the McGowans were a clan of drunks, suspected of involvement with the Irish Mob. "Just keep your distance," he'd warned her one day as he was working on his laptop and cell phone by the pool.

Which had made her pursue Kevin even more intently.

Now, as Bud Love offered up a lame story of a "high-priority" workload—a ruse intended to whitewash the fact that he'd brought a girl to the Hamptons house—Darcy sensed the shifting tides of power. The big, bad McGowans were going strong in the restaurant business, while Dad and the other partners at the firm were being subpoenaed for investigations.

"Darcy, pumpkin . . ." Bud Love strained to keep the annoyance out of his voice. "Can we talk privately for a moment?"

They stepped into the cavernous living room, where Darcy noticed a cobweb swaying from the stained-glass piece. "Now, you know I don't mind you having friends over." His voice echoed, and the emptiness of it all made Darcy hug herself to ward off a shiver. "But really, this young man is not in your league, sweetheart."

"You don't know him, Dad." *You don't know how perfect we are to-*

gether . . . what he and I are going to become . . . the business we're going to build together.

"I know enough. There's no future for you with a McGowan."

"And what kind of future do you have with Stephanie the sycophant? Or am I not supposed to ask?" Darcy didn't usually shoot direct questions at him; their relationship was layered in years of her playing Daddy's Little Girl while he rose to the Daddy role, lavishing her with ponies and private school and cars. The good-girl role had always worked for her, but with Kevin she found herself in need of something Daddy couldn't deliver. It felt strange to take a swipe at her father, strange, but oddly empowering. "You seem to be forgetting your own standards, Daddy. It's always everyone else who has to jump through hoops," she said. "Jump high, higher! Every time you raise the bar, the rest of us go crazy trying to please you."

"I maintain high standards for myself and everyone I deal with," Bud Love said, his voice at a controlled pitch. "And right now, you are over the line, young lady."

Darcy felt her spine stiffen. Her father should know a thing or two about stepping over the line; by all accounts he'd pushed more than a few legal and moral boundaries lately. She was sorely tempted to lash out at him now, remind him of the colossal mistakes he'd made. There'd be some dark, vengeful joy in pointing out how he'd fucked things up royally for their family . . . but she bit back the words, knowing that would bring them to the lowest, grittiest moment of their relationship, to an undignified, hellish exchange without redemption.

And as she fought for control their attention shifted to the commotion in the hallway as Lupe appeared to offer everyone breakfast, Charlie and Tara came in from the pool, and Lindsay groaned about needing coffee.

Turning away to glance toward the hall, Darcy shrugged. "Excuse me, Daddy, but I have a few guests to attend to."

And Bud Love, always a stickler for manners, didn't even try to stop her.

"We'll have breakfast out on the lanai, Lupe," Darcy announced, sliding her hand around Kevin's naked waist and leading the way out to the flower-strewn patio.

Lindsay looked like hell, pale and shaky, and Austin was notice-ably absent. Kevin's eyes were bloodshot and Darcy wasn't at the top of her game, but as she caught a glimpse of herself in the glass of the French doors she was reassured that the long night didn't show in her clear blue eyes or smooth skin. Only Tara and Charlie sparkled with that natural glow that probably had something to do with sexual satisfaction and a slice of happiness.

As she reached up to pluck an orchid from the trellis, Darcy felt a slight twinge of envy. Tara had found something good; Darcy wanted it for herself.

But we'll get there, Darcy thought as she gave Kevin a sniff of the flower and tucked it behind her left ear. She and Kevin were going to get their slice of the pie.

She glanced over the low hedge, to the table by the pool where Dad and Stephanie had decided to take breakfast. Things were changing, and her father had to get with the program.

You'd better start liking Kevin, Daddy, she thought. *Because after your business goes down the tubes, Kev is going to be my savior.*

17

Lindsay

"Can we just not talk about it?" I wrapped my hands around the Mikasa coffee cup and let blur the array of flowers tucked into the latticework about the lanai—white, purple, and lavender blooms swirled in a whimsical design created by Darcy's exclusive florist. I wished that the beauty of it all could wash away the ugliness I was feeling about last night.

"Tell me!" Darcy pressed. At least she'd held off bugging me until the others had gone inside to get showered. "Was he awful? Did you tell him to fuck off or . . . he didn't rape you, did he?"

"No, no." I took a sip of coffee, but it seemed to lodge high in my throat. "If you have to know, we had sex, okay? But he left soon after that. I don't know. It was dark, and when I asked he said he had to go."

"So why is that so wrong? Some guys don't like to cuddle afterward."

"It just seems so wrong. I don't think he's really into me."

"Stop being so self-deprecating."

"He called me Darcy."

"Oh." Darcy pressed her lips together to keep from smiling. "Did he really?"

I nodded. "And that's not the biggest deal. It's just that I don't sleep around like that, not if I'm not into the guy."

"And you're not into Austin? Have you seen him jogging down the beach? He could rescue me any day."

"He's cute." I thought about sex with Austin, his firm, precise hands plying me into response, the steady rhythm that brought me to orgasm. Sure, it felt good at that moment, in the dark of the quiet bedroom. This morning, regret had swept in, and no amount of reassurance from Darcy was going to ease my distress over the choices I made last night. Besides, Darcy had a way of twisting things around, manipulating people and facts to make everything fit into her own agenda.

"Oh, no. I see that look on your face," Darcy lamented. "Don't say it."

"I can't help it. I keep thinking about Bear." I ran a fingertip over the patterned glass of the patio table. "Do you think he'll find out?"

"I don't know, probably. But it serves him right, doesn't it?"

I shook my head as gloom roiled deep inside. "I didn't want to screw things up with Bear, and now, that's just what I've done."

"Excuse me, but you didn't screw up. He's the one who ditched you to stay at his surfing competition. If he wants you, he's going to have to treat you better than that, Linds. In the meantime, go to the beach, talk it up with Austin. I think you two would be great together."

I had my doubts, but since it was my day off from Old Towne Pizza, I figured I might as well check out the surf and test the waters with Austin Ritter.

18

Tara

Despite the best-laid plans to arrive in different vehicles to avoid making her parents suspicious, Tara had just pulled into the driveway at her parents' contemporary beach house when she noticed Kevin's van coming off Dune Road, right behind her.

"Oh, well," she said aloud, waiting at the ground-level door for Charlie to catch up with her.

He waved at Kevin's receding van, then turned to her, his dark eyes flashing with want. "And how are you?" he asked as if they hadn't seen each other in a while.

"Fine."

He moved into the doorway behind her and cupped her bottom with one hand. "Very fine."

She felt breathless as their faces were inches apart. Lord, she wanted to kiss him! She craved him in the worst way, but her parents' house was forbidden territory.

Tara reassembled her composure and proceeded into the house, up the twisting contemporary staircase. "I know you're behind me," she teased, lowering her voice. "Now don't look up my dress."

"Wouldn't miss it for the world."

She reached the main floor and swept onto the landing with a laugh, checking the kitchen for her mother. Instead, the reading lamp in the living room glowed yellow over her father, who sat reading the newspaper.

"Daddy . . . what are you doing here?"

"That's a fine welcome for your father, isn't it?" He lowered the newspaper and motioned her over so that he could place a kiss on her cheek without getting up off the couch. With the gray dusting the sides of his head and the skinny reading glasses, he seemed suddenly old, but then he'd been working so hard this summer, staying behind in Manhattan to defend an African American man who'd been blatantly passed over for promotion to top-tier management in a large corporation. The Blue Bell Corporation and Mr. Tyrell Olney had dominated dinner-table discussion the last few times she'd seen him.

"How's the Blue Bell case going?" she asked. "Have they fallen to their knees yet, pleading mercy?"

"It's status quo." He squinted at Charlie over his reading glasses. "And who's this?"

"Wayne's friend Charlie. This is my father, Laurence Washington."

"Charles Migglesteen, sir." Charlie leaned forward with a curt bow and shook her father's hand. "I've had the pleasure of enjoying your family's hospitality these last few weeks."

"The soldier? Welcome. Forgive me, Charlie. I thought you were a friend of Tara's."

"Tara?" Charlie's eyes fell on her, warming her to the core before he turned back to her father. "We've become friends, sir."

Well, at least he didn't deny her, Tara thought, turning toward the kitchen door.

"Tara's been a huge help, taking me around a few places while Wayne catches up on the latest in Xbox technology."

"Still hooked on that crap?" Laurence folded his newspaper in his lap. "I'd hoped he'd outgrow it."

"Wayne's a dweeb." Tara turned toward the kitchen.

"Don't speak ill of your brother," her father groused.

"I'd say it to his face. It's a talent, Daddy. He should look into programming when he gets out of the army."

"Your mother went into town to the fruit market. What's for lunch?"

Tara opened the fridge, hating that the domestic chores fell on her again while her brother was probably upstairs, thumbing his way through virtual intergallactic battles. "I guess I could make you an omelette. Cheese or bacon."

"Both," Laurence grunted. "With some toast, please."

As her father leaned forward and popped open his briefcase, Tara wondered if it was wrong to hide her relationship with Charlie. After all, her parents always claimed to be free of prejudice, supporters of equality for all, at least on paper. Given the chance, would they accept Charlie, a white man, as an appropriate man for their daughter to date?

She doubted it.

Tara was wise to the harsh realities. It wouldn't look good for Daddy's professional reputation, the champion of slighted black people giving his daughter up to a white man. And Mama would claim that a relationship with a white man would squash Tara's cultural identity. In her mind Tara could hear the animated voices of her mother's sisters, the aunties, pouring on the advice, telling her she was too skinny and flat chested, pushing her to tuck into the corn bread and ribs and sweet potato pie, warning her not to act like a white girl, whatever that meant.

How she missed her Grandma Mitzy, Mama's mother. She felt sure Grandma Mitzy would understand, that she'd be crazy about Charlie, too. Before she'd passed, Grandma Mitzy had been a source of unconditional love, pulling each grandchild into the ample folds of floral fabric and hugging them close and finding something wonderful and unique in that child. For Tara, it had been her ears. "Such a sweet child! Look at the shape of the ears—like little shells. Wouldn't surprise me to find a baby pearl inside. Reminds me so much of my man Willy. Mm-mmm!" And she would hug Tara close, surrounding her with perfume that smelled of peaches and lilac soap.

Lost in the memory, Tara pressed a palm to one ear. Like a perfect shell.

Unfortunately, the rest of the world didn't have Grandma Mitzy's vision. As Tara lined up butter, eggs, cheese, and bacon on the counter, she concluded that her parents would definitely struggle over her relationship with Charlie. Best to keep it mum.

"So where were you two?" her father asked pointedly, as if smelling subterfuge. "Where'd you come from?"

"We . . . well, I was over at Darcy's . . ." *Getting down and dirty with Charlie*. Tara bit her lip and focused on cracking the eggs. "Mama knew about it, and Charlie . . . Where were you?"

"I got reacquainted with an old friend last night," Charlie said, his eyes holding Tara's with a smoky promise. "Kevin just dropped me off out front."

"Oh." Her father seemed distracted again, paging through a brief.

At least he let the topic drop for now, Tara thought as she beat the eggs with a whisk. She didn't need Dad on her case about falling for a white guy.

Still, the seeds of suspicion were planted.

Staring out at the ocean through the wall of windows, Tara counted the days until the end of the summer. It was going to be nearly impossible, living under the same roof with Charlie and her parents, wanting to be with Charlie, needing to keep up the pretense for her parents that they didn't want to touch each other, lie together and talk into the night, satisfy each other . . .

This architectural gem of a house was not big enough for everything that was happening under its roof.

19

Lindsay

"Stupid, stupid, stupid," I muttered under my breath as I ducked into the shady coolness of the screened porch. I'd been stupid last night, and it didn't seem to be any better today. Shaky with a hangover, somehow I'd let Darcy talk me into visiting Austin on the beach. Then, as I was about to leave, someone had called Darcy with an invitation to a blowout beach party held by Anusa Armando, the fashion designer.

"Isn't she the woman who designs those eclectic patchwork jackets?" Tara had asked.

"Quilted jackets and gypsy skirts. At least, that was this year. Anusa throws a great party," Darcy had said. "I think we need to go—all of us."

"We don't have invitations," I had pointed out, hating to have to remind Darcy that not everyone in the Hamptons was "connected."

"Half of the Hamptons crashes her parties," Darcy insisted. "Do you think they have someone checking invitations in the dunes? You have to come, and you have to at least make an attempt to look happy."

Bamboozled into attending, I could now see that my day off would get worse before it got better. I let the door slam behind me with a satisfied "thwack!" I figured the smacking noise could be part of my penance for making such a stupid move, sleeping with Austin.

"Don't slam the door!" came my mother's voice from inside the kitchen.

"Sorry." I paused in the doorway, glad to be home and wanting nothing more than to hole up in my bedroom and swear off guys forever. I was surprised to see Ma up to her elbows in flour amid a steam-filled kitchen. The industrial stove, with its six burners, held five pots and pans, four of them boiling, bubbles smacking.

"It's hot in here." I wiped my brow. "Whatcha making?"

"Kathleen will be here with the baby any minute and I'm trying to make her favorite chicken pot pie."

"In four boiling pots?"

"Ah, no!" Mary Grace turned the burners down to a simmer. "That's to sterilize the baby's bottles. Though I should throw your brother's duffel bag in for good measure. He and Bear spent their entire trip living out of Bear's van. Reeked to high heaven. I sent Stephen marching straight to the outdoor shower. We can't have that in this house, not with a tiny baby around."

"So they're back . . ." I felt the vise squeeze tighter. What if Bear heard about Austin and me? Austin didn't seem like the type to brag, but I wasn't sure.

"Will those two ever grow up? They're celebrating because Bear found some sponsors at the competition. A reporter was there from *Surf* magazine, and apparently he compared our Bear to the likes of Mickey Dora. Can you imagine?"

Since Steve started riding waves, *Surf* magazine has been circulating in our house, so we all knew the greats—LeRoy Grannis, Mike Doyle, Doc Ball, and the Duke. I felt a little sickened by Bear's success, especially at this vulnerable moment. What did it mean?

Ma pushed the crust aside and started hacking into lines of carrots on the cutting board. "Oh! And the most important thing. Elle called. She's back in the States!"

"What?" I squeaked, wondering if one more bomb could drop at my feet. "I can't believe it. She loved London." I took the lightly floured note from my mother. Typical of Elle, to pop up with a phone call after being away for years.

"She's coming for a visit, and I told her she could stay here."

"Ma! You've got Kathleen and the baby staying, and I think Steve promised Napolean's friend he could move into the shed for the month of August."

"The shed! It's not fit for a dog."

"Then it's perfect for Steve's friends. But it's going to be crowded around here. I'll be happy to see Elle. We can share a room and everything, but—"

"I want Elle to feel welcome, with her grandparents' place sold and all." When we were little, my mother was the unofficial neighborhood mom, hauling all the girls up to the beach in a wagon, taking us for ice cream and movies, letting me host sleepovers on the screened porch. It wasn't surprising that Ma felt an attachment to all my friends. "But call her back," Ma went on. "I didn't have time to get the details."

"Got it," I said, snitching a piece of pie crust. "Kind of hot to be baking, isn't it?"

"The things I do for my children, baking in the middle of July."

After a short nap and a long shower, I loaded my board and pointed the Saturn toward Bikini Beach, wondering about Bear leaving and Elle returning. There'd been no answer on Elle's cell phone when I called, and I realized that somehow it was going to fall on my shoulders to warn Darcy that her least favorite friend would soon be back in town.

Although the relationship between Darcy and Elle had ended with a huge showdown, it had never been hearts and flowers between the two of them. Darcy had always managed to make herself the queen bee of every social group, the leader who ruled by instinct and self-promotion, a dynamic Elle never bought into.

I turned up the music, a Hootie and the Blowfish tune, remembering the first time we'd met Elle, at an outdoor fair in July. We were probably seven or eight, and Darcy and I had been riding the small roller coaster, repeatedly, jumping out of the car as soon as the safety bar popped up and scrambling back to the entrance to ride again. One time, Elle had ended up in the back car, the most exciting ride on the train.

Elle was dressed in a neat summer pinafore, like a character from a picture book. Her reddish brown hair was scraped out of her face with a headband so that tiny wisps of baby-fine hair sprinkled a fringe at her forehead. Ducky hair, I used to call it. Like a little brown duckling.

"Hey, that's our seat," Darcy had said, hands on her hips. "Move it."

Elle didn't answer, but her dark eyes flashed on Darcy defiantly as she thrust her bare legs forward and dug in.

"Excuse me?" Darcy scowled, ready to pick a fight.

"Come on. We'll sit somewhere else." I grabbed Darcy's elbow. "Quick! Before everything is taken."

We'd ended up sitting right in front of Elle, who shrieked over every rise and drop. When the ride finished, the ducky girl bolted out of the exit and beat Darcy back to the entrance to ride again.

"I don't believe this," Darcy had steamed.

But I had been a little impressed, surprised that the ducky girl had beat Darcy at her own game.

A few days later, when I found Elle capturing sand crabs in the shallows, I offered to help, and together we threw ourselves into the mission. Elle dove right into activities Darcy wouldn't do with me. She could focus on a task for hours and she didn't mind getting sand in her swimsuit or salt water in her hair. By the end of the week, Tara joined us on the beach, searching for shells and jumping the waves. By the end of the summer, much to Darcy's regret, Elle was a part of our group, joining us for ice cream runs, bike rides, Monopoly tournaments, and sleepovers.

Over the years, Elle moved in and out of the clique, sometimes by choice, sometimes because of Darcy's not-so-subtle manipulations. Elle was brilliant, a math whiz with a photographic memory, a fact that curled Darcy's toes with jealousy. With parents mired in academia and medicine, Elle developed a reputation as a hippie-nerd—another reason for Darcy to keep her out of the group. And yet, despite Darcy's disapproval, I maintained my end of the friendship with Elle, who possessed a certain sparkle that made people enjoy being around her. Unless, of course, like Darcy, you were one of those people who couldn't tolerate sharing the limelight with someone else.

There were a few bad stretches when Elle seemed hell-bent on destruction. She'd searched the dunes for plover eggs to smash; made a game of throwing matches against the foundations of the houses, which once started a small fire at her grandmother's place; and when Darcy insisted that we construct little altars to honor the

Catholic saints, we knew it was Elle who sneaked back and destroyed them.

There'd been days when Tara and I had secretly discussed who would win a competition for craziest, and while Darcy usually won the bossy award, Elle was the ultimate looney. Still, no one anticipated the events of my twelfth summer . . . the slick rocks of the jetty, the fierce battle of words between Darcy and Elle.

Having arrived at Bikini Beach, I circled the parking lot three times, sorely tempted to bolt out the exit. Instead, I parked and stepped out into the oppressive heat rising from the black pavement to unload my board.

Bear's camper was not back in its usual spot on the parkland. That meant he probably wasn't surfing today. My tension eased a bit.

This would be a prime situation to have Elle around, asserting herself without hesitation, chatting people up without worrying what they thought. As I lugged my board over to the lifeguard stand, I went over the carefully scripted lines one more time. I wasn't going to make any reference to last night or the party, didn't want to say anything that would make Austin feel uncomfortable in front of Max, the other lifeguard.

"Hey, guys. How's the surf been today?" I asked casually. Lifting one braid from my shoulder, I dared to look up at them.

But Austin didn't answer. He didn't make eye contact or acknowledge me at all. With a cold, repulsive expression he stared out at the water, pretending I didn't even exist.

The other lifeguard Max was just as cold. "Why don't you ask them out there?" he said.

I stepped back and clutched the blistered post of the lifeguard stand, feeling as if the wind had been knocked out of me. *Breathe, keep breathing. Maybe you misinterpreted.* He couldn't ignore me, not after what we'd shared last night. Okay, I could accept if he wasn't madly in love with me or not ready to commit, but we'd had close-up, naked sex—touched each other intimately. My face was level with the lifeguards' feet, and I noticed Austin shift his legs slightly, those tanned, hairless legs that I'd wrapped mine around last night. This couldn't be happening. He couldn't pretend he didn't know me now.

I checked Austin again, but his stony expression remained. Only now there was a new curl to his lips. A secret, nasty smile underlying the pretense that I didn't exist.

The bastard! Stung, I cast a sad look out at the surf I wouldn't be able to enjoy today and lugged my board across the scorching sand to the parking lot.

20

Tara

Tara Washington had attended dozens of Hamptons parties, with everything from live carousels to psychics providing entertainment. But tonight, Anusa Armando's fete topped everything.

"I have to say, I've never been to a party where you can get your fortune told, your hand molded in wax, and your feet rubbed." Strolling around the "fairgrounds" of Anusa's party was Charlie's first foray into the Hamptons party scene, and he seemed highly amused by the circus atmosphere.

"That foot rub is actually a hot-stone massage," Tara said, "and I don't think you're supposed to call the palmist a fortune teller. Not PC."

"Really? Is that some sort of demotion?" Charlie reached out and pulled her closer, and she pressed into him, loving the feel of his hard body against hers. Ever since last night, since they'd been together, she and Charlie had moved to a new level in their relationship, sharing a closeness she'd never felt with a guy. It was as if they could finish each other's sentences and thoughts, and they'd each shrivel up and die if they were apart for long. Music up. Roll happy ending.

The only downside was that she wanted to be with him tonight and every night. She couldn't imagine sleeping down the hall from him now, far from the warmth of his body against hers, and how would they sit at the dinner table in her parents' home, Mom's eyes narrowing and Dad scratching his chin as their hands touched while passing the butter beans? She and Charlie had to find a way to get together again, soon, especially since Charlie and Wayne had to report back to their post in North Korea before the end of summer.

Charlie kissed her lightly on the lips, then wrapped his arms around her waist so that they could both look out over the lawn full of guests, small tents, torches, and tables.

"It's weird," she said softly. "From here the ocean is just a big, black hole. Without that sliver of moon reflected on it, you'd never know it was there." They found a sign pointing to the beach, leading to a wooden stairway that led down the cliffside.

"Maybe we should get our fortunes told," Charlie said, peering back at the palmist's tent. "I'd like to know what's down the road for us. A cozy suburban house with a two-car garage and 2.3 kids?"

Tara laughed. She'd never talked about getting married before, not even joking around.

"You laugh?" He pressed a fist to his forehead. "I'm wounded. Devastated."

"Don't overplay it," Tara said. "I was just thinking that you've got to feel sorry for that .3 kid. Always getting slighted."

Charlie groaned. "Could it be that I've met someone even geekier than my geek self?"

"I think my brother wins the geek crown for our family." She went in front of him on the stairs, which turned out to be three stories of wooden steps leading down along the dunes. "I'm just . . . serious. Academic, no-nonsense single African American female seeking . . . nonacademic, nonsensical single male."

"At least I fit the male part," Charlie said. They walked down in silence for a minute, her high-heeled Manolo Blahniks clapping on the wood steps. "I noticed you didn't say single African American male, but isn't that a priority for you?"

"Not for me." She paused, feeling the truth, knowing he recognized it. "But my parents are expecting something like that."

"And here I thought your father just hated me because I'm Jewish."

"Jewish?" That hadn't occurred to her; that he would think he was different, that there was reason to discriminate against him. The last step was mired in sand. She stepped off and her Manolos, the skinny-heeled ones with the straps decorated with cutout gold leaves, sank into the cool sand. "It's not that you're Jewish." She sloshed through sand to a boulder and sat down to remove her shoes.

He jumped down the last steps, flinging his arms out as if he'd just stuck a landing for Olympic gold. "That I'm white? Actually, that I'm not black."

"Bingo."

"Aw, you're not like that, are you?" His voice sounded forlorn as he moved closer and leaned down to face her. "You don't treat me differently because of the color of my skin."

"I don't," she said, unable to say the words that lingered between them: *But they do. My parents see you as a white boy, an outsider. Nothing against you, Charlie, but the Washingtons are into preservation of family culture, and you just don't fit the profile.*

"Shit." His chin dimpled as he pressed his lips together tightly. "Well, that's just not fair. Because, the thing is, in here, I got more soul than half the brothers you know. Innate cool. Awareness. I could be black, I could totally pull it off, if I could just change my skin color."

She laughed.

"Again with the mocking laugh? I'm serious."

Pinching her lips together to stifle a smile, Tara recalled a book she'd read in junior high called *Black Like Me*, in which the author had consumed a dye to darken his skin and experience firsthand the way people of color were treated in the South. Charlie wasn't that crazy, was he? Because, much as she loved him, she loved who he was—an angst-ridden, white Jewish guy from the Bronx—not some derivation he could fashion himself into. "It's not just about skin tone, because, brother, you're darker than me." She held her arm out against his, and with the black hair on his arm his skin appeared to be a shade darker than hers. "It's a way of life . . . a culture that we inherit."

"I know that. I do! And it's probably not PC to say it, but I'm more black than your brother, and he was the first to point it out."

"I know." Tara dropped her face into her hands, not sure whether to laugh or cry. She shared Charlie's frustration; Lord knew she'd been railing against the confines of this cultural restriction all her life. "You're right. I've spent my whole life trying to live up to my parents' expectations of 'black behavior.' Ironic, when I'm stuck in this skin that looks so white. It's a constant struggle; a no-win situation."

He stopped pacing and sat across from her, leaning close to study her. "You've fought them all your life. How did you do it?"

"It wasn't really a fight. Just a square peg trying to fit in a round hole."

He shook his head. "Don't throw me out with the reject blocks because of all this. It's so clear that you and I belong together. We fit, don't we?"

"We do." That she knew in her heart. "We fit together well."

Charlie squeezed one eye shut. "I see a big but coming."

"The question is, can a good fit—a solid relationship—be strong enough to overcome the adversity of my parents, your parents, and a society that would always cast a curious, scornful eye at us and our children?"

"I like the way you say 'our children,' " he said, taking her by the hand. "But no more twenty questions. It's a gorgeous night and I'll always kick myself if we don't take advantage of that beautiful beach down there."

With a deep breath, Tara rose to the salt air and lilting music of the party. Charlie was right; there would be time for twenty questions later. For now, they needed to enjoy this summer night ripe with music and friends and possibilities . . . endless possibilities.

21

Darcy

"How long? How much time do we have?" Darcy asked as steel drums shimmered in the warm night.

"I couldn't reach Elle on her cell phone," Lindsay admitted, "so I don't know yet."

When a roving belly dancer came to their group, Lindsay had pulled Darcy away to dump the bad news on her. Elle! Please. The girl was going to be the summer buzz-kill.

"But it's not like the summer is over, Darce. I mean, yeah, Elle is coming and she's going to stay at my place, but everything that happened between you guys was years ago."

"Funny, when I think of her, it feels like yesterday." Darcy could still recall the oddest details. The black, glassy sheen of the water. Elle's Keds with red and blue striped laces. The bottle of Perrier Darcy had clutched as she negotiated the rocks, trying not to spill the drink. And the hateful look on Elle's face, her lips wrenched so tight that Darcy thought Elle was going to spit on her from the jagged rocks. And maybe that was what Elle had been planning when her sneaker slipped, her balance shifted, and a searing panic overtook her malice for Darcy. Panic and a graceful plunge into water so deep it was black as obsidian. "I guess it's not so easy to forget, when you're accused of killing someone."

"No one really accused you. Those fishermen saw everything."

"Whatever," Darcy said, recalling that her own parents hadn't really believed she was innocent. How many times had her mother said: "Thank God Elle survived!"? And her father's staid response: "Imagine the liability! I dread to think of the legal and civil suits." Bud and Melanie Love were all about covering their asses, while Darcy sat over her Max Factor deluxe manicure kit in her room, feeling like a hollow, burnt-out shell of a person as she methodically removed polish, pushed back cuticles, and polished again. Tangerine Scream. Candy Apple Red. Flower Power! She tried one outrageous shade after another, but nothing could comfort or soothe, no Over the Rainbow or Cornflower Explosion could jar the bad feelings that laced through her heart.

That had shown her the scary reality; no one was watching over her, no one was taking care and looking out for Darcy. Oh, they could buy her nice things and bankroll private schools and trips. But when it came down to it, the only person looking out for Darcy was going to be Darcy herself. From Elle's screwup on the jetty had sprung Darcy's search for someone who really cared; someone to ally with. The gorgeous, energetic Kevin.

"Are you the designated driver?" Lindsay asked, her eyes on Kevin as he leaned forward and tipped a drink back against his lips. The orange liquid—a screwdriver, Darcy suspected—rushed into his mouth and down his chin, much of it dripping onto the grass between his sneakers. It was dark enough not to see the drops of drinks splattered on his jeans, but Darcy could make out a stain toward the bottom of his patterned silk shirt.

"It sure looks like I'm stuck driving again," Darcy answered. "And Kevin insisted on bringing that hunk-of-junk van. I hate driving that thing. It's like wheeling in the Mystery Machine." She wondered if other people at the party realized how sloshed her boyfriend was. Of course, when you were standing at the bar beside Lorne Michaels or laughing in a group with Calvin Klein, you tended not to pay attention to B-grade celebrities like the son of a local restaurant owner.

She looked down the great lawn, a wide expanse of grass overlooking the ocean, and wondered if Tara and Charlie had left already. Round, white-covered tables decorated the expanse, along with torches blazing on tall sticks. Anusa had put out a beautiful spread, as usual, but it was disconcerting that they hadn't even started serving dessert and already her boyfriend was listing and losing his footing.

Once again, Kevin wasn't able to put a cork on the drinking. It pissed her off, ruining her good time. He was either sloshed like this, or wired and weird like last night, when he wanted to chase her on the beach and then maul her in bed all night. "You know, sometimes I wonder if the Kevin and Darcy Bliss Package is worth all this." Really, she'd had better offers, from lots of guys. What was it about Kevin that kept her hanging on, even when he embarrassed her and turned into a moronic slouch at parties like this? Just then he let out a loud laugh, giddy and bright. He did have an infectious sense of fun, but . . . "Am I a doormat?" she asked Lindsay.

"You?" Lindsay followed her gaze to Kevin. "No. Never. You're tough and demanding. Not that I don't wonder sometimes what you see in Kevin."

"He's a good guy. Hot, and he makes me laugh a lot." She thought of the old Kevin, the guy she'd fallen for years ago, and added, "When he's not wasted."

"Which isn't a lot of the time anymore. It seems to me you've worked most of your life to snag him, and now that you have, you're getting an inside look. He's got a drinking problem, Darce."

"I know that. But that's the alcohol, not Kevin."

"Did you ever try separating the two?" Lindsay's eyes softened, brown moons in her heart-shaped face.

"He can control it," Darcy said, though she wasn't sure that was true. "I mean, we all drink, like, to party. We've all had too much."

Lindsay shrugged. "Not to pass judgment, but Kevin has taken partying way beyond. He doesn't seem to sober up anymore."

"You're right," Darcy admitted, relieved to let her friend in but alarmed that it was all true. "You're right, but I don't know what the answer is, because the alternative is a nightmare, too. Last night, when I asked him not to drink, he got so fired up, I think he was doing coke, too."

"Yeah, Austin mentioned something about that. I think he saw Kevin doing some lines out by the pool."

"And you didn't tell me?" Darcy snapped, then screwed up her face. It wasn't Lindsay's fault, and the last thing Darcy wanted to do was cry here, right in the middle of Hamptons party central.

A girl in a maroon and pink print sarong came by offering them a tray of different kinds of shooters in test tubes—blue, green, red, and orange liquors. Lindsay waved her off, then put a hand on Darcy's arm. "I'm sorry . . . about everything." Something flashed in her eyes—a tear?—and then suddenly her face was crumpled in a sob.

"Lindsay?" Darcy turned to her, squeezing her arm. "What's the matter?"

"I didn't want to tell you. I mean, it's my fault, but . . ." She swiped at her eyes. "Why am I crying? It's not like I really care, but when I went to the beach today and tried to talk with Austin, he totally ignored me. Wouldn't even say hello." Lindsay sniffed and swiped at new tears. "It was just so humiliating."

"What an asshole." Darcy grabbed a stack of napkins from a nearby table and let Lindsay dab at her face. *This is my fault*, Darcy thought as she rubbed her back between the shoulder blades. "I'm going to kill him. You should have called me."

Lindsay's dark hair splayed around her face as she buried her eyes in the napkins. "I didn't want to talk about it, but . . . when you asked about being a doormat, well, that's me, isn't it? I just got stepped on, big-time."

"That's not true." Darcy felt a tug of guilt. Hadn't she been the one to set Austin up with Lindsay? And she'd thought they'd be okay together. Okay, maybe she realized Austin wasn't going to just drop to his knees and fall for a girl with a weight problem, but she'd relied on him to do the right thing, show Lindsay a good time and be a man about it. "You had a good time with him, right? The rest is his problem. You can't help it if he's a socially maladjusted psycho."

"I should've known." Lindsay's voice caught. "Should've been smarter . . ."

"Don't even say that." Darcy turned her friend toward her and reached around her shoulders to hug her. Although Darcy was so bad at this sort of thing, she could feel Lindsay shaking slightly under her palms, so she rubbed her back a little.

"Woo-hoo! Girl-on-girl love." Kevin growled. "I'd like to get in the middle of that. And I probably can, since one of those girls is mine."

"In your dreams." Darcy lifted her chin to glare at him, realizing a bad night was only going to get worse. "Get lost."

"I was just thinking the same thing." With some difficulty he extracted his keys from the pocket of his jeans and tossed them in the air. They flopped to the ground, and as he leaned down to retrieve them he stumbled. "Come on, Darce. There's a nice, quiet bar up the road with my name on it."

"Give me the keys," Darcy said firmly.

"In *your* dreams," Kevin sputtered.

Darcy stepped away from her friend and squared off with Kevin. "I've had more than my quota of assholes tonight. Don't add to it, Kev."

He straightened up, stumbled, dropped the keys again. "Then get your butt over here and let's go, Pop-Tart!"

Sucking in a furious breath between her teeth, Darcy leaned down quickly and swept up his key ring. "You're drunk, Kev. Don't make it worse by being a dick, too." She dropped the keys into her tank top, tucking them in between her breasts. Linking her arm through Lindsay's, she tugged her toward the beach. "Let's get some fresh air."

"Where ya going?" Kevin called after her. "Darcy! Get back here, 'cause I'm leaving."

"Not without your keys," Darcy said, cutting a path around a busy table where people were waiting in line to have their palms read.

"Shit!" Kevin said loudly behind them, talking to himself. "Did she just call me a dick? Am I a dick?"

"A little slow on the uptake," Darcy muttered.

"I'm okay," Lindsay said, raking her hair back with one hand. "You can drive him home if you want."

"He can wait." Right now Lindsay needed all the nurturing she could muster. "I figure he'll rant and rave awhile. He can go out to the parking lot and bang on the side of his van, but at least he can't get behind the wheel. By the time I'm ready to go, he'll have cooled down. Full of apologies."

"Sorry enough to stop drinking?" Lindsay asked.

"That's another conversation for when he's sober." Which wasn't often, these days. Although Darcy didn't look forward to having it out with Kevin about his drinking, she knew that conversation was coming; it was inevitable, and Kevin was going to have to pull himself together if they were going to make the Kevin and Darcy happily-ever-after scenario happen.

In the meantime, this party was shot to hell because of her pathetic boyfriend and Elle MacWEIRDson and some pretty-boy lifeguard who'd abused her best friend. But Darcy knew she had to stick by Lindsay for a while, put on a cutesy face, and make the most of Anusa's big bash. It was the least she could do for her friend.

22

Lindsay

Sometimes it takes a crisis to bring your friends back. Although to-night was not among those stellar party nights for me, I would always remember it as the night Darcy and I reconnected. As we headed down the steps to the beach, I had to admit that Darcy's staunch support surprised me, especially considering the way she'd begun the summer, ditching me and pursuing Kevin with the single-minded conviction of a stalker. But Darcy was Darcy: headstrong, self-absorbed, obsessed with beauty. Maybe some of those qualities would soften over time, but for now I was relieved to get past the veneer to the sympathetic friend inside.

We were headed down to the beach in search of Tara—Skeeter Fogarty had seen her head down the stairs—but I was relieved to leave the noise of the main party. It wasn't every day I burst into tears at a fashionable fashionista's party in the Hamptons, and quite frankly, making a public spectacle of myself sucked up a lot of energy.

Darcy wobbled, trying to balance in her Gucci sandals on the hard-packed sand, while I just snatched my Rockport sandals off and carried them in one hand. The dark beach was punctuated by the dancing flames of a bonfire, where dark figures were gathered, some on their feet and others sprawled in a meandering circle of light.

"I don't see Tara and Charlie," I said, "but a fire is a good idea down here." The damp breeze off the water lifted the white man-tailored shirt I'd worn over my black shorts and tank top, and the sand was cold as mud underfoot. "Let's check it out and warm up."

"Oh, goody," Darcy said. "We can sing Girl Scout songs and eat s'mores."

"You, Ms. Love, are no Girl Scout." I smiled, glad to have traces of the old Darcy back. Sure, I knew that Darcy would revert to criticizing my clothes, diets, and manicures and chasing after Kevin again, but for now I was happy to seize the moment.

Halfway down the beach I recognized my brother walking in the opposite direction, returning to the party. "Steve, have you seen Tara and Charlie?"

He lifted his chin, as if just recognizing us. "No. And what the hell are you doing here? What the hell's going on with you?"

"Missed me that much, did you?" I laughed, though my senses were on alert. It wasn't like Steve to snap at me like that.

"Sounds like the theme song to *Family Feud.*" Darcy staggered, trying to move through the sand without taking off her Guccis. "I'll meet you over at the bonfire," she told me and headed off to the growing group of revelers.

"So what's your problem?" I launched into my brother. This was the first time I'd seen him since he returned from Hatteras and he seemed edgy and distant. "Christ, you look awful."

Suddenly angry, he dug his hands into the pockets of his jeans, the wind rippling his white T-shirt over his chest. "Don't start with me, Linds. Just tell me if it's true what they're saying about Ritter. Did you really let him?"

Suddenly sick, I pressed a hand to my mouth. "What did you hear?"

"My own sister. I can't believe it, Linds."

"Believe what?" This was agony, but I needed to know what was going around.

"Tell me it isn't true and I'll go rip Ritter a new one."

"Steve . . ." I pressed my eyes closed, frustrated, wounded. Everyone knew. Of course they did. I was reduced to being a score, one for Austin. He was no gentleman; I'd learned that the hard way. "Really, it's none of your business."

"So it's true?" He pressed his palms against his cheeks. "Nice move, Linds. Do you know what people are going to say about you? What they'll think?"

I know, I know. I could read the disappointment in his eyes. "It was a mistake, okay?"

"A mistake is taking a monster wave and tombstoning. Messing around with Ritter? That gets you your own entry in the Book of Stupid. Maybe your own chapter."

"Okay, it was dumb, but I didn't know he'd be such a bastard about it."

"And what's with Tara and that soldier?"

"Charlie? He's got a name, Steve."

"The way she clings to him . . ." He shook his head as if it all left a bad taste in his mouth.

I wondered if he was jealous. Not that he'd ever really expressed an interest, but years ago, when we were in junior high and Steve had spent part of his summer teaching Tara to surf, they'd developed a certain chemistry. Back then when I had teased him about it he'd just scowled, but that had been his typical response to any needling from his little sister.

"What kind of a rap did he pull on her?" he went on. "Better hook up before I have to head back to war?"

"Steve! They're really into each other. It's called a relationship, and it's bad enough you feel the need to meddle in my business. Leave Tara out of this."

"You know how it is with her. She's . . . like a sister to me."

I suspected that was just the tip of the iceberg, but I couldn't think about Steve's feelings for Tara right now. An image of Austin's face throbbed in my mind—that sick, smug grin he'd had as he looked out over the breaking waves, ignoring me. Bad enough that he tried to use me; now he was going around spreading dirt about me. The guy was toxic, and I couldn't let him get away with it.

"Hey . . ." Darcy called. "Are we going, or what?"

"I gotta go," I said, nodding toward Darcy. "We're headed up to the bonfire. You want to come with us?"

Steve seemed disappointed, his shoulders hunched, hands in pockets. "I'm outta here. This party's beat," he said, moving on.

Watching him go, I hoped his bad mood wasn't all about me,

though it did strike me as strange that Steve had suddenly made himself the guardian of my reputation. I filled Darcy in as we walked on the hard-packed sand toward the glow of the fire. "Apparently Austin is talking. Steve's mad at me for lowering my standards."

"I hate when guys do that. Like sex is the big conquest for the guy, the big humiliation for the girl. Don't let him make you feel bad. Believe me, Austin will feel worse when I get my hands on him."

"Like that's gonna hurt him." Darcy was five feet four and a size 2, and the image of her pouncing on Austin like a kitten actually made me feel better.

Ambient light glowed over the heads of the people gathered at the bonfire—forty or more revelers from Anusa's party who'd wandered down here to mellow out, smoke some weed, or listen to some classical guitar by a musician casually perched on a log. Two coolers of beer, domestic and imported, lay open in the sand, and a few yards back toward the cliffs a long barbecue grill was set up. Two chefs wearing white bib aprons and tall hats stood behind smoking skewers of chicken and steak.

"I don't see them," I said as Darcy and I circled the group. "Where do you think they went? I don't think they'd leave without saying something."

"It's not Tara's usual M.O., but now that she's so in love it wouldn't surprise me. I told them they could use my place anytime they want. Dad and his honey left in a flash, probably thinking I'd report everything to Mother dearest. Anyway, now that Dad is gone, the Love Mansion is back in business."

I thought it was a little strange that Bud Love didn't feel comfortable in his own summer house, but Darcy had ruled her parents for years. My eyes flicked over the faces, coming to a dead stop.

Austin Ritter? It couldn't be.

I grabbed Darcy's wrist and squeezed. "He's here," I hissed. "Austin."

"Oh, great." Darcy's brow arched as she spotted him. "Now we can have a weenie roast." She stepped forward, pulling me with her. "Come on."

"No! Let's just go." I didn't like confrontation, especially when the other party had just humiliated me and spread the word to half the guys in Southampton.

"I am not going to let you walk away from this," Darcy whispered in my ear. "He's the one in the wrong, and he's got to pay."

"It never works that way," I lamented.

"Just come on." Darcy kept her hand clamped onto my arm, marching me over to Austin, who sat back leaning on his elbows, his hairless legs sprawled in front of him, crossed casually at the ankles.

In the periphery I could hear meat sizzling on the grill, the guitarist plucking "Stairway to Heaven," and the accented voice of that girl in the sarong circulating among the bonfire crowd with her tray of shots in test tubes. I heard the dull roar of the ocean smashing on the shore, and the occasional shout from down the beach. But all of these sounds blended into a dull blur of background noise secondary to the red hammer thrumming in my head, pounding out pure anger.

"Oh, it's Austin," Darcy said loudly, wrinkling her nose. "I thought there was a bad odor coming from this spot."

I braced myself, expecting him to say something vile, but he just stared through our legs, turning to the guy beside him, a burly, bearded guy with aviator glasses. "It's cooling off, isn't it?" Ignoring us, Austin shook out his red lifeguard sweatshirt and wrapped the sleeves around his neck.

The burly guy's beady eyes flicked from Austin to Darcy and me, then back to Austin, leery and perplexed.

"Go on. Pretend you don't see me. Pretend I'm invisible," I spoke quietly, calmly, like a female metronome. "You can't hurt me, Austin, I'm beyond that now, but you know that saying: 'What goes around, comes around.' "

Austin turned to the bearded guy. "Do you hear someone talking?"

"Oh, that's mature," Darcy said.

"That's funny." Austin cocked his head. "I'm hearing these voices, but it just sounds like 'Blah, blah-blah, blah-blah.' "

The burly guy held up his hands. "I'm outta this, man. A conscientious objector." He pushed to his feet and headed over to the grill, leaving Austin alone, cross-legged in the sand, with Darcy and me standing over him.

Heads turned, and I sensed a few people watching us, seeking an entertaining diversion. Well, tonight I possessed the passion to deliver the performance of a lifetime.

"In some ways, I blame myself." I spoke quietly, my eyes trained on Austin, who seemed to be squirming a bit now. "I suppose I always knew you were vain and narcissistic. Nobody's perfect, and I was willing to overlook a few flaws. But did any of us realize the level of depravity you'd stoop to? The sheer cruelty—"

"And rudeness," Darcy added, clearly impressed with my speech.

"So rude." Looking down on him now, his curled beak of a mouth and his beady eyes, I wondered how I ever found him attractive. He was way too pretty, a spoiled little Lord Fauntleroy dressed in lifeguard's clothing.

Which suddenly struck me as odd. "Wait a minute. What's with the red shorts and T-shirt? You came to this party in your lifeguard uniform?" A few feet away someone snickered. "Oh, but that's your rap, isn't it?" I went on. "Of course! Everyone knows a girl can't resist a lifeguard."

"Excellent point," Darcy added. "Totally vindicating for you, Linds, though it doesn't seem to be working for Austin tonight." She pretended to scan the group. "Poor Austin. All buffed out in his lifeguard gear with no prospects in sight."

"Though it's not that kind of party," I said. "More of an arts crowd. Fashionistas and artists."

"True," Darcy agreed. "Maybe you should have worn your Jackson Pollock mask, Austin. Or John Irving. You could pull off that handsome, sulky look. A total lie, but not beneath you."

We'd hit a vein. I could tell by the way he shifted uncomfortably, his chin jutting out. He checked his watch, and I suspected he was just going to go, leave without giving us the satisfaction of really getting to him.

"Shots here. Anyone like a shot? Wild Turkey or Jagermeister? Green apple or peach schnapps . . ." The tall, thin waitress in the pretty sarong was circulating again, holding out her tray of colorful test tubes. I was about to say no thanks, but then I thought again.

"You know, I could use a few shots." But instead of reaching for a single test tube I grabbed the entire tray, held it over Austin's head and tipped it, slowly at first, so that only the thick, syrupy liquor poured out onto his head, lap, and shoulders.

Stepping back to miss the mess, Darcy let out a roar of delight. "Wah-ha! Yeah!"

"Oops," I said flatly. "My bad. But then again, the only way Austin can be tolerated is with a few shots."

All around us people were laughing as Austin finally lifted his dripping, sticky head and made eye contact, his eyes glimmering coldly.

I smiled. "Now, was it that hard just to look me in the eye? I think not. And in the future you might think twice before dishing dirt about someone behind her back. And manners . . . get some."

In a fit of anger he rose to his feet and snatched the empty tray out of my hand. I held my ground, staring right back at him, silently daring him to try and justify his behavior. "Does someone need a little anger management?"

He retreated, turned, and ran toward the water, sand spraying behind his feet.

Darcy did a little victory dance beside me, swinging her hips, stirring the pot. "Go Lindsay, it's your birthday! Go Lindsay! You dissed him . . ."

It was a first for me, deliberately contriving to humiliate someone—and succeeding. Not my style at all, but today it had seemed necessary.

Then I turned and saw Bear watching from the edge of the crowd, face scruffy with a few days' growth, eyes gloomy and disappointed.

Disappointed with me.

Turning away from him, I bent down to help pick up the test tubes and suddenly wanted to cry. Revenge was a shallow thrill, especially when you just kicked the love of your life in the teeth.

I plunked the sand-coated test tubes into the tray, mumbling: "Stupid, stupid, stupid . . ." Yes, I deserved my own chapter in the Book of Stupid.

23

Elle

"Hey, have you seen three girls who look like Charlie's Angels?" Elle asked a tall, dark-skinned man who'd been directing guests onto the estate.

"Yah, mon. Like . . . everywhere. We got Charlie's Angels, the Breakfast Club, and the gang from Cheers. Oh, and I just helped E.T. find a parking spot for his spaceship." His deep, rich laughter boomed in the night.

Elle liked him immediately. His name tag said Mr. Fitzroy.

"Seriously?" A middle-aged man with a shaved head eyed Mr. Fitzroy intently. "Spielberg is here?"

"Did I say that?" Mr. Fitzroy clapped a hand against one cheek. "Not that I ever drop names, don't ya know."

"Well, Mr. Fitz, you're no help at all, but you do make me smile. But I'm telling you, if the Angels swing back this way, tell them Elle is looking for them."

"Okay, Elle. And what about the devils? You want me to help you find them, too?"

Elle shook her head, her long earrings jangling. "I've been fighting demons all my life." As Mr. Fitzroy turned to greet another guest, Elle ventured onto the green lawn, feeling the Hamptons world open up in a way she hadn't experienced in all her years as Dr. DuBois's charge at the research center or the professor's daughter at academic functions. The jangling steel drum music, the huge lawn teeming with people lit by dancing torches, the laughter and salt air on the breeze . . .

This was an eye-opener indeed, well worth her return to the States.

After a cup of tea and a game of catch-up, Lindsay's mom had insisted that Elle head over to the designer's party to find the others. Good old Mary Grace—her second mom. She'd let out a squeal when the older woman had come to the porch door. Mrs. McCorkle had recognized Elle instantly, of course, and as soon as they got to talking the years melted away in a flash. Sitting in the old ladderback chair in the paneled dining room brought Elle back to countless days and nights lounging in the McCorkle house, playing cards or Monopoly, dreaming up moneymaking schemes, painting each other's toenails, making fudge or popcorn or both. When Mrs. Mick ordered her to go off and find "the young people" at the party, Elle didn't want to burst her bubble and point out that, aside from Lindsay, that group wasn't going to be so relieved to have "Trouble" back in town.

Although Elle had never met Anusa the designer, she'd crashed her fair share of parties and felt right at home strolling the grounds in her short, faded denim skirt and bikini top, a tropical print with a sea of aquamarine dotted with tiny yellow, pink, orange, and purple flowers.

Passing a buffet table loaded with fat shrimp on ice, cheeses, and crudités, she realized she was hungry and grabbed a plate. While she was munching a carrot, a woman with very large amber jewelry insisted she join their group, and she sat down, mostly listening as the guests talked about the soaring real-estate values in the Hamptons and the tight housing market. After that she waited in line at one of the little tents, hoping to have her fortune told. The two gentlemen in front of her in line, one as thin as a pencil with a shaved head, the other solid and well built, with silver hair, struck up a conversation, and she enjoyed talking with them, realizing from the conversation that they were gay and not trying to hit on her.

"I can't believe you don't remember Sag Harbor," the silver-haired man, Frank, was telling her. "It's charming. A little port town with small, colonial architecture intertwined with eclectic homes."

"She should come to one of our parties," said his friend, Kirin.

The other man rolled his eyes. "My place is tiny. Two bedrooms, and Kirin has filled it with baubles. Antiques and shells and driftwood. I keep telling him one more piece of junk and I won't be able to move."

Kirin shook his head. "Don't listen to him, it's lovely. You must come by."

"Just yesterday I stubbed my toe on his latest monstrosity. Can you imagine a desk so small no one can sit at it?"

"It's from a little old schoolhouse, and the desk was never intended for flaming, overfed oafs who'd be happy shopping for furniture at Levitz."

Although she found her head ping-ponging from one man to the other, Elle was entertained by their conversation and glad to meet them. Still, the line for the fortune teller moved slowly— "Someone in there must have issues!" Kirin remarked—and Elle decided she needed to move on and keep looking for her friends.

One more circle around the great lawn and she sensed that they just weren't here. The party was in full swing, but Elle was getting sick of wandering alone and decided to head back to the McCorkles' and unroll her sleeping bag in Lindsay's old attic room. She said good night to Mr. Fitz, then set off to the parking field in search of the minicar she'd rented.

On the way she passed a green van bearing the logo for Coney's, one of the Hamptons' most popular restaurants, which just happened to belong to the father of the one guy Darcy could never catch. What was his name? Kyle? Kurt? Whatever.

As she rounded the van she saw that the side door had been propped open and a pair of legs in washed-out denim dangled out over the running board.

A body? Hopefully just some dude sleeping it off or chilling in the parking lot. Elle glanced at the feet, now bare. As Elle considered whether she should move on or administer CPR, a torso joined the body, revealing a guy.

Spiked hair, tipped gold, maybe from the sun. Attractive in a Moondoggie sort of way. His silk shirt was unbuttoned, letting a shadow of tanned skin show through. Moving slow as a cat, he swung his head around and opened his eyes. "Am I a dick?"

Elle considered. Anyone who had to ask that question probably was. "I don't know you, but from where I stand, I'd say chances of escaping dickdom are slight."

"So I'm a dick?" He crumpled, head against his chest. "Shit!"

Elle stepped up to the van and checked out the interior. Someone had poured pots of money into customizing it with a built-in television, sound system, couch, and surfboard rack, but it could use a good cleaning.

"Come on in." He hoisted himself to his knees and staggered over to a cooler.

Elle climbed in, almost able to stand up straight without hitting the ceiling. She stepped over to the foam sofa and plopped down. "So, have you got a real name or are you sticking with Dick?"

"Kevin." He swayed over a cooler, fished around inside, and returned with two cans of beer.

Setting aside the icky domestic beer he'd handed her, she let her eyes trace his thin lips and stern brow, a Kevin refresher course. "So you're the Kevin of Coney's fame."

"Yeah." His grin was cocky, proud. She liked his perfect Chiclet teeth and the way he touched his tongue to his bottom lip, as if he were about to taste her. "You heard of me?"

The name of the restaurant is on the side of the van, dummy, she thought. But instead, she decided to do a little digging. "Aren't you Darcy Love's boyfriend?"

"That's what she thinks." He launched into a string of expletives, mangled phrases mixed in with some story of how she always reeled him in close, then pushed him off to be with her friends. Considering Kevin's drunken state, the beer spraying as he cursed, Elle wasn't completely clear on the details, but it did resemble the Darcy she used to know, self-centered and manipulative.

"But you're not like that." Kevin slid an arm around her and leaned into her, his face hanging suggestively close to her breasts. Either he was looking down at her cleavage or falling asleep. "You're different," he snorted into her bikini top.

"You don't know me." She didn't mind giving him a hard time, didn't have anything to lose at this point. "I'll bet you don't even remember my name."

He lifted his head, his thin lips curving. "You think I'm drunk, but yo-ho, no. I know that's a trick. You never even told me your name."

She laughed, a little relieved that Kevin McGowan didn't re-member her, wasn't connecting her to the squirrelly thirteen-year-old that Darcy had labeled "Trouble" and "Looney Tunes" and "Elle MacWeirdson." He didn't remember the girl whose junior high classmates had labeled her "most likely to set fire to the school" in the yearbook, the girl who'd been accused of setting trash-can fires in the beer garden of his father's restaurant back in the days when everyone in their crowd was too young to even sneak root beer, let alone the real stuff. Which meant that obviously she had grown from squirrel to elk, allowing her a chance to have a little fun with Kevin at Darcy's expense.

He lifted his head to guzzle the rest of his beer. "Hey, aren't you going to drink yours?"

She put her hand over it. "You don't need it, pal. You're about blown out of your shorts as it is."

He grinned, letting his tongue sneak out to tease his bottom lip. "Nah. I'm just looking to get blown."

His hand snuck around one breast, his fingertips swirling around a nipple erotically, and she laughed again at her good for-tune, having stumbled into Darcy's disgruntled boyfriend and the perfect chance to sting the one girl who'd choked her with criticism, the girl who'd pushed her over the edge, almost literally. Although Darcy's fists had been at her side that gray day, it had been her goading, her relentless need to control and manipulate that had sent Elle clambering over the rocks of the jetty, sliding into the deep, black sea. Plummeting from the safe summer world she knew into a kaleidoscope of foreign places, brisk languages, alien cul-tures.

When Kevin pushed her gently onto the floor and started kissing her, she saw the jagged line of revenge materialize like a thunder-bolt. How far did she want it to go? To devastation level, or just a walloping zing to let know that the power had swung to Elle's favor?

Kevin pressing against her, sort of dry-humping her leg, and Elle figured that if the two of them were here, they might as well rule out a game of solitaire. Besides, his body had that European look Elle had found so appealing, lean and comfortable in worn denim. She'd be willing to bet he wasn't wearing underwear under those jeans, which she loved.

He rolled off her slightly, giving himself an opening to reach under her short denim skirt. Even drunk, he managed to worship the sensitive skin of her inner thighs. He then raised her expectations a bit as he slid a few fingers under her thin panties and teased her to wetness. The way his fingers worked her clit, swirling it around with just the right amount of pressure, was so sweet. Maybe he wasn't as drunk as he seemed.

"This is nice," he whispered, his breath hot on her neck. "So nice."

"Yeah." She sucked in a breath as his fingertips skimmed right down between her legs, driving her wild again. Elle had never been one to play coy or delicate, and she wasn't about to start now, especially when she could have a little pleasure and zing Darcy at the same time.

She popped open his button-fly jeans, reached inside, and cupped his hard balls. "Got a condom?"

24

Darcy

As Darcy wove through cars parked haphazardly in the make-shift parking lot outside Anusa's home, she laughed out loud at the expression of embarrassment on Austin's face. Ha! Vain bastard! Served him right for being a rat to Lindsay.

Score one for Lindsay. Austin: zero.

Even the shot girl had been sympathetic. When Austin ran down to the beach to rinse off and soak his wounded ego, Darcy had handed her a hefty tip and tried to explain about Austin in a nutshell.

"You mean he's an asshole?" The waitress in the sarong thrust a bony hip bone out, taking a stand. "God knows, I've had my share of those. You don't have to pay for the shots."

"But you deserve a tip for being such a good sport." And then Lindsay apologized for dumping the test tubes onto the sand, and the sarong girl was cool with that, and in fact she got off work at eleven, and maybe Lindsay and Darcy would want to meet her? And the girl, whose name turned out to be Ruthie, loved Coney's, and the three girls headed back toward the stairway together.

Now, as her heels clicked on the walkway around Anusa's mansion, Darcy smiled, vaguely aware of the men watching her lithe, perfect body swagger past the patio lanterns. All in all, the party had turned out okay. Now . . . to reel in Kevin and straighten him out.

"You know, none of this would have happened if Bear just came back in time for your party," Lindsay said. She was back in a minor funk again, freaked about the fact that Bear knew about Austin and her; however, Darcy knew that was a minor ripple that would smooth out in a day or two. The worst was over for Lindsay; Austin had burned her, but she had gotten back at him times seven, and revenge was sweet, even from an observer's point of view.

"Bear will get over it," she told her friend. "Maybe this is the kick in the pants he needs. You guys can have it out and clear the air next time you see him at the pizza place. Kiss and make up."

"Like we were ever a couple," Lindsay muttered as she slid her single flat car key out of the pocket of her shorts. "Where is Kevin parked? Are you sure he didn't have an extra key? It would be just like him to drive drunk and leave you here."

"I have a feeling he's sitting in the van, stewing. I'll be fine. Call you tomorrow."

She backed away from Lindsay's dusty Saturn wagon, thinking it was sorely in need of detailing. Sighing, she realized she'd have to talk to her friend about paying a little more attention to maintaining a good appearance all around. The diet seemed to be working for her, but she was wearing last year's sandals, driving a dirty car, and letting her hair grow like a weed. *I'm going to help you pull it together, Linds*, she vowed as she cut down a path that led to a distant parking field.

Spotting his van from a distance, she could hear music blasting out through the open windows—confirmation that Kevin had found his way back and was waiting inside. By now his annoyance would have faded and he'd be putty in her hands, ready to make up and behave as a good boyfriend should.

Another couple passed her, laughing about something. She smiled at them, now picking up the sound of moaning voices. Oh, great, two losers were getting it on in the woods.

But as she got closer, her heels wobbling on the flattened grass, the moaning got louder and the van seemed to be moving.

The van was rocking, like something from a bad comedy film.

Wait a minute . . . was it Kevin's van?

She checked the side, and there was the logo for Coney's, bumping up and down . . . and that moaning! Too weird.

She felt a heavy weight in her chest as her fingertips closed on the door handle. This was a mistake. Maybe Kevin let one of his buddies use the van. She was going to whip open this door and find Fish inside, doing the nasty with some girl.

Well, okay. Not a pretty sight, but she could live with it.

She popped the door handle, slid it aside, and took in the fleshy view of her boyfriend's flat butt jutting forward and back. The gold-tipped ends of his hair touched his shoulders, reminding her that he needed a haircut.

A haircut. Such an odd thought when he was fucking someone else.

"Kevin!" she shrieked, peering around him to see the girl he was screwing, a petite thing who sat back on the couch with her legs limberly lifted to her shoulders like a player in Cirque de Soleil.

"Aw, man!" He pulled out and crumpled to the floor, holding his crotch.

The girl lowered her legs and tucked them casually to one side, sitting upright, looking perky and not at all embarrassed. "Darcy." Her eyes narrowed, catlike. "You know, the last time I saw you, you had that same look. That fury." She straightened, flicking an imaginary speck from the cup of her bikini top. "Have you ever thought about anger management?"

Elle!

The image of the girl blazed, bold and red, in Darcy's fury.

Elle was back.

25

Lindsay

"I gotta hand it to you, Elle. When you blow into town, you really do it with a bang," I told my long-lost friend that night as we draped ourselves over the single beds in my attic room. The windows had been thrown wide open, and outside, moths bounced against the screens, crickets sang, and a breeze stirred the mixed scent of salt and flowers and cool night air that I had come to associate with the Hamptons house.

When Darcy had come running from the parking fields, frantic after finding Kevin's van rocking in the parking lot, I had been relieved to switch gears and have everyone's attention move from my situation with Austin (and my lack of a situation with Bear) to Darcy's debacle with Kevin, brought on by Elle.

"It didn't mean anything," Elle insisted now as she rolled over and pulled her knees to her chin. Curled up like that, she was so tiny, even elfin, an image helped by the emerald stud in her nose and the shiny rings winding up from the lobe of one ear. Her red-streaked hair was now wrapped in a coil and secured by chopsticks, and her green eyes were wide, glazed with something I wanted to call remorse. Or maybe I was just projecting.

"It meant a lot to Darcy," I pointed out. "All these years she's been pursuing Kevin? Don't tell me you've forgotten all that."

Elle rested one cheek on her knees and tried to hold back a catty grin. "Well . . . maybe I remembered."

"This summer she snagged him, finally, and you pop into town and ruin all that in, what? Like, ten minutes?" I tucked a pillow under my chin. "I gotta say, it's not going to make for the smoothest homecoming. Alienate Darcy and you're not going to be so popular in the Hamptons."

"I don't care about popularity. I don't need other people to like me."

And that has always been one of your biggest problems, I thought, *and one of the reasons you don't get along with Darcy.* In very different ways, Darcy and Elle were blazing their own trails, trying to make their own social rules, and failing on different levels. While Elle pursued a scattered pixie image with a bohemian flavor and Darcy favored a more cosmopolitan, prep-school style, both girls had a bad habit of bulldozing ahead, taking out anyone or anything in their path, leaving itinerant peacemakers like me to chase behind them, smooth things over, pick up the pieces. Countless times I had been the one offering the McCorkle house as "neutral ground" for a meeting place; I'd been the one coercing each girl to show up at the beach, come to the movies, go along for slices of pizza, join on for a bike ride to the next town. In some ways I didn't mind being the facilitator as it placed me in a central and essential role, which I felt well suited for.

But this time I suspected the rift exceeded my peacemaking skills. By messing with Prince Kevin, the crown jewel in Darcy's potential kingdom, Elle had committed the unforgivable, staging a coup in matters of the heart and financial security.

"The thing is, you put yourself between Darcy and her ultimate goal, the Kevin and Darcy Bliss Package."

"A pathetic goal, if you ask me. Have you taken a good look at that boy lately? His liver must be pickled in beer."

"I'll give you that, but he's still Darcy's choice. And by having sex with him, you've declared war."

"Really?" Elle flopped back on the bed, lifted her hips, and pushed herself into a yoga bridge. "Well, to quote Michael Jackson, I'm a lover, not a fighter. She can have her precious Kevin back. I'm done with him."

"I'll bet you are," I said aloud, seeing through Elle's ruse. This wasn't about casual sex with an old acquaintance, and it had nothing to do with Elle wanting Kevin in any way. "Did it work? Did it feel good?"

Elle propped herself on one elbow, trying to gauge my question. "Well, for a guy who was half in the bag, he wasn't too bad. He does this little swirly motion with his fingers that drives you wild, and—"

"I'm not talking about the sex, Elle. Did it feel good to take a swing at Darcy? Broadside her when she least suspected it?"

Elle's eyes opened wide, ovals of mossy green that stood out in a field of black eyeliner. "Holy crap, you're good." She fell back onto the floor and laughed. "You've gotten really good at this."

"Between you and Darcy, I get lots of practice." Unfortunately, the two people involved didn't seem to have a clue about their own motives, and the rest of the summer was going to be difficult, split between my two warring best friends.

"Well, if you must know . . ." Elle crossed her knees into a lotus position. "It felt fucking great. All those years she put me down, tried to manipulate me . . . even up to that day on the jetty when she drove me so crazy I almost didn't mind slipping into the ocean. She always pushed my buttons and for once, tonight, it felt good to push hers."

"I'll bet it did. But it's going to make it that much harder to get what you want."

"Get what I want?" Elle cocked her head, tugging on the rings in one ear. "What's that about?"

"You were right about one thing: you don't need to be popular. You don't need mass approval."

"Yup. I couldn't care less what anyone else thinks."

"Except Darcy." I popped up onto my elbows, knowing I was on target. "She's the one you've got to win over. You need Darcy's approval."

"That's a crock!" Elle picked up a pillow and flung it toward my bed.

Fending it off, I knew I'd hit a nerve.

"How could you even think something so stupid?" Elle insisted. "Take that ridiculous idea and just, like, fling it out the window or flush it down the toilet or something."

But I just shook my head. "You'll see." Elle and Darcy were smart enough; with any luck, one day they would both figure it out.

26

Tara

"The most beautiful sunrise I've ever seen was over the hills in Thailand." Charlie spoke quietly, holding their attention so rapt that so far no one had even tasted the pear torte that Tara and her mother had passed out. "Orange, purple, and red. I had the sensation of being on a different planet, millions of miles closer to the sun."

Tara smiled, loving this man. She wanted to slip her slender sandal off and rub his foot under the table, but she still wouldn't chance contact in her parents' home. Tonight, it was progress enough that her parents seemed interested in what Charlie had to say, accepting of his experiences overseas.

"Sounds like you've made the most of your travels with the military, Charlie." Her father lifted his fork and cut into the torte.

"And Thailand sounds like a fascinating country," Serena Washington said. "Did you ever go there, Wayne?"

Tara wanted to groan. Somehow her mother always managed to swing attention back to Wayne, the favored son.

"Mama, I figure I'm doing enough travel just getting myself over to Korea. Besides, I like to dink around on my days off. That computer system they've got on base, it's prehistoric. Better now that I've worked it over, but there's always files to update and viruses to kill. You wouldn't believe the stuff people download without thinking. And then they bellyache when their files are corrupt."

Wayne stabbed at a piece of torte with his fork. "I got my hands full over there."

Just then the phone rang, and when Dad started to answer, Mama shook her head. "Let it go, Larry. If it's important they'll leave a message."

But Dad pressed his napkin to his lips, dropped it to the table, and crossed the room. "Very few people have the number here, Reenie. It must be important."

Dad's deep voice sounded from the kitchen, and Tara dared a secret smile for Charlie. Dinner had gone well tonight; Mama and Dad seemed to be accepting Charlie for who he was, gaining little glimmers of insight into his life.

"The torte is delicious, Mrs. Washington," Charlie said. "Not too sweet."

Mama smiled, but it was back to the church-social smile. "Thank you, Charlie. I always hate that cloying sweetness of some desserts. Lemon is the key."

Dad crossed through the dining room and started opening the built-in armoire in the adjoining living room.

"What is it, dear?" Mom seemed concerned.

"Breaking news upstate." He clicked the remote, surfing to find a news channel. "Alleged beating of a black man in custody. Apparently there's a videotape. I'll need to head up there tonight."

"But it's the start of your vacation! Can't someone else take the case?"

Wayne and Tara exchanged a quick look of "not again . . ." They'd witnessed this argument plenty of times before.

"Anyone want the last torte?" Wayne asked, knowing that no one would even answer. He stabbed it from the platter as Serena left the table to stand in front of the television and express her concerns to their father.

Tara twisted in her chair as the news channel switched to a reporter on the scene in Apple Junction, a small town in upstate New York where the incident had taken place. Her stomach began to ache as the reporter spoke quickly, emphasizing words like "brutalized" and "abuse" and "actual footage." Apparently, this was a juicy story.

Turning back to the table, Tara pushed her dessert away and listened as some of the details of the story spilled out. The suspect, an

African American named Clarence Dumont, was wanted for armed bank robbery. He had been shooting at police officers when taken into custody. One of his bullets had struck an officer, who was currently being treated in a critical care unit.

"The man's got to be defended," her father argued, his voice slightly muted.

"I understand that, but there are other partners in the firm. You just started your vacation. Here it is August and you haven't even spent a full week here at the beach."

"I don't think Mr. Dumont can wait while we sit on the beach and take a vacation, Reenie." And with that, her father was down the hall, packing his things to head back to Manhattan.

When she heard her mother's car pull into the driveway some time later, having dropped Daddy off for the last train back to Manhattan, Tara braced herself against the kitchen counter, wondering if she could dart off to her room and escape a confrontation with her mother before Serena made it up the stairs. The dishwasher was loaded, the counters all wiped down so Mom wouldn't have anything to complain about there, but from past experience Tara knew the extent of her mother's disappointment when Dad blew off vacation or a special occasion to work a case. Mom was not going to be perky, and considering her own issues with the nature of Dad's work, Tara just wanted to escape.

"I'm beat," Tara called down as her mother climbed the stairs. "Off to bed."

"Tara, it's not even eight o'clock."

Caught, she froze.

"Are you feeling sick?"

"I'm okay. Maybe I'll read in bed."

"What's the matter, honey?" Serena paused on the landing and touched her daughter's shoulder gently.

Maybe it was Mama's sweet tone, or the fact that her mother had actually touched her for the first time in years, but the gentleness pushed Tara to open up. "I just hate it when Dad takes on these high-profile cases without having the facts. Dad's turning into a civil-rights ambulance chaser, always defending the black brothers even if those defendants are in the wrong. It's an embarrassment."

"You're talking about your father's vocation." Her mother's eyes flashed with indignation, and Tara could see that she'd made a mistake confiding her true feelings. "Your father defends who we are."

"No, ma'am. He defends criminals. Those people aren't you and I."

"He is out there trying to protect the rights of African American men and women, and you of all people, with your sights set on law school, should understand the importance of that mission."

Tara stepped back against the pillar of the spiral staircase and closed her eyes, wishing she could disappear. "I know it's important, Mama. I just wish it didn't have to be my father looking like a cartoon character . . . a buffoon. Do you know they did a comedy sketch about him on *Saturday Night Live* during the Hunnicutt case? Did you see it?"

Serena turned away, her heels clicking on the kitchen floor as she tucked the car keys into their compartment in the drawer. "I heard."

"And you're not embarrassed?"

"I support your father because this is what he has chosen to do, and it is the right thing, Tara. He believes in his work; we both do. If we don't constantly reinforce our civil rights, people will backslide, and I'd hate for you to ever know the way it used to be with racism and discrimination."

Oh, I've known discrimination, Tara thought, recalling how her aunties pushed her to take bigger portions and get rid of that "white-girl's ass," how darker-skinned girls at school steered clear of her because they thought she was either white or of mixed race; how her own parents didn't want to acknowledge that Charlie might be a possible boyfriend because he was the wrong race for an upstanding African American family like the Washingtons.

"I'm going to have a cup of coffee, decaf of course." Serena turned on the tap and started filling the glass carafe. "Would you like some? Maybe we can interest your brother and Charlie in a game of Scrabble."

"No, thanks." Normally Tara would jump at the chance to mix Charlie into the family social milieu, but not tonight.

Tonight she was going to turn on the television in her room, lose herself in a mindless sitcom, and imagine what it would be like to be born in a wacky family that wasn't all wrapped up in thorny issues of race.

27

Darcy

Darcy leaned onto her windowsill and met her reflection in the glass, diamonds winking in the grandiose splayed setting of the Cortez necklace, the gems shimmering like icicles above the swell of her breasts barely covered by a hot pink bikini. If she looked up she could see Andre's naked chest as he leaned over her and tentatively touched her shoulders. Beautiful Andre . . . sexy, gorgeous, and a little too naïve for Darcy's tastes.

But the diamonds were thrilling—stunning—far more exciting than jewelry-store-heir Andre, a Great Egg boy she'd sought out after her life came crashing down at her feet with the end of the Kevin and Darcy Bliss Package. He'd been involved with another Great Egg girl, some simple Sara whom Darcy had seen around the ritzy neighborhood, a high school lacrosse player. Not too hard to bump out of the picture, when Darcy put her mind to it. But it had been a shallow victory, wrangling Andre, bringing him out here to show off like a tournament trophy. She'd even talked him into finagling the necklace, a loaner from one of his father's stores, thinking that possession of the fine gems would bring their relationship to a new height of passion.

But it wasn't working. The only sparkle in this room was coming from the Cortez necklace. The Cortez heir was definitely lacking in glamor, and as Darcy stared out past her own reflection, she had to admit that she wasn't happy.

It just hurt too much, losing Kevin.

After the incident of the rocking van, Darcy had retreated back to Great Egg, where she'd holed up in her bedroom, turned off her cell, and slept for most of the next day. When she woke up, her mother confronted her, annoyed by Kevin's incessant calls and a bit put out by Darcy's sudden appearance. Meaning, having Darcy in the Great Egg house obviously put a damper on Melanie's social schedule, cutting into quality time with the hunky tennis pro. So Darcy used her father's secretary to book a suite at the Plaza in Manhattan, then drove in for a few days of shopping and spa treatments at Elizabeth Arden.

She'd been in the middle of a cucumber facial when the attendant in pink begged her pardon and an irate Lindsay burst into the room, grabbing a towel to mop sweat from her brow. "Christ, what's the deal with these people? I thought this was a spa, not a maximum-security facility."

Darcy had lifted the pads from her eyes with a gasp. "What are you doing here?"

"You've had me so worried! When your mother told me you left the house I rode in on the Hamptons Jitney to track you down."

"Linds, that is so sweet." Darcy nodded at the attendant. "Giselle, can you get my friend Lindsay some water, please, and add her on for my one-thirty pedicure."

"Of course, Ms. Love." Giselle poured water from a pitcher floating with ice and lemons, handed it to Lindsay, and exited to make the appointment.

Darcy stretched like a cat under her pink robe. "We'll get our toes done together, then I'll take you to Balthazar's for a late lunch. My treat."

"Sounds nice, though it's so hot in the city I think my toenails are even sweating. And when you hear what I have to say, you might want to shoot the messenger. Kevin is getting desperate. He's stopped into Old Towne Pizza every day since you left the Hamptons, and he just sits there at the counter with a Coke and begs for my help getting you back. It's embarrassing."

"Pathetic." Darcy felt a tremor of relief that he was suffering, too, but there was no forgiving what he'd done, screwing around with her archenemy. In Darcy's book, just fucking around with someone else would have been reason to cut him off flat, but Kevin had taken it all to a new level of treason.

"And then, last night, he actually came to my house and said he wasn't going to leave until I got you on the phone."

"No! What did you do?" She shot a look at the door. "You didn't! Tell me he's not outside!"

Lindsay lifted a heavy clump of hair from the back of her neck and shook her head. "He would be if I'd let him. The poor guy doesn't know what to do without you. All those years you could barely get him to look at you, and now he seems to think you're his lifeline."

"How did you get rid of him last night?"

"Mary Grace McCorkle to the rescue. Ma sat him down, served him tea and snack cakes, listened to his tales of woe, and told him how it was when she was a kid. That took, oh, I don't know . . . about ninety hours."

"Well, thank God for your mother," Darcy said, wishing for the zillionth time that she had just one parent with a protective bone in their body.

"He's serious about getting you back, Darce. I don't even think he's drinking anymore. I mean, every time I've seen him he's been on soft drinks and tea. Not like the old Kevin at all."

"Really?" It was all intriguing, but still, there was no going back with him. He'd crushed her dream, smashed it beyond repair. Darcy leaned back on the pillow and replaced the cool cucumber-scented pads on her eyes. "Maybe he can sober up and really feel the pain."

"Darcy! That's just rotten."

"And what he did to me . . . with *Elle!*" She ripped off the pads again. "Whom you're still aiding and abetting, I take it?"

Lindsay took a long sip of water, her eyes on Darcy.

"Now that's just twisted. I'd think that now, finally, everyone in the world would recognize how crazy she truly is."

"You don't know what she's like now, everything she's been through." Lindsay went to the counter and poured herself some more lemon water. "Besides, I like crazy. I'm friends with you, aren't I?"

* * *

Back in her bedroom, Andre leaned up against her, rubbing his hands over her perfect body as if he'd just discovered a hidden art treasure. Could he tell she wasn't into it? She shifted her shoulders and the diamonds shimmered, sunshine on the ocean. So beautiful. All dressed up and nowhere to go. Of course, she had made a point of taking Andre around the Hamptons, to the beach and a few restaurants and clubs, just enough to get the word out that Darcy Love had bounced back, that she was still on top of her game, that neither Kevin nor that bitch Elle could put a ripple in her happiness for long.

But honestly, she didn't feel comfortable taking him everywhere. For a Great Egg boy he was a bit of a bumpkin, and she didn't want too many people to hear him talking about Mommy and Daddy, and his only other girlfriend, Sara, and—God forbid—his dog Florence.

Although hooking up with Andre and the diamond dynasty had helped her save face, it couldn't ease the swelling of her heart, the bad feeling that she'd lost the one thing that mattered so much, the family of two she'd worked so hard to create for herself. Andre was young and a little naive, easily bruised by her sarcasm and so grateful for sex that she could only guess Sara the lacrosse player had kept her legs la-crossed.

Ironic that here she was, decked in diamonds on a beautiful August night in the Hamptons and she couldn't even keep her mind on her new boyfriend, who was trying so hard to please her.

"How's that?" he asked, flicking his fingers lightly over her nipples.

"That's great, but I've got a few other moves you might like to try by the pool." She turned in his arms, noticing his excitement as she pressed against him. Beautiful Andre, the boy with a diamond factory. So young and . . . unformed. Very nice to look at, but the thought of educating Andre made her feel weary.

He pulled her close, breathing heavy, and squeezed her butt so hard it was painful.

She pushed him away, extracting herself. "Stop doing that." Was that too cold? She didn't want to hurt his feelings, something she'd never really had to worry about with Kevin. "Let's go down to the hot tub."

"Do we need clothes, or can we go naked?" he asked.

"Sure." Whatever. Nessie had seen worse.

And nothing seemed too important these days. Hot-tubbing with Andre today, get a hot-stone massage tomorrow; did any of it really matter?

28

Lindsay

Although it was late in the season for fireworks, I fully expected a sonic blast once Elle and I stepped inside the Salt Pond Inn. If everything went according to plan, in about five minutes an unsuspecting Darcy would enter the restaurant with Tara, who was bringing her here under the pretense of having lunch. Once Darcy spotted Elle, all bets were off. I sank behind a white linen tablecloth and adjusted the display of fresh lilies on the table so that they'd block the immediate view of Elle from the door.

"Clever," Elle said. "You don't happen to have a fake mustache in your purse, do you?"

As the Salt Pond was this summer's place to see and be seen, more than half the tables were taken, some with recognizable celebrities. Beside us the anchorwoman for a national morning show shared a table with her two children and husband. They were relatively quiet compared to the polo players at the big round table, lifting pints of ale and shouting rejoinders to each other. The quiet table in the corner was dominated by power brokers of film, two mighty producers, an actor turned director, and an actor who was so recognizable on the streets of New York he didn't even try to hide behind sunglasses or a hat. And those were just the players I recognized.

"Typical Hamptons." I shook my head. "You go for a low-key lunch and you walk onto the set of *Entertainment Tonight*."

"Beg pardon? I'm sorry, but just seeing foie gras on the menu makes me salivate—even if I am nervous about Darcy. You don't think she'd kill me in front of all these people, do you?"

"Relax. She won't draw blood in front of a celebrity crowd like this."

Elle's eyes shifted curiously. "Who? Where?"

"You've been out of the country way too long." Elle had never been a fan of television. One summer we'd had to force her to watch reruns of *St. Elsewhere* to bring her up to speed on "life as we know it," Darcy had insisted. "But don't sweat it. Nothing a few days in front of the TV with a few Blockbuster moments won't fix." With the menu to my face, I filled Elle in on who was dining around us. I was whispering about the anchorwoman/supermom when Darcy and Tara appeared at the patio entrance, Darcy chatting up the maître d'.

A small handbag dangled from her arm, catching the sunshine. Shaped like a duck and covered in sequins and bangles, it was a beacon, leading all eyes to Darcy. Dressed in a spaghetti strap sundress in a beachy turquoise and white print that gave her aquamarine eyes a chimerical quality, her hair swept back from her eyes in golden ringlets trickling down her back, Darcy brought to a halt a few conversations in the room. Certainly the polo players were on point.

I felt their eyes follow Darcy to our table, felt their curiosity over the change in her expression from salacious to furious. The maître d' leaned closer, as if trying to apologize, but she shoved him aside and strode over to the table, right up to me.

"Et tu, Brute?" Darcy asked, twisting her spine into a delicate, S-shaped pout.

So Darcy—ever the drama queen. I tapped the empty chair beside me. "Have a seat, before those producers over there flip you an Oscar."

"I really shouldn't," Darcy said with a steamy hiss, but she did.

Since the table was square, that put Darcy directly across from Elle, who tinkled her fingers in a wave and smiled. Elle had moussed and spiked her red curls that morning, and I bit back a smile, thinking she resembled a fairy who'd gotten a wing caught in an electric socket. "Me again. Your worst nightmare."

"So not funny." Darcy snapped her head to Tara, then to me.

"And I resent the setup. You know I wouldn't have come if I knew . . . *she* would be here."

"Of course. Hence the subterfuge." Tara flipped open her napkin and pressed it onto her lap, cool and unruffled. Today her auburn hair was curled under at her shoulders in a simple A-line—exotic and mystical—and I was struck by her versatility, with a range of looks from surfer girl to Cleopatra.

"Well, now that you're here," Elle began, "let me say how sorry I am for . . ."

Canoodling your boyfriend? I bit my lip, wondering how Elle would bail.

". . . everything. I mean, this last thing was just wrong, I know. I guess I was still harboring some ill feelings from years ago. My bad." She shrugged, as if years of resentment and anger could roll right off her narrow shoulders like springs over the rocks of a waterfall.

This is going better than expected, I thought.

Darcy held up one hand, a wall of cotton candy pink nails blocking off Elle. "Apology not accepted."

"Okay, then," I sighed. "I knew it couldn't be that easy. Guess we need to transfer from the express train to the local."

"But the last thing we want is to dredge up negative issues from the past," Tara said. "Lindsay and I are here because we love you guys and want this feud to end. We've been friends too long—all those years, digging for sand crabs and pouring cold water down each other's backs. You can't tell me you're going to let that all go over a guy."

"He wasn't just a guy to me," Darcy snapped, "and you all know that."

"We do," Tara said, "but we also realize that Kevin has a drinking problem, Darce. He's headed down a scary road, and I'm not sure you want to go there."

Darcy shook her head. "That's got nothing to do with this."

"He's got to be responsible for his behavior," I said. "Okay, Elle was wrong to go for it, but if she didn't come along, another girl would have been right behind her."

Elle snagged a carrot from a plate of crudités on the table. "What they're saying is, be pissed at me, but don't blame me for the breakup with your boyfriend." She bit into the carrot with a cracking sound.

"Exactly," I said. "That's called transference."

"Let's leave the technical terms to the experts," Darcy said. Her piercing blue eyes shot through Elle, then she turned her head. "I've managed to avoid you the past few weeks, and I'm very comfortable with that situation."

"But we're not," Tara said. "We're all friends, and Lindsay and I aren't comfortable splitting our time between two factions, navigating a civil war. Let's get to the bottom of this and move on."

Darcy folded her arms. "Good luck with that."

"I don't think we need to dig too much," I said. "It doesn't take a shrink to figure out that you two compete because you're so much alike. Fucked-up families, the only-child thing, feelings of abandonment—"

"That's pop psychology bullshit, and I *hate* it when you try to psychoanalyze me. Like it's all so easy. Like I'm as transparent as a Twinkie wrapper!" Darcy threw down her napkin and grabbed her adorable duck-shaped handbag from the table. "Forget about the psych major, Lindsay; you're wasting your time."

Stung, I dug my fingers into the straw seat of my chair. Damn, I was only trying to help. I tried to recover and respond, but Darcy was already gone from the table, a graceful exit that attracted its share of attention, especially from the polo players, who were in the midst of good-byes. One of them cut off his conversation and made a beeline after Darcy, following her like a circus clown.

"Where's she going—the ladies' room?" Tara asked.

I bit my lip. "That looks like more than a potty break. I'd say she's outta here."

"But *I* drove," Tara said. "How's she getting home?"

The Salt Pond Inn was half a mile off the highway, at the end of a gravel road that wound through dunes. Not a lot of buses or cabs coming this way.

Elle tore off a piece of foccaccia. "Well, I'd say that went well. She went from hating me to hating all three of us."

"You'd better go after her," Tara said.

But I was already on my feet, weaving through tables, past the concerned waiter to the patio exit. The polo players stood in a half circle, saying last good-byes, but otherwise the parking lot was empty. I cut around a tall, squat Land Rover and scanned the road as it turned past a cluster of scrubby pines. There was Darcy, her heels wobbling over the gravel, her head level and shoulders back like a runway model.

It was going to be a long walk back to Southampton.

Let her go. She doesn't appreciate your peacemaking mission. Don't follow her like a lost pup.

"Looks like your friend forgot her walking togs, eh?" said one of the polo players, a graying man with laughing eyes.

I nodded as he climbed into the Land Rover. Darcy would be fine. She'd find a ride. Probably from some billionaire who'd let her keep the car. It was just Darcy's karma to be rich and unhappy.

Everyone has a different cross to bear, Ma always said. And Mary Grace McCorkle was usually on the nose about human nature.

I had been around Darcy long enough to have more than an inkling of the torment that tugged at her soul. Issues of abandonment.

Which was why I had expected Darcy to come around and forgive Elle. "Do you know her parents ditched her in Connecticut?" I had told Darcy a few days before the lunch. "It's not like she just got bored and hopped on the Concorde to New York. The DuBoises made her leave London because they just couldn't squeeze her into their lives anymore."

Darcy had reacted with silence.

That was when I knew I'd hooked Darcy, caught her on a barb of compassion.

I knew that Darcy fought with her own demons on the issue of abandoment, always getting sucked in when her parents would appear to want time with her . . . a country club luncheon with her mother or a company Christmas party with her dad. Darcy complained about her parents and appeared to have dismissed any emotional connection with them, but I had seen her drop plans at a moment's notice to be with them. Only to realize later that her presence was all for show—the trophy daughter, the innocent, youthful beauty who would lend an air of "family" legitimacy. When we were little kids I had envied Darcy, watching longingly as her parents bought her anything she wanted: designer jeans and outrageously priced swimsuits, pagers and cell phones, expensive jewelry from the elegant shops on Main Street. But over the years, as Darcy bargained to spend nearly every night at my house because she couldn't stand the roaring quiet of her distant parents, I began to understand. Darcy's parents were long gone, and though they'd left the checkbook behind, it wasn't enough to keep a girl going. Darcy needed love, just like the rest of the human race.

The other day when I explained the crux of Elle's recent dilemma, that Elle had been sent back to the States because there wasn't room for Elle and her father's girlfriend in the London flat—or even, apparently, in the entire city of London, since the DuBoises could have rented a second flat—something clicked in Darcy. Her anger for Elle lost its edge, her complaints fading out like a movie soundtrack. And though Darcy had retorted with an obnoxious, "Why are you telling me this? You know I don't care," I knew it was a big lie. I also knew when to press my point and when to shut up and let a message resonate.

Here in the sunlight, I felt the top of my head baking in the sun. Shielding my eyes, I watched as Darcy disappeared in a dip in the road.

Let her go . . . let her walk home. Maybe it would teach her to appreciate her friends.

I turned to go back out to the patio, but my mother's voice niggled at my mind.

You know you can always rely on your friends . . .

Goddamn that voice.

By the time I reached Darcy, her newly pedicured feet were gritty with sand. "You know," I called, negotiating a pile of loose gravel, "I don't usually like to work out right before I eat." I wiped my sweaty palms on my culotte shorts, a flattering, loose cut in navy with khaki leaves.

Darcy let out a snort, then turned back. "Why do you always have to be the fucking United Nations?"

"You guys always do that to me. What else can I do when I'm friends with China and the Soviet Union?" I took a breath and pulled the khaki linen blouse away from my waist. "Look at me. My hair is melting and my pits are soaked."

Fists on her hips, Darcy cocked her head to the side. "Yeah, and you're one of the best goddamned sights I've ever seen."

Her gush of sincerity took me by surprise. This was the girl who'd just told me to give up dreams of being a psych expert? "So . . . are you coming back? I'd hate to have to fall to my knees and beg. This gravel looks sharp."

"Honestly? I don't know if I can forgive her. Or him. I don't know what to do."

"Take it one step at a time," I said. "Start by having lunch with her. Work your way up to going steady."

There was a new edge to Darcy, the wariness of frightened prey ready to bolt.

"Hey, it's been a summer of mistakes, for all of us," I added. "And you've been there, too. You know the power of forgiveness, Darce. Can't you try?"

"Okay, I'll do it." She threw her hands up in surrender and started marching back toward the restaurant. "But only for you."

I fell into step beside her, wanting to complain about the heat and the sandy road and the fact that I always had to play the mediator. But I sensed that it wouldn't take much to make Darcy flee again, so I gritted my teeth and plodded on.

By the time we returned to the table on the shady patio, Darcy had regained her old composure, cool as a summer breeze. She sat down beside Elle, propped her sequined purse on the table, and leaned into Elle's personal space. "I'll be civil. But you can't make me like you."

Elle worked hard to contain a grin, unsuccessfully.

"Wipe that smug look off your face."

"This isn't me being smug." Elle pointed a finger at her face. "This is me being highly amused by your vain attempts to resist my delicious personality. I've won over tougher cases than you, Darce. It may take some time, but you'll come around."

Darcy squeezed her eyes shut. "Okay, right now your delicious personality is grating on my nerves. Can we just have lunch and talk about something else?"

"Sure." Elle handed out menus. "I'll even buy."

Heads tipped down as we studied the salad and sandwich selections with a collective feeling of relief.

Darcy put her menu down. "And just one more thing. Just to get this on the record so we're square, if I ever catch you with my boyfriend again, I'll have to kill you."

I felt my brows rise, wondering how Elle would take it.

But she just nodded. "Sounds fair to me. Now who wants to split an order of calamari?"

29

Darcy

"This is Dr. Samuel Mehta calling from East End Hospital. Is this Darcy Love?"

The voice seemed so out of context in the small Bridgehampton bar where Darcy had gone with her friends to shoot some pool that she wondered for a minute if it was some kind of lame joke.

"This is Darcy. Who's this again?"

The doctor repeated his name, adding that Kevin had been brought in unconscious, an apparent overdose of drugs and alcohol. "He's conscious now. We're not sure of long-term prognosis, but I'd say he's very lucky to be alive."

Darcy shrank back against the rack of billiard sticks, not sure what to do. When her friends turned from the pool table and asked her what was wrong, she whispered, "Kevin's OD'd."

Elle's head shot up and Lindsay froze midshot.

"Is he okay?" Tara asked.

Darcy waved them off. "I . . . I don't know what to say. I'm not really next of kin or anything."

"Yours was the only name he'd give us. Let's put it this way, if you don't give him a ride home, we're going to have to put him in a cab from Riverhead to . . . wherever it is you live. Southampton? No one's going to be happy with that cab fare."

"I'll come," she said before she could talk herself out of it. And suddenly she was neatly replacing her pool stick and retrieving her ornamented duck purse from the midst of beer bottles and spinning slightly in search of the door.

"You're going to the hospital?" Tara spelled it out. "Is it serious?"

"He's conscious now, but he told them I was his next of kin."

"You can't go alone." Lindsay slid her stick onto the table. "We'll drive you."

Darcy shrugged. It didn't matter how she got there, as long as she did.

"I'd come along," Elle offered, "but I guess we'd all think that's a bad idea."

It took Darcy a minute to unravel Elle's dark humor, but she found herself letting out a macabre laugh on the way to the parking lot. Sometimes Elle's twisted humor was a relief.

Dr. Mehta's words floated through her mind as Lindsay floored it down the expressway toward the Riverhead hospital. Emergency room. Overdose. Next of kin.

"Was he trying to kill himself?" she asked aloud, "or just pushing the party too far?"

"That's a good question." Lindsay fiddled with the dash, lowering the air-conditioning. "Something you'll have to ask Kevin."

At the hospital, the clerk at the desk paged Dr. Mehta, a short, dark-skinned man with braces and the wide, dark eyes of a five-year-old. "Darcy Love? Come with me."

Lindsay peeled off to sit in the waiting room while Darcy followed Dr. Mehta back, past beds blocked off only by thin white curtains. "I've been hoping your friend will talk to us now that you're here. He's been rather stingy on the details."

Kevin was propped up in the bed, his lips chapped, the collar of his hospital gown stained black from having his stomach pumped, Darcy assumed.

"Tell us, Kevin," Dr. Mehta began, "what did you take?"

Kevin turned away. "Just some stuff. I think I drank too much."

"Oh, cut the crap, Kevin." Darcy stepped up to the bed. "Stop being a mary and tell the doctor what you took."

Kevin rubbed his eyes with the butt of his hands. "I snorted some coke. I was drinking. One of my friends had some Vicodin. I was supposed to take one, I guess. But I didn't."

"Vicodin is a powerful pain reliever," Dr. Mehta said. "Too much of it can kill you, but I suppose you already knew that."

Kevin shrugged one shoulder, turning to Darcy. The corner of his mouth drooped slightly, as if he was biting his lip to keep from crying. "Thanks for coming. Can you get me out of here now?"

"First, I want to know . . ." She swallowed against the thickness in her throat. It hurt to see him this way, so fragile, his eyes burning with empty light. "Kevin, did you try to kill yourself?"

His eyes flickered down, his face crumpling with pain. He was crying.

Dr. Mehta's head dropped down to his chart. "You know, over time you can kill yourself with alcohol alone. The Vicodin, it just speeds things along, if that's your goal."

"How could you do that to yourself?" Darcy demanded.

"I just . . . just didn't want to feel the pain anymore." Kevin lifted one arm, pushing his face into the crook of his elbow. "I missed you, Darce."

"This isn't about me," she said. "Not entirely. You've been on a pain-kill mission since junior high, Kev."

"Yeah, babe. Haven't we all?"

"Not like you, with your friends partying all night on the beach, the endless rounds of drinks on the bar, and popping drugs like they're Skittles. You've lost control of your life, lost the ability to judge what's right and what's the biggest bonehead move you've ever made."

He snorted. "That would be Elle?"

"No, that would be you nearly killing yourself."

"I just thought . . ." He swiped at his wet cheeks, then pushed his tongue against his lower lip, making Darcy want to cry. The gesture was endearing, somehow; the old Kevin was there, the kid who used to tease and connive just to get her to make out with him. "I thought if you couldn't stand me anymore, I didn't want to be here."

"I could stand you, Kevin," Darcy said, her voice hoarse with emotion. "I love you. But I don't like you very much when you're wasted. After a few drinks and a couple lines of coke, there isn't a lot of Kevin left. Just this blithering asshole that nobody likes."

He sighed. "What if that blithering ass is the real me?"

"It's not." Darcy moved up to the bed and reached for his hand, which seemed rough and bonier than she remembered. "And I want the real Kevin back. The guy I knew before cocaine zipped him up too tight."

"You want me to cut the drugs?" His eyes were hemmed in dark lines.

"Cut the drinking *and* the drugs," Darcy said firmly.

"We can provide some assistance, Kevin," Dr. Mehta said, looking like a teenaged Yoda. "Certainly a detox program would serve you well, and we offer therapy and support groups. We have a chapter of AA that meets here, but we can also refer you to many groups that meet right in your own community."

"I can't do *that*." Kevin's forehead creased. "My old man would kill me. Son of Coney's in Alcoholics Anonymous? It's not gonna fly, Doc."

"If it's about cost and privacy, we can work something out," Darcy said. "My therapist can give you a referral for Betty Ford or someplace in Manhattan or . . . or even in Vermont, near Bennington. I'll take you up myself . . ." Darcy was fast-forwarding to the advantages of having Kevin close to college, away from his influential friends and dysfunctional family. They could spend weekends together, driving through the fiery reds and oranges of the autumn foliage, warming by the fire in quaint bed-and-breakfast inns.

"I'll do everything I can to help you, Kevin, if you're willing to do it."

"And ultimately, it is your decision, Kevin," Dr. Mehta cut in. "We can support you, but you are responsible for your life."

Kevin sucked in a wincing breath, as if it were painful just to breathe. "Yeah, okay. I'll clean up my act. But nothing too radical until after the season ends. My old man will give me hell if I just up and disappear now."

"Okay," Darcy said, squeezing his hand and wondering if this could possibly work out. Wisps of hope swirled around the old dream, the Kevin and Darcy Bliss Package. Could it really happen after all?

30

Darcy

"You're a good helper." Timothy McGowan climbed to the third rung and pointed down at the stack of plywood. "You know, last time we had a hurricane, everyone on the staff pitched in to close up the place. Buttoned it up so well, we had minimal damage. Minimal. But this year, with the end of season so close . . ." He sputtered a raspberry and flicked his hand as if batting away a mosquito. "I let them go. Let them go back to their winter jobs, get out of the path of the storm. Things can be replaced, I say. But people, people are one of a kind. The human condition must be protected and guarded at all costs! At least, that's what I say."

Among other things, Darcy thought, feeling a bit numbed by his constant barrage of chatter. Staring up at him, balanced on the ladder, she wondered why his wife didn't get after him to cut that shaggy gray hair, especially the strands that curled around his ears and collar like wild ivy. She'd never noticed inside Coney's, which was dimly lit, but out here the sunshine cast Kevin's father in a whole new light.

"Hand up another board, there, Darcy," he said. She hoisted up a plywood board, glad for the leather gloves to keep splinters out of her hands. Damn, these boards were heavy, even after Kevin trimmed them down to size with a power saw.

"Thank you, darlin'. I appreciate it." He fit the board neatly over the window, pulled the hammer from the loop on his pants, and began driving nails. "My son . . . he gets sick of hearing his old man rant and rave, on and on. I know it, but I can't help myself."

"You're not ranting," Darcy chided him, although he'd been babbling on so long about social security, union wages, preservatives in bread, and the cheese surplus that she'd tuned out everything but the big exclamations long ago. She hoped there wouldn't be a quiz.

After three hours spent assisting as father and son unloaded plywood, cut it down to size, and tacked it over the windows of Coney's on the Beach in preparation for the incoming hurricane, she was starting to see how the old man drove Kevin crazy, always criticizing and snapping at him. Kevin was sawing the boards too narrow/too wide, moving too fast/too slow. No doubt about it, Timothy McGowan was a cranky old man, but Darcy was still counting on winning him over with her charm and maybe even smoothing things over between the man and his son. Darcy had always had a way with adults—parents, teachers, store clerks, even the Great Egg supermoms who headed the school organizations and Girl Scout troops had loved her. Whether it was her saccharine manners or her thousand-watt smile (courtesy of two orthodontic specialists), Darcy had a gift for sucking up, and she intended to utilize it on Kevin's father.

"Darcy's got some ideas for renovating the restaurant, Pop. Good ideas."

"Renovations? Oh, really now?" Timothy McGowan's pale blue eyes blinked suspiciously at Darcy.

She wasn't sure she liked the way this was going. "Kevin . . ." She scowled at him, then cocked her head in deference to his father. "You have a lovely place, Mr. McGowan. I've always adored Coney's."

"But you'd change a thing or two given the chance?" Mr. McGowan slid a piece of plywood off the cart. "So like a woman. And how would you change my establishment, Darcy?"

Now that Kevin had put her on the spot, she figured she might as well share her ideas. "Those bay windows on the south end? The ones with the plants in them. I'd take them out and replace with a solid wall. You could put in a big gas fireplace, which would be a big draw in the winter months. Besides, the southern exposure is too hot for unshielded windows at the beach. And if you close up the wall it will be better insulated; a savings on air-conditioning, fuel bills."

"Is that right?" His face was rigid. "Not for nothing, Darcy, but who asked you?"

The sting of embarrassment was so sharp, she couldn't muster an answer.

"*You* did, Dad." Kevin dragged a sheet of plywood across the porch. "You asked her."

And the place needs it, old man! she wanted to shout. Darcy had come up with dozens of ways to renovate the building, change the menu, and upgrade the business. Renovating Coney's was all part of the master fantasy in which she and Kevin married and became a premier couple of the Hamptons, the restaurant gurus, hosts to movie moguls and actors, TV personalities and dignitaries and any celebrity who seemed to be the new flavor of the month. Sure, Coney's was popular now, but with her input and vision the restaurant could become a Hamptons event, the hottest place to see and be seen out East, on a par with four-star restaurants in Manhattan.

As Timothy moved his ladder to another window, Darcy flexed her fingers inside the leather gloves, feeling very small. Suddenly she understood how Kevin felt, though she imagined this was a minuscule sampling of the degradation his father passed down on a daily basis.

"Goddamned changes," the older man grumbled. "Everybody's an expert." He banged a nail, as if to emphasize his anger.

Kevin joined Darcy, swiping the beads of sweat from his forehead with the hem of his T-shirt. "Not for nothing, Dad, but I think Darcy's got some great ideas. This place could use some new vision."

"Vision. Now that's a buzzword if I ever heard one." Timothy came down the ladder and swung around toward Darcy and Kevin, pointing the hammer at them. "My father had this business since before the two of you were born. How's that for vision?"

"Fairly insightful, I'd say. I mean, to open a good-sized restaurant and bar on the beach, not knowing how the community would develop?" Darcy felt as if she were reading a script for a college workshop, the assignment: act whimsical and polite. Honesty hadn't worked with Mr. McGowan; time to grease the pan. "That was brave."

"You're darn tootin'." Timothy lowered the hammer, but his pale eyes were full of rage. "Do you know what was on this stretch of beach before we got here? Do you know? It was nothing. Dunes. Lumps of sand. My father built a business out of lumps of sand . . ."

"Look, Dad, if you want to get all these windows covered, including the big ugly bays on the south side, we don't have time for the long version of Coney's history." Kevin wheeled the cart of plywood down the porch, turned the corner, and vanished from sight.

Darcy headed after him awkwardly.

"Your grandfather was a man with vision," Timothy shouted, swinging his hammer against a boarded-up window.

A clatter of glass sounded. Something had broken under the plywood.

"Damn it to hell!" He started prying the board loose with the prongs of the hammer.

But Darcy didn't want to stick around to watch the billowing wrath of Timothy McGowan. Checking her gloves, she edged toward the corner of the building. "I guess I'll just go help Kevin . . ." Rounding the corner of the porch, she saw Kevin working furiously, picking up boards and flicking them against the side of the building as if they were playing cards. With his shirt off, she noticed again how thin he'd become, his ribs stretching his chest, his washed-out jeans barely hinged on his hip bones. Although thin was in, Kevin was starting to look sick. For the millionth time, she wondered when he was going to start therapy, refusing to accept that he'd just go on drinking all winter. Hadn't he promised her to start rehab as soon as the season ended? Every day, each morning she woke up wondering if this would be the day he'd ask for her help, tell her he was ready to go.

Darcy folded her arms across her chest. "Better watch it, or you'll break a window, too."

"Why do you suck up to him?"

"I never suck up," she said indignantly.

"You're the queen. The Jedi Master of Suck Up."

She cracked a smile. "That good, am I?" Darcy waited for Kevin to calm down, to turn around and tell her he was sorry for losing his cool, that he didn't mean to blame her.

But he kept hammering away.

She wasn't used to being upstaged like this; when a temper

tantrum was thrown, she was usually the one throwing the tirade. The role reversal was not pleasant for her.

Shucking off her gloves, Darcy crossed the porch to the main entrance where Kevin had left a cooler full of beer and water. She cracked open a bottle of water, sat down on the wooden steps, and recalculated. As if it wasn't enough that she needed to talk Kevin into getting sober, now she'd have to figure in a lifetime of dealing with his obstinate father, a royal pain in the ass. She wondered if all this was worth the dream . . .

To be the future Mrs. Kevin McGowan.

To be a restaurateur, a Hamptons personality.

To be with Kevin. She still felt a little wounded at times, still lapsed into a blue mood occasionally when she recalled that horrendous spectacle in Kevin's van. At least he'd had the good grace to trade it in for a truck, against his father's wishes, of course, but the bad memory mobile was history.

Yeah, Kevin was worth it, even if he was a workout. Peeling some sweaty gunk out from between her fingers, she figured she could hack it. Every family had its dysfunctions, and she wasn't about to let a grouchy, middle-aged man ruin her future. Let the old fart rage on and on, like the hurricane winds.

He could huff and puff, but he wasn't going to blow Darcy's house down.

31

Lindsay

"Have you seen the forecast?" my mother asked, leaning into the laundry room where I was folding colors. "The hurricane is picking up strength, a category four now. Maybe you should go back to school today. Get ahead of it."

"And spend extra time in the dorms?" There was nothing more dweebish than arriving on campus too early, especially since I had signed on to live in the dormitories as a resident assistant instead of taking a share in a student rental house. Though I'd love to be hanging with friends, I'd chosen to reduce my student loan by working for free housing. Always penny-pinching, the way of the McCorkles. Still, I couldn't stand to be back in the sterile dorms early. "I'll be okay driving on Tuesday, Mom."

"Not if some of the roads wash out. You know, the Shinnecock Inlet was created by the hurricane of 1938. You can't underestimate the power of a storm."

"I'll be okay, Ma." I shook out an oversized red T-shirt and held it under my chin to fold it. "I want to be home right now, to make something out of the last few days of summer. My birthday, Ma." Of course, I couldn't tell her that I needed some closure with Bear before I left. Ma and I didn't discuss the fact that I'd been crushing on him for years, that he hadn't returned to work at Old Towne Pizza after the Hatteras competition. That we hadn't really talked, either at the dinner table or out in the surf line.

That my heart was breaking.

Some days I wallowed in dark thoughts, viewing the tragic turn of events as one of the daytime soaps Darcy was glued to. I blamed my brother for sweeping Bear off to the competition that forced me into the wicked Austin's arms. I imagined the sponsors to be unsavory, wretched men who promised Bear a glowing treasure chest only deliver a piece of driftwood on a crowded Honolulu beach. The evil sponsors.

How could they take Bear away from us?

Ma pulled a navy sheet out of the laundry basket and handed two corners to me. "Why don't you drive back to Brooklyn, then?" she suggested. "That'll put you halfway back to school."

"You trying to get rid of me?" I pressed the edge of the sheet to my mother's hands, getting in her face.

"I've been trying for years, and still I've got two clinging like there's no tomorrow." With a wry grin, my mother snapped the sheet into a compact square and placed it onto the dryer.

"Oh, come on, Ma. You love having us around. If Kathleen and all the others would move back in with all the grandchildren, you'd be in your glory."

"Wouldn't I?" Mary Grace smiled. "The human race is the only animal that doesn't know when or how to kick its young out of the nest."

I folded a white sweatshirt and loaded it into my duffel bag. "Well, if Steve were mine, I would have drop-kicked him years ago." I mimed punting a football.

Ma just shook her head. "Such a wise guy. You'll see when you have your own, my dear. You'll see."

32

Tara and Darcy

A fat ribbon of wind and rain blew up onto the covered porch of the Love Mansion, sprinkling Tara's skin and feathering her dark hair back. She crossed her arms and hugged herself, wondering if they'd made the right choice to stay here. No one else seemed fazed that she and Charlie were holing up in the path of a hurricane, but Tara was sure it was the most reckless, adventurous decision she'd ever made.

Surprisingly, their scheme had been masterminded by Wayne, who'd spent a lifetime wandering the path of least resistance. "Why do you think I care if you two are together, and why do you keep trying for Mama's approval and Daddy's blessing? Get a motel. Tell them you're going back to Princeton early, to beat the hurricane. Lord, girl, you were supposed to be the brains in this family. Don't they teach you strategic operations at Princeton?"

"You know, with devious minds like yours, maybe the U.S. stands a chance in maintaining itself as a superpower," Tara told him, eyeing him curiously.

"Is that supposed to be funny?" he sniped.

Instead of letting him engage her, Tara had hugged her older brother. "Now that you're leaving, I'm going to miss you."

"I'm just going back to Manhattan," he said flatly. He planned to wait out the hurricane in the city and meet Charlie at JFK Airport for their flight back to Korea.

"Yeah, but I probably won't see you before you go. Take care. Keep those computers virus free."

Wayne had just rolled his eyes and told Charlie to be packed by noon. The two guys would say their good-byes and head off together, then Wayne would drop Charlie anywhere he wanted.

Since a hotel would be expensive, hard to find on this evacuated island, and easy for her parents to trace in credit card bills, they had decided to barricade themselves in the Love Mansion, which fronted the beach but had an expansive lawn and massive bulkheads, able to withstand the storm.

Darcy was fine with it, even reassured somehow. "It might do this old place some good to have a couple who's actually in love staying here," she'd muttered.

They'd said their good-byes a few hours ago, Darcy's car packed to the windows for her trip back to Bennington, a five-hour drive even when the Hamptons weren't being evacuated, probably more today. Kevin had been quiet, propped in the passenger seat; Tara hadn't been able to tell if he was sulky or nervous or both.

As the taillights of Darcy's lipstick red convertible had shrunk to small dots, Tara had stood on this wide wooden porch, considering the storm that had ended the summer so abruptly. Elle had already left for Connecticut and classes at Yale, Darcy and Kevin were on their way to Vermont to begin Darcy's senior year and Kevin's drug and alcohol rehab program. As soon as the storm subsided Lindsay would head back to Seton Hall for the last time.

One more year . . . they each had one more year before real life was supposed to begin, and yet Tara found herself in the throes of adulthood, as if she'd cracked out of the egg a year too soon and found Charlie waiting there, Charlie now imprinted upon her psyche.

Enjoying the fury of the wind, she clutched the smooth white porch rail and tried to imagine what the future held for them while Charlie prepared a dinner of avocado salad and roasted chicken in the Love's enormous state-of-the-art kitchen.

Wonderful Charlie, the only guy to make her feel that combination of passion and joy to be with him. He wanted her to join him when she finished school. He wanted to get married and start a family and make each other happy all the time.

Although her parents would have conniptions, she and Charlie didn't share their hangups about race. She could picture herself with Charlie, as Mrs. Migglesteen. She would research tort law while he taught sociology, and on weekends they would paint the trim on the house together or plant tulip bulbs in the garden. She would serve up a tall pitcher of lemonade after he cut their grass under a hot summer sun . . .

Or maybe, instead of growing closer this year, they'd drift apart. The daily e-mails would spread out over two days, then three or four. Snail mail would stop altogether, and phone calls would become awkward, full of difficult gaps and distant silence.

She wiped the spray from her face, swiping off the tragic vision. Maybe her cynical scenario was incorrect. For now, she was content to savor these last dwindling days of summer and ride out the storm with Charlie.

Open your fucking eyes.

Her knuckles were white as she gripped the steering wheel, not from traffic stress or worry over the approaching storm, but from the ridiculous change of Kevin's temperament around the time they left New York City behind on the Throgs Neck Expressway and headed north on the Hutch. As they flew past streets packed with rowhouses tight as books on a library shelf, Kevin's remorse over his drinking problem shifted to a worry over the timing of his detox program.

"What if they don't think I need the program?" he said.

Oh, you need it. Darcy gritted her teeth but restrained from answering.

"I can see one of these doctors saying, look, you drink too much sometimes, but who doesn't? Start flying straight. Hit the road and save the looney bin for the real lunatics."

Fat chance.

"And then what? What if I have to turn tail and head back? I'll be stuck until the hurricane passes through and roads open again."

"I wouldn't worry about it," she muttered.

"Yeah, well, you've got a car, so why would you worry?"

"Kevin . . ." She tried to be patient, tried not to steam as a car cut in just inches from her bumper and zoomed ahead of her. How many times did they have to go over this same argument? Didn't he get what a huge inconvenience this was for her, having to talk with the doctors and make arrangements for him and reassure him that this was the right thing to do? And all along he sat there sweating all over the passenger seat of her car, even with the air-conditioning blowing cool, whining about being stuck without a car. "You're not going to a looney bin. Green Valley is a treatment center dedicated to people with drug and alcohol problems, and I have it on good authority that some very famous people have spent time there. Celebrities. Actors and senators' kids. It's like the Hamptons of New England."

"I don't know about this." He folded his arms across his chest, his tongue sliding out to touch his lower lip. Somehow, the gesture that had once seemed so sexy now turned Darcy's stomach. "I know guys who drink a hell of a lot more than I do, and they don't need a program. *Fucking* program. Something tells me I'm gonna regret this."

"Green Valley has one of the leading programs in the Northeast," she said. The treatment center was also one of the priciest, requiring a commitment of thirty grand for the first three months, but Darcy didn't care. She'd given the nurse her father's Amex card number over the phone, pretending she was Kevin's stepsister. She'd do anything to help him get through it, and footing the bill was inconsequential, except for the inevitable talk she'd have to suffer to offer up some lame excuse to Daddy. "If anyone can help you, they can."

"Yeah, well, we'll see about that." He frowned, turning to stare out the window, once again giving her the feeling that she'd lost him already.

Just get better, she said silently, wishing she could make the words strong enough to penetrate his thick skull for absorption in his brain. *Do it for yourself. Do it for me . . . for us.*

33

Lindsay

Although it wasn't raining as I drove to Bikini Beach, strong winds battered my Saturn wagon, giving me the sensation of swimming against the current. Another example of how difficult it was to have a relationship with a guy like Bear Harmon; you had to drive into hurricane force winds just to say good-bye.

A fitting send-off for Bear, who'd always been out of reach—the floating ring bobbing on a riptide. He'd been threatening to leave the Hamptons for years, leave the old surf crowd and pursue tournaments around the world, surfing south of the equator during the winter months in the north, chasing the endless summer.

"Don't know where I'll land next summer," he'd told the guys one night as everyone roasted dogs on the barbecue outside his camper. "California, or maybe Aruba."

Of course, Skeeter and John couldn't resist taunting him with that latter-day Beach Boys song: "Aruba, Jamaica, ooh, I wanna take ya . . ."

Personally, I couldn't believe Bear was really leaving, didn't want to believe that he wouldn't be back in the Hamptons next June just as he was every year. His VW pop-up van was one of the few vehicles left in the camp area as I pulled into the parking lot, but he'd already taken down the tarps, packed up his possessions, and collapsed the roof in preparation for his escape from the hurricane and the Hamptons. The windows were dark, apparently vacant, which was no surprise. Knowing Bear, he was on the beach, trying to harness a ride on some of the killer waves caused by hurricane-force winds.

The roar of the wind whistled in my ears as soon as I got out of the car. I plodded toward the beach, overwhelmed by a sense of missed opportunity. All these years, Bear had been hanging around my family's summer house, a regular at the dinner table, one of the few helpful surfers on the beach, my brother's best friend, and the closest I'd ever gotten to revealing my feelings for him was inviting him to Darcy's party this summer. All those years, all those intimate talks, and I'd never been able to reach out and link my arm through his, touch his hand or lean on his shoulder?

What a failed flirt I was.

But my life had never been like the scenes in the women's novels I'd read, where the women knew just what to say to snag their men, even after they'd acted like comic clowns. Those characters had their happy endings, and I was left chasing Bear down in a hurricane just to pressure him into a good-bye scene I could hold on to over the years.

Sand stung my bare legs and whipped back my denim jacket. Ahead of me, waves rose in great walls of gray water, curling and rallying along until they slapped against the packed gray sand with brute force. The magnitude of it all was breathtaking—the power of nature, all that fury—but I felt too tangled inside myself to feel the appropriate awe. Damn the hurricane; it blew into town, cutting my summer short and chasing my friends away. My twenty-first birthday was two days away, and how would I celebrate now? I'd be lucky to score a beer with Milo at an off-campus pub.

Two guys in wet suits stood on the beach, watching someone in the surf, and as I approached them I recognized my brother and Skeeter Fogarty, both in dripping wet suits.

"Steve!" I shouted, breaking into a run. "Aren't you supposed to be at work?"

He looked beat, his face windburned, his dark hair swiped flat against his skull. "Not with waves like this. It's a little whipped up now, but for a while there I do believe we harnessed the perfect storm." He waved his arms toward the surf. "We're going, Bear. You're on your own!"

As if Bear, the lone head bobbing in the wild water, could hear him. I shook my head. All along the coast beaches were closed and the Coast Guard was broadcasting warnings for people to stay out of the water, but wild surf always attracted wild surfers. The very reason I'd known I'd find Bear here. "Where's Johnny?" I asked Skeeter.

"He's whipped." He zipped a block of Sex Wax into his backpack. "Marriage sucks."

"Yeah?" I gave a bitter laugh. Considering the way the Fogarty brothers had been headed full throttle into trouble, I'd say their wives saved their sorry asses.

"We're outta here." Steve pointed to a backpack and short board propped against the dune. "Bear's cell phone is in there. If you see him go down, call 911. Don't make the mistake of thinking you'll save him. It's hellacious out there. I almost went down in the soup."

I felt my hands tighten to fists, annoyed by his pompous big-brother act. "I think I could hold my own."

"Neophytes like you have no business being out there," he said, jabbing a finger in my face.

I pushed his hand away. "You ought to know."

"Just go back to school and learn to shrink somebody else's brain," he snapped, following Skeeter to the path through the dunes.

"Yeah, since yours is already Barbie size," I muttered into the wind. All this was Steve's fault, anyway. He was probably the major reason Bear kept his distance from me. And Steve, lacking in the diplomacy department, had never done anything subtle or overt to help foster a relationship between Bear and me.

I shielded my eyes against the wind, now carrying a spray of drizzling rain. Between breaks in the surf, I saw him bobbing out there, a lone surfer. I waved, but it was hard to tell if I got his attention since the whipping mounds of ocean required some negotiating.

Damn. With hours of sunlight left, there was no telling when he'd come in, and I couldn't wait here in this miserable, biting wind.

I thought about waiting in his camper—though the inner sanctum had always been sacred ground—and then considered just leaving. Wouldn't it be better to cut out than to wait here, a simpering, lovelorn groupie?

Another missed opportunity.

I pressed my palms to my face, trying to ward off the sandstorm and wondering how I'd get through the winter months without at least a shred of hope that I'd see Bear again. The wind pushed the board against my feet, and I looked down and saw the answer. Duh! Why was I standing here like an observer of my own life?

I shed my jacket and sandals on the beach, grabbed Bear's board, and pushed into the water. Paddling out was difficult since the waves were slamming in hard and the undertow sucked at my legs, toppling the board. I forged on, arms aching as I ducked my head against slapping salt water. The bottom dropped off abruptly, setting me in the churning water without any footing for balance.

A shot of panicked adrenaline whipped through me as I clutched the board. *You can do this. It's just surfing times ten.*

Waves kept breaking around me, and I lowered my head and paddled through, thinking that the onslaught would have to end eventually.

I heard Bear before I saw him.

"Lindsay! What the hell are you doing out here?"

When I found him he was a few yards away, both of us rising and falling in a lopsided dance on unformed swells.

"I came to say good-bye." It was supposed to be romantic, but somehow when the words were shrieked over roiling swells, it just sounded desperate.

"You shouldn't be out here," he yelled.

"Neither should you!"

Oh, great! Chastise him like you're his mother; that'll win him over.

Not that it mattered, as the wall of water that came spraying toward us was probably going to kill us both.

In a flash I saw Bear hop up to a crouch, and I did the same, trying to balance while watching the wave creep up behind me. Bent over, my fingers skimming the suds, I kept low and raced away from the breaking part of the wave.

It worked.

I was riding a killer wave.

Until I stalled, losing momentum as the wave crumbled all at once into a smashing twist. In seconds I was doing a header over the board, plunging into the cold salt water.

There was a yank on the leash at my ankle, dragging me along underwater. Frantically, I tried to find the surface, but as I pushed up a torrent of water pushed me over, rolling my body into an underwater somersault. I flailed wildly, popping through the surface for a hungry breath of wet air.

That was when I realized it was gone. My board. The leash must have broken. I tried to find it in the surrounding hash of suds, but I was sucked down again by the back of a wave.

I held my breath, arms flailing in the gray undersea world, swirling in a violent, deadly maelstrom. I was caught in the soup, the foamy water that prevents buoyancy. Bear once called it surfer's quicksand, and yet I thrashed my arms like a wild woman.

What if I never breathe again?

The thought seemed suspended in time just as I lingered under the surface, suspended in the churning water.

Something grabbed me hard under the shoulders and yanked me up. My head shot into the wash, into salt-sprayed air, and I sucked it all in greedily, coughing.

Bear . . .

"You okay?" He swam beside me, one arm tucked around my shoulders, the other clutching his board. "You got sucked under. Lots of riptides today. We're going to ride my board in together, okay?"

Too caught up choking on salt water to answer, I nodded. He pushed the board to my chest, holding it while I pulled myself up.

Kneeling there, I could see the board I'd been using as a wave tossed it brutally. Long gone. "I'm sorry," I gasped.

"Don't think about it." He was already on the board behind me, his chin pressing onto my shoulder. "Just stay low. Keep in a crouch."

Together, we rode and bobbed and paddled back to shore. I felt sick and cold as I slopped in through the shallows, my wet clothes smacking.

A wave struck me from behind, knocking me to my knees. I braced against the sand and hung my head down, exhausted and chilled through to the bone, relieved to be breathing again and alarmed at how close I'd come to drowning.

"Come on." Bear was behind me again, propping me up, half dragging me away from the surf. My feet felt so heavy, my arms aching from fighting the tide. I was still in a daze as he opened the side door of his camper for me.

"The heat's pumping," he said. "You go on in and get that wet stuff off. There's some towels and blankets to wrap up in."

I climbed into the van and hunched beneath the ceiling as he closed the door behind me. The welcome warmth made me collapse onto my knees for a moment, and I sobbed a little, tasting the salt from my wet hair and tears. Funny how a death-defying experience isn't so scary until you look back on it and think of the what-ifs.

The sound of the boards sliding onto the side rack brought me back. I rose up on my knees, tugged off my wet clothes, and dropped them into the small sink. My skin felt clammy and cool, and I pressed into a soft, worn blanket that smelled of fabric softener, pressed my face into the smells of home and land and warm bedding. God, I'd been so stupid.

I shook the folds out of the blanket, wrapped up in it, and huddled in front of the warm vent. The inside of the van was compact and surprisingly neat, with a small kitchenette wall across from a bench seat that I assumed opened into a bed. I was wringing my long braid out into the sink when the door opened and Bear appeared, a dark, solid figure against the gray beach of swirling sand. His chest was bare and a towel was wrapped around his waist. He tossed his wet suit inside, climbed in, and closed the door on the storm's fury.

"You okay?"

"Fine." I nodded, trying to cover the telltale squeak of my voice. "Just mortified at myself." The worn silk edging of the blanket slipped over one breast, and I tugged it up with a fist. "Steve was right. I'm a neophyte asshole."

"Don't let him bring you down. You held your own for a while."

"I had no business being out there."

"None of us did. You gotta respect it, but we're always trying to shave off a small piece for ourselves, just this next wave. And as soon as that's over the rush is so huge that we're all paddling back out like the lunatics we are."

He knelt down to fish through a duffel bag and I felt my eyes on the knot at his waist, sure that the towel was going to stretch a bit too far and fall to the floor. Not that it would be a bad thing. In fact, I found myself wishing that the laws of nature would just help me out here and loosen that knot.

Bear turned back, towel in place. No such luck.

"But something tells me you didn't come out to surf today. Not dressed like that. Why'd you come down?"

I bit my lower lip, knowing that ten years of denial would shatter with my answer. "I came to say good-bye, Bear. I came for you. God, you're heading off to Hawaii, maybe never to return. It's like you're stepping off the end of the earth."

"Sometimes change is good." He lifted his chin. "I see these tournaments as a positive development for me."

"Good for you, a major downer for me. Bear, I'm going to miss you."

He grinned, dimples showing in the partial smile that had probably evolved to hide his chipped teeth. "You trying to get me choked up, squirt?"

I knew he was teasing, and I didn't want this entire conversation reduced to a playful joke. "Don't you feel anything for me, Bear? When we're together?"

"Sure, I do. I've always liked being with you, but I knew we couldn't go there with you being Steve's little sister and all."

"What would you say if I told you I want to go there?" I asked him.

He squinted, then rolled back, his hands in the air as if I'd exploded a grenade in front of him. "Wow! I mean, that'd be great. Awesome. But don't you think we might feel bad about it later? I mean, there's something special between us, and I kind of like having that to think back on. I've known you since you were a little squirt, riding your Big Wheel over your brother's surfboards."

"I wasn't that young," I protested.

"But the thing is, I'd hate to ruin it by taking advantage of you, just because you're sitting all naked and sexy in my van."

Sexy . . . did he really see me that way? Suddenly brave, I let the blanket drop from my shoulders, revealing the swell of my full breasts.

He blinked, openmouthed, suddenly not so lighthearted as I gathered the blanket to my middle, hobbled closer to him on my knees, and pressed my lips to his.

It was the most serious kiss of my life, intense and hungry, punctuated by the sounds of our breathing and the roaring winds outside. His tongue teased my lips gently and played at the edge of my teeth, drawing emotion up from my soul.

Together we fell back onto the carpeting, our bodies pressed skin to skin as we kissed time and again. *The longest, sweetest make-out session in the history of the world*, I thought as my hands explored the solid muscles of his shoulders, down his smooth back to the tight butt I'd watched for years.

He responded to my touch, growing hard against my stomach. For a while, his hands remained on my breasts, stroking my nipples until they tightened and puckered. Then one of his hands smoothed down along my hips, letting his fingers dip between my thighs, and he groaned.

"God, you're so wet," he whispered.

"Because I want you," I said honestly. "I want you bad, Bear."

He closed his eyes, letting his fingers glide over me so sweetly. "Are you sure? Are you really, really sure?"

How could he even ask when he was making my body sing with such pleasure? I knew that making love wouldn't change our separate futures; it wouldn't keep Bear in New York. But I wanted it, wanted him, even if it was going to be only for this moment in time, this single night. "I've never been more sure of anything in my life." To let him know I was serious, I dared to reach down and touch him, my fingers closing around his hard shaft, making him gasp.

"Okay," he breathed. "In that case, I'd better find some protection . . . fast."

Turned out he had a pack of condoms in a duffel bag. I pulled the blanket back on, still feeling a little self-conscious about my weight, and watched him roll it on with ease, a little impressed by his adeptness, his comfort with his own body. The way he tucked his chin into his chest and leaned down over his flat stomach to make sure the rubber was in place.

Something sparked in his clear blue eyes as he leaned over me again, dipping one hand under the blanket to glide over my breasts. My taut nipples stung with desire at his touch, and I swept the blanket aside and reached up to his shoulders.

He positioned himself over me and pressed between my legs, nudging and bobbing, teasing me with taut control. "How's that?"

I lifted my knees, opening myself to him. "Amazing. Awesome. Killer."

"You're talking surfer talk."

"When in Rome . . ."

"Do you like it?"

It was getting to the point where I could barely talk, being so wrapped up in the pattern of probing, the steady rhythm. "Yes. Yes!"

"Then how's this?" He pushed past the sensitive folds and plunged deep inside me, causing me to gasp.

I squeezed my eyes shut in ecstasy. "Very good," I gasped. "And you'd better keep going or I'll have to kill you."

He laughed and started the steady rhythm again, pumping into me with such energy and warmth I couldn't help the sensations that were building, warming the distant chill, filling my body, all from the touch of Bear.

I closed my eyes and let it all go, existing in this moment with this boy I'd mooned for and crushed on and followed secretly in my heart for so many years. Bear Harmon, the chip-toothed surfer with the silly name, was making love to me, touching me inside. In my yearning to move with him I felt the reality around us slip away. I lost track of any single sensation and gave way to the steady flow that mimicked the surf, the tug and pull, the plumbing of the deep and the swirl of pressure against boundaries, probing and smashing and gently caressing. Bear was loving me, stroking me, again and again and again, and the sheer pleasure of that intimacy and the rising sensation in my body suddenly welled up, causing me to let out a thrill-filled yelp. His cry followed soon after, an elongated sigh of release. He found the blanket and pulled it over the two of us. Then, easing one hip down beside me, he lowered his head to mine, keeping body contact as he dropped a kiss on my cheek, still close and warm and sexy.

"Lindsay . . . you're so beautiful."

And in that moment, I believed him.

PART TWO

When Life Hands You a Bucket of Sand, Start Building a Castle

Summer 1998

34

Darcy

"All rise for the Honorable Judge Cletus D. Szchenowski," the court clerk announced in a bored voice, and everyone in the courtroom stood up. Darcy rose demurely and smoothed down the pleats of her plaid linen skirt, thinking that the judge for her father's case had an unfortunate name and wondering if he'd ever thought to change it.

As Judge Szchenowski led the lawyers through the opening protocol of her father's trial, Darcy tried to find a comfortable spot on the hard wooden chair in the visitors' section of lower Manhattan's stuffy old marble courthouse. These guys sure could talk, and none of it came close to the impassioned speeches of television courtroom dramas.

Aside from the protestors outside, former employees circled the bottom of the courtroom steps with signs complaining: THIEF! or WANTED—MY JOB BACK! or U-OWE-ME $290 MILLION!—it was all very lacking in drama. Of course, the underlying drama was quite intense. The notion that Bud Love and his family could lose it all, their money, the extra houses and fancy cars, all status and respect in the community was a real ass-kicker, but pretty unbelievable.

She wondered if they'd bring in one of those artists to sketch. Would there be photographers outside as the trial proceeded? Maybe they'd catch her in a few shots. She could imagine a newspaper editor—a handsome older man—circling her face in red pencil, barking, "Who's the chick? I want to see more of her. Now!" And the flashes would blind her as she walked out onto the row of steps. And if the day in court wasn't too draining, she'd pause and pose. Recrossing her legs, she composed captions that might accompany the outfit she'd chosen to wear today.

PRETTY IN PINK, DAUGHTER DRESSES FOR DAD'S DEFENSE
PINK SYMBOLIC OF INNOCENCE, SAYS CEO'S DAUGHTER
PLAID SCHOOLGIRL SKIRT WINS OVER JURY

With a sigh she let her head tip to the side, her blond hair falling over one cheek, shy and yet sultry. From her petal pink lipstick to the toes of her Ferragamo mules, Darcy's wardrobe, makeup, and hair were carefully choreographed to show support for her father, compassion for all those poor people who lost their jobs when the money went missing, and youthful innocence—underlining *innocence* for the jury. It was hard to believe that her father was being blamed for missing money just because he was head of the corporation. Did anyone think a CEO like Bud Love actually went into the office and counted dollars, made deposits, kept ledgers? It was totally ludicrous, but here was Buford Love, looking more handsome and earnest than any defendant she'd ever seen on *Law and Order*, his wife and daughter behind him dressed like high-fashion saints.

Darcy straightened a crease in her skirt, the sweetest pink plaid that ever landed on the racks at Bergdorf. It was not something Darcy would even try on during a normal shopping trip, but yesterday she'd set her goals tight and right on courtroom attire: innocent daughter.

She felt a hand touch her shoulder. That would be Kevin, as her mother had retreated into her shell, colder than a clam on a February morning. But the scandal had brought Kevin closer to her than ever before, and with his months of group therapy and meetings he had learned twenty million ways to spell "support." Sometimes he seemed unrecognizable when he spoke about "giving it all over" or "taking personal inventory" or "taking things one day at a time."

He touched her arm gently and leaned forward, his green eyes flashing with concern. Those eyes . . . and that smile, so broad with two crooked dimples. And now that he'd stopped abusing drugs and alcohol the gray of his skin had given way to a healthy peach hue—model material, that boy. Sometimes her heart got a squeeze just from looking at him.

"You okay?" he mouthed.

She nodded, trying to make her boredom seem like forbearance in case anyone was watching. Whoever had the brilliant idea of opening a trial on the Friday of Memorial Day weekend? Well, she realized the trial hadn't officially opened today, with jury selection and everything, but still, today's court date had to be putting a crimp in hundreds of vacation plans. Tara was probably helping her mother open the beach house, and most likely Lindsay was already out surfing on this spectacular day. They'd been all over her about their graduation party tomorrow, but Darcy wasn't sure she could stand to celebrate that landmark when her life had snapped in so many pieces. Not to mention the fact that the Hamptons house had been damaged in that Labor Day hurricane, and in the heat of the trial preparation, her parents hadn't driven out to assess the damage.

In front of her sat her father, his head bowed reverently as if he were sitting through Sunday mass. His hair was shot through with sterling gray, a charming shade actually, and Darcy wasn't sure if he'd had it colored before or if the threat of twenty years in prison had turned him gray. She wasn't sure if he was folded over because he'd lost hope or because he was trying to remove himself from the proceedings. She really wasn't sure about much when it came to her father anymore, and it wasn't easy to even look at him without the glaze of anger over how he'd thrown their social reputation and family money into an uproar.

"I can't believe they'd start a trial just before Memorial Day weekend," she told her father last week while they were waiting for Darcy's deposition in a conference room at the firm. "That's dumb. Don't those people have any social life at all?"

Bud Love had shot her an icy look over the file of papers he was signing. "I blame your mother for comments like that."

The men and women on his legal team had tittered a little or awkwardly looked away, as if it were way too personal to watch when in fact, there was nothing personal at all between Darcy and her father. He was the moneymaker, the great provider, who was falling down on the job, stumbling along with this trial. Sitting in that conference room, Darcy folded her arms with a tight grin as one of Dad's business philosophies—one of the many Bud Love–isms that the corporation cherished—ran through her mind: "If someone can't do the job, you gotta let him go." Didn't Dad see that those giggling lawyers weren't doing a very good job? She would have fired them all, months ago.

How could they let the grand jury decide that Buford Love had violated such a big law? Didn't these imbeciles see that a huge corporation was at stake—lots of jobs, lots of reputations?

Apparently not. So began the era of "Daddy the Criminal"—a time of endless depositions, tempers flaring between her normally comatose parents, snide smirks from former friends when she ran into them at the gym or the Great Egg bagel shop, and panic over how far the final verdict might cut into the family finances.

In the humid courtroom, Darcy felt her jaw aching to yawn. She was tired. God, she'd love to yawn, but that would look bad.

If only she'd worn that navy picture hat today. She'd picked it up at Bendel with the plan to wear it for a later court date since it was much too mysterious for the first day. Inside the delightful brown and white striped fitting room, she'd tilted it back on her head and immediately saw herself as a blond Jackie Kennedy Onassis or even Madonna, playing coy for paparazzi.

The hat was a find, and if she had it today it would help to hide the yawn that insisted on bubbling up. She bowed her head to her chest and pressed a fist to her mouth, as if it were all too painful to bear, though she'd tuned out from the legal speak long ago. Damn, the yawn felt good. How late were they up last night?

Kevin had driven into Great Egg from the Hamptons so that he could be with her for the opening of the trial. Mom said he could stay in the guest room. Not that it mattered, since Mom drugged herself to sleep early on and Dad stayed in a hotel suite in Manhattan, to be closer to his lawyers and handlers and probably to also remove himself from the wrath of his family.

Mom disappeared around eight-thirty, and Darcy and Kevin had the screening room in the basement all to themselves. She'd poured them Cokes from her father's wet bar, sneaking a shot of rum into hers, then pretended to go to the pantry for corn chips and salsa. Instead, she took a left turn into the cedar closet, slipped off her clothes, and wrapped herself in a brown fur stole that used to belong to her great-grandmother.

She didn't own any fur, of course, since the idea of hurting little bunnies or seals was disgusting. But she had to admit the sensation was glorious as she slung it around one thigh, then up over her bare breasts. Quite the turn-on.

Kevin had been engrossed in the sitcom, but his attention shifted quickly when she danced out wrapped in a skimpy swathe of fur. She told him to undress while she popped an Anita Baker CD in, and for once he didn't mind taking orders.

His body was in better shape now that he was sober. His daily runs on the beach had built some muscles into those legs, and she enjoyed rubbing the fur against his abs, over his shoulders, then down again to tease him with it.

Ever since he'd finished with rehab, he'd been insatiable, always ready to go. Usually Darcy didn't mind. With her father under fire, the family fortune at stake, and school on hold, it was nice to be in control of one part of her life, always able to coax Kevin into wanting her. In other matters, such as socializing at bars or clubs, Kevin had hatched a new agenda that was diametrically opposed to Darcy's life philosophy, but when it came to making love he would submit to her wishes, and Darcy liked the feeling of power over him. She'd realized that with this level of activity it was going to be a challenge to keep condoms in stock, so after Christmas she called her gyno and switched to birth control pills.

They'd danced around and tickled each other with that fur for more than an hour last night. At one point she was moaning so loud that Kevin pressed a hand over her mouth, and she bit into the flesh of his fingers defiantly just as she came.

Afterwards, thrumming with satisfaction, she took him to the guest room and slid into bed beside him, safe in the crook of his arms. Although he was asleep in a few minutes, she'd lain awake, thinking of the many ways her father had screwed things up.

First, the money issue. Mom said funds were drying up fast, especially since investigators had put some sort of hold on most of Dad's investments. When the cash ran out, it was really going to suck.

And then there was college. Education held sparse appeal for

Darcy. Not that she couldn't do well, but when there were poetry readings and student performances and spontaneous road trips to New York City from the placid Bennington campus in Vermont, it didn't seem so important to complete her student projects and papers. As she'd told one faculty advisor, so what if she graduated in five years instead of four? Although the professors did expect her to assert herself academically, Darcy was usually able to loop together a student production or pull off a new interpretation of a Shakespearean role. Life on the commons, overlooking the hills of New York and Pennsylvania, was sweet; why not stay another year?

"Because we just don't have that kind of money anymore," her father had told her on the phone toward the end of the fall term. His voice was craggy and chipped, the voice of an old man who didn't care that she was focused on her final project, working late hours in one of the studios videotaping a one-woman show. "Finish the semester and come home."

Leave Bennington? Her second home? And why . . . because he'd fucked everything up with his careless accountants? She'd argued with him on the phone, without success, but the threat of leaving campus made her dig in a little deeper and gave her the impetus to spend more time on her end-of-semester project, her monologue of a deranged shopper. Late that night, she was between takes in the studio when she heard the shrieking sirens of emergency vehicles. Stepping out into the snowy night, she saw a truck from the local fire department cruising slowly down the lane in front of her, its flashing red and white lights spiraling odd shadows on the midnight blue snowscape. Across the meadow, an old-fashioned ambulance whooped, its red lights blinking like a Christmas tree.

Not an emergency. The vehicles were announcing Midnight Breakfast, a Bennington tradition, when students took a break from the looming deadlines of finals and assembled in the dining hall, where faculty members served them waffles and eggs and coffee.

Without hesitation she grabbed her coat and headed toward the dining hall, her boots crunching on the frozen crust of snow. This would be her last Midnight Breakfast, her last chance to be a part of this community. She'd always mocked the superstudents who holed up in the library or science lab; she'd rolled her eyes over the vixens who slept their way into good roles and grades, but now that this world was being snatched from her, she wanted it in the worst way.

Tears formed in her eyes as she headed toward the golden rectangles of the dining-hall windows. It was so unfair—the prosecution of her father, the failure of her father to protect her lifestyle and her future.

Her reckless father and his stupid, stupid accountants were going to ruin her life, and she couldn't think of a way to stop them.

During that walk along the snowy path, she resolved to do her best to play the game, show support in the courtroom, pose as the perfect daughter and give the jury a picture of the defendant's family that might tug on their heartstrings. She'd do her best to save the family fortune and reputation.

And if all that failed, Kevin was her plan B. He'd been doing well in rehab, though the counselors limited her visits, and his father's restaurant was a Hamptons institution, a gold mine, and the Hamptons had a strong social network, where she'd quickly rise to the top.

Tuning back into the courtroom activity, she checked out Kevin's suit. The pants appeared painfully short when he sat down, and the fabric was shiny, the sign of cheap, synthetic material. If he was going to be with her, he'd have to do better. Kevin put a reassuring hand on her wrist, fingers that could use a manicure. Maybe she could get him in to see Andrea before he left Great Egg. He needed work, but the boy had potential. He was a diamond in the rough, her diamond, and she was willing to make a few cuts to maximize his value and make him sparkle.

35

Lindsay

"The problem with hosting parties is that you're so focused on getting it right, you don't have time to have fun." I squinted at the blue dots of paint I was dabbing onto the yellow butterfly on my niece's face. Even with all my careful planning and luring Elle and Milo out to stay in the McCorkle house for the weekend, the graduation party gave me the jitters. Not helped by the fact that Darcy seemed to be a no-show.

"Speak for yourself," Elle said, painting dragon scales on Shea Handwerger's face with a flourish. "I am all about fun, like a sea otter. Did you know they make a game of everything? Fishing, eating, exercise, building their homes. I am the otter. If it's not worth it, I'm not there."

"Aren't you having fun, Aunt Lindsay?" Kyra asked, her brows arching into her strawberry blond bangs. "It's your grad-you-lation."

"Graduation, honey. And I'm having a blast." I knew it was a big lie, but I figured it was better to sound positive and spare the six-year-old her pathos. I leaned close to dry the butterfly on Kyra's face with a few puffs of breath. "You're done. Ready to fly away."

Kyra pressed her freckled face close to the makeup mirror borrowed from Ma's vanity and grinned, revealing a gap in her bottom teeth that made me long for those days—six-year-old innocence when the worst that could happen was a scrape on the knee or candy deprivation. "Thank you!" Kyra said. She flipped open the screen door and skipped off to find her cousins, twirling a fluorescent stick in the air.

Dotting the back of my hand with blue paint, I wished I could muster half as much enthusiasm to fly off and be a butterfly. These past four years I'd been so focused on getting good grades, earning extra money, and scoring attention from my lit professors that I hadn't prepared for real life. The whole job thing and the feeling that I should be leaving my mother's home—despite the fact that I couldn't afford anything within a hundred miles of New York City—somehow, it all crept up on me and smacked me in the face the week before graduation.

At last, I was done with college—finito! Unfortunately, all my studies hadn't prepared me to start having a life. Unlike my friends. Tara always seemed to know she'd get into the world of law and politics, and Elle seemed to be a walking gold mine, with her professors talking about publishing her senior thesis and colleagues of her parents bending over backward to create entry-level positions for her wherever she went. Watching Tara and Elle get involved with their new jobs, make new contacts, and hang with new friends, I felt a pinch of envy. They'd sped ahead into the grown-up world, while I was still licking a lollipop at the bus stop.

With a degree in psychology, my prospective paths seemed clear. If I went back to school for a masters in social work, I'd be qualified for various government jobs with the Department of Social Services, the Department of Child Welfare . . . the various agencies that served people in various ways. A steady living, but the thought of becoming a cog in one of the many bureaucratic wheels held little appeal. An MSW would also allow me to hang a shingle and do counseling, but I didn't feel qualified. How could a twenty-two-year-old with limited life experience advise people suffering through emotional crises I'd only read about? Much as I enjoyed psychoanalyzing my friends, I wasn't up for being a professional shrink.

So I'd put in my time at the college placement office. I'd e-mailed my résumé to a hundred places and met with two employment agencies, but no one seemed to know what to do with me.

What had I been thinking, majoring in psych?

My lips pursed, I started painting ridges of little blue waves up my arm.

"Excuse me," Elle pointed her paintbrush at me accusingly, "don't waste our paint."

"We're done. Shea the dragon is the last." Tuning out the music and laughter, I blew on my hand, then started capping the paint pots.

The McCorkle house was brimming over with family and friends, many of whom used the graduation party as an excuse to make the trip to the beach on this weekend of dawning summer. The street was lined with cars and minivans, the lawn was lined with flaming torches. The adult guests wore plastic leis and the children's faces were painted like cats or tigers or exotic birds or Batman. There was croquet in the side yard, badminton on the back lawn, and a makeshift pitching clinic in the driveway.

It was all good . . . a walloping fun time all around, but somehow I couldn't wait for it to be over. Family parties were fine for the first hour or two. After that, I was always trying to jump in my car and remove myself from brothers with epic tales of their heroic adventures as firemen or cops, sisters who knew it all, and diapers that needed changing—the hazards of being the youngest in a large Irish family. In this case, being the guest of honor, I felt even more pressure to circulate and accommodate—the way my mother always did. Except that Mary Grace McCorkle had a gift for hosting a party, while I just wished everyone would go home.

"What's with the puss?" Elle said. "If you don't watch it, we're going to have to paint a big red clown smile on you."

Shea laughed. "Yeah, a clown smile. Paint one on Aunt Lindsay!"

Elle put a streak of green on his nose and nodded with satisfaction. "You're done, dragon. Go breathe fire on some marshmallows."

Shea scowled into the mirror, then bolted off, letting the screen door slam behind him.

I continued capping paints, but Elle grabbed the red brush and brandished it in front of my face menacingly. "I'm not kidding. Snap out of it or I'll paint you happy."

"I just wish I had a job. Graduation is sort of anticlimactic when there's nowhere to go."

"I thought you were going to wait tables at Coney's?"

"That's a way to make some cash," I said. "I'm talking about a career, like you going into foreign service, springing forth from your job at the Lithuanian consulate. Great aspirations."

"You think I wanted that job? It fell in my lap and I only took it so that my parents wouldn't hatch any schemes to pull me back to Europe or Africa." Elle picked at some glitter on her palm. "It's not like I'm planning a job in foreign service."

"Yeah, but if I could only get a half-decent job like that . . ."

"That's just so you, Lindsay. That 'if only' thing. If only I had a boyfriend. If only I had a ten-speed bike. If only I could lose fifteen pounds. You're totally stuck in the future."

"That's not totally true," I protested.

"It totally is, and I'm telling you, you've got to think otter. Be an otter. Enjoy the moment. Play at your job, and have fun at your own party or else move on to something that is fun. Don't you think you'll love working at Coney's?"

"I doubt that." I hadn't started yet, and it would certainly be better than slinging pizza at Old Towne, which wouldn't be the same without Bear. "I do know that it's not a career, and I can't believe I worked so hard for four years to wait tables."

"Would you shut up already? You've been out of school for, like, ten minutes."

"And now it sounds like I'm complaining, and that's part of the problem. I know I've got it good with my family, friends, opportunities—even this party. I know it's great but I'm not loving it and I feel guilty for not appreciating it, especially considering everything Darcy is going through now." I dropped the last of the paint jars into the plastic bin. "So that's my problem. What does an otter do when she's not having fun and she feels guilty about it?"

Elle threw up her arms, bangles jingling. "It's remedial otter training for you."

"Is that a twelve-step program?" I stowed the bin of paints in the corner of the porch. "Because if it is, I'm sure Kevin McGowan can tell me all about it . . ." Ever since Kevin went to rehab last fall he'd become a walking testimonial about the AA one true way.

"You're evil." Elle grinned, revealing dimples.

"I know, and I'm trying to enjoy that about myself."

Elle nodded. "Spoken like a true otter. So what do you say we blow this popsicle stand and hit the beach?"

I winced. "Not without clearance from Mary Grace McCorkle. Don't you know anything about party etiquette?"

"That's what happens when you're raised in a jungle. But really, let's find Tara and Milo and do something. We'll hit the beach or we can even track down Darcy. After you cut the cake and kiss all the babies, no one will miss you around here." Elle pushed open the door and led the way down to the path of scattered slate stones cut into the lawn. The driveway had been taken over by toddlers, who rumbled on Big Wheels and loaded dolls and stuffed animals into mini–red wagons.

I navigated around their sticky fingers to the rose arbor and was headed toward the back door when I caught the low drawl of male voices on the other side of the thick green laurel that shielded the driveway from the street. A few new cars were sprawled on the street—bright red and metallic blue SUVs and sports cars. Boy cars. I grabbed Elle's arm and tugged her to a stop. "Who's that?"

Elle peered through the green leaves. "The lifeguards. They must have come straight from the beach."

I checked my watch—almost six, the beach would be closed. "Nobody invited them." I pressed my face closer to the leaves, peering at the patchy images on the other side. The sight of Austin with his too-pretty face brought back that sickening feeling from last summer, the guilt and embarrassment, and the complications between Bear and me. I'd heard from Bear twice over the winter, once because I'd made Steve call him around Christmastime. "All the travel's a little disorienting," he'd told me. "But it's fun to get paid for surfing." Somehow, I'd hoped he'd find his way back to the Hamptons by the start of the summer, but the latest news from Steve wasn't so hopeful. "Bear's really digging Hawaii," Steve had told me while I was unloading my carload of junk from the dorm. "I think he's going to stay there."

Bear in Hawaii . . . a few thousand miles away. It was such a huge disappointment, I didn't even want to think about it.

Since that night we'd spent together, I had barely even looked at another guy. I knew Bear was the person I wanted in life, the person whose star was crossed with mine. At last, I understood the relentless commitment Darcy felt toward Kevin. And so my senior year had been academic and social, but not sexual at all. "Celibacy is a very fine thing, if you're doing it for a reason," my friend Milo had told me during one of our many late-night discussions at college. "If, however, you just can't muster a partner—like some of us who will remain unnamed—it sort of sucks."

I've been so good, so faithful to Bear all these months, I thought as I eavesdropped on the banter beyond the laurel hedge. I didn't deserve to feel guilty about Austin anymore.

"I never realized lifeguards were such assholes," Elle observed.

"Please . . ." I squinted into the hedge. "The sight of Austin Ritter makes me want to hurl—and I'm only getting a partial view!"

"Shh!" Elle separated two leafy branches for a better view. "He's right there."

"Gentlemen? What the hell are you doing here?" asked my brother Steve.

"Lindsay asked us," Austin said.

The big fat liar! I would have loved to reach through the laurel hedge, thrust my nails at his face, and grab him by the scruff of his tropical shirt, but it wasn't worth getting scraped by the branches.

"She told us to come. Sort of."

"Yeah-huh." Steve remained cool. "No, really. What are you doing here?"

The other lifeguards laughed. "You're so busted, Ritter."

"Honestly?" Max spread his fingers wide in a peacekeeping gesture. "We heard there was beer, we know the hotties hang here, and everyone knows the McCorkles have a rep for throwing some kick-ass parties."

"Ahh, at last, the truth." Steve's arms rose like a preacher's as he surveyed the group. "And the truth shall admit you to the party. Go, drink and be merry."

"Oh, shit," I muttered as the lifeguards whooped with joy.

"Thanks, man." Max high-fived Steve.

"Yeah, right," Austin said, slinking by until Steve's hockey stick rose like a railroad-crossing barrier.

"All except you, Ritter."

Austin eyed him with disdain. "Huh?"

Elle nudged Lindsay with an elbow. "This is going to be good."

"Sorry, but we don't allow assholes." Steve lowered the stick. "Nothing personal."

Austin's hands balled into fists. "You're kidding, right?"

"Just go," Steve said, "before I call the cops about all your cars blocking the entrance to our driveway."

"Try it!" Austin growled, but the other lifeguards were in his face, backing him toward the street, saying things like, "Be cool," and "Take it easy," until he was escorted to his car.

Elle pushed away from the hedge with a shriek. "Go, Steve . . . it's your birthday! Go, Steve, big brother . . ." Elle swung her hips, doing a happy dance with her cheer.

I felt a swell of embarrassed affection. Twenty-two years on this planet and today was the first time I'd ever seen Steve exercise the protective instinct associated with older brothers. "Not bad," I admitted. "Not bad at all."

36

Darcy

Impatiently punching the gas pedal with her sandal, Darcy turned up the driveway to the Love Mansion with that desperate feeling of being late and left behind. She'd missed her last semester of college, lost her shot at a Bennington degree, missed her exit on the Long Island Expressway, and now, thanks to her mother's bitchiness about loaning Darcy her Land Rover, Darcy had probably even missed her friends' goddamned graduation party.

"Right now a party should be the least of your concerns," Melanie Love had said as she finally handed over the Land Rover keys. "You should be thinking of how you're going to pay for the repairs on your convertible. Really, I don't know how you could do so much damage just driving down Northern Boulevard."

Her mother always managed to swing conversation back to the car accident—Melanie's favorite topic lately. Darcy realized that this was the absolute worst time to plow into a parked car—her fault—but that stupid Cadillac had been double-parked, it had been raining, and she'd had a load of things on her mind when the Honda's tail had suddenly been on her, the hood of her Saab folding before her eyes, right up to the dashboard.

The lipstick red car she loved crumpled like an accordion.

"Be careful with the Land Rover," her mother warned. "Extra careful. Christ, I don't know why I'm letting you use it considering the way you've been driving, but someone's got to meet with that realtor and get the house listed. George says we'll get to keep the Great Egg house, but he thinks the courts may try to liquidate the Southampton and Aspen houses, so we're better off beating them to the punch." George was the lead attorney on Dad's legal team, and from the way her mother drooled over his name, Darcy wouldn't be surprised if Melanie Love had the hots for Mr. Law and Order.

"The realtor's name is Gladys Kevalian, and you're to call her as soon as you hit Montauk Highway. She'll meet you at the house."

Not in this life, Darcy thought as she cruised down Montauk Highway three hours later. The thought of selling the Southampton house floored her, and she figured if she threw a few harmless obstacles in the path of the sale, maybe she could hold on to the mansion for another summer or two. Darcy pushed the brakes as Mom's chunk-assed Land Rover rolled past two stonework pillars that had mossy green stuff growing in the cracks. Where the hell were the gardeners? The grounds were overgrown with dry brush and tall, bushy weeds trounced through the beds of red and yellow Dutch tulips. Amazing how they took advantage when her mother couldn't get out here. Well, Darcy would deal with that later. Right now she wanted to dash into the house for a quick shower, freshen her makeup, and get over to the McCorkles' for the tail end of the party. Kevin wouldn't be there, of course, as he was no longer able to engage in social situations where liquor was being served, but right now she just wanted to put everything else aside for a few hours and catch up with her summer friends.

But as the Land Rover popped over a pothole in the driveway, Darcy noticed a sleek silver Mercedes parked in front of the house. The woman beside it, who turned and glared at Darcy, cell phone to her ear, was obviously the realtor.

"Are you Darcy?" the woman said in an accent so thick, she resembled one of the Gabor sisters. "Yes, yes! Your daughter is here now! I call you back."

Darcy blinked at the woman, who tossed her phone in the car and brought out a clipboard. "And you would be . . . ?"

"Gladys Kevalian, with Gold Estate Realty." The woman thrust her business card out, stabbing Darcy with the edge. "How much do you want? What price was in your head?"

Darcy didn't have a clue, but she answered, "Four million."

"Ach! This is the thing. People so in love with their houses, they expect an ungodly price for them." Gladys rolled her eyes for dramatic effect.

"But, Gladys, this is the ungodly Hamptons." *Unlike the dead market in Transylvania,* Darcy thought, fully expecting the woman's dark brown lips to part and reveal vampire fangs.

"If you want a high price, then you must do repairs," Gladys said. "And I must say, it will cost you a pretty penny. That hurricane did more damage than your mother mentioned."

Darcy turned to the house, which wasn't at its best. Three shutters were gone, giving the impression of missing teeth. A neighbor's quick assessment had warned them of burst pipes in the guest house, and Tara had told her that the roof had blown off over one of the peaks. Now the roof resembled her father's hairline; a haunting reminder of the many things that had gone wrong in her life. It was as if the house were conspiring with her parents against her, standing in the way of her happiness.

"Look, Gladys, I'd give you the grand tour, but I'm already late for another appointment."

"Not necessary. I've been through the house; your mother mailed me a key. Not so bad inside, but there is damage caused by the roof. And you have pipe problem in the guest house. Very bad. You have lots of work to do."

"Thanks for sharing that." Darcy climbed onto the wraparound porch, stepping over roof shingles that had fallen. "So, if you've got everything you need, why don't you go off and make your list and call the repairmen or . . . whatever it is you do."

"My inventory is only for the listing." Gladys tapped her clipboard. "It is *you* who must make repairs." The ire in her voice made it sound as if she were delivering a sentence.

"I just live here," Darcy said. "Talk to my mother."

"Yes, of course!" Gladys reached into the Mercedes again for her cell phone and dialed. "Hello, Mrs. Love? Gladys Kevalian . . ." In a cold, somewhat accusing voice, the realtor implied that Darcy's mother had misrepresented the sale, lied about the condition of the house.

Picking at the peeling paint on the porch rail, Darcy could almost hear her mother barking on the phone.

"She wants to talk to you," Gladys said, handing over her slender flip phone.

"Tell me you are going to handle these repairs and get this woman off my case," Melanie Love said.

Darcy turned away from the realtor. "Mom . . . decorating is your thing."

"It's a matter of repairs, and I can hardly ignore the trial proceedings to spend time in the Hamptons. That wouldn't play well for your father, would it?"

"No. But what snake pit did you pluck this woman from?"

"Gladys comes highly recommended. She'll get us top dollar. All you have to do is supervise the repairs on the house. It's all cosmetic, honey, something you should understand."

Darcy gritted her teeth. She wasn't the one who'd gotten an eye job last year. "This isn't my thing."

"Find some handymen, and probably a licensed plumber. Ask your friends for references. Maybe Mary Grace McCorkle knows someone. The insurance adjustor assessed the damages and they'll pay us six thousand. If you handle it right, there may be enough left over to get your car fixed."

Was her mother asking her to pinch pennies? Darcy felt her mouth pucker in disgust. "Why did you spring this on me now? And did you realize what a mess this place is? I haven't been inside yet, but the yard is littered with roof tiles and everything is just . . . yucky." Darcy stepped over a torn screen, noticing the chipped paint on the banisters of the wraparound porch and the dirt and dead bugs jamming window tracks. "Can't you get Nessie out here for a few days?"

"Nessie has another full-time job, and we can't afford to pay a maid, even for a few days. It's up to you."

She turned back, glaring at the nosy real estate agent. "This is so unfair."

"Ha! Welcome to the real world, honey."

Darcy considered saying no. She could step around the mess, live in this rattrap for the summer, just to spite everyone. But the possibility of getting her car back loomed before her, a mirage of a lipstick red sports car . . .

"All right, I'll do it."

Gladys threw her hands into the air. "Good for you! Now, can I have my phone back? You're using up my anytime minutes, young girl."

Darcy waved her off like a fly. "How soon can you get the in- surance check?" she asked her mother.

"Two weeks, maybe three. Till then I think our credit is still good out there."

"I should hope so!" Christ, Mom made it sound as if they were criminals or worse . . . poor!

"Just do the minimum to make the place sell, okay? I gotta go." Mom clicked off, leaving Darcy alone with Transylvanian Gladys, who quickly snatched her phone away.

"Okay, so now that you got kick in the pants from Mommy, we go out back and I show you where mold might be growing near burst pipes."

Darcy crossed her arms. "That sounds disgusting. Do we have to?"

"Come. I have very busy schedule." Gladys snapped her fingers, as if training a poodle.

And much to her dismay, Darcy obeyed the command.

37

Lindsay

"Get me out of here before I wrap my fingers around this realtor's skinny neck and shake her till she spits out her commission."

I was glad to get the call from Darcy, but confused. "A realtor? Are you buying something?"

"Apparently we have to sell the Love Mansion before the courts take it away, and Mom has hired Cruella von Whippenstein to make the deal. I'll explain later, just get over here."

Promising to head out as soon as I could politely escape the party, I turned to Elle and hung up the kitchen phone.

"Where the hell is she?" Elle asked, having realized it was Darcy on the phone.

I explained the situation, then sent Elle to find Milo. "I'll go get Tara to cut the cake. Hey! Are you sure you don't want to be included with us? You graduated, too."

Elle shook her head emphatically. "No, and promise me you'll never, ever put my face on a cake. That's just scary."

I smiled. "Scary is completing two years' worth of course work in just nine months." Elle had torn into Yale with her usual nonconformist zeal, reading twenty classics and devouring her junior and senior workload in one big bite. "Okay, so if we cut the cake and do a toast, maybe we can duck out without too much attention."

Shaking her head, Elle backed out of the phone nook, a small little booth off the kitchen paneled in cherrywood. "I don't know what you're worried about. With all the McCorkles around here, it's pretty darned hard to get attention."

"Hey, I resemble that remark!" Paul, my dentist brother from Poughkeepsie, pushed his worn Yankees cap back on his head and pointed toward the dining room.

"Don't get your panties in a bunch," Elle told him. "I'm actually jealous. I wish I had ninety brothers and sisters."

"Don't forget the nieces and nephews, who are crying for cake." Paul put his hands on my shoulders and guided me toward the dining room. "Would you get in there and cut the cake already? Another ten minutes and those munchkins will have their fingerprints all over it."

"We'll have to bring in crime scene to dust for prints," added Timothy, my oldest brother, who'd been an NYPD detective for years.

"I'll cut it already, before it melts like me." I lifted my hair, twisted it up, and fanned the back of my neck. It was too hot to be inside, but maybe if I cut the cake and schmoozed a few more family friends I could cut out of here with my friends and locate Darcy. I ducked inside, finding Tara, her parents, and a handful of others paying homage to the blessed cake.

"Look at this lovely masterpiece!" Mary Grace McCorkle framed the sheet cake with her hands. "Hilda did it, the bakery on Main Street. Did you get a picture? It's almost a shame to cut into it. Lindsay, love, you and Tara squeeze in behind the cake so we can get a picture. Our two graduates."

Tara cocked an eyebrow, then followed me behind the table, where we bent down, our faces inches from the sea of buttercream. I could feel the fat molecules wafting into my pores, heading straight for my butt.

"Just what I spent the past eight months starving myself for," I muttered as cameras flashed. "My face emblazoned on a sheet of frosting."

"Yeah, and now it'll find its place in the family photo album, along with all the other cakes," Tara said. "The one with the purple roses that turned out black, and the Jurassic Park dinosaurs . . ."

"Remember the confetti cake that we made ourselves? And when we squirted chocolate syrup onto the vanilla icing and it looked like a murder scene?"

"The *Psycho* cake." Tara pretended to hack away in a stabbing motion.

"You can laugh," I said. "I've got all of them in Kodak moments, like the archive of McCorkle cake history. And the worst part is, I didn't even want a cake today. I asked for those little cheesecake tarts Ma makes, but does my opinion matter?"

It had been Hilda the baker's idea to imprint the faces of the graduates on the cake. I was only glad this bit of baking technology had not been available when my sisters were passing around birth photos.

"Who wants cake?" Mary Grace asked, shooing the girls away from the table. "Got to have a piece of cake if you want to wish the graduates good luck."

"Is that right?" Tara's father, looking cool and crisp in his smooth black silk shirt, approached the table. "In that case, I'd better take two."

"That's a wedding superstition, Ma," said my older sister Kathleen. "Nobody ever heard of a graduate cake."

Mary Grace sawed through the cake with a knife. "That's the beauty of superstitions; you make them up as you go along." She deftly doled half a dozen squares of cake onto paper plates, then paused to smile down at the cake. "Here's a superstition for you. I say anyone who takes a taste of this cake tonight will appear in my daughter's first novel." She turned to Tara's mother, Serena Washington. "Did you know our Lindsay is a writer?"

"Aspiring," I corrected, "but that's just a hobby. I majored in psych, which is very different."

"She wants to fix people's brains." Mary Grace rolled her eyes. "If it were only possible, I'd have had mine overhauled years ago."

"Actually, I'd need a medical degree to mess with your brain," I said, searching for plastic forks.

"But writing is your talent. Call it a mother's pride, but I do enjoy reading Lindsay's work. What's Tara doing this summer?"

I ducked away from the table, eager to grab a slice of cake and get out of the dining room before Ma asked me to recite the poem that had won the Knights of Columbus award in second grade.

"Tara's working in the New York offices of Senator Wentworth,"

Mrs. Washington responded, her posture so regal, shoulders back, neck elongated. Tara's parents didn't step out in the Hamptons too often, and I was pleased that they'd attended the graduation party.

Cake in hand, I clamped onto Tara's arm and pulled her out through the kitchen to the screened back porch, fending off friends and family along the way with: "Can't talk now!" "No, you can't have her." "We'll have to get back to you on that."

Out on the porch, I cleared a few empty beer bottles off the glider but remained on my feet, feeling too hopped up to sit. "Darcy called. She's freaking about the hurricane damage on the house, but I think it's really about being there without any staff to fix it up and the fact that her mother is putting it on the market. Elle is getting Milo and we're going to head over there."

"I was getting worried." Tara sat beside me, poking at a section of the photo frosting with a plastic fork. "I called her cell three times and got her voice mail."

"I don't think she could show her face at this party. I mean, considering . . ."

"That she didn't graduate?"

"Yeah, that, and the charges against her father, and her mother freaking over finances. Did you hear the one about Bud Love hiding cash in coffee cans? Someone thinks he buried a stash somewhere on the grounds of the Hamptons estate, just before the feds came to arrest him. One of the housekeepers saw him digging."

"Sounds like the stuff Hamptons legends are made of." Tara scraped at some frosting with her fork. "Do you think that would work? I mean, would a coffee can protect money? And what would happen if Bud Love turned up at the Hamptons Diner in, like, ten years with a mildewed thousand dollar bill?"

With a laugh, I sampled the cake. "Ooh, sugar rush. The cake part is okay, but the frosting . . . gag." It clumped on my tongue like a pat of butter, and I'd learned not to bother indulging unless there was a delicious payoff. I put the plate aside. "I'm done. Let's get Milo and Elle and head outta here."

Tara stood up. "Do you think it's a good idea for all four of us to descend on Darcy? I mean, she's got all that baggage with Elle, and she's barely met Milo."

"What, you think we might overwhelm her? Darcy Love?"

"You're right." Tara gathered up a few discarded plates and

headed toward the kitchen. "So we'll go and pretend that none of it really matters and we're just hanging out. And she'll pretend that she doesn't care that we're even there. And we'll just have one big I'm-too-cool-to-care fest."

I held the screen door open for her. "Exactly."

38

Elle

"Is this the scene where I'm supposed to fall to my knees, grab a handful of dirt from the rose garden, and vow that we'll never go hungry again?" Darcy let the front door slam behind her and crossed the porch, demurely stepping around wads of leaves and mud and roof tiles.

Apparently Darcy hadn't lost her edge over the winter. Elle climbed out of the car and stared up at the majestic old mansion. Though the storm had taken its toll, the structure gave a strong impression of permanence, a quality Elle had always loved about old buildings.

"It's good to see you, too!" Lindsay laughed, jogging up the stairs to give Darcy a hug. Elle was glad to see that Lindsay had lost that college weight; it had dragged her down and poked holes in her self-esteem.

After a quick air-kiss, Darcy pushed past Lindsay and headed down the steps. "Get me out of this dump. Where are we headed? Coney's? Bahama Jack's? The Mad Hatter?"

Elle leaned back against Lindsay's wagon, squinting up at the damaged roof in the setting sun. "Actually, we wanted to check the place out. Milo's father is a carpenter back in Queens, and he might know some people who could get your work done for a fair price."

Milo stepped forward and reached toward Darcy. "Hey."

"You remember Milo?" Lindsay prompted. "My friend from Seton Hall?"

There was no recognition in Darcy's eyes, but she shook Milo's hand and forced a smile. "Maybe your father can come out another time." She swung her purse onto her shoulder—a leather log, shaped like a baguette. "I'm ready to party."

"Just hold on a second," Elle said, walking down the driveway to get a better look at the damaged roof peak. Not that she was an expert, but she'd had some construction experience when her mother was in the Doctors Without Borders program in Russia and again when she and her father spent one autumn in northern Georgia building houses for Habitat for Humanity. As a result, Elle loved the sharp smell of freshly milled lumber. She could spend hours going through bins of screws and nails, nuts and bolts and cabinet handles in a hardware store.

Milo and Tara followed, shielding their eyes against the orange sun blazing toward the horizon. Darcy marched to Lindsay's car and took the passenger seat, underscoring her desire to leave. Lindsay talked to her through the open window, ever the mediator.

"It doesn't look too bad," Milo said, "though getting to it is half the battle."

"There's some damage inside, too, in the attic room," Tara said. "Charlie and I tried to cover things with tarps and batten down the hatches, but I'm sure some water got in."

"Interior work is easy," Elle said as images of smoothing creamy plaster over nail holes soothed her.

"No one will ever find a ladder that goes that high," Darcy shouted from the car. "It's three and a half stories. We'll have to get a goddamned crane out here."

Milo shrugged. "A scaffold and some safety harnesses would work."

"I just want someone to get up there and nail on those shingles," Darcy called.

"But make sure they replace the wood base," he said. "You don't want to tack shingles onto a rotting roof."

"I don't want to tack anything, except maybe a sailboat," Darcy shouted impatiently, then pulled herself back into the car.

Milo bent over and picked up a roof tile. "Slate shingles? I love a slate roof, but no one's going to be tacking these down."

"Expensive," Elle said.

Milo ran his fingers over the thin slab of slate. "You can reuse a lot of the shingles that fell, though it requires a special process. Hot tar, I think."

"Sounds gooey!" Elle squinted, trying to gauge Milo's thoughts. She didn't know him well at all, but from his careful examination of the tile, his awe of the roof, she sensed that he shared her excitement.

"I never did a slate roof before," he said, adjusting his glasses. Designer eyeware, with frames in various shades of orange, red, and yellow. Elle figured that no straight guy would be caught dead in such elegant eyeware, but she didn't know Milo that well.

Elle giggled. "Me, neither."

"What are you two saying?" Tara crossed her arms. "You think you can fix that roof yourselves? You want to climb up there and monkey around nearly forty feet off the ground?"

"We'd use a scaffold and safety harness," Milo answered without looking up from the slate. "It's probably safer than taking a bath in your own tub."

"But . . . but there are other repairs," Tara said breathlessly. "The drywall inside."

Elle raised her hand. "Been there, done that."

"And some pipes burst in the guest house. There's water damage. I haven't seen it, but—"

"I'm handy with a wrench," Elle said. She giggled again when Milo looked up, his wide lips curving in a smile. "Wrench, I said. Not wench."

"We might need a plumber," he said.

She shrugged. "Maybe, but we could see how far we get first."

"Are you serious?" he asked. "You'd try this with me?"

"As long as you don't try anything with me," she teased.

He let out a crisp laugh. "I can safely say that isn't going to happen."

"Good." Elle liked to know where she stood with a guy, and since her incident with Kevin McGowan she'd steered clear of sex and relationships, concerned over the power of sex to harm and dissuade people from their true goals. "So, when can you start?"

"Wait one minute." Tara held up her hands. "You guys are already booked. You're working in Manhattan at the embassy, and aren't you working as an apprentice for your father? And don't you think you should run this harebrained scheme by Darcy? It's her house."

"I can do the consulate work with my eyes closed," Elle said. "They only like me because I speak Russian and I'm cute. And Darcy will go for it. We're cheap labor."

Although she hadn't been in touch with Darcy over the winter, Elle had followed the news reports regarding Buford Love's pending trial, and for the first time in her life she felt sympathy for Darcy. Elle had suffered through the social ramifications of her own father's bad behavior, but at least that wasn't a public trial and it didn't hurt the family finances. Considering the way she'd hurt Darcy last summer, Elle figured she owed the girl a sizable karmic debt, and it would feel good to start carving away at it with a hammer and some nails.

"My old man will probably be happy to get rid of me," Milo said.

"You'd better run it by her," Tara said, pointing at the car.

"Fine." Elle extracted another piece of slate from a bush and took it to show Darcy, explaining about the slate roof, Milo's experience, her love for craft projects. "So Milo and I would like a shot at the repairs," she finished.

Darcy's blue eyes scraped from her to Milo, then back again. "Is this some kind of joke?" She turned to Lindsay, who shrugged. "Why are you being so nice to me?"

"Call it professional interest," Milo said. "You'd need to pay for materials up front, and if everything works out we'll charge you a fair price. Half of what you'd pay a contractor."

"Okay, I guess."

"Ooh!" Elle clapped her hands together gleefully. "This means I can quit my boring job in the city!"

"You can't quit!" Lindsay said. "I thought you loved that job. Just out of college and you're working at the Lithuanian consulate. Isn't that a huge opportunity?"

"It was interesting for the first week. Now it's just routine."

"Can I have it?" Lindsay pleaded. "I need a job."

"We should collect as much slate as we can find; salvage what we can," Milo said, gathering a few pieces that had fallen into the tulip beds at the edge of the driveway.

"And we should take a look at the damage inside." Elle was already bouncing up the porch stairs, thinking back on the floor plan of the house from years ago. As she recalled, there were plenty of bedrooms, and Darcy usually didn't like to be alone. It would be convenient if she and Milo could stay here, close to the work site. Darcy's parents were tied up with the trial in the city right now, and she felt sure Darcy would go for it.

"Does this mean we're not going out?" Darcy asked.

"If you want a clean bed to sleep in, I suggest we get busy inside." Lindsay opened the screen door and removed a wad of dirty straw that had lodged in the doorjamb. "Come on, Darcy. If we work together it'll be fun."

"Please . . ." Darcy pressed a hand to her forehead. "Let's not make this like an episode of *This Old House*. You can't make me enjoy home repairs, and it's going to be a long summer stuck in this place without my car."

"Who needs a car in the Hamptons?" Elle said, holding the door for Darcy. "I bet you've got a bunch of bikes in the garage that work perfectly. Put some air in the tires and you can ride that thing all over town."

"Just what I need: wheels with a little bell on the handlebars."

Darcy's deadpan delivery made everyone laugh—everyone except Darcy.

"You guys don't seem to get that my life is over," she lamented.

"Life as you know it." Elle nodded. "But it gives you a chance to re-create yourself, form a better you."

"As if there was room for improvement," Darcy said.

"You'll see." Elle skipped through the house, stopping at the fireplace to clang a tool against the grate. "Like the phoenix . . . from the ashes, Darcy will rise!"

39

Lindsay

"North Carolina is a long way from the Hamptons," I told the lifeguard who stood over the giant beach blanket that held many sunbathing friends. Super polite and handsome as a Ken doll, Drew Browning had homed in on me when I was wading in with my board. Now he seemed to be addressing all his comments to me, and as I responded the words seemed to roll off my tongue, as if I'd inherited the gift of gab from my mother. "How did you end up being a lifeguard on Bikini Beach?"

"That's the name for this place? I thought I heard Chad call it B.B., and I figured it was an inside thing." He turned toward the surf, the wind feathering dark hair over his forehead. Drew was classically handsome, and not as show-offy as the other lifeguards, who insisted on pulling off their sweatshirts and sitting bare chested in the tall chairs, even on chilly days. "My cousin owns a seaplane business up here. I've worked for her during the summers but then got certified in lifesaving and decided to step out a little more."

"That's pretty adventurous," I said. "And surprising, since I've heard the Carolinas have some great beaches." And where did that comment come from? It was as if I'd kissed the Blarney Stone, just after Ma.

"Hatteras has miles of pristine beaches," he agreed, "but there's no place on earth quite like the Hamptons."

We chatted for a few minutes until Drew had to get back on duty. He told me he'd check in later, then jogged down the beach.

"Well, look who won the lifeguard lottery," Elle crowed. "I'd say that boy likes you, Linds."

"Do ya think?" I bit my lower lip, watching him climb nimbly up the ladder of the lifeguard chair. "He seems nice and every-thing, but he's a little too interested, if you know what I mean, and I definitely don't want to get involved with another lifeguard. I keep wondering if it's all about the way I look now that I lost weight. Or maybe he heard about Austin and me and he thinks I'm easy. Or maybe he heard that Bear is gone and figures I'm avail-able. I don't know . . ."

"Or maybe he just likes you," Tara said. "Come on, Lindsay. Can't you give the guy the benefit of the doubt? Not all guys are horndogs."

"True," Milo said. "Though in my experience, I'd say most are."

"You guys aren't being fair," Tara said. "It's never right to judge a group of people based on their gender, size, or color. You have to treat him fairly, Lindsay, even if he is a man."

"Who died and made me the spokesmodel for gender equal-ity?" I adjusted the waistband of my bikini and sat up. "All I'm say-ing is, I don't trust the guy. And honestly, I'd rather stay home and watch reruns of *Cheers* than meet a guy like Drew Browning in a bar."

"But he's just so cute," Elle said. "Am I the only one who sees that?"

"I see it," I admitted. "I'm just not ready to act on it." I rolled over onto my tummy. "Somebody's got to do my back."

"Got it." Elle popped up and grabbed the tube of sunscreen. "I'm done baking anyway. Time for some sand sculpture."

The sky was a rare shade of royal blue, and from my perspective on the beach blanket Elle and Milo seemed to be playing in front of a blue screen as they packed sand into mounds, adding seawater from buckets borrowed from some kids playing nearby. As they worked with the sand Elle asked Milo about his family, his friends back in Queens, his life. Her questions were fast and furious: "Do you have brothers and sisters? Do you get along with your parents? What would your dream job be? When did you know you were gay?"

I eavesdropped on their quiet conversation, enjoying the sun's heat on my back. "I think I always knew I was gay," Milo said, "just as you always know your favorite color and the foods you like. The only real conflict for me was coming out, since my family is pretty old school on that stuff and all the other guys in my neighborhood were big sports buffs and athletes, guy's guys. If I'd worn glasses like these to high school, I think someone would have tried to flush me down the urinal in the men's room."

"No way!" Elle said. "People aren't really like that anymore, are they?"

That had been my reaction when Milo had approached me at the beginning of senior year in college, looking for a room in the dorms. He was sharing a house with three other guys he'd known since freshman year, three friends who'd turned on him when they learned that he was gay. "I thought it was obvious," Milo had said. "All this time, I assumed they knew. But no . . . Jay hears a rumor from one of his teammates and confronts me, acts as if I'd murdered somebody. When I told him it was true, he nearly cried. Then he acted as if I was going to pursue him. Sexual abuse, he said. As if. I told him he isn't my type, he told me to get out of the house, and here I am, looking for a room in the dorm, surrounded by freshmen."

Although I had offered to talk with Milo's housemates, to strike some sort of compromise, Milo had stopped me. "I'd love to see Jay and the others jump on the enlightenment train," he said, "but I'm not willing to pay the fare."

As a resident assistant, I was able to get Milo a single room in the dormitory I worked in, "though you *will* be surrounded by freshmen," I'd said apologetically.

"Fine, as long as I don't have to play drinking games and pull all-nighters with them."

So Milo had moved in down the hall from me, and we'd started walking together to the dining hall for lunch, then spending evenings together in the empty student lounge, watching *Friends* and *Seinfeld*, proofreading each other's papers, and playing Tetris on our laptops. He helped me design and sew a formal gown for a Barbie doll as part of my project for design class, and I helped him write a psych paper comparing the characters on *ER* to Greek gods and goddesses. My friend Grace had moved in with her boyfriend and was rarely around, leaving me with a hole in my life, and Milo moved easily into that space without being intrusive. Soon we started going into Manhattan together to catch museum exhibits or Broadway shows at half price. Some weekends we shared a ride back to Brooklyn, where I had awkwardly met his parents one evening when I arrived early to drive him back to school.

"That management scum will take anything you give them! Don't cower to them!" an older man in a shapeless undershirt and athletic shorts railed at the television. His thick white hair whirled in various directions, not comb friendly. He was a frightening sight through the front screen door of Milo's porch, but by the time I had second thoughts he was already backing toward me, his eyes still on the television.

"That's right! Don't give them your firstborn. The bastards." He unlocked the door and held it open for me. "Hello, dear," he said in a more subdued voice. "What can I do for you?"

"I'm here to pick up Milo," I said sweetly.

"Of course you are. Have a seat." He gestured to the furniture, but the sofa and matching chairs were covered with laundry in various stages of folding. I moved some towels and perched on the edge of an armchair as he shouted "Milo!" up the stairs.

Very scary . . .

I sat up on the beach, where the sculpture of a sea sprite was taking shape. "Now that's art. You guys work well together. I can't wait to see what you do to the Love Mansion." They had measured and ordered supplies yesterday and planned to start right after Memorial Day.

"So what do you think your father's going to say when you tell him you want to spend the summer out here?" Elle asked Milo.

He shrugged. "As long as I'm getting paid, he won't care."

"What if he was counting on you as an apprentice?" Elle said. "Or maybe he's hoping for a summer of father-and-son bonding."

Milo shot a look at me, and I said, "I don't think so."

"My father and I have issues," Milo told Elle quietly.

"Is he antigay?" Elle asked.

"He's anti-everything."

"Except unions," I said. "I remember that he's a big proponent of labor unions. Defending the workers."

"Working stiffs." Milo squeezed a crease into a ridge of wet sand. "Management-bashing is his passion. Other than that, he's like the original Archie Bunker. Add on my mother, who takes in kids for day care during the week, and my two sisters in high school, and you've got a house of chaos."

"I love that!" Elle beamed. "I would love a home like that, a real family. I want to be adopted. Take me home, Milo, and make me your little sister."

Milo shook his head.

"Really, it's what I crave," Elle insisted. "My parents are so low key. For them an exciting day means reading two books instead of one."

"You wouldn't like it, would she, Lindsay?"

I shielded my eyes with one hand. "Oh, I don't know. You never know with Elle. She loves to assimilate into other cultures."

"You have to bring me home with you, Milo," Elle insisted. "Parents love me."

Milo dropped the bucket into the sand, shaking his head. "Elle, it's not you I worry about."

40

Tara

A gull shrieked, rousing Tara from her catnap in the sun. She stretched, savoring her day off. Tomorrow morning she'd take the early train back to Manhattan, to her new job in the offices of Senator Sterling Wentworth. So far her job entailed fairly menial tasks like making copies, answering phones and e-mail from his constituency, but one of his aides was going on vacation next month, which would allow Tara some input on the senator's e-mail newsletter and policy writing. Not bad for a recent college graduate.

So much had changed since the last time she'd been on this beach, a sunny day just before last season's hurricane when she'd splashed in the surf with Charlie. After he'd returned to Korea their relationship had fizzled too quickly. She'd found it difficult to connect with him through the mail—his writing was so corny—and every time he called her on the phone she felt trapped, as if caught in the bubble of last summer, unable to break out. The truth was, she was changing, growing every day, exploring new options, and being with Charlie closed those options. Maybe she'd feel different if he were here beside her, but he'd been transferred to Fort Benning, Georgia, and Tara's New York roots ran deep.

As a wave smashed onto the shore below them and sent a mist of cool spray their way, she remembered how they'd once played on this beach together. Thank God Darcy and Elle had ended their feud, at least for the time being. Elle seemed to be embracing Lindsay's friend Milo, though her twenty-questions game was a little invasive. Elle just didn't know when she was stepping over the line.

"People still have issues with gay men," Milo confided in Elle. They were still building a sand sculpture—a buxom mermaid, from Tara's perspective—which meant Tara couldn't have been dozing too long. "One of my friends had his apartment robbed, and the burglars actually stuffed his copies of the *Gay Free Press* into the toilet."

"Fucking burglars," Elle said. "They must have been Republicans."

"I heard that," Tara said, propping herself up on one elbow, "and you're in big trouble, Elle." To everyone's surprise, Tara had declared herself a young conservative and had landed a job as a clerical assistant in the Manhattan office of a staunch Republican senator.

"Oh, go back to sleep, Tara," Elle said, hopping to her feet with two buckets. "I didn't make any libelous statements about Senator Poopy-pants."

"You know," Tara propped herself up on her elbows, "go on and tease me, but I went after that job because I really believe in everything Senator Sterling Wentworth stands for."

"Ix-nay on the olitics-pay," Elle said. "I'm apolitical." She headed down the sloping beach to get more water, Milo following with another empty bucket.

"Elle's gotten better, but she's still lacking in empathy," Tara told Lindsay, who sat up and dug through her net beach bag.

Lindsay's brown eyes were thoughtful. "Is she stepping on your toes again?"

"It's just her blithe attitude toward everything. Like Senator Wentworth. My job is important to me, and I had to fight for it. I prepared well for the interview, and even then I'm not sure I would have gotten it if one of the senator's staffers didn't make a huge blunder."

"Really?" Lindsay paused, her lip gloss in midair. "I didn't hear about this. What happened?"

"It was one of the guys sitting in on the panel interview—James Melvin is his name. He joked that I had a learning disability because I checked the wrong box on the form. I thought it was just a dorky joke, until he slid the application across the table and pointed out that I'd checked the African American box."

Lindsay winced. "Ooh . . . egg on his face."

"You'd think so, but he never apologized, even after I advised him that I am, in fact, an African American with a light shade of skin."

"How awful for you. How'd he weasel out of that one?"

"He just mumbled something unintelligible and went on with the interview." Tara sighed, remembering the feral look on Melvin's face, his beady eyes soulless and cold. "Later, when I heard that I got the job, I was a little worried that they felt pressured to hire me. Maybe they thought I'd use Mr. Melvin's blunder as grounds for a lawsuit. But I've gotten over that now. I'm just going to give them my best, prove that I'm up to the job, and focus on the important matters."

"Like Josh?"

"Like civil rights and the senator's proposal for welfare reform." Since Tara's relationship with Josh Cohen was in its early stages, she was reluctant to bring him around her friends.

"But when are we going to meet Josh?" Lindsay asked. "Doesn't he have a summer place out here?"

"His parents are in Hampton Bays, but we weren't able to hook up this weekend."

"So who made the first move?" Lindsay asked, cracking open a bottle of water.

"Definitely Josh." Tara laughed. "He asked me to join him for lunch the day I started work. We went to Burger Heaven and split the bill, but we've been lunching together ever since, catching movies and free concerts at night. It's been an intense two weeks. Already he's calling me his girlfriend."

"Then we have to meet him. How about this week? I've got to bang on some human resource doors, and we promised Darcy we'd stop in at the trial and keep her company."

Tara shook her head. "Leave it to Darcy to treat a corporate fraud trial as the social event of the season."

"Would it be too weird to invite him to lunch with us?" Lindsay laughed and her eyebrows shot up. "Oh, that would be pushing it."

"Way too weird." Especially considering Tara's mixed feelings about her attraction for Josh. Was this pattern of falling for white men rooted in some psychological need . . . or was it just a matter of circumstance? She knew Lindsay would be sympathetic, but she also didn't want her friend overanalyzing things until Tara had a better grasp of the situation. "Why don't you stop by the senator's office to pick me up for lunch," Tara suggested. "I'll introduce you to everyone, including Josh."

"Okay," Lindsay said, "and I won't bite. I promise."

41

Darcy

"I know you miss the housekeepers and the gardeners and all, but we could never do this when they were around." Kevin strutted out to the end of the diving board, beads of water sparkling on his bare skin. "This is fucking great!"

Shielding her eyes from the sun, Darcy watched as he dove into the pool, his lean body an arrow into the water. Perfect form. With new muscle tone and voracious energy, the reformed, clean and sober Kevin was delicious eye candy. She loved to feel the muscles of his shoulders as he leaned over her, pumping into her as he'd done that morning in bed, and whenever he passed by she could barely resist touching his tight butt.

"Why don't you come in?" he called. "The water feels great."

"Maybe later." The polish on her nails was chipped and two nails had broken in the process of sweeping the front porch and pool area, then wiping down all the lounge chairs and tables. It was disgusting, dirty work, and right now she was doing her best to triage her manicure, filing and removing polish.

Kevin was correct about the housekeeping staff; she missed them desperately. Funny that you never realized how filthy a house could become until people stopped cleaning.

While Kevin swam laps, she filed her nails down to presentable crescent shapes and thought of the challenge Kevin had presented last night. "Before this summer is out, we are going to do it every which way, in every single room of this house."

She'd laughed, backing into the turquoise room with gaming instinct. "It's a pretty big house. Maybe it's more than you can handle."

"Do you doubt me, woman?" he'd growled, tumbling her onto the turquoise bed and trailing kisses down her neck to the crease between her breasts. The rooms were dusty and laced with cobwebs, but in Kevin's arms the creepiness dissipated and she felt alive and loved.

In terms of sex Kevin had become amazing since he'd gone through rehab. In the past she'd been annoyed when he couldn't finish the job or when he passed out before things even got started, but now he was on top of his game, playing her body as if she were a priceless musical instrument. Darcy felt the muscles between her legs tighten at the sight of his nude body streaking through the water. He seemed to want her all the time, and she was ready and willing.

A few minutes later he emerged with a splash near her feet.

"That felt great." He climbed out of the pool, water cascading down his body to the cement.

"If we're having everyone over later, we're going to need some food to serve," she said. "Got any ideas?"

"I'll fire up that rotisserie grill in the kitchen. Maybe I'll let you taste my specialty. Skewered chicken and vegetables."

"Really? Is it good?"

"Tastes just like chicken." He came to her side and bent over her for a kiss.

"Eee! That's cold! You're dripping on me!" she squealed, but nipped at his lower lip seductively.

"Cold?" He straightened, touching his tongue to his bottom lip defiantly. "How about the hot tub?" He grabbed her hand. "Come on."

She rose from the lounge chair, padding upon the decorative tiles beside him. They would always look so good together, she thought, catching the reflection of their perfect nude bodies in the French doors. She could see it—their photos in newspapers, the subject of society columns when they became the premier Hamptons couple, Darcy and Kevin, the darlings of the celebrity crowd. Everyone loved a beautiful couple and a popular place to hang out, and once Coney's was under their care, Darcy and Kevin would provide both.

She slid into the hot tub, her breasts buoyant and slick in the bubbling water. Kevin dropped into the water beside her and sighed with contentment. "I'm in a really good place now, Darce." He moved closer, and in the effervescent water she felt his fingers slide up along her thigh. "Thanks to you. I know I wronged you in the past, honey, and I'm sorry for that. I'm really sorry. I hope to make it up to you now."

Leaning back, she breathed in the chlorine-scented air and gazed beyond the patio to the hedges, the rose garden, the towering cypress trees that bordered the winding driveway. Though so many things about this summer really sucked, Kevin had come through as her savior. "You'll have plenty of chances to be nice to me," she said, reaching for him. "Over and over again."

42

Lindsay

Two weeks into the summer, and it's as if he never existed, I thought as I paddled into the lineup. Skeeter and Johnny were horsing around and a few other guys were popping up on their boards, but the days of surfing beside Bear, of talking in the lineup or taking a break on the beach were a distant memory, like an old videotape frozen in the worst scene.

Our lineup was missing two guys. Bear was living in Hawaii and Steve was so busy with his new job, he would only make it out for a few weekends and a week of vacation. And though I tried to throw myself into my job search, I couldn't stop thinking about Bear. He was the missing link in my summer.

The first two weeks of June set everyone in a routine that I suspected would replay all summer. Milo and Elle extracted themselves from other job commitments and got to work on the Love Mansion, where Darcy was happy to have them move in and keep her company. Darcy commuted into Manhattan three or four days a week to attend her father's trial, show daughterly support, and strike a pose for the cameras outside the courtroom. Tara stayed in Manhattan for her job working for the senator during the week but spent every weekend in the Hamptons. And I surfed whenever the weather allowed during the day and spent five nights a week waiting tables at Coney's.

Although I had worked as a waitress in a small Mexican restaurant in Brooklyn, that experience hadn't quite prepared me for the challenge of Coney's. It was one thing to keep my station covered, checking in on tables without appearing overbearing. Opening wine bottles in front of graying men with hard jaws and critical eyes was intimidating for me, especially coming from a family of the beer and whiskey sour persuasion. There was the ever-constant refilling of the water glasses, as well as the bread baskets, from which rolls disappeared so quickly I was convinced women were stuffing them into their purses to gnaw on for breakfast the next morning. Tables that ordered ribs or crabs or crab claws needed hot steamed towels, and Coney's Banana Flambé had to be ignited tableside with a flourish, a sideshow that I always dreaded.

And yet, I persisted—flaming bananas be damned—and I enjoyed the feeling of accomplishment at the end of each night and the tips, which varied from a measly two dollars in pennies from college guys to crisp fifty-dollar bills from the high rollers. So what if it wasn't my dream job? So far it had paid for a new surfboard, and it would tide me over while I waited for all those H.R. people to call.

Although my friends and I had always steered clear of Timothy McGowan and his legendary "shenanigans," as Ma called it, I had certainly gotten an eyeful working at Coney's. The man enjoyed being treated as royalty, dining in his private booth every night, making the staff wait on him without ever tipping. He always had to be informed when a celebrity came in so he could stop by their table and shmooze, and he thought nothing of bursting into song as he strolled through the bar, like some drunken troubadour.

No wonder Kevin had trouble getting along with the old man. Aside from Mr. McGowan's daily snarl sessions criticizing the way Kevin handled the bar, the older man was now on a campaign to get his son to start drinking again. "You've got to loosen up and enjoy life," Mr. McGowan told his son. Code words for "get wasted."

A devil in disguise, Mr. McGowan served complimentary rounds to customers Kevin had cut off and berated his son in front of customers. Once I saw Mr. McGowan shadow Kevin in high drama, a finger to his lips and a bottle of whiskey behind his back. The old man sneaked up behind his son and actually poured a shot of whiskey into Kevin's coffee when he wasn't looking. Sly as a fox and quite the showman, Timothy McGowan somehow came off as cute while trying to entice his son back to drinking.

"I know you're still pursuing the Kevin and Darcy Bliss Package," I whispered in Darcy's ear one night when she occupied her usual bar stool, lending her elegance and support while waiting for Kevin to get off from work, "but in case you haven't noticed, there's a toxic battle going on between father and son. Your future father-in-law is a narcissistic alcoholic who's determined to drag his son with him down into the depths of a whiskey vat."

"And that's your professional opinion?" Darcy's smile grew tighter. "I've had my run-ins with Mr. McGowan already. I know the man can be a royal pain in the ass, but I don't think he'd do anything to knowingly hurt Kevin."

"Yes, but he probably thinks he's doing the right thing. As he puts it, 'How can a man succeed in the bar business if he doesn't sample his own goods now and again?' "

"He's a problem, I know he is," Darcy said, shaking her head sadly. "I keep asking Kevin when he thinks the old man will step out of the business, but Kevin's got too much on his mind right now to worry about the future. 'One day at a time,' he keeps telling me. He needs to think that way to keep going. But personally, I can't wait for the day when the old man steps out of the business so that Kevin and I can take over."

I nodded, a little surprised at Darcy's imperialist desires. "Does Kevin know about this? That you're planning to take over the business?" Lately he seemed focused on getting out of it, determined to separate himself from the sordid business of getting people buzzed.

"Let's just say Kevin's on board."

When I brought up the conflict between the McGowan men one day over lunch at home, Ma wasn't at all surprised. "That Timothy McGowan has always been a big boozer, ever since he was a young man. He and his friends had their very own rat pack going—a bunch of liquored-up, gambling ladies' men who would perform a song or two into the wee hours of the morning. That's how Coney's got its start, opened as a cabaret all those years ago.

Timothy was a fine tenor, a very sweet voice till the smoking choked him all up."

"A tenor? The man barely speaks above a growl." I had heard stories about the Hamptons rat pack—the Raccoon Pack, some people called them—but didn't realize it had all started with Kevin's father. "No wonder Coney's is such an institution. I knew it couldn't be the food." I sliced a hard-boiled egg and set it aside for myself, leaving the rest for Ma to gunk up with mayo and sweet pickles.

"Your father and I caught a performance there one night, back when they still performed. Your grandparents didn't approve, of course. They believed performers belonged onstage, restaurants were meant to serve food, and never the two shall mix. But your dad and I found the show quite enjoyable. Timothy McGowan did make a fine host, and when he was bartending the liquor flowed like water, though that was back in the days before the host law and consciousness of the dangers of driving drunk."

"Well, from what I've seen around the bar, Mr. McGowan doesn't seem too happy that his son isn't forming his own rat pack," I said. "I wouldn't be surprised if Darcy isn't taking him back to rehab before the summer ends."

Ma shook her head, screwing the lid back on the pickles. "Poor Darcy's got her hands full, what with being tangled with the McGowan clan and her father on trial. Last I read, it wasn't looking so good for Bud Love. Sad how a man can build a huge business and see it all come tumbling down, leaving his family nothing."

"Poor Darcy's too lazy to get herself a job," I muttered. "I keep telling her she's going to need the money. With the way things are going, she's not going to be living off her father much longer. But she doesn't get it."

"Denial," my mother said. "You studied that, didn't you, dear?"

I let out a breath, refusing to cut Darcy any slack.

"And how's our Elle fitting in this year?" Ma asked, changing the subject.

"Better than ever. She and Milo seem to enjoy working together. So far I think they've got the roof so that it doesn't leak."

"Maybe they can have a look at our porch door, the one that always sticks," Mary Grace said. "And I haven't seen much of Tara."

"She works for a senator in Manhattan, so she's only here on weekends."

"And the boy she brought around last year? So lovely and polite . . ."

"Charlie?" I winced. "That's over. But she's seeing someone from work. I met him in the city. Seems nice."

Mary Grace smiled. "I did like Charlie, but you girls are too young to be getting serious, and I have to say, it riled your brother to see Tara with that young soldier."

"Steve?" I squinted. She knew he'd liked Tara years ago, but it was a goofy puppy love thing. "That's all over, Ma. He and Tara are just friends, barely that."

"That's what I thought, until I spied him turning green with jealousy."

43

Darcy

"Have you seen it yet?" Lindsay asked.

The jangling cell phone had jarred Darcy from a catnap leaning against the bus window. Having been up late partying with Kevin, Darcy was unable to resist the steady thrum of the bus traveling west on the Long Island Expressway. She planned to take the Jitney all the way into Manhattan, where she'd head downtown to make an appearance at her father's trial.

"Seen what?" she asked, gravel voiced. She turned toward the window, feeling woozy and slow from sleep.

"That means you haven't." Lindsay paused. "Okay . . . when you get to the city, stop at a newsstand and pick up the *Daily Apple* and call me back."

"Why? What's in it?" Darcy rubbed her eyes, careful not to smear her mascara.

"Suffice it to say the Loves made it to the tabloids," Lindsay said before hanging up.

Although Darcy hated teases, she suspected that this was a case in which seeing was believing. As the Jitney plodded through the Midtown Tunnel, she wondered what designer outfit would appear in the photo.

But when the newspaper opened to the titillating family photograph, it wasn't at all what Darcy had expected. Instead of showing Darcy in her Dior suit or Ralph Lauren plaid separates, sporting a

Kate Spade bag and a new "Rachel-style" haircut from *Friends*, it was a bland, very bad shot of two naked, fleshy people in a hot tub. Darcy was about to toss the paper aside when she noticed the caption: LOVE, CORPORATE STYLE: Bud Love Demonstrates His Management Style with a "Close Aide."

That flabby man was her father!

The woman beside him, with her naked boobies blacked out, had to be Dad's assistant, Stephanie.

She got Lindsay on the line and yelled into the phone, "Why didn't you tell me about this?"

"Don't kill the messenger. Ma found it, and I had to call you before you walked into the courtroom unarmed."

"Well, thanks for that, I guess." Darcy pitched the paper into a wire trash can and kept walking. "How could he be so stupid, fooling around with this trial going on? Doesn't he know people are watching, that his behavior has to be scrupulous?"

"The photo could have been taken years ago," Lindsay pointed out.

"You're right." Darcy had recognized the background of the photo, the herb garden and wrought-iron lantern of the Aspen ski villa, and Dad hadn't been there for months. His lawyers had kept him in the New York area, trying to avoid the perception that he was still spending corporate funds traveling lavishly.

Darcy wasn't surprised to find her mother absent from the courtroom that day. After weeks spent suffering through testimonies dry as mothballs in a balmy courtroom, Melanie Love wasn't going to endure the added scandal of being the cheated-on wife, and Darcy couldn't really blame her.

When Darcy's father filed into the courtroom with his lawyers, she rose to greet him . . . but didn't offer her cheek to kiss. And he didn't step close to take her hand but only barked "good morning" as he passed.

As if it were her fault he got caught fooling around with Stephanie the sycophant.

Sitting in the courtroom with her legs demurely crossed at the ankles—all the better to admire her Manolo Blahnik sandals—Darcy thought over the evidence the prosecution had presented: one interoffice memo after another expressing concern over unorthodox accounting practices. "And was the defendant, Buford Love, copied on this correspondence?" the prosecutor asked over and over again.

"Yes, he was."

"Did Buford Love attend the meeting during which this fraudulent accounting was discussed?"

"Yes, he was there."

"Did the defendant authorize this transfer of funds?"

"Yes, he did."

Darcy wasn't a legal expert, but based on the testimony she'd heard she sensed that things were not going well for her father. Maybe he would actually have to go to prison for a while. Probably one of those "country club prisons" with tennis courts and nine holes of golf. Dad would be fine in a place like that . . . but what about Darcy and her mother? Without her father's salary, his savings and stock options and properties, how would they continue to live?

Darcy planned to stay the night in the Great Egg house to lend her mother moral support. She figured they could have a girls' night out, go for mussels at Frisco's on the Bay or just grab salads at A Way With Green in downtown Great Egg. Mom could thank her for getting the repairs done on the Hamptons house. They could assess Dad's situation together and make a plan for the worst-case scenarios. But when Darcy arrived that afternoon Mom was gone, disappeared without a note. When Darcy finally reached her on her cell, Melanie said she was upstate at a friend's house, taking a time out to reevaluate her priorities. During an awkward pause Darcy waited for something—an invitation to join her mother, curses for Dad, a word of advice—but silence buzzed on the line. Darcy wondered how she figured into her mother's future life, if she even figured at all.

"It doesn't look good for Dad, does it?" Darcy asked quietly.

"I've given up hanging my future on the outcome of his trial," her mother said, as if she were dropping a name from the guest list of her annual garden party. "How's the renovation going? I'd like to get that house on the market soon."

"Fine," Darcy said, grabbing her purse and slamming the kitchen door of the Great Egg house behind her. She'd walk to the Great

Egg train station and ride west to transfer trains in Jamaica—anything to escape this suburban hell.

By the time her mother hung up, she was already walking down Main Street, mounting the ramp to the Great Egg Long Island Railroad Station.

44

Tara

"Have a great weekend, everyone," Tara told her fellow office workers, trying not to linger too long beside Josh Cohen, whose head was bent over Michael's desk as he tried to help the clerk figure out the online shipping program for a package that had to get to Washington, D.C. by Monday morning. Although the other staff members knew that she was seeing Josh, she tried not to lord it in front of them, especially since Josh had heard that Senator Wentworth didn't think it good office policy for workers to "fish off the company pier."

"You're going." Josh straightened, his dark eyes flashing with warmth. "Let me walk you down to the subway with that."

Tara looked down at the garment bag hanging from her shoulder. "I'm okay. It's not heavy."

"No problem. It's the only way I'll see sunlight before this eternal day from hell ends." They'd had a power outage that day, a brownout caused by air conditioners sucking up electricity on the local grid, and it had doubled the workload in the office. Senior staffers had to stay late to make sure priority tasks were completed before the week's end.

"I've got this covered." Michael waved them off. "As long as the power stays on. Otherwise, this package is going by pony express."

Josh hoisted her bag onto his shoulder and led the way out of the office suite to the elevator. It was already after six on a summer Friday, and most of the tenants on their floor had emptied out.

"How's the school funding policy going?" Tara asked him.

Stepping onto the elevator, Josh squeezed his eyes shut. "Like a slug. I'll be here past midnight. God, I wish I could take this train with you."

"You'll come out first thing tomorrow." She turned away from him and looked up at the lights moving down over the floor numbers. "But it's not like we could be together tonight, anyway. I know my parents wouldn't approve."

He slid an arm around her waist and tugged her close in the empty elevator. "And my parents would let us sleep together, as long as we got married by a rabbi before sundown."

She laughed. "Get out!" She wasn't thinking marriage. Right now she couldn't get past the day-to-day details of their relationship, the fact that they'd become so close so quickly, spending most nights together. Resting her head on his shoulder briefly, she remembered how it felt waking up in his bed this morning, in Josh's small, tidy Hoboken apartment. With her mother out in the Hamptons, Tara had been able to manage not being at home most nights, and she enjoyed the sinfully delicious pleasures of staying up late with Josh, sleeping beside him, and brushing her teeth beside him in the morning. Amazing how a string of lunch dates could lead two people to live together, but here they were, girlfriend and boyfriend, sharing just about everything.

The elevator doors slid apart, and they separated and headed through the lobby, the heels of D & G mules clacking on the granite tile.

"So I'll call you as soon as I get out east," Josh said.

"I'll pick you up at the Jitney stop, if you want," she said, wondering if this would be the right weekend for Josh to meet her parents. After last summer's lukewarm reception of Charlie, she doubted they'd be thrilled to discover that their daughter was involved with another white man.

Falling for another white man.

She could already imagine her parents' reaction: that cold, alienated look in her mother's eyes, and her father would turn away to hide his disappointment.

Why did she keep falling for white guys, putting her family in this difficult situation? Sometimes Tara felt like a traitor to her own race. Other times, she felt like a fraud, an African American masquerading as a white person in the Anglo world.

It was always confusing, always fodder for guilt and discomfort.

When she'd brought it up with her friends last weekend, Elle and Lindsay had assured her she wasn't doing anything wrong.

"Isn't culture something we embrace because it helps define who we are?" Elle proposed. Having traveled the world, learned to speak Russian and Swahili, Elle had great respect for different cultures but didn't feel bound by cultural expectations. "If you choose to live differently from your forefathers, why do people take offense?"

Lindsay had reminded her that the clash and mesh of culture was the stuff of great literature. "It's an age-old conflict," she insisted.

But Tara didn't enjoy conflict in her personal life; she craved peace and resolution . . . the balanced scales of justice.

"Why so glum?" Josh asked when they paused at the street-level subway entrance. "You look like you've got the weight of the world on your shoulders." He pulled her to the side of the entrance, out of the way of pedestrian traffic, and into his arms for a hug.

"I'm going to miss you," she said, avoiding the real matter pressing on her thoughts.

"I'll be there before you know it," he said. With a grin, he slipped the strap of her garment bag over her shoulder. "Save me a frosty piña colada with a straw and an umbrella."

"You got it." Holding her breath against the hot stench of the subway stairs, she headed toward her train, eager to get out of the sweltering city and head east to the land of sandy beaches, ever-mutable light, and crisp, salty breezes.

45

Darcy

"The prosecution probably won't introduce the photos of your father and his friend," Tara said when Darcy asked her about it that Friday night. With a father known to take high profile cases, Tara was considered the legal expert in the group. "The prosecutor might not want to appear petty and hurtful to the jury," Tara added.

They were hanging at the bar at Coney's, Darcy happy to be there with her friends, able to watch her boyfriend behind the bar and send him positive vibes. If Dad's was a lost case, at least she had Kevin, and if she poured all her energy and faith in him, how could they fail?

"Do you think they need the photos?" Lindsay said as she transferred drinks onto a tray. "I mean, it doesn't help make the case, and they seem to have loads of evidence. Have you seen those boxes of files marked as evidence on TV?"

"Lindsay's right," Darcy said. "The damage seems to be done. My father's moral character is shot to hell." Surely the rest of his life would come tumbling down in due time. All the more reason to separate herself.

"Still . . ." Tara put a hand on Darcy's wrist. "In the end, it's all up to the jury. Our legal system is flawed, but I still think it's the fairest in the world."

Darcy nodded, trying to swallow a sip of wine that had turned bitter in her mouth. Although it was clear that life as she knew it was over, she still struggled with the loss of her financial freedom. "Part of me still can't believe this is happening, but regardless of what happens with my father, I've got to move on. Today I realized I can't rely on my parents anymore. My father let me down on so many levels—didn't even pay my way through college—but what good would it do for me to sit around and blame him? I've got to move on."

"That's so true, Darcy," Lindsay said. "We all need to climb out from under the parents' wings and think about what we want."

Tara squeezed her hand. "I'm proud of you, honey."

"I can't really take credit. It's survival instinct. Besides, I've known what I wanted for years . . . and he's standing right down the bar."

Her friends' heads swung left, to where Kevin stood in a heated discussion with his father, who scowled as he hung glasses upside down in the overhead rack.

"I was thinking more along the lines of a career," Lindsay said. "Something you can accomplish on your own and a way to be financially independent."

Darcy shook her head at Lindsay, who always had trouble getting the big picture. "You sound just like your mother. But don't worry, I've got the career thing waxed. When Kevin and I take over this place, we're going to make it a Hamptons institution. I figure I'll start off hostessing and Kevin can manage the place."

Lindsay squinted at her. "You want to be a hostess?"

"Of my own place, sure."

"Then why don't you start now? Get off that bar stool, learn the business and make some money in the process," Lindsay suggested. "You could wait tables or bartend. This is what I've been telling you about, Darce. You need a job."

"How hard can it be? A little conversation as I lead people to a table. Of course, it'll give me a good reason to spend a fortune on my wardrobe, and probably write it off, too. With my personality and the solid reputation of this place, Kevin and I are going to become big names in the Hamptons' scene. You'll see. In a few years, you'll be able to say, 'I knew her when . . .' "

46

Elle

"I knew her when she was crazy in love with a big buffoon and staking her future on some honky-tonk bar," Elle muttered under her breath, astounded by Darcy's naivety. She'd been listening to the conversation next to her at the bar, horrified that her friend could be so in the box.

"What was that, mumbles?" Milo cracked a peanut shell, split it open, and offered it to Elle.

She pinched a peanut with a scowl. "I was just finishing Darcy's sentence in a realistic way. I know you can't always choose who you fall in love with, but can't she see that Kevin doesn't belong in this business? He tries to talk people out of ordering a second round. He spills his guts to anyone who'll listen, when it's supposed to be the bartender who listens to the problems of the world." She squeezed lime into her Corona, then shoved it down the neck of the bottle.

Milo leaned forward to check the two McGowans, who were arguing at the end of the bar. "Putting up with his old man, I'd say he's a candidate for sainthood." He grabbed another handful of peanuts. "Actually, so am I."

"Hey, you two," Darcy said, leaving her bar stool to stand between them and slide an arm around each of them. "How're my favorite contractors doing?"

"Great," Milo said. "Have you seen the roof? We're almost done with the exterior."

"Hallelujah, because that scaffolding worries me. Every time I walk by it I think of giant Tinkertoys clattering to the ground."

"It's actually very secure," Milo said.

"And next we'll get started with the interior walls of the attic," Elle said, hoping to distract Darcy. "You should start looking at paint swatches to get an idea what color you want."

"That'll be fun." Darcy leaned closer and lowered her voice confidentially. "And I've got a little tip for you two. As long as you hang together at the bar, you're not going to meet anyone. You're so cute together, you look like a couple. But you're scaring off possibilities."

Thank God! Elle thought, restraining her sarcasm to flash Darcy a sweet smile. "Thanks for the tip, Darce, but right now I just don't have room in my life for relationship complications."

"Me thinks Elle doth protest too much," Darcy said, amused by herself.

"I think she's just on a break," Milo jumped in, defending Elle. "Give her another month or so and I'm sure she'll be lifting her skirt for strangers again."

Elle smacked him on the arm. "You are so wrong! When was the last time you saw me wearing a skirt?"

Just then Kevin stomped down the bar and tossed two metal mixing vats into the sink with a loud clatter. "Get off my back, okay? Jesus H. Christ! You think I want to be here? You think I asked for this?" His face was ruddy, his pale eyes ablaze with anger. "Believe me, it's no prize, being your son."

Elle leaned back from the bar reflexively, then sensed Darcy in a panic behind her, fingernails digging into her bare shoulder.

"Cool it, Kevin," Mr. McGowan rumbled in his deep voice. "This is neither the time nor the place."

"That's the thing, Dad. There's never a good time for you to talk about alcoholism, because that's what it is when someone drinks too much. We have drinking problems, and I can't sit back and ignore it and keep pouring out poison when I can get these people help."

"What? What are you arguing about?" Darcy shot a stern look at Kevin.

"Same old, everyday bullshit." Kevin balled up a rag and flung it into the sink. "I'm done with the crap."

"So quit, why don't ya?" His father bellowed from down the bar. "You'll be back in the morning, begging forgiveness, if I know you." Dismissing Kevin with a wave of his hands, he left the bar and climbed up the steps, disappearing in the reception area.

"Whew!" one of the guys sitting at the bar blustered. "Family fireworks, and it's not even the Fourth yet."

A few people laughed, but Elle and Milo remained quiet, sympathetic to what Kevin was going through. He'd managed to fight off his own consuming habit only to return to a world surrounded by drinkers, a world where his father's business fed into drinking problems. It couldn't be easy for Kevin, taking his father's criticism on the chin while trying to redefine attitudes toward drinking.

"Kevin, honey . . ." Darcy pushed her drink away and leaned her elbows on the bar. "It's okay. He just needs to let off steam."

"Don't you see? It's not just tonight; we go through the same drama every fucking night. I can't take it anymore." Kevin yanked at the strings of his apron and pulled it over his head. "You! Lindsay, can you bartend?"

She winced. "I make a mean Bloody Mary."

"That's good enough. Most of these customers are beer and wine drinkers, anyway." He tossed Lindsay the apron and hopped over the lip of the bar. "Back behind the bar, Linds, and don't take any crap from my old man."

Lindsay caught the emerald green apron in midair and held it up, looking at Darcy and the others for some clue as to how to proceed.

"Kevin, please . . ." Darcy pressed her hands together in prayer position, tears sparkling in her eyes. "Don't do anything rash. I know you're going through a rough time now, but . . ." Rushing forward, she embraced him, whispering something in his ear.

Biting her lower lip, Elle watched. Was this going to be the fall of Darcy's savior?

Kevin was shaking his head, but Darcy persisted, whispering, pulling him closer to the bar, pressing her face to his so he was forced to look in her eyes.

Meanwhile, Lindsay sat the apron on the bar behind Kevin with a shrug. "I've got tables to take care of." And she went off to the kitchen.

A few minutes later, after much private discussion with Darcy, Kevin hopped back over the bar and resumed taking orders. Things seemed to be back to normal, but Elle sensed that the threat remained for Darcy. More trouble in paradise.

47

Lindsay

"I know you need to dress for the interview, but I'm just not used to seeing you buttoned up in little suits like that," Elle said as she took a seat across from me on the westbound train to Manhattan. "You're so . . . Gidget Goes Corporate."

I straightened the lapel of my beige jacket, a polyester linen blend, hopefully enough polyester not to wrinkle. "Don't make fun of me. I need all the confidence I can get so that I don't do something embarrassing during this interview."

"You look like a young Audrey Hepburn," Milo assured me, "and I'm sure you'll do fine. What are you worried about? You're eminently overqualified to file papers and answer phones in the textbook division of Powder Publishing."

"Don't be surprised if I take a powder at Powder. I don't give good interview," I admitted. "I'm always worried that there's a stain on my blouse or toilet paper trailing from my shoe. And when it's time to talk, my words get all gummed up and I sound like an idiot. It's a wonder I can manage a yes or no."

"Well, I'm impressed, and I'd say your interview karma is about to change," Milo said sweetly.

"Suck-up," Elle muttered, slinking down low in her seat. "And if you don't get the job, I'll call my father's friend at Island Books, Uncle Jorge. I didn't think of him, but then I didn't think you were interested in publishing, Linds."

"Only because I've exhausted all other options, unless I want to be a camp counselor or volunteer for the Peace Corps."

"I would *love* that," Elle insisted.

"I thought you were happy to be back in the States," Milo said.

Elle twisted her mouth to one side. "Yeah, I guess I am. Especially since I'm going to be adopted by a Brooklyn family." She clapped Milo on the shoulder. "I'm so excited."

I shot Milo a look of horror. "You're letting her meet your parents?"

"She insisted on it, and I figured it was the least I could do since she got me a free ticket for the matinee. Elle got free *Lion King* tickets, can you believe it?"

"I'm impressed. That's a very hot ticket."

"How do you know this producer, anyway?" he asked Elle.

"Oh, he's some kind of assistant production something, but we went to university together in England. He's a fun guy. I can't wait for you to meet him."

"You know, between your Uncle Jorge and this producer, you're starting to look pretty well connected, Elle," I teased. "Who else do you know? Got any uncles who work as Park Avenue shrinks—maybe a nice Jungian therapist who's looking for a protégé?"

"Believe me, I know plenty of shrinks, but you don't really want into the crazy industry, do you?" Elle laughed. "Depression is so depressing."

"Yes, but being around us, Lindsay must have a deep understanding of neurotic behavior," Milo added.

I nodded. "And let me say, my family laid a strong dysfunctional foundation." I wriggled in my seat, trying to keep the skirt of my suit from creasing. "I'm glad you guys are taking a break today. You've been working pretty hard on Darcy's place. Not even taking weekends off?"

"We will," Milo said. "We're just on a roll, figured we go with it."

"And we wanted to finish off the roof before more rain or wind damaged the house," Elle added. "It doesn't really feel like work when you don't have to dress up and answer to a big boss."

"Hey, I thought I was the boss," Milo said.

While they argued I unzipped my bag, took out my new cell phone, and checked for messages. It wasn't like anyone even knew my number, but I enjoyed checking for voice mail, then scrolling through my address book, lingering on one name . . . Bear.

"What's that?" Elle asked.

I turned to her. "My new cell."

"I know what a cell phone looks like. What's that name in your address book—Bear?"

"It's his cell number. He had a cell phone before any of us, remember?"

"But you just got yours. You programmed his number in?" Elle pressed. "Have you been in touch with Bear?"

"I wish. We've talked, like, twice over the winter, and I got a few postcards," I admitted, but Elle's intense gaze made me squirm. "So what if I have his number. It's not like I'm waiting for him to call."

"Here's a revolutionary idea," Elle said. "Why don't you call him?"

"In Hawaii? I . . . I don't know if my cell goes there."

"Bullshit. You're just afraid." Elle snatched the small black phone from my hands.

"Elle . . . give it back. I think Hawaii has roaming charges."

"What do you care? What good is a cell phone if you never use it?" She held the phone back, out of my reach. "What's the point of having his number if you never call it?"

"Just give me the phone back," I pleaded. When Elle didn't budge I turned to Milo.

"I know nothing," he said, holding his hands up defensively. "I don't own a cell phone and I met this Bear man, like, once."

When I turned back to Elle, Bear's name was on the screen and Elle was pressing the call button. "No!"

With a giggle, Elle listened to the phone a second and handed it back to me. "It's ringing . . . you can't hang up now, or he'll know you chickened out."

My nerves burned in anticipation as I pressed the phone to my ear and waited through three excruciatingly long rings until Bear answered in a gravelly voice.

"Bear? It's Lindsay."

"Hey, Linds." He cleared his throat. "What's up?"

He sounded so casual, I felt as if we could instantly pick up where we'd left off. "I'm on my way into Manhattan for a job interview."

I pushed out of my seat and moved down the aisle, back two rows to an empty seat. "I got a new cell phone and I was thinking of you and, I don't know, just thought I'd call."

"Cool. How's the surfing there?"

I told him about an offshore storm that had brought some big waves in last week.

"And what's it like for you?" I asked. "Is Hawaii really as amazing as they say?"

He groaned. "Even better. It's really paradise, Linds. You can live in a shack without electricity but you don't really care because you've got this amazing ball of sun and waves that are totally irresistible."

"Really? So I guess you're not heading back anytime soon."

He laughed. "How's everyone? Your ma?" I gave him an update on my mother, Steve's new job that was sucking up his time, and how Sal was complaining that the new deliveryman could never find anyone's address.

And most of all, I miss you, I wanted to say, the words lingering on my lips. But even though I'd turned away from my friends and had ample privacy on the deserted late-morning train, I didn't know how to make the leap from the mundane to something so personal.

Muffled sounds came from his end of the line. "Hold on a second," he said, and there was the sound of movement, his voice, her voice. I couldn't catch the words, but the intonation was clear. Something like: "Is everything okay? Are you all right? Who is it, honey?"

A woman. Bear is with some woman.

"Sorry," he said, coming back on the line.

"Where are you?" I asked pointedly.

"In bed. It's pretty early here, and surf isn't up till afternoon today."

In bed with a woman.

I felt a wound, deep in my chest, so painful I had to pretend we were going into the tunnel and end the call. The train threw me to one side as I made my way back to my friends. I held on to the seat rail, feeling off balance, knocked out of normal planetary orbit.

"Aren't you glad you called?" Elle asked as I returned to my seat.

"I'm not so sure about that. I got him out of bed, and I don't think his girlfriend appreciated it."

Elle winced. "Crap."

"At least I know; he's moved on." Fighting tears, I focused on the landscape racing past the window, the rows of houses edging up to the train tracks, the cars waiting at streetlights or shooting down a parallel highway, everyone in a hurry.

Like the speeding train, Bear had forged ahead. So why couldn't I? Why was I the one left behind at the station?

48

Tara

"Whose idea was this, anyway?" Tara asked as she dug through her father's bag of clubs.

Backtracking, she recalled that Elle had initiated the outing when she learned her mother was still paying for a membership at the Sandy Hills Country Club. And since it was already ten A.M. on a Sunday morning, Tara was fairly sure she'd been stood up by Josh once again. This weekend marked the third time he'd planned to meet her out here but had cancelled at the last minute, and it was all so disappointing. Last time, she'd taken the train back to the city with the plan to blast him for being so rude, but all that fizzled when faced with the logic of their situation, their jobs. Josh was a key staff member and his job was a high priority in his life, and when they were both in the city, their lives together were easy, fun . . . fulfilling on an everyday level. Although she felt slighted about the weekend thing—after all, it was summer and they had such a great chunk of the planet to enjoy out here—she didn't want to flip out on him.

So golf, she decided, would be the perfect distraction.

"Oh, the Sandy Hills . . ." Darcy had rolled her eyes, recalling that her father was a member. There'd been an awkward moment or two when the girls had been making tee-off arrangements and one of the staff had pulled Darcy aside for a private chat. Darcy returned, slightly sulky and annoyed.

"What was all that about?" Tara had asked, and Darcy told the girls that the woman felt the need to inform her that her father was "no longer a member of this club."

Immediately all four girls shot a scowl at the offending woman.

"Well, that really rots," Elle said, steaming. "Maybe we should just go."

"Don't let it ruin our day," Darcy said under her breath. "I'd especially hate to let that woman think that I give a flying fuck about her membership roster."

"Good for you," Tara told Darcy. "You've got the power."

Once they teed off, Tara felt herself notching into competitive gear. Her father belonged to the Shinnecock Hills Golf Club down the road, where she had taken lessons all through high school—lessons that seemed to be paying off, based on her performance today. Of course, that didn't put her on a level with Elle, who had an amazing follow-through.

Lindsay was the beginner of the group. "I really suck at this," she said, rocking from one foot to the other as she lined up a shot. She swung, lost her grip, and sent her club flying.

Tara ducked. "Good thing you've got surfing down, honey."

"I can't believe we're actually playing golf together," Lindsay said, hustling back to retrieve her five iron. "And I can't believe you're wearing those shoes."

Elle did a little jig, showing off her high-top Keds that had been tie-dyed purple and red. "Shoes do not make the golfer," Elle said. "So far I'm shooting below par, and you have yet to keep a ball on the green."

"What do you expect when my only experience is from playing miniature golf?" Lindsay replied. "I can handle a windmill and I can whack it in between the vampire's teeth, but what idiot builds a pond in the middle of a golf course?"

Darcy and Tara leaned on each other, laughing. Darcy was crisp and cool in a black, A-line culotte skirt, relaxed despite the downward turn her father's trial had taken.

"It's called a water trap," Elle said. "Now stop complaining and take your swing."

Lindsay swept her club back to wind up and accidentally knocked the ball, sending it flying behind her.

"Ouch!" Darcy jumped away as the ball bounced off her backside. "Right in the ass, Lindsay!"

"I am so sorry!" Lindsay rushed to her friend and grabbed her arm as the other women huddled close, all staring at Darcy. "Are you okay?"

"Fine!" She rubbed the sore spot, gesturing the girls away. "Quit staring at my butt and take your shot!"

"Maybe I'm better off sitting this one out." Lindsay pulled the club against her chest. "Or I'll be your caddy. I can carry your clubs . . . and wash your balls," she added with a sexy grin.

Tara held up her hand for Lindsay to stop. "Something tells me this is your first time . . . your virgin golf outing."

"You guys were my first!" Lindsay giggled. "I always knew there was a special bond between us."

Elle was up next. She wiggled her skinny hips, then swung back and through, sending the ball loping ahead gracefully to bounce a few feet from the ninth hole.

"Where the hell'd you learn to do that?" asked Lindsay.

"Japan. Everyone there was obsessed with golf. We used to go to driving ranges on the rooftops of buildings, all covered with nets. It was like yoga there—gotta do it every day. I guess it just stuck with me."

"I'll say," Darcy said, taking a shot. Hers cut slightly to the left but bounced onto the edge of the green.

Tara stepped up, smoothing down her peach shorts and peach-trimmed golf shirt. Although it was just a friendly game, Tara thrived on competition and at that moment she wanted nothing more than to take the lead from Elle. Focusing on the ninth hole, she tried to imagine her ball arching through the air, straight to a hole in one. Forget the mechanics, forget the shot . . . just plan a path for the ball.

She swung back, made contact and sent the ball soaring . . . right into the sand trap.

"No!" Tara lifted her club toward the sky and went running like a madwoman, making her friends crack up.

"Ach! I feel so much better now," Lindsay said, hoisting her golf bag onto the cart.

As they rode back to the clubhouse after nine holes, Lindsay couldn't get over the world of the country club, a phenomenon all her friends were privy to. "All these years, and I thought the best part was that cheesy pool at Shinnecock Hills. When did you guys learn to golf?"

"It's sort of a lifetime of learning," Darcy said.

"And how come your mother is a member here?" Lindsay asked Elle. "She hasn't been in the Hamptons for years."

"I guess my grandmother got the membership, and Mom just kept it going," Elle said. "It's probably all about Grandma's money. Gram was loaded, and she left very specific orders about what to do with her money. Like her house; my parents kept it for years after she died. I think Gram really wanted us to have a place here in the Hamptons, but it's just not geographically desirable for my parents."

"I remember your grandmother," Tara said, flashing back to when they were kids, eight or nine, and Elle's grandmother used to take them berry picking. "She would bribe us to sing 'Frère Jacques,' always correcting our French accents. If we sang it right, she bought us cones at the Southampton Ice Cream Parlor."

Elle turned to Tara with a smile. "That was Gram."

Thinking back, Tara quickly flashed to Elle's crisis summer, the year she plunged off the jetty into the roiling waters of the Atlantic Ocean. What a difficult time it must have been for her, to have felt so alienated, then plucked from everything she knew to go off to a foreign land, making friends of strangers.

After all that, it couldn't be easy for Elle to come back here, and yet, sometimes it felt as if she'd never left. "What did we ever do all those years without you?" Tara said suddenly, shaking her head at Elle.

"We were, like, so fucking bored," Darcy said in her Valley Girl voice. "No multiple body piercings, no unexplained fires. No one even dreamed of tie-dyed sneakers until Elle came around."

"Shut up, Darcy," Elle said, her cheeks growing pink, but Darcy just reached forward from the back of the golf cart and grabbed Elle's shoulders.

"We missed you, honey!" Darcy shouted, her voice ringing out across the golf course, and they laughed as Elle steered back toward the buildings.

Later, in the country club dining room, Tara found her mind

drifting away from her friends' conversation as she tuned into the men who'd sat behind her, their conversation so loud it was hard to miss.

"It's a pity just a few of them are ruining it for everyone," the man said. "Last year, when we were looking to host a tournament, one of the national guys told us point blank it wasn't going to happen if we didn't change our club charter and accept blacks."

"There it goes," his friend said. "And that's just the beginning. Let them in and the others will come running."

Tara shot a look over her shoulder at the two men—one bald and rubbery looking, the other a crisp handkerchief that had turned gray with time. They actually had the nerve to smile at her, even as the rubbery man said, "Call me racist, but I like to see a good place like this protected from people like that."

Tara turned back to the table, her fingernails digging into the linen tablecloth.

"Okay, Ms. Washington," Lindsay said, "you look like you just saw a ghost."

Tara darted her eyes to the left. "Tune in on the conversation behind me."

Trying not to stare, her three friends fell silent and listened.

"None of this would be a problem if Tiger Woods hadn't come along," said Rubber Man. "It's too bad, because I wouldn't mind opening the doors for someone like him, but they don't write the rules that way. Let him in and you've got to let in all the others."

"Excuse me, sirs?" Elle said politely. "But do you mean that this club doesn't accept African Americans as members?"

"Members?" Gray Hanky snorted. "We don't even let them in as guests."

Tara turned back to her plate, stung. If those men realized her race, wouldn't they be appalled? And that woman was worried about Darcy playing here, with her father's lapsed country club dues. The place would be in an uproar when they realized that she was black.

"Really?" Elle blinked at the two men. "And to think they let in dickwads like you."

The men sucked back, off guard.

Across the table, Darcy let out a laugh. "Nice one, Elle."

"I'm so disappointed," Elle said. "Gram must be turning over in her grave. She marched with Martin Luther King Jr. She sponsored sit-ins to protest the Vietnam War." She looked up at the heavens. "Sorry, Gram. I'll get your membership dues back, even if I have to squeeze it out of Frick and Frack, here."

Lindsay was cracking a smile, too. "I've sort of lost my appetite for Sandy Hills." She scooted her chair out. "All this racism is stinking up the place."

"I definitely have to go." Tara stood up and slammed her napkin to the table with a scowl for the men. She was tempted to lash out at them, but didn't think it wise to waste her energy on such a lost cause. "I don't want to be late . . . for my date with *Tiger.*"

Seeing their jaws drop in astonishment, Tara smiled. *That will give those two old codgers something to think about.*

49

Darcy

It would be hard to let this place go.

Darcy sat back in a lounge chair by the pool, one of the many lounge chairs she had scrubbed and buffed with her own hands, and let her eyes wander up the cedar shingles of the house, now stained dark brown, up to the peak that Elle and Milo had repaired, its slate shingles now gleaming in the August sun.

Ironic that she had found this summer mansion as lonely and cold as a mausoleum in the past, and now that she was about to lose the place it finally felt like home. It didn't hurt to have Milo and Elle installed in two of the guest bedrooms, keeping the place noisy with the clanging of hammers and the jolt of nail guns, the roar of rock music, and alive with the smell of pancakes and bacon, ramen noodles, or meat on the built-in barbecue grill. Milo had become a kind, steady confidant and Elle had stomped back into Darcy's life, endearing herself in her distinctive way—Darcy's summer savior. Kevin found her overbearing and although he wouldn't admit it, Darcy suspected he was uncomfortable about Milo's sexual preferences. He'd complained about having them here, about the lack of privacy, but Darcy had kept telling him she needed the repairs done—a valid excuse, but also a way to keep Kevin more at bay now that the novelty of doing it in every room in the house had faded.

Strains of a Smashing Pumpkins song echoed from the open window of the attic, where Elle and Milo were applying another coat to the trim. Darcy still couldn't believe how they'd come through for her.

"Spectacular work," Darcy's mother had pronounced just this morning when she'd made the trip out to the Hamptons to inspect the repairs—the white-glove test, as Elle called it. "Are you licensed? I could hook you up with some interested parties, if you're looking for more work."

"We did it for fun," Elle said, running one hand along the freshly painted trim of the attic room. "But we'll use you as a reference, if that's okay. Milo's thinking about getting into theater craft shop, so it might help him."

Darcy had hired a licensed plumber to fix the pool house, but the carpentry work and painting had also been completed by Elle and Milo, with Darcy pitching in to help with cleanup and taping, errands and lunch runs. Although she didn't find the work "fun" as they did, she'd enjoyed being a part of the team and was proud of the end result.

"The pool house looks better than it ever did," she told her mother when they were inspecting the small, cozy building. "Elle had the idea to use this fabric over the walls, and we ditched the curtains for these privacy shades."

"Very nice," her mother agreed.

"Don't you think they deserve a bonus?" Darcy asked. "They did this work for a rock-bottom price, and super fast."

"Darcy . . ." Her mother shot her a stern look. "I'll throw in a little tip, and you'll get your money for car repairs, but a bonus is out of the question." She examined a ceramic bowl, a swirl of geometric designs in summery greens, yellows, and pinks that Darcy had found hidden in the kitchen pantry. "I've always hated this bowl. I'll be happy to let this place go. Furnished." Her lips puckered as she scanned the four walls, then turned toward the door. "Good riddance."

"I don't feel the same way," Darcy said, daring to speak her mind and try to get through the glass wall her mother always hid behind. "I've spent my whole summer scrubbing this place up, sweeping and dusting, killing bugs and pinching dead leaves off the rose bushes. This house has become my home, Mom. I know we're in deep financial doo-doo, but isn't there a way we could hold on to this place?"

Melanie Love turned back to her daughter, her face puckering like a prune. "I can't believe you'd even ask such a question. According to George, we're lucky to be keeping the Great Egg house."

"Maybe the court would allow a trade," Darcy suggested. "We could sell the Great Egg house and live here . . ."

"In this bog? A hundred miles from civilization? Get real, Darcy." And she'd walked out of the pool house, leaving Darcy with the clear message that her desires and needs really didn't matter now in Melanie's plans for financial recovery.

That moment underlined the loneliness that Darcy used to feel when she was alone in this house or closed into her princess-style bedroom in the Great Egg house. That moment helped her realize that she could never, ever go back to being her parents' daughter, the show horse under their thumb . . .

"The second coat on the attic trim is finished," Elle said, lugging a large paint can across the pool patio. "We'll store the extra paint in the tool shed. You never know when something will need a touch-up."

"The new owners will appreciate it," Darcy said glumly. "But thanks. Really. You guys have been great."

Milo appeared in the rose arbor behind Elle, doffing a white painter's cap. "Was that the final verdict? Your mother's determined to sell?"

"I'm afraid so." The summer roses about Milo's head had just opened, unfurling their pink petals, and the realization that this would be the last season she'd see them bloom made Darcy's eyes sting with tears.

"Well, that sucks monkey butt." Elle dropped the paint can on the stones and sat on it. "What's the deal with our parents and disposable homes? As soon as you get vested in a place, they turn around and sell it or rent it and cart you off to some other strange corner of the world."

"Sorry, but I don't relate." Milo perched on the edge of a lounge chair, crossing his worn white painters pants. "I wish my parents would sell that suburban hellhole in Brooklyn."

"I get it," Darcy said. "We've been displaced, but I think that it's symbolic of the fact that there was nothing to keep our families together in the first place."

"Crap, I think you're right." Elle stood up, stripped her denim overalls down to her emerald green one-piece and walked to the edge of the pool. "We're pushed off, shuffled away because they don't know what to do with us."

Milo winced. "Am I the only one who finds this depressing?"

"Someday, dear Milo," Elle told him, "you'll grow wise and sage—able to handle conflicts heavier than your Jackson Five tunes." She dove into the pool, splashing water over the side.

An hour later, Lindsay ran up to them poolside, waving her hands frantically. "You're never going to believe this." She motioned Darcy, who was thinning out pansies in a planter, to sit down. "Big announcement: I got the job."

"Island Publishing?" Elle asked.

Lindsay nodded, jumped up and down, then did a happy dance around Darcy's lounge chair. "I'm so excited! They wanted me to start Monday but I told them I have to give two weeks' notice at Coney's, and they understood."

"Didn't I tell you to wear that purple tank top to the interview?" Milo asked, adjusting his glasses. "Was I right, or was I right?"

Lindsay's head bobbed. "It worked. They liked me. I'm starting as an associate editor."

"I'm happy for you, honey, but not surprised," Elle said. "I told you Uncle Jorge would come through." She jumped up and hugged Lindsay, pressing a wet spot into Lindsay's purple silk tank top.

"Elle!" Darcy scowled. "You schmutzed her."

Lindsay looked down at the stain and shrugged. "Doesn't matter. I got the job!"

"In that case . . ." Elle threw her arms around Lindsay, nudged her to the pool's edge, and leaned in until they plopped into the pool together.

Sputtering and smoothing her hair back, Lindsay surfaced. "God damn it, Elle! These shoes are Dolce & Gabanna!" She treaded water long enough to pull them off and toss them onto the shining tiles.

"But you got the job! You'll buy more!" Elle said, splashing Lindsay.

"No splashing!" Milo said, poised at the edge of the pool in his boxers.

Elle frowned and sliced a torrent of water in his direction.

"Hey!"

Darcy fell back in her chair, laughing. "Still a beach pest, Elle."

"Easy, Princess," Elle called, floating onto her back, "or you'll find your lounge chair floating downstream."

"Just try it." Darcy jumped out of the chair and ran into the pool shouting, "Look out below!" The water seemed to fizz around her skin, refreshing and clean. She swam to the side and leaned her arms back on the ledge, kicking gently, joking with her friends. Too bad Tara wasn't here, but she was stuck in the city during the work-week, committed to the senator's causes.

When Kevin appeared sometime later, Darcy and her friends were still in the water, in the thick of a game of water volley-ball.

"Spike it!" Elle coached Darcy, who gave the ball a pounding that sent it bouncing off Milo's head.

"Not fair!" Lindsay shouted. "We said no spiking!"

"Darcy . . ." Kevin called from the side of the pool.

She knew he'd been standing there a while, but the game moved fast and she couldn't look away for a second. "Hey, Kev!"

"Come here." He motioned her over, a huge, almost hypnotic grin on his face. Had he just come from an AA meeting where he had an epiphany? "We need to talk."

"We're right in the middle of a game," she told him.

"Oh, go on!" Lindsay smacked the water. "You were winning, anyway."

Darcy climbed out with a wariness she didn't usually feel around Kevin. What had he been up to? He was dressed up and obviously busting a gut over some kind of news or secret, dying to tell her. Didn't he realize she didn't like surprises? Didn't he know her well enough to see that she was not the sort of person you sprang news on?

She pulled a towel over her shoulders and squeezed water from the ends of her hair. "Okay, Kev, let's talk."

"Can we take a walk in the rose garden?" he asked, and panic plummeted through her. This was big news, really big.

And she had a sneaking suspicion that she wouldn't want to hear it.

50

Tara

Getaway Friday.

Tara clicked open her e-mail one last time to see if there were any urgent messages that couldn't wait until Monday. She was ready to go. Josh, however, was still in the conference room going over notes on the senator's child-welfare policy with one of the aides. Since Congress wasn't in session now, Tara didn't think it was crucial to have the policy rewritten today, but then she was still a novice in this world. Her eyes flicked to the time on the computer—four-fifty. They'd have to leave soon if they were going to catch the five-thirty train.

Or maybe Josh would bail, which wouldn't surprise her. She'd told him to stop making weekend plans if he wasn't going to keep them, but he'd sworn that this time he was going to stick to the plans.

The phone was ringing, and Tara realized Penny wasn't at her desk. Most of the staff had left an hour ago, a tiny concession for one of the last summer weekends. Tara picked up the phone and clicked on line one. "Senator Wentworth's office."

"Give me Josh, dear." The voice belonged to an older woman.

"I'm sorry, but Josh is in a meeting. May I take a message?"

"This is his mother. Tell him to call me."

Josh's mother! Tara had never met her, but Josh said he'd told his parents all about her.

"No, wait," Mrs. Cohen went on. "I won't be here if he calls. I'd better leave a message."

"Of course, Mrs. Cohen," Tara said, grabbing a pen. "This is Tara Washington. I'm sorry Josh hasn't made it out to the Hamptons this summer. He's like a superhero around here, and it seems like we've fielded one crisis after another."

"Yes, my Josh is a real decision maker, a spin doctor," Mrs. Cohen said. "But don't let him tell you he's suffering. He's been out here plenty of times, dear. Josh gets his beach time in."

"What?" Tara snapped before she could stop herself. "Excuse me, but I . . . I guess I believed him when he complained about not making it out."

"I tell him not to whine, it's so unattractive. But really, the reason I called, dear, is to ask him to do me a favor. Would you ask him to stop at Liebermann's for a loaf of marble rye? Have them slice it, of course. I don't know what it is with these Hamptons bakeries; you just can't get good bread out here."

"I'll give him the message." *Mom.*

Tara was already on her feet when she hung up. In a flash she was opening the conference room door, interrupting what appeared to be a very boring meeting with Josh staring out the window shaking a bottle of Perrier and the policy writer scribbling doodles on his pad.

"We have to talk," Tara said.

"Did the senator call?" Josh stood up.

"No, it was someone more important—your mother."

Josh moved around the table and left the room without even acknowledging the other aide. "Is everything okay at home?"

"Peachy. Before I forget, she wants you to stop at Liebermann's and pick up a loaf of marble rye. Sliced."

He followed her over to her desk. "And for that you got me out of a meeting?"

She crumpled the pink message slip and tossed it into the trash can. "No, I wanted to let you know that a huge lightbulb just went on over my head, and that I'm not going to miss my train for the Hamptons thinking that you'll make the next one with me."

"Come again?" He winced. "You're talking crazy."

"I finally figured you out. You're afraid your parents will find out about me."

"They know I'm seeing you."

"Do they know I'm black?"

He perched on her desk and curled foward, crossing his arms. "No . . . but they also don't know that you like pad Thai and black pugs and Woody Allen films. I don't tell my parents everything."

"But you've kept me from meeting them because you don't know how they'll react to me. You've been going out to the Hamptons without me—and lying about it, I might add—to avoid a confrontation."

"Let's just say that I think they'd be disappointed." He frowned, then rushed to add, "In *me*. Not you. That I've hooked up with someone unacceptable. To them. See, they've always had this thing about me marrying a nice Jewish girl . . ."

"Don't pull that one out of your ass," Tara interrupted. "It's not about being Jewish or Christian, and you know it. This is about accepting me as I am, and about lying to me because you're ashamed of who I am."

"No, I'm not—"

"Just stop, okay?" She pressed her fingers to her temples, feeling crushed, dazed . . . unable to navigate through this.

"Tara, I'm crazy about you." He reached for her hand, bringing it to his lips. "You know that. But honestly, I don't see us as a long-term thing. I wasn't thinking marriage or—"

"Neither was I. I just wanted to ease into your life in a natural way, and I thought we were doing that, till you started drawing lines and lying."

He shrugged. "A few white lies."

"Lying is unforgivable." *And racism is intolerable.* She yanked her hand away and snatched up her purse. "I've got a train to catch." Without looking back, she hitched her garment bag onto her shoulder and walked away.

51

Darcy

Amazing how a cool dip in the pool will quench desire, Darcy thought as she adjusted the towel around her neck and smiled up at Kevin. She was dripping wet, her hair hanging behind her in ratty locks, and he was actually wearing a suit—a khaki linen mix, definitely a step up from the shiny one he'd worn during the first few weeks of her father's trial. He was definitely handsome, but she was in no mood to do anything about it.

"You are going to love this," he said. "I didn't want to tell you until it was all said and done."

She squinted at him. If he weren't making her so nervous she'd enjoy the way he looked with a backdrop of budding pink roses climbing the wall behind him and curving overhead.

"I don't like surprises," she said, searching his profile for the bulge of a jewelry case. *Please don't let it be an engagement ring!* She wasn't ready for that yet.

He put his hands on her shoulders, staring intently into her eyes. "You know how I've been struggling lately. Not so much with sobriety, but with the old man?"

She nodded.

"Well, I've gone over it in group and everyone agrees that it's a no-win situation. I realized that my employment situation had to change, what with my father wearing on me. And it's not healthy for me to be in a bar, with the booze all around me and my old friends who'd be happy to hook me up with some coke."

"We've talked about this a million times, Kev. You know you need to stay away from Fish. And the thing about Coney's is, it'll be worth so much to you if you just ride it out."

He shook his head. "I'm talking about survival here, and it's just too hard to be there every day. But it's okay, because I figured out a way out. Back in December I got a call about a civil service test I took two years ago. They wanted to start doing a background check on me, processing me to be a firefighter in New York City. Well . . ." He clapped his hands together, doing the tongue thing in a smug way. "I made the cut, and this morning I went into the city to be sworn in."

"What?" His story was so twisted, Darcy could barely follow it.

"I'm in the Fire Academy." He spread his arms wide, as if ready to take a bow. "You're looking at a probie in the Fire Department of New York City."

"A fireman?" Darcy winced. "Why would you want to do that?"

"Good salary, great medical benefits, a much better work schedule, and—best of all—financial independence from the old man."

She didn't know what to say. Kevin becoming a civil servant . . . it seemed so unappealing, sort of low class and definitely not in keeping with her plans for him—the Kevin and Darcy Bliss Package. She didn't want to burst his bubble, but she wasn't about to jump in his arms and kiss him as he carried her off to the firehouse.

"You seem very happy about it," she said carefully.

"I am!" He leaned down to hug her from a distance, avoiding the body press to keep dry. "And I knew you'd be happy, too. Just think about it. We can get an apartment in the city. Probably not Manhattan, but I hear Queens and Brooklyn have some good spots. I'll be in the Fire Academy for the next six weeks or so, but after that we can start looking for a place far away from here."

"Oh, Kevin." She tried not to let disappointment tinge her voice. "This really *is* a big surprise. Huge."

So huge, she didn't know how she'd ever get around it.

52

Elle

Elle pulled her legs onto the smooth, oversized leather chair and tucked her knees under her chin as the lawyer went on about the codicils in Gram's will, the odd specifications, the trust fund, foundation, and hold on the sale of her house.

"I thought Gram's house was already sold," Elle said. "That was why I couldn't live there." Not that she'd want to, since the nightmarish images of her worst summer were tied into that place. Besides, the two-story colonial on Shelter Island had been renovated to include two meandering wings that created a rabbit warren of hallways so confusing, once Elle chose a bedroom she could never seem to find it again. It was no place for a single woman to live.

"The house can never be sold." The lawyer, Edgar Shoefield, reached into a wood-paneled box on his desk and extracted a cigar, which be popped into his mouth and let droop above the sagging skin of his jaw. Elle suspected he'd been one of Gram's contemporaries, maybe even a boyfriend. "Right now it's rented, being kept available for your father's return to the area. However, if he does not occupy the house within the next ten years, it will become the property of the foundation, to be used as a nonprofit summer camp for children."

"That sounds totally cool." Elle had always liked the way Gram worked.

"I'm not sure your father quite agrees, but there you have it. That's the house."

"But what about Gram's estate?" she asked. "She always told me I'd be well taken care of." Those words had popped into Elle's head when she'd so desperately wished to help Darcy hold on to the Love Mansion.

"The cash disbursements are another story," Edgar said grumpily. "Your father has received his, but you're not entitled to yours until you reach the age of twenty-one."

"Which happens this October." Duh.

"Yes, of course."

"So why didn't my parents tell me about any of this?"

His steely gray eyes flashed over his reading glasses. "You're asking me?"

"Yeah, I am, Ebenezer."

The man sighed, a raspy sound. "In my checkered experience, I've seen parents worry about their children receiving an infusion of cash. I've seen children burn away said infusions of cash. Perhaps it's the obvious."

"Maybe. So, how much is my inheritance?" Elle was thinking along the lines of a hundred thousand dollars . . . enough for a down payment on a small condo.

He held his cigar away from his mouth as he read from her file. "Ten million dollars, U.S."

"What?" she shrieked, jumping up in the chair. "Are you yanking me?"

"A little decorum, Ms. DuBois," he growled, though a smile tugged at his mouth. "I assure you, no representative of this firm has ever 'yanked' a client."

"Ten million dollars?"

He nodded. "U.S."

She slid out of the chair and went to read the file on his desk. "Edgar, I could just kiss you."

"I know," he said dryly. "But I'll settle for a resolution of our meeting so that I can make my two o'clock tee time."

"Goody gumpers!" Elle kickboxed her shadow, then jumped in a circle. "I can pay full price for the Love Mansion and still have money left over."

"We'll talk in October about inheritance taxes and other ramifications," he said, extending his hand.

Elle shook, then snatched his cigar from his mouth. "You know, smoking can kill you."

"I'm eighty-one, Ms. DuBois. Something is going to get me sooner or later."

"Okay, then." She shoved the cigar back onto his spotted lips. "See you in October!"

53

Darcy

"What time is the realtor getting here?" Lindsay asked as she reached under the hood and turned on the stove light.

Darcy had read that a place should be well illuminated when you're showing it for an open house, and since the September afternoon was overcast, that meant throwing dozens of switches in the Love Mansion.

"Thirty minutes till Cruella the realtor, and the open house starts in an hour." Darcy flipped through a stack of mail on the cooking island, pausing when she came across a newsletter from Hunter College in Manhattan. She was trying to clear up clutter before the potential buyers arrived, but she wanted to check the calendar to see when auditions were scheduled for their fall theater production. "Did I tell you I'm registered for Hunter this fall? I'm going to finish off my degree, at a more affordable price than Bennington."

"That's awesome! So you'll be in the city. We can meet for movies or dinner."

"Yup. I'm even going to try out for the next production."

Lindsay said something about putting out fresh-cut flowers, but Darcy was only half listening, focused on the page that showed calendars of August, September, and October. Auditions were the weekend of September twenty-third. Perfect, except that she'd have her period. Oh, well, she'd deal with it during tryouts.

Except, when was the last time she'd had it? She didn't recall anything the whole month of August . . .

"Oh, God, I'm late." Her heart hammered in her chest.

"Don't worry, we'll pull it all together before the open house," Lindsay said, breezing into the dining room. "In fact, we've still got time to get a pie in the oven, or cookies. That fresh-baked smell is supposed to be irresistible."

"I'm not talking about the open house." Darcy followed her into the next room, rolling the college calendar into a tube. "My period is late."

Lindsay placed the Mikasa crystal bowl on the mahogany table and turned to her. "How late?"

Sick with panic, Darcy hugged herself. "Very."

"Okay." Lindsay checked her watch again. "Go out now and get a test kit. Neither of us will be able to stand it till we know the truth, and anyway, we need some frozen pie or cookie dough to stick in the oven." She turned Darcy around and pushed her toward the kitchen door. "Go now, and don't overthink it. It could be just some change in your body. Stress. You've had a lot of that."

By the time Darcy returned, Gladys the evil realtor had arrived and was already taking command of the house that Darcy had nurtured all summer.

"Get the flowers out of the dining room. It's the room for food," she said, pointing to the fresh-cut roses Lindsay had floated in the Mikasa bowl. "In there! Much better."

Darcy plunked the package of cookie dough in Lindsay's hands. "I'm going upstairs to do this," she said, unable to think of anything else.

The suspense was excruciating, her nerves so shattered that her fingers fumbled when opening the package.

A ten-minute wait, maybe twenty.

She paced in her bathroom, over the pearly marble tiles her mother had been so insistent upon when they'd renovated so many years ago. Italian marble and gold fixtures. A multifaucet shower big enough for an orgy. Well, the shower had certainly come in handy this summer, though it had only been Kevin and her, screwing like bunnies. They'd given up on condoms, but she was on the pill, right?

Sliding open the vanity drawer, she found the pill pack and popped it open. Three white pills remained, along with a blue one in another row. Okay, she'd missed three days at the beginning of the month, but that shouldn't matter, right? She'd heard that after you were on birth control pills for a few months, you were protected from pregnancy if you missed one now and then.

There was a knock on the door. "It's me."

Darcy unlocked it and let Lindsay in.

"How's it going?" she asked tentatively, closing the door behind her.

"It's just about time to check." Darcy stepped toward the little stick balanced on the white box, but she didn't need to get any closer to see the pink line.

Very pink.

"Oh, no." She sank down to the marble tile as Lindsay stepped around her to take a look.

"I take it that means you're pregnant?" Lindsay asked.

Darcy nodded.

"Oh." Lindsay sat on the edge of the Jacuzzi tub, her tanned legs dangling, her toes working to keep her red flip-flops on. "I know that wasn't in your plans."

Tears stung her eyes as Darcy shook her head. "I was on the pill. Sort of."

"You know what?" Lindsay slid off the tub and kneeled beside her. "It's all going to be okay. Whatever you want to do, whatever you decide, it'll be fine. And I'll be beside you all the way, Darce. I won't let you go through this alone."

This . . . this pregnancy. A baby inside her?

How could that happen?

Darcy reached out to hug her friend, but as Lindsay's hands patted her back she broke down in tears and sobbed on Lindsay's shoulder.

"It's okay," Lindsay whispered. "You're not alone."

54

Darcy

"We find the defendant, Buford Love, guilty." The fore-woman of the jury turned her squarish face toward Darcy's father and glared at him from behind her glasses, her lip curled like a Doberman ready to attack. The bitch.

Darcy wanted to stride over to her and strip that unfashionable eyeware off her face, but she figured that one criminal was enough for the Love family. In front of her, Dad's lawyers muttered to each other, the lead counsel, George, turning to her father with a hand on his back and whispering in his ear. Darcy imagined he was giving Dad the "we did our best, gave it the old college try" speech. She'd never know, because ever since Mom dropped out of the scene Dad's attorneys had stopped acknowledging Darcy.

Sliding down on the wooden bench, Darcy felt as if she were sinking in a black hole, the lawyers and court officers, the protestors, jury, and New Yorkers of the courtroom swirling around her, a teeming mass of chatter and sweat, hot breath and disapproving, curled lips. She was sinking, being sucked into the vortex of the noise and indignation and disapproval.

She couldn't take it . . . the bitter animosity toward her father, who'd now left her with nothing.

How was she supposed to survive *and* take care of a tiny baby?

She felt herself gag and worried that she was going to throw up in the courtroom—which would make the angry mob that much more repulsed by her.

Something pressed on her shoulder, and she lifted her heavy head.

"You okay?" Lindsay asked, leaning close. An angel over her shoulder.

"I feel sick," Darcy said.

Bending low, Lindsay slid an arm around her back and helped her up. Turning to the back of the courtroom, Darcy braced herself for more indignant faces. Instead she saw compassion, support and love in the faces of Tara and Elle, who stood waiting for her. When had they arrived? She hadn't noticed, but she'd never been more relieved to see her friends. She wasn't going to fall away into the vortex; her friends would help her find a way out of this.

"Looks like feeding time at the Bronx Zoo," Elle said.

Tara touched Darcy's cheek gently, then took her hand. "Let's get the hell out of here."

55

Lindsay

"Lunch is on me," I insisted behind my menu. The four of us—Darcy, Elle, Tara, and I—sat at a small, square table in Pigalle, a bistro in the theater district. "I love this place. They serve breakfast all day." Maybe my voice sounded a little too chipper and cheerful, considering that my friends and I had just come from the courtroom where we'd heard about the big G verdict for Darcy's dad, but in the scheme of importance, I figured Buford Love's jail sentence paled compared to the other news Darcy was going to have to share with our friends.

"Should we order a bottle of wine?" Elle asked. "A zesty French cabernet? I'll spring for that. I've actually got some good news . . . but that's for later. Right now Darcy could use something to take the edge off."

I choked on my water, prompting Tara to tap me in the center of the back. "How can you choke? We haven't ordered yet." Tara asked me.

"I'm okay," I insisted.

Elle ordered a bottle of cabernet, Darcy sticking with water. We ordered steaks and hearty beef burgundy and eggs Benedict, and the waitress, Natalia, went on her way.

"Sorry about the verdict," Elle said. "I know it was no surprise, but, well, sorry."

Leaning close over the table, Tara pinched off a piece of olive bread. "I'm proud of you for sticking by your father till the end."

"Not that he noticed," Darcy said. "But honestly, I felt so out of it in that courtroom today. I've got bigger problems now." She looked at me, and I nodded encouragingly. "The thing is, I'm pregnant."

Elle's eyes popped in shock. "Really? Are you sure?"

"Oh, Darcy . . ." Tara squeezed her wrist. "And what timing."

"Okay, I'd say that's bigger news than mine," Elle said as the waitress poured her a taste of the cabernet. Instead of sipping she downed it, placed the glass on the table, and nodded at Natalia. "That's what we need, and lots of it."

Natalia laughed as she filled three glasses. "Don't worry, we have plenty in the cellar."

"Have you made an appointment with your gynecologist?" Tara asked. "I'm sure they could help you terminate the pregnancy, if that's what you want to do."

"I've thought about it. I've been turning this around and around in my mind, inside out, trying to run through all the possible scenarios." Darcy tore off a tiny piece of roll. "Ending the pregnancy seems to make the most sense, but every time I think about it, the idea makes me sick. It's, like, a huge sin in the Catholic Church, and I just know it would destroy my father, who's already feeling ruined."

"When was the last time you went to church?" I asked. "And how would your father find out you had an abortion? It's not as if they'd print it in the prison newsletter."

"Linds . . ." Darcy scowled at me.

"Okay, bad joke," I said. "But when did you become antiabortion?"

"I think it should be a legal, safe option for pregnant women," Darcy said sadly. "Just not for me."

"And what about Kevin?" Tara cradled her wine. "Have you told him?"

"Kevin knows. He said we could get married right away. I could be the wife of a firefighter. That's what he wants, I think, but he's leaving the final decision up to me."

I knew that middle-class living was the stuff of Darcy's nightmares. "He means well," I said. "Even if he's not part of the Kevin and Darcy Bliss Package."

"Not anymore." Darcy buttered a piece of roll, shaking her head. "He's not the guy I fell in love with, if that guy ever existed. I know my stomach is a little rocky, but the prospect of a lifetime with Kevin makes me want to hurl."

"How about a lifetime with a baby?" Elle said. "A baby who's going to grow into a little kid, then into a pain-in-the-ass adult like us. How does that make you feel?"

Darcy lifted her chin and smiled, her eyes a play of blue light. "That sounds sort of good. Promising, somehow."

"Then you have to follow your heart," Elle said, as if it were all so obvious. "Lose the father, have the baby."

Chewing her roll, Darcy nodded. "I think that's what I have to do."

We were silent as everyone tried to absorb the ramifications of Darcy's life-altering decision . . . Darcy as a single mom. I swirled the red wine in the long-stemmed glass, wishing I could see Darcy's future. Darcy hadn't even finished college yet. She didn't have a job or a place to live. Her father was going off to prison and her mother had shut down emotionally and closed the credit lines. A very bleak picture, I thought, wondering how Darcy would get through it all.

"Wow." Elle twisted the rings on one hand. "My news is going to sound like some lame consolation prize now. But the bottom line is . . ." She screwed up her face and spewed out the words, rapid-fire: "I'm inheriting a few million dollars from my grandmother and I'd like to use some of it to buy the Love Mansion so we can all have a place to spend the summers together."

Staring at Elle, Tara sat back in her chair and folded her elegant arms across her chest. "You gotta be kidding me."

"It's a joke," I said with a laugh. "Right?"

Elle shook her head frantically. "Turns out I'm loaded, and my dipshit parents weren't going to let me know till the last minute because they thought they'd save me from the evils of excessive fortune! I don't want to step on your shadow, Darce, but when Milo and I worked on that house this summer, I fell in love with it, too. I want to sink some roots. I want to be able to go back next year and the year after that and after that, and since it's in the Hamptons, Gram would have gotten a large charge out of it."

Everyone looked at Darcy, who was now wide-eyed and pink, jarred out of her misery. "Since when did you become my fucking fairy godmother?"

Elle cocked her head. "You're going to need more than a fucking fairy to fix your life, honey."

Darcy took a deep breath. "I see that now. I've got my work cut out for me, but at least I'm calling the shots. Buy the house, Elle. I'd feel good about that, and I'm totally awed at your ability to turn straw into gold. You, girl, are a walking lucky charm."

"Green clovers, yellow moons, pink hearts . . . big surprises!" Elle chirped, mimicking the cereal commercial.

"Here's to next summer," I said, raising my wineglass. "Oh, God, Darce. You're going to have a baby next summer!"

Darcy clinked her water glass against the others, smiling despite the tears that glistened in her eyes. "I know," she said as if it were a miracle none of us could fathom. "I know."

PART THREE

And Baby Makes Six

Summer 1999

56

Darcy

"Oh, look! Another one-piece snap-crotch thingy," Darcy said, holding up the cotton garment, so tiny it seemed impossible that a human body could squeeze into it. This one was striped, in yellow, lime and emerald green, with a trainfull of little animals riding one of the stripes across what would be the baby's belly.

"Another set of onesies . . . from Nancy!" Lindsay said, dutifully jotting down the neighbor's name on the gift list so that Darcy could be sure to write her a thank-you note. "And that, I think"—Lindsay kicked at a few mounds of crumpled gift wrap on the floor—"is the last of the gifts. So we'll put the coffee on and let the guys in." Boyfriends had been sent down the street to wait out the first part of the shower at Coney's "because the sight of diapers and breast pumps makes single men run for the border," Lindsay had insisted, and as the shower's planner and host, she seemed to know best.

"Thank you so much . . . everyone," Darcy said sincerely. Before today she'd had no idea half of these things existed, no sense that she wouldn't be able to survive the next six months without a breast pump from a college friend or an ear thermometer from Mrs. McCorkle's neighbor or an Exersaucer from Elle. How could she have known that the hospital wouldn't release her infant without a proper car seat, which the baby would promptly outgrow in six months? It was all a tad overwhelming and extremely alienating for Darcy, who couldn't imagine that this bold, nudging ball growing inside her was going to really make its way out as a baby she loved.

"Don't they just warm your heart? There's nothing like little baby clothes." Mary Grace McCorkle sat down beside Darcy and began refolding baby garments that spilled out of gift boxes. "Of course, you'll want to wash them all first, in a special detergent. Some baby skin can't tolerate our harsh detergents."

Darcy had been planning to leave the tags on. "I was thinking that I might have to return some of the gifts that were duplicated," she said quietly, so other guests wouldn't hear. The breast pump looked like a Gothic torture device, and what baby would need wardrobe changes to warrant all these outfits? "You know, like, who needs twelve onesies?"

"You will, my dear. Just wait and see." With a laugh, Mary Grace reached over and patted Darcy's cheek. "Babies soil their diapers and spit up so often, you'll be amazed at how many times you'll reach for a new outfit. Could be one every hour."

"Really?" A dirty diaper every hour? Was this Wonder Ball inside her really going to wreak a path of destruction on the cute Calvin Klein boxers Kevin's mother had sent? Darcy couldn't imagine anything that came from her body messing in its diaper every hour, but then, lately, she'd had lots of trouble imagining her future.

In a brief flash of sanity last fall she'd realized she had only eight months left to get her bachelor's degree sans baby, and so she'd pushed on at Hunter College through morning sickness and maternity clothes and weekly ob-gyn appointments scheduled around classes and final exams. Her June due date seemed to spark a deadline unlike any she'd faced at Bennington, and so she'd attended every class, completed every project and paper. In the spring production of Shakespeare's *Romeo and Juliet* she was cast as the nurse, and though she brought a more youthful approach to the role than most people envisioned, she felt that it was balanced with due authority toward her young charge. That production had been a turning point for Darcy, the readings and rehearsals, opening night and maintaining energy for every performance. She was well suited for the rhythm and excitement of theater; getting paying work after the baby was another story, but for now it was exciting thinking of the possibilities as an actress.

"Isn't this precious?" Lindsay's mother held up a navy velvet jumpsuit with a white collar, the Little Lord Fauntleroy outfit Darcy's mother had sent, gift-wrapped from Saks. "Too bad your mom couldn't be here," Mrs. Mick said, squeezing Darcy's arm.

"It's a shame," Darcy said, though she was actually relieved her mother had called to decline the shower invitation, claiming she had a previous engagement. They'd had some explosive arguments when her mother first heard about the baby in late September. Melanie Love was angry at Darcy for screwing up her birth control pills, furious that she was planning to have the baby and keep it, disappointed that she wasn't going to marry Kevin. "What am *I* supposed to do with you?" her mother had asked at one point, as if she couldn't bear the inconvenience of having a pregnant daughter in her life. By October, Melanie Love made it clear that she had no plan to remain attached to her daughter when she put the Great Egg house up for sale and purchased a one-bedroom co-op on Madison Avenue. "I really couldn't afford a two-bedroom," she explained to Darcy, "and besides, it's time for you to make your own way. Especially if you're going to start a family."

Thank God for the McCorkles. Lindsay had driven her Saturn out to Great Egg, packed Darcy's possessions inside it, and moved her into the McCorkles' Brooklyn home, where Mrs. Mick was delighted to have not just another mouth to feed, but one who was eating for two. Hunter College, on the upper east side of Manhattan, was an easier commute from Brooklyn, and after two weeks with the McCorkles Darcy could feel the stress draining from her body. Mrs. Mick seemed so appreciative of the smallest things—picking up milk from the deli, helping with the dishes, inviting her to catch a matinee at the multiplex, and Lindsay seemed to enjoy catching up with her best friend each day when she came home from work.

The winter months had passed quickly as Darcy focused on staying healthy, drinking skim milk, and attacking her schoolwork. Life with the McCorkles had been wonderful . . . but Darcy knew things would change once she had the baby. Mrs. McCorkle was happy to have her stay on, but living arrangements were the least of Darcy's worries.

Motherhood was the problem.

With the baby due in a month, Darcy had expected to feel some sort of maternal feelings, a welcoming glow toward her infant.

Unfortunately, whenever talk of diapers and baby baths and nursing came up, any mothering instinct was chased off by feelings of inexperience and inadequacy.

How could this baby come to her if she didn't love it?

At first she'd thought it was just her lack of exposure to children that bugged her, so she checked out a dozen books from the library and researched contemporary mothering. She learned that breast-feeding could provide the baby with extra immunities, that baby powder could actually harm the baby's lungs, that the cords of blinds were hazardous to toddlers . . .

But none of these facts could make her feel any love for her baby.

And now, with all these women gathered here to celebrate the new life coming into the world, Darcy felt like a fraud, a flimsy actress propped up to play the mommy role, only to disappoint her audience.

Would she ever start feeling some sort of attachment for the shifting noodge in her belly?

She was afraid not. And the idea of playing out the same flawed relationship she had with her own mother was devastating. She was jarred from her painful thoughts when Nancy, Mrs. Mick's neighbor, took the seat beside her with a plate loaded with desserts.

"You okay, little mommy?" Nancy asked. "You look overwhelmed."

"Just amazed at all these gifts," Darcy lied. "You guys shouldn't have gone to so much trouble."

Really, they shouldn't have, because Darcy knew that cold, detached mothers like her mother, like the mother she was becoming, didn't deserve any of this.

57

Lindsay

"Behold, the Diaper Genie—magical processor of poop!" Skeeter Fogarty lifted the plastic contraption, which reminded me of a lunar space module for a mouse, and placed it on the table with a grin. The presents had been opened, the sparkling cider served, and most everyone at Darcy's baby shower had finished eating, and the conversation paused now as Skeeter captured the guests' attention. "I shall demonstrate. God knows, I've packed enough of these with my kids' diapers. Does anyone here have a doody?"

"I do!" His brother Johnny pressed his right hand over his chest. "I was a Boy Scout. I promised to do my duty, every day."

"Not that kind of doody, you bonehead." Skeeter rolled his eyes. "We'll have to improvise. Okay, so what else can we stuff in? Old socks? Styrofoam packing chips? Mrs. McCorkle's Irish meatballs? Just kidding, Mrs. Mick. Okay, so you start by opening the hatch here, stuff in the baby's poopy diaper, though in this case these packing peanuts will work just fine. Press 'em in as far as you can—really get your arm in there. Then you put this little top on, twist and . . . voila! No smelly diapers in sight!"

People clapped and laughed.

"But wait!" Skeeter interrupted.

"There's more!" Johnny added.

"The next time you got a doody diaper, you pop it in, twist the top, and just go about your business." He demonstrated with balled-up gift wrap, repeating three more times. "Easy as that, folks. And then, here's my favorite part, the final product." Skeeter opened the hatch on the bottom of the Diaper Genie and pulled out a string of white plastic bulges. "Sausage links."

"Only it's not really sausage," Johnny added. "So don't eat it."

"Stanky! Who'd want to eat lumps of baby poo?"

"You called it a sausage. Lots of people eat sausage links. I love those little half-smokes."

"Speak for yourself," Skeeter said to his brother. "Personally, I like my links full size, if you know what I mean . . ."

"Okay, guys, let's keep it clean," Steve McCorkle interrupted, taking the diaper machine from Skeeter and walking it over to the heap of gifts.

"Who invited them?" I asked Ma as I stacked empty paper plates.

"Everyone is welcome at the McCorkle house, you know that." My mother laughed at the demonstration as she adjusted the brakes on the Rolls Royce of strollers and moved it behind the couch. "You boys are too much!"

"I have a trick I can do, if anyone can loan me a fifty dollar bill. Anyone interested?" Skeeter announced, but people shook their heads. "Oh, come on. What have you got to lose, besides fifty bucks?"

Watching them joke around, I felt a sore spot for Bear. Of all Steve's friends, why was he the one who'd left town and shacked up with some girl in Hawaii? "Bear's got an island bride," Skeeter was saying one day in the lineup, much to my alarm. "He truly is the Great Kahouna." When I went to Steve for verification, he just shrugged. "I don't know. I think he would have mentioned if he got hooked up with her. Why? Did you want to send a blender or something?"

It would be two years, this September.

Sure, I had moved on, and I was dating a really great guy now, but I still missed Bear. Maybe because we'd been friends, too.

"I hope you boys appreciate all the work that went into this affair." My mother pretended to scold Skeeter as he helped himself from the buffet table. "My Irish meatballs included."

I grabbed an empty tray and headed into the kitchen. "At least we managed to keep them out until after all the gifts were opened,"

I told Tara, who was gathered at the kitchen table with her boyfriend, John Sharkey. They sat across from Milo and Darcy, the four of them lapping up the last of the Coney's Banana Flambé that I had made for the group.

"I like this new tradition of having men at baby showers," Ma said as she rinsed glasses in the kitchen sink. "In my day, it was all women, and the amount of oohs and aahs over each little pacifier that was opened was enough to put a person in sugar shock."

"I think that's how showers still go in my family, Mrs. McCorkle," Sharkey said. Tara had met attorney John Sharkey through her father almost six months ago, and much to Mr. and Mrs. Washington's delight, one date had evolved into a steady relationship. I found Sharkey very entertaining, always regaling us with tales of people he'd helped and injustices he'd righted. An active proponent for equal rights, Sharkey had emerged over the years as a spokesman for African Americans at rallies and marches, boycotts and fundraisers. While Tara agreed with his mission in theory, she had confided to us that he sometimes made her feel guilty for not being as involved in the campaign as he was. Today he was in fine form.

"In my family," he went on, "men are kept away from the business of child rearing, and that's fine by me. My sisters have had three babies in the last five years, and they wouldn't let me within a mile of the baby showers. That's female business."

"And did the dads help in the delivery room?" Tara asked.

"You kidding me? They want nothing to do with it. My brother-in-law, Vince, he thought he'd step up and help my sister out, but one look at Mother Nature and he was out. That brother went down—all two hundred pounds of him."

Ma and I exchanged an amused look. "I hope I can hold it together for you, Darcy," I said. Darcy had asked me to be her labor coach, and we'd been attending childbirth classes together—a new experience for both of us. We practiced the breathing techniques in class with a great deal of skepticism. One day Darcy even raised her hand and asked, "Can't we all just get a whopping dose of pain meds?"

"Just make sure you're there," Darcy told me now. "I'm not going to be very kind when some nurse tells me to blow tiny breaths and forget that my body is being torn in half."

"Can we not go there?" Wincing, Milo dropped a fork onto his empty plate. "I swear, men just aren't built to tolerate thoughts like that."

"I'm with you, Milo," Sharkey agreed. "When I'm a father, I'll be quite content to wait outside with a box of cigars."

"You're so old school," Tara teased him.

He pushed away from the table and untucked his tie from his shirt pocket. "You got that right. Now, if you'll excuse me, I'm going out front to talk about manly things. Baseball and circular saws. Not to mention Brownie Beaver. My nieces will be devastated if I don't get an autograph." Elle was outside with her boyfriend Ricardo, who played a beaver on *Woodchuck Village*, a PBS show that was gaining popularity among preschool kids.

"He's not in costume," Milo told him, "but look for the tall, winsome gentleman who could be Antonio Banderas's twin." Milo also worked with Ricardo, as Elle had brought him into the studio a few months ago to assist the set builders and he'd worked his way up to assistant set designer.

"Ask him to sing you the one about Beaver's teeth-brushing tips. It's very cute," I said.

Sharkey headed out the screen door, adding, "I live for it."

"Aw, he's a keeper," Ma crowed. "Very polite."

"Thanks, Mrs. Mick," Tara said.

"Ma, you like every boy who comes around here." I was careful to reserve my own comments as I removed a tray of cheese tarts from the oven and set them on the stove to cool. Zack and I had gone out with Tara and Sharkey a few times, for dinner and drinks, and I'd found the man just a little too flashy and full of himself for the judicious Tara. Everywhere we went, he tried to monopolize the conversation with stories about cases he'd taken pro bono. He insisted on ordering apple martinis for everyone, then stuck Zack and me with the bill.

"If a man has good manners, I admit I'm a pushover," my mother admitted.

"He's got my vote, Tara," Darcy said, pushing herself up from the table. "Okay, I'm going to go out there and act maternal again. Madonna's got nothing on me."

Milo followed her. "I'm going with you. Time to say my good-byes if I'm going to meet my friends on Shelter Island."

Steve passed them on his way in and went straight to the tray of tarts. "I love these things," he said, grabbing one.

"They're for the guests!" I insisted.

"So? I'm a guest, Gidget. Man . . . this is hot." He juggled it over to the table and took a seat beside Tara. "Hey, T. What's new in the world of politics?"

She shrugged, a light in her dark eyes. "Same old bureaucratic bullshit."

"Sounds tedious. You still thinking about a career change?"

"She already took her LSAT," I butted in. "Columbia Law wants her in the fall."

"I've been accepted there," Tara said, her eyes on Steve. "But it's not like I was their number-one draft choice or anything."

He nodded. "So it'll be law, like the old man."

"Yeah, the apple falls near the tree. I know it's boring, but I think it's a good match for my skills."

"It's a great match." Steve broke the tart in two and held one steaming half up to his lips. "You deserve better than what you've got. I mean, in the senator's office."

My eyes went wide at the obvious chemistry between them. Steve was flirting, and Tara was flirting right back at him.

"You should give me a call sometime, in the city," he was saying. "Maybe we could hook up for lunch or something."

"Maybe . . ." She glanced over at the screen door, obviously thinking of Sharkey. "Did you meet my boyfriend? John Sharkey. He's a civil rights attorney."

"Heard about him," Steve said. "But who hasn't? His face is on the evening news every time there's an allegation that someone farted in the wrong direction."

"Steve!" I said.

"All I ask for is a modicum of manners . . ." Ma shook her head. "My own children . . ."

But Tara was laughing. "I agree, New York's flatulence statutes are simply archaic."

Steve swiped another cheese tart and headed into the living room. "So call me sometime."

"What was that about?" I asked Tara as I dished the tarts onto a platter.

Tara laughed. "I really don't know."

"Flirtation is harmless," Ma said, drying a bowl.

"But you've got Sharkey," I said.

"And you've got Zack," Tara said. "And Elle is in love with Ricardo, and Darcy is with Kevin . . . some of the time." Darcy was less than enchanted with Kevin's position as a New York City firefighter, a job he'd embraced wholeheartedly, loving the excitement, the hero potential, the camaraderie of the firehouse. I suspected it was probably a very good thing for Kevin to be far from his father and his Hamptons crowd, but all Darcy could see was that he was working in a civil service job, living in an apartment on Staten Island. "Staten Island . . . didn't they secede from the rest of New York City? Aren't they part of Bayonne or Jersey or something?" Although Darcy focused on criticizing his choices, I suspected the real issue was that he kept pushing her to marry him, and she wasn't comfortable with that idea.

I wasn't sure if Darcy and Kevin belonged together, but for now, it was kind of fun to see my friends paired off with guys. "Finally, a summer when we're all dating someone," I said. "And professional guys. Lawyer, actor, stockbroker, and firefighter. I feel so grown-up."

Although I had planned to stay behind and help Ma clean up while my friends went ahead to Elle's house, my mother pushed me out, insisting that she had plenty of help from her neighbor Nancy and two other friends who'd seemed happy for an excuse to get together. "You just scoot and let the old crones handle this," Ma said. "Besides, your boyfriend doesn't seem to know anyone in the group."

"Zack isn't shy," I assured her. We'd met at a Hamptons party a few weeks ago, where Zack was impressed that I actually stripped down to my bikini and jumped in the pool when temperatures soared to triple digits (as opposed to the other women, who sat around wilting but didn't dare ruin their makeup and hair). He'd challenged me to a race, and I'd almost beat him in the backstroke heat. "You're good," he'd told me that afternoon. I'd smiled and, surprising even myself, zinged him with, "You have no idea how good I can be . . ." And we were off and racing into a relationship.

Back at Elle's, everyone had settled in around the pool, recuperating from too much food as Prince's "1999" played over the pool speakers. "Whoever thought we'd be hearing this song in 1999?" I said as Zack and I crossed the patio. "When it came out, it seemed the year would never arrive."

Zack squinted at me. "What were you, like two?"

Darcy sat at the edge of the pool, swirling her feet in the water while Kevin paced behind her. Obviously, they were arguing again, but no one dared get into that. Elle and Ricardo sat under an umbrella table with earphones hooked into her laptop, picking songs from CDs to make a party mix of music. Tara and Sharkey looked every inch the *Ebony* couple in their straw hats and dark sunglasses, reading quietly and sipping Sharkey's favorite apple martinis.

One look at the complacent pool scene was all it took to send Zack into a twitch. "We need to do something. All this sitting around is getting to me. How about a jog on the beach? Or a round of tennis? Your friend was just saying that no one uses her tennis court."

I agreed to a set of tennis, though I knew he'd win handily. Zack was extremely aggressive and competitive—assets when it came to trading on the floor of the New York Stock Exchange, annoyances during a friendly game of tennis.

"Is that the best you can come back at me with? I'm closing you out," he cried.

"I thought we were playing for fun." I ran backward, jumping to return his serve.

He swiped at it as if the game were effortless. "Fun doesn't mean you stop trying."

Annoyed, I whacked at the ball and sent it driving right for Zack's head. He returned the shot, but I let it bounce past my feet.

"What's wrong?" he asked.

"Listen to yourself. You're goading me."

He retrieved a ball, shaking his head. "No, I don't goad. You're just overly sensitive. You know . . ." He stuffed his pockets with balls. "I've been watching and I've got a word of advice. It's your backhand. You're twisting the racket, angling up. You need to control the ball by controlling your racket. Doesn't that make sense?"

How about I backhand your ass, I thought as a ball sailed past my racket.

"Lindsay?" He adjusted his visor on his dark brush cut. "Are you with me?"

"How about a run on the beach?" I suggested. *I know a towering cliff where I can give you a little push.*

He jumped the net and slung an arm around me. "What? Are you pissed at me?"

I sighed, feeling his muscled body beside me, his hand fingering my ponytail. *Give Zack a little time, he knows not what he does,* I thought. "I'm sick of competing with you," I said. "How about a little indoor exercise?" I went up on my toes and nibbled at the lobe of his ear. "This time, I want you on my team."

58

The Love Mansion

"Tell me, Elle." Hands clasped behind him, Ricardo surveyed the gallery of small postcards from around the world that Elle had framed and mounted on one of her bedroom walls. "Why do your friends call your home the Love Mansion?"

Elle laughed. "Well, it used to belong to Buford and Melanie Love, Darcy's parents, but she's always said that there was no love under this roof. So . . . after I bought it, I made the joke that it would really become the love mansion, now that my friends and I were going to live here." As she spoke she popped in the new CD, found the track for "Pink" by Aerosmith, and cranked up the volume.

Ricardo started moving in time to the music, subtly at first, but even the smallest movement of his tall, lean body seemed so expressive. Perhaps it was because of his theatrical training, or because he'd spent the past two years inhabiting an oversized Beaver costume and performing physical humor, but Ricardo possessed total control of his body. He knew how to move to elicit various reactions on the dance floor, and this gift, Elle had discovered, much to her delight, translated well in the bedroom. She snuck up behind him, moving in synch until the song ended.

"I can't believe this is all yours," he said, gesturing to the house. "What I mean to say is, I'm very happy for you, but why would someone with this extent of wealth want to be a line producer for

Woodchuck Village? Why would you want to listen to those inane songs all day and put up with Isabel's vile temper on the set? Why would you want to toil for a single summer day in the oven of Manhattan when you can live here as a princess?"

She rose on her toes, reaching up to hang from his shoulders. "Sometimes princesses like to escape their castles," she said, thinking how the job on *Woodchuck Village* had given her something she could sink her teeth in, a demanding job that consumed her time and her focus whenever they were taping, which was usually four days a week. "I get bored easily, and that job keeps me out of trouble. Besides, I like some of your songs."

"Please . . . they're not my songs, I only sing them." He rolled his dark eyes. "Preschool drivel."

"Who's the beaver with the pudgy brown nose?" Elle sang as she worked Ricardo's T-shirt up over his lean abdomen.

"And another thing I've been meaning to ask you, Elle." His voice wasn't accented, but it held that Latino lilt that always made Elle smile. "Must you always introduce me as Brownie Beaver?"

"Who's the beaver who is losing his clothes?"

"Hey . . ." He raised his arms so she could pull the shirt over his head. "Those are not the words to my theme song."

"It's . . . Brownie Beaver, every girl's best friend, Brownie Beaver, watch his paddle spank your tail end—"

He pulled his lips away from kissing her neck to end her song with a kiss. "Enough of the bastardized song," he said, plunging his slender fingers into her bikini bottoms. "Let us locate the real beaver among us."

Lindsay

The first time I had sex with Zack reminded me of my first session with a personal trainer at the gym. He was patient, but he pushed me hard, wanting the best for me, encouraging me to try new positions. I was just getting used to his habit of stopping the momentum to call a switch, barking, "Get on top!" or "Let me get you from behind!" or "Raise your hips!"

Zack was truly a workout, but he also drove himself hard, and just running my fingers over his rippling muscles or leaning into his six-pack abs was a supreme aphrodisiac for me. Tight butt, flat stomach, muscles like stone—Zack had the body, all right, and I felt sexy just cuddling against him. Inside the bathroom I could hear the shower still running. "Hurry it up in there!" I called, kicking off my sneakers.

Standing in front of the oval mirror in the attic room, now my official summer abode, I slipped out of my white tennis skirt and pale pink tie-dyed shirt and stretched to the ceiling. My shoulders were a little pink, but the rest of my skin already had the warm golden tan of summer, stark against my white sports bra and bikini underwear. It was such a relief to have normal-sized breasts and a body that responded to a low-fat diet and regular workouts. Zack would never had been attracted to my former fat self, and the chubby Lindsay would never had stripped down and jumped into the pool the day we met.

I crossed to the gazebo turret, the tall window that afforded a view of the dark blue ocean nipping away at sand, probably half a mile away. Folding one leg under me, I sat down and considered opening my laptop. When I'd moved my summer clothes out here last week, I'd spent a few hours writing at this desk, putting together notes that, I hoped, would string into an outline, then into a novel. This would be the summer of my inspiration, the summer I created a best-seller. About what, I wasn't quite sure, but I'd begun by writing about a series of dates from hell, the last six guys I'd dated before I'd met Zack. Six losers. Some of the accounts were funny, others downright pathetic. Too offbeat to match up with my current job, working on manuscripts for Island Books' new Windswept Island line of romance. Category romance. "It's a huge market in book publishing, and Island Books needs to get in it," Jorge had told me when he'd taken me off hardcover editorial and assigned me to assist the new editor, Allessandra Beckett. The idea had seemed so exciting until I spent a week watching Allessandra finger her toes as she read, photocopying manuscripts because everything was "Rush, rush!" according to our publisher Jorge Melendez, and ordering tuna sandwiches and turkey burgers to keep Allessandra from having low blood sugar. That was the extent of my last three months. (That and answering the phones for "Windswept Island Romances," but since Allessandra apparently had no life beyond romance publishing, the only calls came from my mother and friends.)

I pulled my knees up to my chin and stared out at the foaming ocean, thinking of Allessandra, the romance editor with no romance in her life. Poor girl.

Just then Zack emerged from the shower, a towel draped over his shoulders as he raised his arms in victory. "Let the games begin!"

I sprang from the chair and jumped into his arms, loving the way he could catch me with one arm. Poor Allessandra the spinster could wait. Right now, I needed a workout.

"You ready to ride?" he asked.

I smacked my thigh with a decadent smile. "Giddy-up, cowboy!"

"While I'm out here, I'd like to check out some of the local establishments, see if they're complying with hiring practices." Sharkey sat up, the sheets bunched below his waist. The silvery sheen of perspiration on his chocolate brown skin gave Tara thoughts of running her tongue over his chest yet again. "Want to come along?"

"Maybe." Tara stretched leisurely, her body still thrumming pleasantly from their lovemaking. The sheet fell down, revealing one tawny breast, but Sharkey didn't notice anymore; he turned and slid his feet to the floor, calculating his next plan. "I'll bet a lot of the restaurants out here hire illegal immigrants. Those people need to be apprised of their rights, though it's going to be difficult to get to them without scaring them off."

Tara reached for him but her arm fell on flat sheets as he was on his feet, pacing.

"I need to research the demographics of Suffolk County . . ."

She sat up in bed. "Can't you ever turn it off?"

"There's been a black community out here for years, but I'm not sure if—"

"Hello? Sharkey . . ."

"What? What is it?" he snapped.

"I sort of wanted to cuddle for a few minutes," she said plaintively.

"Oh." He lifted the sheets and slid back into bed. "How's that?" he asked, stretching out beside her, still tense.

"Better. But I can see I'm gonna have to work you over to make you relax." She pushed him onto his belly and straddled him. "Maybe a little massage? You need to work the kinks out."

"Mmm. Feels fantastic. Girl, you just start pounding me if you hear me reciting labor law."

"Are you sure it's still okay?" Kevin asked as he slid off the bed to remove his shorts and Jockeys.

"I'm still a month from my due date and the nurse in my child-birth class says intercourse is fine." Darcy lifted her hips to peel off her bikini underpants. When they'd fallen back into the marriage argument, Darcy never expected this day to end with a lovemaking session, especially when Kevin started with the ultimatums: "Marry me or else . . . I'll never speak to you again . . . I'll take off in that Jeep and never look back . . . I'll go back to drinking." She didn't believe any of it, and in any case, she had to stick by her instincts, which strongly indicated this was not the time for marriage. "Give me one good reason not to get married right now . . . today?" he'd insisted, and she'd answered, "I'd look fat in my wedding dress."

After she'd convinced Kevin not to mess with a pregnant woman and her raging hormones, he'd apologized so sweetly and he'd started kissing her and touching her. And when she suggested that they do it, he didn't seem at all repulsed. Just cautious.

He stretched out alongside her. "You're sure I'm not going to, like, bonk the little guy?"

She laughed as she reached for him. "Don't flatter yourself."

"Okay, then . . ." He pressed her back into the pillows and they picked up where they'd left off kissing and caressing.

When Darcy thought she could wait no more, she slid down to the edge of the low bed, turning away from the mound of tummy looming before her. Kevin kneeled on the floor, positioned himself between her legs, and pushed in.

With a happy gasp, Darcy let her fingers close over the ruffled edge of the shams. She'd been wanting this, wanting to make love, and even if she and Kevin didn't always see eye to eye, she did enjoy being with him.

"Everything okay?" Kevin asked, breaking the rhythm.

"Perfect," she assured him. Her life was spinning out of her control, her belly expanding into a Wonder Ball, but at this moment, everything seemed just fine. Closing her eyes, she imagined she was back in time, suspended in a lazy, warm afternoon of last summer.

59

Lindsay

When I made the appointment to meet with Island Books publisher Jorge Melendez, the agenda had been career guidance, a move back to hardcover editorial and tips on how to break in as a writer. Elle's "Uncle Jorge" had a reputation for mentoring people in publishing, pushing employees up from the ranks, bringing editors into sales and marketing meetings to give them a full picture of the industry. But when I stepped into his office, I made the key mistake of forgetting that the romance line, Windswept Island, was his pride and joy.

"So how goes it with Allessandra?" Jorge asked, gesturing for me to take a seat. "Are you learning all kinds of new things?"

Only that Allessandra liked to kick off her shoes and run her fingertips over her toenails while she read manuscripts. That and where to get the best tuna sandwiches in town.

"I'm trying," I said enthusiastically as I perched on the edge of the love seat. As publisher, Jorge had a full suite of furniture in his office, while lowly assistants like me worked in a cubby with a two-drawer file cabinet, desk, and secretarial chair. "Allessandra is kind of quiet, though, and it's hard to learn from watching someone read."

Jorge's laugh was like a rumbling tuba. "I suspect that's true. We're very happy with Allessandra."

So much for lodging my complaints, I thought, queasy at the thought of those tuna wrappers stinking up the office.

"She came on board, brought in some heavyweight romance writers—figuratively and literally, I hear—and she got those manuscripts in the pipeline right away." As he spoke, Jorge pinged a small statue on his desk, making the hula girl dance. "We've gotten great feedback from the field. Orders higher than anticipated. Fingers crossed, but if this takes off the way I anticipate, you'll have a nice future with Windswept Island books."

"Great!" I forced a smile, though the romance line was the last place I wanted to be working. I'd read the first fifty pages of Allessandra's acquisitions to write cover copy, and the books possessed a cookie-cutter sameness that drove me mad. That and the fact that the two protagonists—"the hero and heroine," Allessandra continually corrected me—were just about perfect, their big flaws being a weakness for chocolate or their inability to say no when someone abandoned yet another lost kitten on their doorstep, or fear of falling in love again because they'd been hurt so much before. Big fucking deal.

"So . . ." Jorge glanced up from the hula girl statue. "You said you have a few questions?"

"Right." Quickly reassessing, I knew it would be a mistake to beg him to get me away from Allessandra and the cookie-cutter romances. "Actually . . . I'm working on a book of my own," I blurted out, surprising myself.

"Fabulous." He was unfazed. "I've published two of my editors before, both successes. What genre are you writing in?"

Genre? "Well, right now it's comedy. Comedy sprinkled with angst."

"They say there's always truth and pain in the best comedy," Jorge said. "But comedy isn't really a category of fiction."

He extended a hand as if waiting for me to pick up the ball.

"Oh, sure . . . right." I nodded in that bullshitty way I knew he would see through.

"Is it romance? Suspense? Romantic suspense? A thriller? Fantasy? Sci-fi?"

Again, the bullshitty nod. "So far, I'm leaning toward satirical fiction . . . sort of like the early Susan Isaacs."

"Aaah!" Now he was giving me the bullshitty nod. "Women's fiction. Excellent, but maybe difficult to market as a first novel."

My bullshitty nod was losing momentum, much like the hula dancer on his desk.

"You may want to think about trying something easier to market, and branch out from there." He tweaked his chin thoughtfully. "I've got it. How about a category romance? A snappy short contemporary? You can incorporate your rapier wit and your new knowledge of the rules of the genre."

Those damned rules. Allessandra kept talking about them as if they were listed on the cover of each book. "You can't have a romance where a child dies; it's against the rules," she'd say. Or, "The hero can't sleep with another woman, unless, of course, it was in the past or he's doing it to save the heroine's life." A shake of the head, a look of scorn. "You just can't break the rules that way."

I half expected Allessandra to drop a list of rules on my desk one morning, but then that would divert her from the steady mechanics of reading, editing, reading, editing . . .

"Would you like to try your hand at a romance?" Jorge prodded.

"That's a great idea," I lied. Honestly, I couldn't think of anything worse.

"Here's what I propose." He clapped his hands together in prayer position. "You set to work on your category romance. With our summer hours you can spend extra-long weekends at your Hamptons getaway, writing to your heart's desire. Put something together over the next few months and I'll take a look at it personally."

"Jorge, I'd really appreciate that," I said, secretly horrified at the slippery romance chute I'd just fallen down. I stood up, realizing the meeting was over, that I'd have to return to old Tuna Breath and spinning cover copy about candy-coated dilemmas.

"I must say, I'm simply delighted with this development." Jorge straightened his tie as he walked me to the door.

"Me, too," I said in the squeaky voice of a liar. Then, realizing my grammar gaffe, I corrected, "As am I."

With a nervous smile, I turned and trudged down the hall, realizing my future in publishing, as both an editor and a writer, was doomed.

60

Elle

Elle sat cross-legged in the chair at the console, rocking along with the music being recorded by two of her favorite people in the world, Darcy and Ricardo. Darcy wore a black A-line dress with white piping that could have been Dior, the pleated skirt demure under her large belly. Ricardo, in his low-slung jeans and avocado green T-shirt, looked like a tall tree beside her.

> *"Look both ways before you cross the river,*
> *Look both ways before you head for land,*
> *Don't turn back, don't shake and quiver,*
> *Just look both ways and things will be just grand."*

Darcy and Ricardo sang together, their eyes on the music, their ears capped with headphones as Elle nodded in time from the other side of the glass at the studio control panel.

The volume lowered on the musical accompaniment, and Darcy turned to Ricardo, looking genuinely perplexed.

"But, Brownie, uh . . . just one more thing . . ." Darcy said in the giddy Delilah Fox voice she'd been hired to do in voice-over. Delilah's body was a small puppet, a silvery fox with an orange bow, played by a heavyset male puppeteer known as Jukes, whose heavy, burly voice was just unacceptable for the role. But Jukes had already been hired on to play two other puppet characters in

Woodchuck Village, so Elle convinced the executive producer, the wicked Isabel Slater, creator of Brownie Beaver, to let her hire Darcy to do Delilah's voice-overs.

"What's that, Delilah?" Brownie asked.

"Now that I'm across the river, I forgot where I'm supposed to go! I think I need to go back and ask Daddy Fox for directions," Darcy chirped.

"That's fine, Delilah," said Ricardo in a voice so warm, Elle wanted to burst into the studio and grip him in a huge hug. "But before you cross the river, what are you going to do?"

The music swelled again as Darcy and Ricardo sang, "Look both ways before you cross the river . . ."

Elle closed her eyes and grooved to the corny, warmhearted tune. Whenever she met twentysomethings who found out that she worked on *Woodchuck Village*, they razzed her and mocked Brownie's popularity, but Elle didn't care. She'd grown genuinely attached to the warm, homey quality of Brownie and his *Woodchuck Village* friends. The sweet, earnest characters, the innocent, instructional songs, and the tidy miniature village itself, a mishmash of nature and cubism done in brilliant blues, bold greens, and warm oranges and pinks—it was all the perfect home, a place where characters cared about one another and problems could be easily fixed with a song or an apology. For Elle, Woodchuck Village was the place to be.

Okay, so the executive producer was a bitch, and Elle's day was always riddled with a zillion obstacles . . . like how to transport a walrus into the studio when no refrigerated trucks were available. Or how to come up with enough work for the puppeteers so they could afford to quit their other jobs to be on set full time. Or how to get underwater footage of real beavers eating that wouldn't appear too frightening to toddlers as they eviscerated fish. But Elle rose to each challenge. She'd learned that boredom was dangerous for her, and the demands of producing a low-budget show kept her hopping.

Of course, there was the added bonus of falling in love with Brownie Beaver himself, Ricardo Bonet. A classically trained actor, Ricardo was a master of physical humor, and often Elle felt that his expressions could give voice to her own emotions as he portrayed Brownie feeling left out by his friends, feeling alone in the world, or romping merrily at a party. Sometimes, admittedly, she confused the actions of Ricardo and Brownie, but Elle rationalized that Ricardo had to have a deep understanding of this material to interpret it so well.

As the song ended Lloyd, the studio engineer, gave Darcy and Ricardo a thumbs-up and they took off their headsets and emerged from the glassed-in studio.

"Nice job," Lloyd told them. "Your vocals work well together. I think Isabel's going to like this. She might want to include this on the CD."

Executive producer Isabel Slater was a cranky spinster, former schoolteacher who considered herself an expert on children and entertainment. Although Elle thought she was a miserable person, she figured Isabel must have at least a scintilla of love in her heart to have created the world of *Woodchuck Village*. But was that any excuse for treating her staff like dirt?

"Isabel will criticize my voice and claim that Elle hired Darcy out of nepotism," Ricardo predicted. "Then she'll go home, drink a glass of sherry, and decide that it was a brilliant idea to hire a woman to do Delilah's voice. Her brilliant idea."

"I don't care if she takes all the credit," Darcy said, shrugging. "Just as long as I get my cut on the CD."

"Actor's Equity . . . you're in!" Elle assured her as they headed out of the recording booth to hook up with Milo, who was working on set downstairs.

A few minutes later they were seated at a small Greenwich Village restaurant just around the corner from where the show was taped, a mandarin red–themed room with tables so close you could share your spring rolls with the people dining beside you.

"Cozy," Darcy said, struggling to pull closer to the table without bumping it with her belly.

"We call it the Woodchuck cafeteria. We eat here so often, I could recite the menu in my sleep, but the food is great, and we love Chioki and Kim," Milo said, smiling up at their waitress, apparently Chioki.

As they ordered a few dishes to share, Ricardo's cell phone rang. "It's my mother," he said, recognizing the number. "I must take it." He flipped it open and moved away from the table.

Elle watched him pace nervously as he talked in rapid-fire

Spanish, turning away and finally ducking out the door to the street. "Mom's apron strings are thousands of miles long," Elle said. "It's a wonder Ricardo hasn't been strangled in them yet."

"But she's in Puerto Rico, isn't she?" asked Darcy.

"His whole family is still there. And I do like the fact that he respects his parents. I just feel like it's hard to break in. Families usually adore me, but I don't have a chance with his. Unless I can get them to come for a visit." She split her chopsticks apart and rubbed them together. "Now there's an idea."

"They could all stay in the Love Mansion," Milo said as he passed around the beef satay. "They'll think you're a wealthy American princess."

"She is a wealthy American princess," Darcy said, grinning at Elle. "The title I used to aspire to."

"Darce, they retired the crown with you," Elle shot back at her as Darcy took a beef stick from the platter and bit her bottom lip. Elle wondered if she'd gone a little too far.

"Oh, don't get weepy on us," Elle said, trying to play it cool. "You've been through a string of bad luck, but you're still the princess in my book."

"Just having a cramp. My back has been aching all day. I guess I'm just not used to the commute to Manhattan anymore." Darcy squeezed her eyes shut and gripped the table.

"Cramps?" Milo winced. "Pregnant women don't get cramps." He swung toward Elle. "Do they?"

Elle exchanged a panicked look with him and shrugged. "What the hell do I know? Darcy, are you okay?"

She nodded. "Yeah. It's going away now." She took a deep breath. "I'm fine."

"Do you want to call your doctor?" Milo suggested. "I mean, feeling sick and we didn't even get to the appetizers yet."

"It's a little too early to call," Darcy said. "I mean, if it's the beginning of labor, the hospital probably won't admit me for another twelve hours."

Milo's satay froze on the way to his mouth, and Elle swallowed an ice cube. "Labor?" they cried in unison.

"Don't flip out. I said *if*." Darcy put the meat stick on her plate and stood up. "I'm going to hit the restroom while you two try to calm each other."

One minute Elle was dipping her beef in hot sauce, the next she noticed Darcy just standing there, standing over a puddle on the restaurant's red tile floor.

"What the hell . . ." Elle looked at the puddle, then back up at Darcy, who seemed equally surprised that her legs were dripping wet under the perfect pleats of her black Dior maternity dress.

Darcy pressed her hands to her face and spoke the words that incited panic in Elle's heart: "Looks like my water broke."

61

Darcy

"**Y**ou guys make about as much sense as Fred and Ethel in a rerun of *I Love Lucy*," Darcy said as they finally were strapped into Elle's Jeep and headed uptown. "Don't you know that babies aren't born in five minutes? Especially to a first-time mother."

"I don't know nothin' about birthin' no babies," Elle said.

"Wrong genre, wrong medium," Darcy said from the back seat.

"Can I be Ethel?" Milo asked. "I've always found Fred so abrupt and domineering."

"Don't you want to stretch out back there?" Elle suggested, looking in the rearview mirror.

"It's better if I stay upright, keep active, so that I dilate. Now that the water's broken, the baby really needs to come in the next twenty-four hours."

Milo gripped the armrests in the front seat, staring forward. "All this technical talk is making me really, really nervous about this. Darcy, you don't want the baby born in the backseat of Elle's Jeep between Park and Madison."

"Just get me out of Manhattan and back to the sanity of the Hamptons." Darcy had already spoken with Lindsay, who had this Friday off for summer hours and was writing away in the attic room. "Call me as soon as you get to Montauk Highway and I'll meet you at Southampton Hospital," Lindsay told her. Holding on to the handgrip as another pain seized her, Darcy mentally reviewed the things she was supposed to do when the contractions started. Stop eating. Stay hydrated. Don't bother calling the doctor or timing contractions until they start coming closer together. "First-time mothers take hours, sometimes days to go through the stages of childbirth, the dilation and thinning," her childbirth instructor had said. "So be patient, and don't run around like a crazy person."

As Elle and Milo were doing.

"Last chance," Elle said as the car crawled toward the Midtown Tunnel. "Are you sure you don't want us to check you into a hospital in Manhattan?"

"I've heard New York Hospital is the best," Milo said, "but Bellevue can work if you're a downtown girl."

"Southampton Hospital is perfect," Darcy said. "Just keep driving."

Traffic was slow. They rolled to a stop in the tunnel, where the air felt stuffy and stale. Darcy wasn't sure how long they were stopped, but she was starting to break a sweat despite the air-conditioning, and the labor pains seemed to boomerang back all too fast. By the time they made it out of the tunnel, the pain was hitting her hard, pummeling her through the middle.

"How long is this trip going to take?" she asked, squirming to find a more comfortable position in the car seat.

"On a summer Friday afternoon? I'm afraid to think about it." Elle bit her lower lip as she glanced at the dashboard. "Are you sure you're okay? Darcy, you're dripping with sweat."

Darcy was looking at the clock on the car dashboard, timing the contractions. "I think it's happening too fast. It hurts like hell, and at this rate, we're not going to make it to the Hamptons."

"Call the doctor!" Elle barked.

"I'm timing the contractions," Darcy gasped, trying to breathe through the pain.

Milo fumbled with his cell phone. "I'll call, I'll call. What's his number?"

"Dr. Stacey White." She handed her cell forward, unable to focus on numbers now.

When Milo reached the doctor, it was decided that they'd better get out of traffic and stop at a hospital on the way. "Stop at

North Shore," Milo repeated from the phone. "Or LIJ. LIJ? What's an LIJ?"

"Long Island Jewish," Darcy said, remembering the lay of the land from her Great Egg upbringing. "But we're closer to North Shore now. Take the Manhasset exit . . . you'll see a hospital sign."

Just knowing relief was closer helped Darcy cope a little better. By the time Elle pulled up to the ER entrance she felt able to walk, but the nurse insisted on a wheelchair.

While Elle waited outside, a resident came into the curtained area to conduct a torturous exam, pronouncing Darcy dilated to eight centimeters. "That's fairly far along for a first-timer," she said encouragingly. "Have you been doing your breathing?"

"The breathing is crap." Darcy propped herself up on her fists and growled, "Get me the epidural."

There was a bad patch of pain, wheeling to maternity. Elle jogged alongside her, tucking into the oversized elevator and following down the hall to the maternity ward and her very own birthing suite.

"Wow, you get a room with a couch?" Elle said as she washed up and slipped scrubs over her clothes.

"I need drugs," Darcy cried, split by pain.

Elle flagged down a nurse, who tried to keep Darcy focused on breathing. At last, Dr. Jennifer Cho, the ob-gyn on call, introduced herself, along with the anesthesiologist, who appeared with his kit to administer the epidural. The magic potion was inserted, to almost immediate relief, and Darcy relaxed, happy to breathe and be human again.

"Is that better?" Elle asked tentatively when the room quieted at the end of a contraction.

"Much." She suddenly noticed her petite friend, swimming in oversized scrubs, her green eyes wide with curiosity. "I can't believe it's down to the two of us. After all this, you're going to help me deliver this baby."

"Stuck with me again." Elle gave a nervous laugh. "Are you scared?"

Darcy shook her head. "Not about this." She took a breath as the pressure mounted. "It's all the stuff that comes after that frightens the hell out of me."

"I'll be there," Elle said as the doctor ordered Darcy to take a deep breath and push. "I'll help you with the baby."

"Sounds like you have an experienced friend here," Dr. Cho said through her mask.

"Who, me?" Elle shook her head, her silver earrings wiggling. "Nope. No experience. But lots of good intentions."

"No experience required," Darcy said before bracing herself for a major push.

62

Tara

"I can't wait to meet her." Tara pressed her shoulder up to hold her cell to her ear while she caught a stack of bills from the ATM. "A baby girl!"

"Maisy Chayse Love," Darcy said, sounding a little tired. "Chayse after my grandmother, the one who used to take me for tea at the Plaza. Everyone thinks she's very sweet."

"What's she doing right now?" Tara asked as she tucked her wallet away and headed toward the subway.

"Sleeping. She tends to sleep all day and wants to party all night."

"Just like her mother," Tara teased.

"Not anymore. Honestly, when three in the morning rolls around and she stares at me and gives a little howl, I'm in no mood to party." Darcy paused, yawning. "But I wanted to make sure you're coming tomorrow."

"I'm on my way to meet Sharkey right now and we're headed out that way. Going to some church social tonight near Freeport, but we'll be there tomorrow. If you're up for it."

"Looking forward to it," Darcy said. "I'm glad Elle arranged for everyone to get together. I'd never be able to do it now; I can barely hold a thought for ten seconds. What was I saying?"

"I'll be there, and I'll take that sweet baby out of your hands while you go and take a nap or something."

"Like that's going to happen."

* * *

"I'm here to see John Sharkey," Tara told the heavyset older woman who worked as the receptionist for the Harlem firm.

The woman, Zelda, Tara recalled from previous visits, eyed her suspiciously as if she'd never laid eyes on her before. "And you are . . . ?"

"Tara Washington."

Zelda announced her over the intercom and told Tara to have a seat.

As Tara waited, people passed through the lobby—messengers and attorneys, some familiar faces for Tara. She decided to use the restroom and flipped her jacket onto the banquette but took her purse.

Inside the lavatory stall, she heard two other women come in, complaining about the heat and the fact that they'd used up all their summer vacation days. Then one of the women said, "What's with the white girl sitting in the lobby?"

Tara's hand froze on the stall door.

"Sharkey's girl."

"That brother got him some white ass?"

"That's what I'm saying."

"He ought to think about practicing what he's preaching."

Tara felt cold inside. She knew they were talking about her; she'd been the only woman waiting in the lobby.

And the gossip was all so wrong. She wasn't white, and what would be wrong with John Sharkey dating a woman of another race? Wasn't he a proponent of equal rights for all people—not just African Americans?

That conversation haunted Tara all the way out to Freeport, where Sharkey pulled onto the lawn of a Baptist church, parking amid ranks of cars.

"What's this picnic about?" Tara asked as she negotiated the lumpy grass in her heels. "Since when did you find religion?"

"I was invited by a friend," Sharkey said, smoothing the lapels of his tan suit coat. Tara followed him around to the side of the church, where she spied a banner that read: COALITION FOR THE ADVANCEMENT OF AFRICAN AMERICANS.

"Sharkey . . . no! You've dragged me to one of your political arenas?"

"Just a little barbecue among friends," Sharkey said, waving at someone over by the dessert table. "I just happen to be the guest speaker."

And she'd thought her day couldn't get worse.

She suffered through the speeches and testimonials, the brothers patting each other on the back, and the call to drive racism and Satan to the dark corners of the earth. Finally, Sharkey was introduced, and she had to admit, he was a dynamic motivational speaker. But all the time he spoke, she found herself thinking of the sheen on his dark brown skin, the fine lines of his face and short-cropped 'fro. He was a classically handsome man, but what did people think when they saw him with Tara? Did everyone believe he was dating a white woman?

She wanted to believe that it didn't matter; who cares what people think! But in her heart, she cared. She wanted to fit in somewhere. She wanted to be just a little bit normal.

After the fanfare, their hosts insisted that they partake in the savory barbecued meats. Tara took a few of the smallest ribs she could find, and Sharkey grabbed a barbecued turkey drumstick. After a few guests socialized, she and Sharkey found a spot at the end of the picnic table and settled in to eat, Tara feeling positively wrung out by the events of the day.

She wiped barbecue sauce from her fingers, checking the crowd. "How soon can we leave?" she asked quietly. "I'd like to get to Elle's by midnight."

Sharkey tore a hunk of meat from the turkey leg. "Let's not be rude. I know you didn't want to come here, but it's the sort of thing you need to do if you're going to be with me."

Tara felt stung. Not only had he dragged her here unknowingly, he was now punishing her for not liking it? "I didn't know that being your social secretary was a requirement for dating you. But then I also didn't know I was scandalizing you at the firm." When he gave her a curious look, she went on. "I overheard the receptionist talking with someone. They think you're dating a white girl. And they think it's wrong."

"What do they know?"

"Apparently, they know a few facts, and they've got some very strong opinions for you." She couldn't believe he could just slough it off. "Aren't you going to defend me? Don't you think it's wrong of them to gossip—to judge me that way?"

He kept his eyes lowered, picking at the huge turkey leg. "Really, I don't know what you expect when you dress white and surround yourself with those lily-white friends of yours."

Tara couldn't have been more blindsided if he'd hoisted his turkey leg and whacked her in the head with it. "They're my friends, and what the hell does that mean—dress white? Would you prefer that I put cornrows in my hair and squeeze into something two sizes too small to show off my big black ass?"

He gave her a stern look. "Would you pipe down?"

She lowered her voice but refused to be silenced. "Or maybe I should just strap on an apron and stay at home in the kitchen, where I can refine my recipe for fried chicken, black-eyed peas, and collard greens."

Sharkey laughed. "You caught me on that one, and I am duly chastised. Your friends are very nice people, but I think there's a subliminal pull going on here. Your friends are pulling you away from the issues of people of color. You can make all the excuses you want, but I see you avoiding the Black Caucus, staying away from the community meetings in Harlem, steering clear of events like this. You're not on board, Tara. Now when are you going to stop hiding among your white friends and take a stand for your people?"

"My people?" Tara clenched her fists in frustration. "First off, I think you're hammering a little too hard with your message. I don't think equality is something you can pound into people; social change comes in small growth spurts. It's a long-term process, a growing awareness."

"So you think we should slow down the message?"

"No, but I don't think you should badger people and guilt them into concessions. And I don't think you should label me as the enemy because I'm not on board with all your choices. You know, when my ancestors were singing 'Follow the Drinking Gourd' and looking to the sky to chart their escape from the South by finding the North Star, they couldn't have anticipated the complexity of issues that would evolve from their freedom. I have to admit, I envy them their concrete struggle for freedom."

"Now, don't diminish our cause. The current struggle is concrete, too."

"But you act as if every issue is clear, as if it's all black and white. Don't you see the gray areas?" Tara asked. "The way some individuals use race as an excuse to cash in on lawsuits? The irresponsibility of so many black fathers who fail to be there for their children, let alone support and teach them?"

Sharkey's nostrils flared. "Easy for you to criticize, from your cushy home."

"How about the way I am treated by blacks and whites because the color of my skin makes them unable to determine my race?"

"Back to that." He nodded knowingly. "Your own personal race card. Maybe that's why you don't truly understand the plight of African Americans in this country. When you look white, people are going to treat you better."

"That's not fair," Tara said defensively, but though she protested she knew that no apology could undo the damage. Sharkey, a man who pledged his life to fight for fairness, was being totally unfair toward her.

She stood up from the table, folding her napkin neatly. "Whatever my skin color, I'm still a person." She leaned close, lowering her voice. "And though I used to be your girlfriend, that doesn't give you the right to treat me as anything less."

And with that, she straightened her back, held her head high, and walked away from John Sharkey.

63

Darcy

"And baby makes six," Mary Grace McCorkle said as she snapped yet another shot of the friends posing in the rose arbor.

"Let's take a few." Darcy held her pose on the wicker chair beside Lindsay, who held the bundled baby Maisy as if she were juggling a precious vat of liquid gold. Tara stood behind them, her hands reassuring on Darcy's shoulders as Elle and Milo clowned around on either side, displaying a progression of goofy faces.

"Such a lovely group," Lindsay's mom proclaimed, checking Darcy's camera. "You've only got a few shots left."

"We'll use the whole roll," Darcy told her, feeling as if they'd better get it all down in a snapshot before the earth spun round again and sent them all careening in different directions. She'd had that odd awareness since Maisy's birth, the sense that everything could change in a single moment, and it made her anxious about the future . . . her future.

Since the birth Darcy felt like a ghost of herself, as if her body was going through the motions of life but her soul was floating off in some distant place, waiting to find some meaning in all of it.

The maternal feelings never did kick in at the hospital, and Darcy had struggled on trips to the nursery with other new moms who could find their infants immediately and swore that the bald, skinny baby bawling in its blankets was the best thing ever created.

But Darcy's eye didn't go to her daughter automatically, and when she did find her among the row of infants she was horrified that the little girl to her right was so much prettier and the infant on her left always slept so soundly. And what were those red splotches across her face? Pink bumps with white pus? Infant acne, the nurse said. Definitely unattractive.

Although her friends made a fuss over Maisy's perfection, Darcy just didn't see it. The baby made her tired. The baby wanted to nurse all the time, or so it seemed, and when Darcy tried to soothe her to sleep at night Maisy fixed those luminescent dark blue eyes on Darcy and howled furiously, as if she recognized Darcy's total incompetence as a mother, as a person, and could only proclaim it in a catlike shriek.

You've called my bluff, Darcy wanted to tell the baby, and she had to wonder what was wrong with her, what critical element was missing from her composition, preventing her from loving this little howler she'd created.

"Ma, you need to get into a few shots," Lindsay called out, and Mary Grace handed Milo the camera and gently snatched the baby from Lindsay, cooing to her softly as he snapped a photo. Mrs. Mick was a godsend—a living pacifier.

"And that's the end of the roll," Milo announced.

"Good, because I'm starving." Elle directed the group toward the patio. "Go on and open the wine. I'll put the fish on the grill and Milo's going to toss a salad."

As they headed out of the rose arbor, Tara slipped an arm around Darcy's waist. "How's it going, Mommy?"

"I don't know what the hell I'm doing," Darcy admitted. "I think Maisy hates me, and I can't say that I blame her."

"Getting any sleep?" Tara asked.

"Here and there. Elle's a big help when she's here, and Mrs. Mick is, like, the dream nanny. I'm not complaining. I've got more support than most new mothers, but somehow I just have this horrible feeling that everything I do is wrong."

"I've had a similar week," Tara told her. "Sharkey and I broke it off."

"What?" Darcy was surprised. "I was wondering why he wasn't here."

"He dropped me at my parents' last night," Tara said, "and I don't expect to ever see him again. Which might not be a bad thing."

Darcy and Tara took chairs close to each other, and while Lindsay and her mother cajoled the baby, who was starting to fuss, Tara shared the details of her issues with Sharkey. As she listened, Darcy found it hard to imagine functioning in the dating world again, setting limits, dealing with unfulfilled expectations. But through it all, she felt for Tara, who had been treated unfairly.

"I'm glad you broke up with him," Darcy said when Tara had finished her story. "You're way too good for him."

"And now that it's over," Lindsay added, "I gotta say, he always made me a little uncomfortable, waving those apple martinis around and asking so many questions. I felt like he was going to sue me for some injustice I didn't know I'd committed."

"Sharkey can be intimidating," Tara agreed. "He doesn't realize that I won't let you guys get away with anything."

"You are our voice of reason," Lindsay agreed. "But the way he treated you . . ." She reached into the blanket and raised one of Maisy's tiny fists. "It's just wrong!" she said in a baby voice, shaking the fist.

"Who can understand the mind of a man . . ." Darcy leaned back in the chair, searching the voluminous blue sky for answers. A line of lacy pink clouds skirted the western horizon over a golden sunset, and east, over the ocean, the blue deepened into gradations of mysterious darkness. Yin and yang.

"Do you miss Kevin?" Tara asked.

It was the first time one of her friends had mentioned that Kevin hadn't been around since Maisy was born. He'd slipped into the hospital briefly, dropping off flowers and taking a peek in the nursery, but he didn't seem capable of embracing fatherhood if he couldn't be a full-time father, and Darcy understood. He'd met a girl on Staten Island, he was planting the seeds of a new life that didn't involve Darcy or a newborn baby a hundred miles away. She didn't begrudge him his freedom; the decision to have the baby had been hers alone.

Darcy pulled her blond hair back and twisted it in a knot. "I was just thinking about how some men and women are like oil and water, that they just can't ever mix well. We can coexist together, but that's the best we can hope for. So I guess the answer is that I'll probably miss certain things about Kevin, but right now I don't have the patience to give him attention."

"What a shame, the baby not having a father," Mary Grace said thoughtfully.

"But she has plenty of love," Darcy said firmly, surprised by the conviction in her voice. "Look at all of you, so many aunties and her uncle Milo. It will be enough." *It has to be.*

As if to argue against the motion, Maisy let out a howl.

"I think it's feeding time." Darcy propped up the back of her chair and reached for the baby as Lindsay brought her over. Darcy adeptly lifted half of her loose batik print shirt and nestled the baby onto one breast. Maisy could be very vocal, but when it was time to eat she got right down to business.

"I'm going to see if Elle and Milo need any help getting things on the table," Tara said, and Mrs. Mick followed her inside.

"I still can't believe I missed the delivery." Lindsay flopped a lounge chair flat and stretched out beside Darcy, staring at the sky. "I figured I'd be safe, holed up here. But no, you had to go into labor in the city."

Darcy smiled. "Believe me, I'd much rather have taken the short ride to Southampton Hospital. I don't think anyone believed how fast it happened, but the doctor thinks I was probably having back labor long before I knew what was going on."

"Christ, how many types of labor are there?" Lindsay shook her head. "A million ways to torture a woman."

"So how's the book going?" Darcy asked, yearning for conversation that didn't involve baby stuff.

"I'm just polishing right now. Three chapters and an outline for a romance."

"Really?" Darcy said. "Did I miss a beat? I thought those sickening sweet, pat characters were ruining your days?"

"Jorge thinks it's a good way to start, so I'm knuckling down and giving it a shot. I'm planning to bring it in this week." Lindsay pressed her hands over her eyes and sucked in a deep breath. "If it sucks, at least I'll know I was rejected by the best of them."

"He'll love it," Darcy said encouragingly, "I know he will."

"We'll see. At least with this done, I'll be able to meet Zack at the gym over lunch again. I haven't seen him all week."

"Not even at night? Why don't you plan a dinner?"

"I've been writing at night. Besides, every time we go out to eat Zack obsesses over the carbs in the rolls or potatoes, or the amount of fat in the salad dressing or meat. Not the best dinner conversation."

Darcy laughed, trying not to jostle the baby. "I am so glad I won't have to deal with boy problems for a while."

"What do you mean? It's not like you've entered a convent or anything. In a few months, Maisy's going to be taking bottles and rice cereal. She'll be walking in a year, and you'll be back on the Hamptons party circuit, falling in love with someone new."

"It won't be the same." Darcy shook her head as a tiny vision of the future opened up for her—her future with Maisy. "And you know what? That's not a bad thing."

Looking down at Maisy, her body so tiny Darcy could support her with one arm, Darcy found it hard to imagine that she'd outgrow this onesie in a few months, that the small pink booties Mrs. Mick had knitted for her would become too small for her chubby little feet.

And yet . . . she knew it would happen. Just as the seasons would change, Maisy would grow and insinuate herself more and more into Darcy's world, until Darcy would find it hard to remember life without her.

You're a part of my life now, little one, Darcy thought as Maisy gave a little kick. Caressing the pink bootie, Darcy finally got it, full force.

She was a mother. Maisy depended on her. A brand-new, miniature girl was in her hands now, and she couldn't fuck up Maisy's world the way she'd screwed up so many things in her life.

It was an ominous responsibility, and yet it was the most hopeful twist of fate Darcy had ever experienced.

As Maisy finished sucking, Darcy supported her head and patted her back.

"I love you," Darcy said softly, rubbing her soft little back.

Maisy let out a million-dollar burp, and Darcy smiled. It was all good.

64

Elle

"I have to admit, this is the easiest money I've ever made," Darcy said as she and Elle watched baby Maisy gurgle and coo for the cameraman. "Of course, the money's going into a trust fund for Maisy, but it's a fabulous start for her college fund."

"Look at her, making raspberries for Jeff! We'll schedule a few more sessions over the next year," Elle said. Videotaping baby Maisy as she slept had been her brainchild when she saw that the concept for one of the future scripts involved sleep. She'd presented the idea in the production meeting, and for once the executive producer gave Elle credit—at least for a few seconds. "I want to edit footage of sleeping children in, that's definitely my plan," Isabel said. "And when we get to the concept scripts involving eating, laughing, etcetera, I want to do the same." So Elle had been able to "hire" baby Maisy, and Darcy had been happy to bring her into the city for a short session at the studio.

"And your contracts should be in any day for the new Delilah voice-overs," Elle told Darcy. "In fact, remind me before you leave and I'll see if Patrick has them ready for you."

"I can't thank you enough." Darcy's blue eyes sparkled with energy. "I didn't plan to audition for any roles until after the summer, but with those new contracts I'll have enough credit for Actor's Equity. Once again, Elle, you've delivered the pot of gold at the end of the rainbow."

"Everyone helps each other in Woodchuck Village!" Elle pro-claimed.

"Don't get cute with me. I've seen what it's like working for Isabel Slater."

"Her bark is worse than her bite," Elle said, tucking her clip-board under her arm and crossing to the cameraman. "How's it going, Jeff? Got what we need?"

"More than enough." He stepped away from the camera. "She's a cutie. Take good care of her, Mom," he told Darcy, who beamed with pride.

As the technicians brought down the lights, Elle kneeled beside the stroller and brought her face close to Maisy's. "Now you just give yourself a pat on the back and have a great nap during that ride home."

Maisy squinted at Elle, the corner of her mouth lifting in a smirk.

"Are you messing with me?" Elle teased.

"Thanks, Elle." Darcy unlocked the brakes on the stroller. "Tell Ricardo we said hey. Are you guys coming out to the Hamptons when the show goes on hiatus?"

"Actually, I have a devious plan up my sleeve. A trip to Puerto Rico." She explained that, since Ricardo was so attached to his family there, she thought she'd surprise him with two round-trip tickets to his island home during the break. Elle thought it would be thrilling to steal him away to an exotic place, and she realized that acceptance from his mother was a key element if they were going to have a long, healthy relationship.

"Could be fun," Darcy said cautiously. "But I thought he turned you down when you suggested the trip a few weeks ago."

"Oh, he's gotten over that." Elle walked them down the hall, past posters promoting the first two seasons of *Woodchuck Village*.

"When are you going to tell him?"

"Today's the day. Our flight leaves tomorrow night!"

"We'll miss you." Darcy gave her a quick hug. "But have a great trip."

"We will." Elle waved good-bye to Maisy, then sighed as she turned face-to-face with a larger-than-life poster of Brownie Beaver waving in front of the windmill of Woodchuck Village. God, she loved that man!

* * *

That afternoon Elle was too wired to take her usual seat behind the director on set. She'd worked with the show's writers and Callie, the director, to plant the surprise about the Puerto Rico trip in the script, and she could barely contain herself as the puppeteers taped the scenes leading up to the big reveal.

This was the only way to take their relationship to the next level; Elle was convinced of that. It had been difficult to get Ricardo to let her move in with him, but she'd conquered that one. She'd even taken over a tiny corner of the medicine cabinet for her toothbrush and box of tampons. Although she only spent part of her week in Manhattan, she was happy to carve out some progress and move things forward, despite his roommate's glum reception.

But Ricardo's family was the turning point. He was very close to his mother, talked with her on the phone a few times each day, and he seemed to adore his younger sisters, three of them still living at home in a lovely sounding house on a cobblestone street in San Juan. Elle had dropped a few obvious hints about meeting these wonderful people, but, as usual, Ricardo had kept her at bay, vaguely saying that it would happen when the time was right.

Well, now was the time. Elle was crazy for Ricardo, and she longed to be part of his family, holding hands at the dinner table as they said grace, taking turns styling hair with his sisters, helping his mother deadhead buds in the lovely garden that blossomed and twined along their veranda.

She'd told Ricardo of how she'd always longed for a family, how there'd been no family dinners for the DuBois clan, with her father teaching late classes at the university and her mother on call at some hospital or embassy in a foreign land. With no siblings, there'd been no late-night talks or giggle sessions or games of hide-and-seek in the house. Just books, and her father's stinky cigars, and occasionally Mom's recordings of Italian operas, so baroque and brassy to Elle's ears.

Ricardo knew how much she needed this. Would it hurt to push him, just a little, to make it all happen now?

As the big moment of revelation neared, Elle circled one of the cameras, moving closer to the animals posed in the giant cabbage patch.

"Well, what could that be?" Brownie Beaver asked with a spry tilt of his head, definitely aware that they'd traveled off the script as Red Rabbit discovered a large letter inside a cabbage plant. Brownie opened the envelope, leafed through Elle's note and the travel folder containing the tickets, and paused.

"What's it say, Brownie?" Green Toad goaded him.

But Brownie shook his head, removing it. And suddenly there was Ricardo, eyes blazing as he glared beyond the cameras. "Can we cut? Please . . ." His dark eyes were distressed, his mouth a stern, straight line.

"Stop tape," Callie, the director, shouted, then she took a step toward Ricardo. "Don't sweat it, Ricardo. It's a special surprise for you from Elle."

Elle's heart pounded as she hurried onto the cabbage patch stage. "I wanted to surprise you," she explained quickly, trying to defuse the doleful look in Ricardo's eyes. "And everyone agreed to help me. We thought it would be fun. You know, just squirreling around."

"Please, don't reduce it all to juvenile lyrics. Did you think I would feel shamed into this trip if you presented the tickets in front of my friends and colleagues, in this unprofessional display of grandiosity?"

"No!" Elle insisted as the director turned away, pretending to check a note with one of the assistants.

"Why do you do this?" he burst out, then, as if reconsidering, lowered his head to stare sadly at the cheerful, chubby-cheeked beaver face in his arms. "You're choking me, Elle," he said quietly. "I . . . I can't even breathe anymore, your fingers are so tight around my neck!"

"No, Ricardo!" It wasn't that way. He had total freedom.

Two of the grips who'd been hanging on set, waiting for taping to resume, now grew wide-eyed and receded into the shadows. Elle suspected that they were all huddled around the craft table, slathering peanut butter on celery sticks and taking odds on who would win this showdown, and knowing the delicacy of Ricardo's male ego, she suspected she was the dark horse.

"'Cardo . . ." She reached her arms out to him in a conciliatory gesture, but he refused to make eye contact. "Don't be angry. We'll be on hiatus, and you know how much I want to meet your family. When I hear you talk about your mother's garden or that spicy chicken dish she makes, or the way you stay up late and dance all night, it's just that . . . sometimes I feel like they're the family I never had, the family I always wanted."

"They are not your family." His voice was low, edged with frustration. "I say no, I try to hold you back when I need room to breathe, and you push right past me and go and buy the tickets. And this is just the latest. You pushed your way into my apartment, and let me tell you, my roommate, he is still furious. You get the theater tickets when I say I am exhausted. You tell all your friends that I play a beaver when I ask you not to. Every day, you push, push, push." He bent over, as if he couldn't bear the weight of this burden. "I am here to tell you, Elle . . ." He straightened, his dark eyes rueful. "I cannot take it anymore."

He swung round, his flapping, four-foot beaver tail nearly hitting her as he started loping toward the dressing rooms with uncharacteristic awkwardness.

"Where are you going?" she called.

"Out of here. Away from you."

"We still have to tape the scene . . . with the correct ending, of course. Just a little bit different, but we knew you'd be able to pick up the lines in no time."

"I'm finished, Elle." He reached back to lift his tail over the director's chairs.

"But what about the tickets? 'Cardo . . . can't you just, just this once . . ."

"No! You go. Take one of your friends."

"What about you . . . and your family?" She felt herself sinking fast. "I just wanted to meet them. Ricardo . . . we're going on hiatus. What do you want to do?"

"I want you to leave me alone," his voice rang out clearly as he left the stage area. "I'm going to Disney World."

65

Tara

It would be Tara's last trip to the Hamptons, at least for a few weeks, until she figured out her law school classes and got back into the rhythm of a student schedule, especially since she'd heard that the old intimidating practices of yore were still very much alive in the Torts lecture hall, especially for first-year students. She didn't mind buckling down and looked forward to being in an academic environment again, but it was wonderful to have one last weekend of freedom, cruising in her mother's borrowed Beamer convertible since her car was in the shop.

Lindsay was going to take the train out after work, and Elle promised to make lemon twisters for anyone who showed up. Beyond that, the weekend would be a lazy, pitch-in affair, with nothing planned and no demands beyond the strain of a stiff game of Scrabble or a real-estate trade in Monopoly.

A line of red lights loomed ahead—beach traffic, she suspected—and Tara pressed on the brakes and rolled to a stop. As soon as the truck in front of her moved up, she could see that it was pedestrian traffic gumming things up, some sort of demonstration. The protestors didn't have the road closed, exactly, but the crowd billowed into the street just enough to make negotiating treacherous without nicking a handbag or the billowing sleeve of a choir robe. They were singing "Amazing Grace," and Tara could make out a few female voices belting out some bluesy riffs.

Great. Stuck in a slow-crawling revival service.

She bit her lower lip, maneuvering carefully as heads turned and stared at her. Women nodded at her and commented to their friends. An older man scowled. A young man shook his head, heavy with disapproval. Although sunglasses shielded their eyes, she knew what they were thinking: there goes the fashionably thin woman driving her expensive convertible without a care. The electric blue BMW convertible sparkled obscenely, the glare off the hood shouting: "I'm rich and greedy!" Tara felt the heat of humiliation suffuse her face. She wanted to shout that this car was borrowed, that she worked hard for a living, that she suffered her own share of racial issues. She didn't deserve their scorn.

If Tara could have turned around and peeled out of there, she'd have done it in a flash, but as it was it seemed that it would be fastest to proceed ahead and inch her way through to the front of the pack.

One of the protestors broke away from the crowd and darted ahead, narrowly missing the front bumper of her car. The young man jogged ahead, as if on a mission. Tara maintained her steady pulse on the brakes, trying to focus on the squeak of a wagon wheel and the cry of a baby in a stroller over the quiet hum of the engine. A minute later the jogger returned, leading John Sharkey, walking at a good clip in his Sunday best.

Of course. She should have known he'd be at the center of all this.

"Tara." He stood in front of the car, forcing her to slam on the brakes.

"Thanks for the heart attack." She pushed the car into park and got out, waiting beside the door for him to come to her.

His shirtsleeves were rolled up politician style, and the cotton of his shirt was starkly white against the chocolate brown of his skin. He squinted against the sun, and Tara suspected he had forgone shades in anticipation of media shots; John had always said sunglasses made a brother look too slick and elusive. "Sister . . ." he said, giving her a stiff hug. "I'd like to invite you to join our quiet little march. We're protesting the Savant Greens Country Club's policy of not promoting people of color to upper-level management."

"This is about the Savant Greens?" Tara felt stung with surprise. "But my parents are members there." It sounded so lame, when what she really meant was that she felt that people of color were welcomed there.

"Yes," Sharkey said, smiling smugly, "I imagine they're happy to take your money. But giving back to the black community is another issue altogether."

"I wouldn't be so sure about that." Images of the staff at Savant Greens passed through her mind. Max, the attractive head waiter whom she and friends had crushed on, whose meticulous sense of order and suave sense of fashion had prompted the girls to speculate about his sexual preferences. People of color were employed there—a handful of African American caddies, a few bar waitresses, some of the locker room staff . . . they didn't seem to be treated unfairly. Had they been passed over for promotions? Tara didn't know, but she did have to wonder if a protest like this would bring backlash toward those people, none of whom she'd recognized in the crowd. Yes, she knew that wrongs had to be righted, but was this the way? Intimidation and negative attention?

"We are here on a mission, in defense of people of color." Sharkey lifted his chin, his eyes hard, black stones. "I would expect you to join us in this, Tara."

"It's not quite as simple as you'd like to make it," Tara said. A woman behind Sharkey looked on with interest, her brows arching, but she kept moving down the road. "These issues are complex, and they affect a multitude of people in different ways. I'm not sure your approach is the most beneficial to people of color."

"Mmm." His eyes went to her shiny car, the back loaded with two coolers. "That and you've got somewhere you need to be?"

"That's not fair. I should be entitled to live my life, even if it doesn't coincide with your mission."

"I wouldn't be so sure. Not when you're a member of this racist establishment. A resident of this closed community."

"For a man who specializes in affirmative action, you throw that R-word around a little too easily. I'd be more careful before making false claims about racism."

"And ignore injustice? Live like a fat cat in this bastion of racism?" He gave a mock sigh. "Okay, sister. I hear ya. You just tuck in there with your eyes closed. Ignorance is bliss."

"I am not ignorant," Tara ground out, facing him squarely and balling her hands into fists. In that moment, she hated John Sharkey.

He held up his hands defensively. "It's okay. We're cool."

"Listen to me, Sharkey. You might think you have all the answers, but apparently you don't know a few facts about the history of the Hamptons." She pointed down the road. "Keep heading east, toward the south fork, and eventually you'll hit Montauk, where a ship of forty-nine men captured in the Atlantic slave trade waited on the *Amistad*, a ship they'd won in a mutiny. Forty-nine slaves whose case made it to the U.S. Supreme Court, with the help of a few whites, I might add. You may have forgotten that little history lesson, but they won their freedom and returned to their homeland. A hard-won victory for people of color, I'd say.

"And since you've targeted a country club, let me point out that the Shinnecock Hills course, just down the road that way, hosted the second U.S. Open Championship in 1896. And did you know that John M. Shippen Jr., an African American laborer who helped construct the course, played in that tournament? The brother finished in fifth place. Way back in 1896. So don't be talking to me about bastions of racism, Mr. Sharkey. Racism exists, but so do leaps and bounds toward equality."

"Amen, sister!" a passing woman called out as she mopped her face with a handkerchief.

"Amen is right." Sharkey let out a forced chuckle. "Sounds like someone woke up cranky today."

"No, someone woke up armed with some facts."

The end of the line of protestors was passing them now, but the people in the crowd, who no longer seemed allied against Tara, remained silent, watching and listening.

"Sorry to interrupt, Mr. Sharkey," said the young man who'd jogged up to get Sharkey, "but we gotta go."

"We do." Sharkey wiped his brow with the rolled-up cuff of one sleeve, suddenly not so crisp or cutting as he shot one last look at the convertible. "Don't want to keep the media waiting. Drive carefully."

Is that the best you can do? Tara thought as he turned away and joined the end of the parade. But really, did she expect him to say he was sorry? Not Sharkey. He wasn't a big enough man to manage an apology.

And all this was affirmation that she was better off without him in her life. Back in the car, she eased ahead to the end of the group, where she threw it into park again, got out, and reached into the cooler in the back.

"You must be thirsty," she said, tossing a bottle of Gatorade to one of the young men who'd scorned her. When he thanked her, she asked him to give her a hand passing out the drinks. While she wasn't on board attacking Savant Greens, she did recognize thirsty people. Sometimes, you just had to pick a small, tangible battle that you could win. Thirst, be quenched!

66

Lindsay

The last weekend of summer, and I've got nothing to celebrate.
The cab dropped me in the driveway of Elle's house and I me-
andered around to the rose arbor, having spotted some activity by
the pool. The Long Island Railroad had been right on schedule,
and yet it had felt like one of the longest trips of my life as I'd kept
replaying this morning's appointment with Jorge throughout the
entire ride.

Summer hours—I could have actually stayed in the Hamptons
last night—but I'd dutifully scuttled into the office since today had
been the only time the publisher could fit me into his busy schedule. And all for what? Rejection.

"Lindsay! Yeah!" Elle sprang up with a clear plastic tube of
water, checking the chemical balance in the hot tub. "You're here!
Let the Labor Day weekend festivities officially begin!"

Darcy smiled up at me from the shallow section of the pool,
where she was swirling Maisy around in a floating chair. "You look
like you had a rough day."

"Well, I have good news and bad news. Which one do you want
first?"

"Bring on the bad." Darcy motioned her closer. "Let's get it
over with."

"Jorge rejected my romance proposal. He was very kind about
it, but apparently it's a lifeless piece of crap. He said I got all the

mechanics right, the format down, but the writing lacked freshness and spontaneity." *At least I didn't break any of Allessandra's rules*, I'd wanted to tell Jorge as my soul sank in disappointment. I'd worked most of the summer on that proposal and staked my hopes on getting it published. Motivated by visions of success—Lindsay McCorkle, published author—and dollar signs dancing before my eyes, I'd turned down party invites and dinner dates to stay at my computer, pushing into my story.

Ironically, I'd even lost my boyfriend over this romance novel, although I acknowledged that Zack's own compulsions also contributed to our drifting apart. The man was like a shark, compelled to keep moving, running, pumping, climbing. When I needed my lunch hour at work to write and had to cancel my gym date with Zack, he'd gotten a little too personal. "Don't think those abs are going to stay tight sitting at a desk," he told me. "And that ass— cute though it is—it's very likely to turn to flab in a matter of weeks."

Painful words, especially for a former fatty like myself, but I'd taken the high road, deciding that obsessive exercise compulsion was Zack's problem, something I had tried to help him with. One weekend in August, when I'd stayed in the city to spend some time with him, I'd waylaid him to Central Park, suggesting a quiet walk up past Strawberry Fields to the boat pond. Even though we could have clocked it in a few miles, Zack seemed undone by the word "quiet." "Don't you ever want some quiet space in your day?" I'd asked him. "Just a moment or two to experience some peace in your life?" He'd shaken my arm off. "What are you, the Dalai Lama? If I need quiet I'll shove some earplugs in. I like noise, stimulation, action." "What about introspection?" I'd asked. "I don't go for that touchy-feely crap. Now, if we run this path, we can probably make it to the reservoir and back in thirty minutes. Ready?"

Zack ended up running alone that day, and we hadn't bothered to call each other since. I had been relieved to break free of him so easily and had turned all my attention and energy toward my romance novel, the story of a very proper editor (who did not eat tuna sandwiches at her desk) who, against her will, falls for a sanitation worker, a hard-core Yankees fan New Yorker who is also a secret millionaire because his grandfather invented a sorting device for recycling.

"That must be a bummer," Darcy said as I sat down on a lounge chair by the pool and kicked off my sandals. "And you put so much time into it."

"You know," Elle hurried over, shaking the tube of pool water, "you could send it around to other publishers. Maybe Uncle Jorge is wrong."

I recalled Jorge's comment that had cut me the most: "I sensed that your heart just wasn't in it," he'd said, sliding the clipped pages across his desk. "It's sort of a paint-by-numbers as opposed to a work of art."

His words had stung, probably because I acknowledged their truth. Although I'd vested quite a bit in the success of my work, I hadn't squeezed any of myself into the story. How could I, when the characters had to be so perfect, so neatly drawn so that they could fit into their formulaic capsules like those tiny dolls you bought from twenty-five-cent gumball machines at the supermarket?

"Actually, I think Jorge is right." I let out a breath. "It just about kills me to admit it, but I don't care about those creaky characters, that prissy editor and the millionaire trash slinger. I could care less about the story; I just wanted to have something I wrote published. You know, the way you want someone to peek into your life and discover you have this amazing hidden talent?"

Darcy hung low in the water, smiling as Maisy blew bubbles. "That's the fantasy. The reality is that you have to scrape every ounce of yourself together and put it out there and hope for the best. At least, that's the way acting is."

"But wait—what's the good news?" Elle asked.

I laughed as I pushed my sunglasses onto my head. "Apparently, my romance was so godawful that Jorge realized Windswept Island is not well suited to my editorial sensibilities. He's moving me to a new imprint next week—mysteries. Maybe not as lucrative for the company, but I am thrilled to get a shot at editing mysteries and re-lieved to be away from Tuna Breath Beckett."

"Ha! You've been liberated!" Elle said.

"I just might enjoy going to work next week."

"Speak for yourself. I'm starting on the crime show Tuesday— *Truth and Justice*. I feel like I have to take it since Isabel pushed so hard to get me another production job, but I'm not looking for-ward to it. Cops and crime scenes are a far cry from the gentle creatures of *Woodchuck Village*, and I hear the E.P. is even an odder egg than Isabel."

"Who, you must admit, was surprisingly judicious in the end," Darcy said.

Elle wrinkled her nose. "Do you think?"

"Oh, cut her a break!" Darcy splashed water at Elle, who danced out of range. "I was working there this week when Isabel gave a speech to the whole staff," Darcy told me. "All this rationalization about how things happen when people work together in close quarters, and that she hates to lose Elle. She was totally on Elle's side, but Ricardo gave her an ultimatum, and she couldn't do *Woodchuck Village* without her star beaver. But she promised to give Elle a good recommendation and look—already she's got this."

"Judd Siegel is his name," Elle said as she lifted the skimming pole from its hooks. "He's got a reputation for devouring young production associates and spitting them out. I heard he went through three interns in one week."

"He'll get more than a mouthful with you," I teased. "Come on, Elle! You've never been afraid of anyone before."

"I'm not afraid. Just disappointed."

"I'm sorry about you and Ricardo." I shielded my eyes to shoot her a sympathetic pout. "Really. I know you had a lot of hope for that relationship."

"I just can't believe he snapped like that," Elle said. "He went crazy."

"Better to know that now than down the road," Darcy said.

"And maybe this whole experience made you a little more aware of the way you try to control things," I said gently. "The way you push, hard and fast, in your eagerness to pull everyone together and create a family."

"I do that?" Elle paused, the skimmer in midair. "Tell me more, Dr. Lindsay."

"Nothing more to tell, except I'm guessing that the worst part of the breakup with Ricardo is having to leave *Woodchuck Village*. The bright, cozy set, the warm, sweet storylines, the people and the positive attitudes there—all combined, I think it became a second home for you. Your TV family. It's got to be hard to say goodbye."

"Yeah." Elle sat on the edge of the pool and plunged the skimmer down to the bottom. "Everything you're saying, a lot of it's valid, and it makes me so mad at Ricardo, that he would pull a power play to take away one of the things I love, that show."

"He's probably hurting, too," I said, "but that probably doesn't help you much, does it?"

Elle stood up, extracting the skimmer from the water, hand over hand. "I'd like to see him get his fat beaver tail caught in a paper shredder." She looked up, her green eyes full of anger. "Does that make me a bad person?"

Darcy and I laughed. "I don't think so," I said as Darcy coasted Maisy toward the steps and out of the pool.

"It's not going to be the same there without you," Darcy said. "I know I'm going to feel a little funny going in to do the Delilah voice-overs, standing right next to Ricardo, that traitor."

"He'll be a gentleman to you, I'm sure," Elle said. "But give me a week or two to get my bearings and I'll see what parts are being cast on the crime show. Milo wants to jump ship, too, and he already has a buddy working in the shop on *Truth and Justice*. Just wait and see, in a couple of months we'll all be working together again."

Bundling Maisy into a fluffy towel, Darcy held her close and rubbed noses. "That's your aunt Elle—the lucky charm."

67

Darcy

When Tara arrived a few minutes later with a surprising tale of the demonstration she'd encountered, Darcy sat back with her towel-bundled baby in her arms and tried to soak it all in—the sweating people, their watchful eyes locked on Tara in her mother's BMW, and John Sharkey at the heart of it all, stoking them up, lauding their cause.

When Tara's story was done, she and Lindsay went inside to change into swimsuits while Elle went to mix up a batch of lemonade twisters.

Hugging her daughter, who now wailed as if she had just seen the ending of *Beaches* for the first time, Darcy recalled sitting by the pool around this time last year, moping about losing this house, worried about Kevin's addictions, stunned from missing her last semester of school and being kicked out of the local country club.

And she'd thought she'd had big problems.

As Maisy latched onto a nipple and settled down, Darcy sighed and settled into the chair. She'd leaped a few obstacles this year, with the help of her friends.

Adversity is the first path to truth. She recalled the quote, Lord Byron, from some reading she'd been assigned at Bennington. So much had changed for Darcy and her friends over this last year, and she had no doubt their lives would be transformed again and again, just as the beach eroded and reformed with the shifting tides.

What would they all be up to next year? No predicting that, but Darcy was grateful to have these good friends. During this time when her life revolved around Maisy's hunger cries and diaper changes, she felt fortunate to have friends who brought flashes of their lives to her, even if just to complain and commiserate.

"Okay, Maisy, now we're going to go for a walk outside." Darcy tucked the baby into the perambulator—"the Rolls Royce of carriages," Mrs. Mick insisted—putting her on her tummy since she seemed ready for a nap. "First we're going under the rose arbor. Can you smell the roses?" Darcy's voice was not the high-pitched tone of "baby talk," but gentle and soothing. Or so she hoped. Ever since Mary Grace had convinced her to talk to the baby she found herself blabbering on about absolutely nothing—the color of the sky, the taste of fresh raspberries, refreshing relief of plunging into the pool on a hot summer day.

"The ones in the arbor look like they're just about to bloom," Darcy said, smoothing the back of Maisy's downy blond head. "Any day now, pumpkin. Just be patient. And when they open up, you'll see all these tiny explosions of color. Oh, look! That one there is beginning to bloom."

Darcy felt a stirring in the carriage. As if on cue, Maisy lifted her upper body with her arms and flung herself over, her eyes brightly glimmering at Darcy.

"You rolled over!" Darcy gasped. "Your first time!" She jostled the baby's tummy and tugged on the ruffles over her padded bottom as Maisy responded to her delight with a wet, gummy, baby smile.

Darcy was all smiles herself, face-to-face with the most wondrous creation on the planet.

PART FOUR

Truth and Justice

Summer 2003

68

Darcy

It was not a good day for an audition.

New York City was embroiled in a fit of early summer humidity, making its citizens that much more prickly. Drivers were quick to hit horns, pedestrians ducked through building lobbies to absorb a few seconds of relief, and the stench of a million bad days snaked up from the street in rotten heat waves.

Darcy felt something pooling in the hollows under her eyes and suspected it was her makeup. Her hair had frizzed and lost its curl the minute she left the closeted coolness of the Little Red Schoolhouse Day Care Center, where she'd left a slightly disgruntled Maisy making a collage of buttons for Grandma Mick's refrigerator. Four-year-old Maisy had resigned herself to serving time at the Red Schoolhouse, though this time of year she preferred to be barefoot and sand-caked, having her run of Elle's house in the Hamptons. The kid had a point, but Darcy tried to explain that sometimes choices were out of your hands . . . like the decision to hold an audition for this low-budget film on the hottest June day New York had encountered in decades.

The address posted in *Backstage* magazine was fronted by a dingy entrance on Forty-seventh with stick-on numbers that seemed to be slipping down the facade. Inside, down a narrow hallway she found the usual scramble of disorganized boredom of an open call: actors waiting their turn, tense and frustrated, a table of sign-in sheets and forms, someone arguing with one of the casting people, and the ubiquitous assistant with her clipboard.

As Darcy filled out the form for the role of "midtwenties, white female," she wondered if the film's director, Noah Storm, would be sitting on the panel inside. Two years earlier, his dark comedy about a large family of children who prop their dead grandmother in the attic and proceed to raise themselves had caused a buzz at Sundance. Despite mixed reviews when the film opened, *Bad Children* had become a cult favorite on video, and Noah Storm, a scrawny Jewish kid from the Bronx, was now a "name."

"It's still a low-budget film," Darcy had pointed out when Elle raved about the up-and-coming Noah Storm. "I doubt it pays much," she'd said, tossing the *Backstage* into the paper recycling bin of their Hell's Kitchen apartment. After Elle's breakup with the Beaver, she'd realized she needed a place to hang her hat in Manhattan, and Darcy had already been searching out reasonable apartments near the theater district, since she'd been getting a few minor roles in Broadway shows. When Darcy found a rambling three-bedroom over a delicatessen that was a great deal, she and Elle decided to take it.

"Stop making excuses and just go to the audition," Elle had insisted, plucking the ad from the bin and handing it back to Darcy. "It's great exposure, and unless you're Nathan Lane, film work is the way to go. You perform once on camera and people all over the world can see you. That's gotta beat dragging your butt to the theater every night at five."

"I like the stage work," Darcy said. The nervous excitement when the house lights went down and the curtain rose, the ringing energy of a dozen actors quickly taking their places onstage, the satisfaction of laughter or applause when a scene hit its mark. "The only drawback is, it keeps me in the city." Granted, it also kept Maisy up late so Mommy could tuck her in at night, but it didn't matter since they were both able to sleep in each morning. In a year or two, when Maisy started school, late nights would be a different story.

"Just audition and see what happens," Elle bellowed in typical overbearing Elle fashion.

Thus Darcy was here in this dank basement, following the casting assistant down the hall, unable to hear well as she told Darcy exactly who would be sitting at the table, but then the assistant was mumbling and facing the wall.

"Excuse me, who did you say?" Darcy asked as she wiped away the beads of sweat and makeup under her eyes. No time for a compact or a bathroom break.

"The casting director Trish Sanchez, who's my boss, the director, and the British actor Bancroft Hughes, who'll be playing the leading role in this film." The assistant wiped one palm on her shorts.

Darcy didn't know who Bancroft Hughes was, but she didn't want to say that. "And they'll give me instructions inside?"

"Just do your best and follow instructions, okay?" the girl snapped, pulling the collar of her sleeveless blouse away from her neck.

Darcy felt her own white lace camisole top sticking to her midriff, though it was a little cooler here on this underground level. Still, Darcy would rather be out of the city, walking along the beach, and she felt sure everyone stuck in this basement audition was blistering with discomfort.

The previous candidate, a middle-aged man with sweat beading on his dark brown skin, emerged from the room, Darcy's cue to enter.

"Bring me your paperwork and I'll give you sides," the woman called. Darcy closed the door and crossed to the woman, presumably Trish, who seemed miserable under a huge black smock speckled with red dots. Darcy couldn't be sure if she was painfully large or pregnant or both, but either way she felt for the woman, who was obviously suffering in the heat. She recognized Noah Storm sitting next to Trish from newspaper photos, and the classically handsome man to his left seemed vaguely familiar.

"Would you please read the role of Nia," Trish instructed, handing her two pages of dialogue.

Darcy frowned down at the papers in her hands. "Any tips? Would you like me to play it warm or sarcastic? For comedy or drama?"

"We want you to read it cold," Noah Storm said, as if it were a challenge. "And I'm getting sick of fielding all these questions, aren't you?" He swung toward Trish. "Who's prepping these people, anyway?"

"They're being told what we expect," Trish assured him.

"That's not true." Darcy shook her head, realizing it was probably a mistake to point out the casting crew's failure, but from the lackluster interest of this panel she was fairly sure she wasn't getting a part anyway. "The instructions aren't too clear out there, but I'll do my best."

"Go talk to them, would you?" Noah groaned. With a heavy breath, Trish moved to the door, while the British guy, whom Darcy recognized from small parts on TV and film, seemed to be programming things into a PalmPilot.

Although Darcy knew she should use this time to study the part finally in front of her, the words were a jumble when she looked down. Instead, she smiled awkwardly at Noah Storm, a beanpole of a man, wiry and gaunt. He could have been a soccer player except for his exquisite eyeware, thin rectangles with luminescent frames. Something about him shrieked intensity—his high, chiseled cheeks or his stark gray eyes. Or maybe it was his impatience.

"Let's just go on without her, so we don't waste time," he told Darcy. "We're evaluating your raw qualities, not interpretation."

"I see." Darcy took a deep breath, knowing that it was the death knell to read without the casting director present. "Okay, then . . ." She proceeded to read the monologue, a woman explaining her disappointment with men by describing one failed relationship after another. Just as she finished the two pages, Trish returned and settled back into her chair.

"Would you like to hear something else?" she asked, trying to read their reactions. Noah's hands were pressed to his face—good? bad? tired?—and Bancroft Hughes was smiling like a barfly hoping for her phone number.

"Thank you," Trish said, holding out her hand for Darcy to return the pages as she turned to Noah Storm. "The important question is, where should we order lunch from?"

Darcy bit her lips together to keep from tearing into all three of them as she shot out of the room, heading for the familiar blocks of the theater district.

It was not a good day for an audition.

By the time she got home, she was making a mental list of

things to pack for the train ride out to the Hamptons. She was un-zipping the large duffel bag as she checked her voice mail—one beep and a woman's voice, polished and smooth.

It was Trish Sanchez. "The film is called *Life After iPod*," her voice said, oozing restrained annoyance. "And we'd like to messen-ger a script over right away. You're our Nia."

69

Tara

"The coast is clear, Mugsy. You'd better step on it and hightail it over here."

Tara laughed, despite the questions looming on her computer screen, the timer ticking off seconds that she should be using to finish this practice test instead of talking to her secret boyfriend on the phone. "I wish I could, but I'm immersed in this online review course. I shouldn't have even answered the phone," she said, selecting "C. Felonious Assault" for question thirty-eight. "I promised myself I wouldn't leave the house till I aced the multistate practice test just once."

"Sounds like a bar review course for idiot savants," Steve said. "Why do you make those bizarre goals for yourself? You know, if you pass the bar, no one's going to know whether you got a 98 percent or 100."

"I know, but I just want to get it right." She'd taken the summer off from work at Senator Wentworth's office to knuckle down and study for the September bar exam.

"Well, since it's June and the exam isn't till August, I'd say you'd better pace yourself. Don't want to peak too soon."

"Actually," she said, selecting an answer for question thirty-nine, "I know you're just trying to tempt me, but that's a genuine concern. Sort of like a pro athlete who blows all their energy in practice."

"I rest my case, Counselor." Steve snorted. "Besides, Ma's been gone to Kathleen's in Poughkeepsie all week, and Lindsay has some banquet to attend in the city, though she'll probably stay at Elle's when she comes out. The place is ours, at least for tonight."

"As I said, I know you're trying to tempt me . . ." And the thought of getting out of her parents' house, sliding out from under these hefty law books, was truly sweet.

"You've been at it all day, right? It's time to take a break."

"A convincing argument. Okay, I've got less than ten questions left on this practice test. Soon as I finish, I'm on my way over."

A lilting ocean breeze cooled the summer night, and she noticed Steve had all the windows open as she parked behind the shed and went in through the screen door without knocking. Years ago Mrs. McCorkle had instructed kids to just use the back door—"I can't be running downstairs chasing after the likes of you every time the doorbell rings"—but back then Tara had never dreamed she'd be sneaking into the house to see Lindsay's brother Steve.

How long had it been now? For more than three years they'd been seeing each other on the sly. It had started with a phone call from Steve one day in October, just a few months after Tara had ended her relationship with John Sharkey. He'd said something about meeting at the Avalon, a bar at Union Square, and she'd gone there that night, thinking he just needed the familiar camaraderie of his kid sister's best friend. He'd brought a friend, a coworker from the sports equipment company, and they'd talked and joked effortlessly. She'd just started law school, and Steve brought up the subject of liability issues on sports equipment—the bats and gloves, masks and helmets he tested—wondering where the line should be drawn between the vendor's responsibility to consumers vs. the implied contract that the consumer would use equipment safely. "I love my job. I give this equipment a workout, violate it in dozens of ways to make sure it'll stand the stress of extreme sports. But no amount of testing is going to make a football helmet safe for a biker or prohibit a baseball bat from being used in an assault. You'd be amazed at what people come after us for." She'd never had a conversation on this level with Steve before. And when did he trim his shaggy brown hair so that it fell softly over the tops of his ears, a subtle wave over his forehead? Gone were all remnants of white zinc sunblock from his nose. And that stubble he used to scratch was now a strong pale jaw with just a hint of five o'clock shadow. She'd crushed on him when he was a shiftless surfer dude; now the attraction tugged at her like the undertow in a storm.

"What?" he'd said, screwing up his face. "What are you staring at?"

"You, Steve." She'd always seen Steve and his friends as the Lost Boys, an irresistible gang of malcontents who would always defy authority and the aging process, but here before her was a mature man. "All these years, I never thought it would happen, but it did. You grew up."

He balled up a bar napkin and tossed it at her. "Get out! You were scaring me, staring at me like that. I was worried you were going to jump up and start singing a Celine Dion song or something."

"But you did, not in a bad way. You matured when I wasn't looking," she said. "Unlike the Fogarty twins, who are still stuck in adolescence."

"I think it's called the junior high wormhole," he said. "When thoughts of naked girls, surfing, and meatball heroes just keep spiraling through the brain."

Tara cocked her head. "Junior-high wormhole . . . Is that the clinical term?"

He nodded sagely. "Textbook case."

That first night at the Avalon, they kept talking long after Steve's friend headed out, Tara still sipping at seltzer when the bartender announced last call. "We'll have to do this again," Steve had said, and then he'd found her a cab and sent her home without any pretense of romance, leaving Tara more than a little miffed. She'd remained that way for the next year, as they'd get together for drinks nearly every two weeks at the Red Eye or Joe Allen's, the Paramount or the Oak Room—bars that did not have pounding music and lines of celebrity hunters out the door, bars where they could sit and just talk. Tara enjoyed her "meetings" with Steve, the biweekly check-ins, but she didn't mention him to Lindsay or the other girls, not sure what it all meant or where it might be going. After all, what did it mean when a guy met you twice a month for a drink and never touched your hand or even kissed hello? Having grown up with Steve, she doubted he was gay, and she didn't think he was lonely, with all his surfer buddies, his friends from Brooklyn, and now his work colleagues whose anecdotes he shared. So . . . what was the deal?

It was more than a year after that date until things broke, and now, nearly four years later after that first meeting, Tara still hadn't undertaken sharing this relationship with her friends or family. It was all a big secret. Tara had always considered herself a private person, perhaps more protective of her privacy because of her father's visibility in the media whenever a scandalous case was breaking. Private, yes, but secretive . . . no. At least, not until Steve. She knew that someday, soon, she was going to have to let her friends in on this one. But for now, she was holding tight. For some reason she still felt the need to protect and coddle this relationship, afraid that too much attention would make Steve and her feel self-conscious or guilty, jinxing everything.

The screen door gave its familiar creak as she stepped onto the screened-in porch, passing the metal glider that used to hold Tara and all three of her friends at once, swinging on a lazy afternoon, lamenting that there was nothing to do.

"Hello, hello?" She saw him ahead in the kitchen, rinsing something in the sink. "I noticed the door open and thought I'd stop in and rob the place," she said casually.

"Nothing to rob. Ma cashed in the family jewels to fly off to Carnivale in Rio." He handed her a martini glass with a sugared rim. "Lemon drops—tip number one in the Steve McCorkle guide to bar review."

"Lemon drops! I can't drink these!" she said, but she took the frosted glass and let her lips sink over the cool, candied rim.

"Just one. Relaxation is key. When your brain isn't wrapping around torts and con law, you've got to give it a rest." He picked up his own drink from the counter and led the way into the den off the dining room, where a cozy nook was filled by a sectional sofa that rivaled a small island and an entertainment center.

Steve flopped onto the sofa while Tara put her glass on a side table and snuggled close. "So, where is your mother again?" She caught his scent, the smell of soap and fabric softener mixed with salty sweat, and she smoothed her palm over his flat chest, loving the feel of his abs under the worn cotton T-shirt. This was her life with Steve—stolen moments spent talking and laughing, holding each other as they watched a TV sitcom, great, screaming sex and sleeping close, their bodies spooning they shared their worries and fears, hopes and dreams for the world. At night, in bed, Steve was not the cynic he portrayed to the world, and she'd become inexorably attached to the kind, gentle person within.

"Poughkeepsie. Kathleen went with her husband to the orthodontists' convention in Atlantic City, so Ma's been corralling the grandchildren all week."

"So you're the king of the castle." She smiled. "I don't know what happened to our generation, none of us able to leave the nest. You, me, Lindsay—we're all still living at home."

"It's called the price of real estate in the New York metro area. You can't save if you're throwing a thousand bucks to rent every month."

"So we're living in our parents' pockets." It had worked for her the past few years, going from work to law school at night, just checking in at home to sleep. Fortunately, her mother had eased up a bit, releasing her from household duties and allowing her nights away without torturing her to disclose her whereabouts. Of course, Tara always let her mother know when she wouldn't be home, and she always manufactured some convenient lie, usually claiming to stay with Lindsay or Elle, just to alleviate her mother's worries.

"It's a temporary thing." Steve slid a hand over her thigh, cupping the inner muscle with affection. "But I've been saving, planning to buy a house in Brooklyn. Something small, maybe attached. Or even a condo. That old schoolhouse in the neighborhood is being converted to condominiums. Could be good."

"Really?" Tara blinked. This was the first she'd heard of this plan. "Do you have a down payment?"

"Pretty much, though I hear the closing costs are a killer." He sipped his drink, then put it aside and turned to her, a lock of dark hair crimped and falling over his eyes sexily. "You might want in on it. It'd be a great investment."

"Buy a house with you?" Her heart beat a little faster. This was like a proposal of fiscal marriage. "That'd be great, but what kind of money are we talking about? I mean, I've been saving, but look at me now, with the summer off. And it might take a while to find a job in my field, *if* I even pass the—"

"I wouldn't sweat the numbers; we could figure that out," he said, catching her eye. "If you're game."

"Well, sure, but . . ." She paused, somewhat overwhelmed. "Let's talk about what it would really mean—the implied commitment."

Steve winced. "The C-word. Every guy's buzz-kill."

"But it's real. If we buy a place together, it implies some commitment, that we're going to live there together."

"Well, duh. Of course." He squeezed her thigh.

"But long term, Steve? Are you really thinking about this?" He seemed so cavalier, she didn't think he was getting the full picture. "That you'd be involved with an African American woman?"

"Tara . . ." He squinted at her as if she were speaking an indecipherable language. "I *am* involved with you. That part's a done deal. What do you not get about buying a house together?"

"It's a huge step." She bit her lower lip, thrilled and a little concerned. A house—their own place where they could be together without having to make complicated arrangements or explanations. It was hardly a romantic proposal of love, but from Steve this was a raving declaration of commitment. And despite his fortitude, she worried that he didn't know what he was getting himself into.

70

Lindsay

All right already, just open the damned envelope. My neck was stiff from turning from the large banquet table to stare at the podium, but I didn't want to move my gilded gold chair and turn my back on Susan Bamford, the author I'd come to support at the annual Mystery After Dark Guild Inc. Awards Banquet. Susan was up for a MADGI award for her second mystery novel, a book that was already edging up the extended *Times* best-seller list, and receiving an award like a MADGI could help the publicity department get Susan more national attention: review quotes, maybe even syndicated radio spots or—the publicity plum—a segment on a TV talk show like *Today* or *Good Morning America* or, heart be still, *Oprah!*

"This is a very special award, not only our top honor, but it also often gives a mystery the 'push' in the market to make it a bestseller," the emcee said with grave importance.

Okay, okay, on with the show. I had been hoping to catch the last train out to the Hamptons. We'd made it through salads, entrees, cheesecake, and twenty-some awards, but, checking my watch, I wasn't going to make it if this woman said one more word to inflate the importance of the mighty Mystery Guild.

I straightened my neck and shrugged expectantly at Susan, who bit her lower lip, a bundle of nerves. She'd been a joy to work with, earnest and full of good humor, unlike the first author I had seen rise to the best-seller list with an increasing list of demands that ranged from audits of the publisher's accounting department to first-class tickets when she went on tour. Pain in the ass. Diana Hargrove always delivered her manuscripts late, then spent weeks rewriting her page proofs, changing "lavender" to "lilac" and "simpering" to "sniveling." She drove everyone crazy, but now that she was a best-seller we needed to keep the sniveling lilac bitch happy.

"And the winnner is . . ."

I crossed my fingers, hoping to see success come to one not so wicked.

"The MADGI goes to Susan Bamford!" The emcee's voice rose three octaves. "For *A Clue for All Seasons* . . ."

Susan popped out of her seat with a squeak, and I stood up to hug her.

"Gift of the MADGI," I joked before she went running toward the stage. This was an author who deserved the accolades, her mystery a tight, compelling story that had made me laugh aloud the first time I'd read it. I was happy for her, pleased that *A Clue for All Seasons* would probably rise up the best-seller lists now. Susan was supporting three teenaged kids and a dog and working per diem as a nurse in a depressed mining town of western Pennsylvania; she could use the dough.

Best-seller status would also mean another bonus for me—a tradition at Island Books to reward the editors of best-sellers. (The staff joked that Allessandra Beckett was probably a secret millionaire; she could afford to move from tuna salad to sushi, if she so desired.) Applauding madly with the audience, I took mental inventory of the upcoming weekend. If I missed the last train to Southampton—and I probably would, since there'd undoubtedly be a MADGI afterparty—I could return to the office and go through some of the manuscripts stacked on my windowsill. The security guard would let me in, and working in the office late at night could be productive, without the ringing phone, cavorting colleagues, and meetings to distract me. Although I already had two manuscripts in my bag under the table, which I'd planned to take home and edit over the weekend . . .

"I want to thank my editor, Lindsay McCorkle, who is a walking lifesaver," Susan was saying. "The day she called to buy my first manuscript, that very morning I had posted flyers on all the local community bulletin boards to sell my car because I just couldn't afford the insurance anymore . . ."

I glanced up at her, glad I hadn't completely tuned out and missed this part of Susan's speech. In the past year or so I'd come to realize that you could never completely catch up in a job like mine, with manuscripts arriving in the slush pile every day, scheduling issues, manuscripts to be line-edited, cover copy to be rewritten, marketing calling for next season's concepts and catalog copy.

"I'd told my kids that either the car or the grocery bills had to go, but they just refused to stop eating," Susan went on, causing a rumble of laughter in the audience.

My mind turning back to office tasks, I made a mental list of all the people to e-mail regarding Susan's MADGI award. Marketing, of course, and the sales force would want to know, field reps . . . I closed my eyes, trying to turn it off. I loved my job and I was good at it; finding three best-selling authors in four years was not a bad track record. But lately I'd realized that, even if I spiraled to the pinnacle of an editorial career, it wasn't going to bring me fulfillment. Social status, money, job security . . . sure, the bennies were sweet. But a voice deep inside me had begun to shout: More! I needed more. Something kinetic inside me needed to bust out and get moving, and I knew that the evolution of Lindsay wasn't going to be brought about through an editorial career or, the more likely mistake, a man.

"Thank you for this esteemed award," Susan wrapped up her speech, "and thank you for helping me continue to do the thing I love best . . . writing."

As I joined the audience in giving the lovely woman a standing ovation, Susan's words resonated for me. Writing . . . I'd always enjoyed it. Granted, I'd been stung when my romance manuscript was rejected, but I'd also been disappointed in myself for following a formula that didn't feel right.

I'd held the Muses at bay for a few years, but maybe this summer was the time to let them out. At last, a little something for myself . . .

71

Elle

I know I'm going to hate myself for this, but . . .

Elle rolled the mouse back and forth, letting the cursor hover over the Submit Payment button on PerfectPair.com. What did it say about her life that she'd encountered such a dearth of single, straight guys that she was about to resort to an online dating service?

No, she wasn't that desperate.

On the other hand, she needed to pay to get any more information on the guys whose profiles she'd "sampled" on the site for free: the cyclist who wanted to show his special friend Manhattan from two wheels (cute), the java junkie looking for someone to hang with in coffee shops and share favorite books (hairy cute), the Yankee fan who had season tickets for two and needed a voracious Bronx Bomber to hold his mitt in his box seats behind home plate (very good seats). Plus she needed to pay to submit her own profile—the only way anyone was ever going to find her toiling away in this basement of a Chelsea brownstone, the wall-unit air conditioner whirring with a steady purr that was probably acceptable in the sixties when it was built but, here and now in the new millennium, was giving her a headache.

Although the production offices of *Truth and Justice* were fairly standard desk-and-chair corporate cubicals in a suite at the Chelsea Pier, these offices for Judd Siegel Productions were dank holes in the basement of Judd Siegel's brownstone, which Executive Producer Judd Siegel touted as the roots of his business and his childhood. "But when your roots turn gray, you're supposed to get them colored, Judd," Elle told him to his face, more than once. "New carpeting. Some fresh paint on the wall. Did'ya ever hear of interior design? It's this post-Neanderthal technique for making the cave feel like a home." The main floor contained a rather standard living room of black and gray leather sofas that reminded Elle of a therapist's office, which was used for short meetings. Beyond that was a door to the back of that level and the upstairs—Judd's living space, which few had seen. Elle cringed to think of how that area might be decorated, but she'd heard rumors of everything from a shrine to Judd's ex-wife to mattresses on the floor surrounded by stacks of old newspapers and VCR tapes. Scary.

She leaned back and the desk chair buckled under her.

"For crying out loud!" She popped up and kicked the chair away, pulling over a free-standing file box to sit on in front of her laptop. On the screen the art deco flowers and diamond shapes—subliminal bride bait?—flashed at her from the home page of PerfectPair.com. Yes or no? Find love ... or plug through the night all alone in this dark, creepy basement office?

She wasn't even supposed to be here. Her shift had started at six this morning and she was supposed to be out by six P.M. and headed east on the Long Island Expressway to Southampton's beaches and breezes and friends and fruity frozen drinks. But when Becca had started stressing because her friends had set her up with a date and she'd been the unlucky production assistant chosen to wait for a messenger delivery, well, Elle crumbled. Becca had someone to meet; Elle had no one, no prospects, no friends of friends, no interested barista at the Starbucks she frequented, no single hygienists dashing about in white coats when she got her teeth cleaned. Pathetic.

Just then her cell phone rang—Darcy. Elle flipped it open and said, "Do you think I should sign up on PerfectPair.com, or am I just going through a dry spell?"

Darcy laughed. "You're asking a woman with a four-year-old? The last time I dated, subway tokens were a dollar."

"They're phasing them out, you know." Elle rolled the cursor over the box again, back and forth. "Subway tokens."

"Oh, now I feel really out of it," Darcy said. "When are you getting off? Maisy wants to say good night."

"I don't know. They swore they were driving this package straight from the warehouse in Hunts Point. I wouldn't mind waiting if I had something productive to do and if Judd would bring in Merry Maids once in a while." She squinted in the shadows at a crack on the ceiling that reminded her of a map of Italy. Something black and furry seemed to be growing toward it, looping around a bookcase that contained dozens of overstuffed binders, production logs from days gone by. No . . . Judd needed more than a maid service. More like a demolition.

"I called because I read the script," Darcy said, "and I had to tell someone. It's wonderful. Like, scary wonderful."

"Really?" Elle went to the Submit box and clicked. There. Now she could start making up the sales pitch to sell herself. "Didn't I tell you that Noah Storm's star was on the rise? Is the script funny, though? His last comedy was a little dark."

"I laughed, I cried, I peed my pants," Darcy said. "Oops, maybe that was Maisy."

"Was not! Mommy!" Elle heard Maisy's voice from the background.

"And here she is to say good night." Darcy promptly put her daughter on the phone, and Maisy proceeded to pin down the schedule for the following morning: pancakes and chocolate milk, followed by tooth brushing and then the ride out to the Hamptons. "Press any harder, Maise, and I'm going to make you a production coordinator."

Maisy giggled. "Okay."

The crack of the ancient door knocker sounded upstairs, and Elle hiked up the skinny, twisting staircase. "Gotta go, honey. See you soon!"

After Elle had signed off on the package and ripped into it, she realized that its contents needed to be handled right away. The package, messengered from the casting director, contained a CD with auditions of out-of-town actors for parts in the *Truth and Justice* episode to be cast Monday morning. No one had mentioned that the incoming package would need immediate attention, but she suspected that Becca didn't even know what she was supposed to be waiting for. She had no choice but to stay and e-mail the audition files to everyone who needed to see them.

"Shiitake mushrooms!" she cursed, returning to the basement to get the work done. Elle had forced herself to clean up her language when Maisy started talking, knowing that the little girl learned so much through mimicking.

Downstairs she turned on the cranky old office computer and set to work downloading the CD and compiling the list of e-mail addresses for everyone who needed the disk. As she was working, she heard another noise upstairs—the door opening and footsteps—and she suspected it was another staff member.

"I'm down here!" she yelled.

"Who's trespassing in my office?" came the booming voice of Judd Siegel.

Elle moaned but kept typing on the keyboard. The last thing she needed was Judd staring over her shoulder.

"Elle, what the hell are you doing here? I thought you went home hours ago." His broad shoulders and tall frame filled the small office the moment he stepped in. Judd was one of those producers who'd come into the business with an established name— Judd Siegel, all-star quarterback for Boston College. After an injury sidelined him in the pros he'd gone to law school and worked as an ADA in Boston, just long enough to gather enough juicy material to spin into storylines of *Truth and Justice*.

"Well, I'd like to say I came to read the future in that funky mold you've got growing on the ceiling, but alas, I had work to do. You wanted out-of-town auditions? You got 'em!" She nodded at one of the auditions, which she'd opened in a box on the monitor while the rest downloaded. "These just came in from Xavier Casting. Check out this guy's hair—very Albert Einstein."

He folded his arms and hunkered close to the screen, staring intently. "Could work for us. But why is this coming in so late? Xavier knows I want audition materials no later than Wednesday."

She held up her hands. "Not my fault."

"I might have to let Xavier go. They've been getting lazy, lethargic." Arms folded, he paced across the small office, his heels clumping on the threadbare oriental rug.

"Whatever you say, boss. But while you're making a note of it, you might want to make an appointment for a haircut and an industrial cleaning crew. Your hair is getting way too shaggy to be respectable, even in film circles, and this place . . ." She pinched her nose. "Stinkeroo."

"You just finish those auditions, Elle. I can handle my personal life."

When the team doesn't handle it for you. Elle had become accustomed to the "handling" of Judd Siegel in the years she'd worked on *Truth and Justice.* A writing producer, Judd would be running 24/7 if his team didn't protect him from the smaller details, the crises of an actor too sick to shoot or a reel of film stolen from a PA's car. Having seen Judd's genius at work, Elle understood his success, but she refused to be fazed by the barked orders and suck-ups creating a bubble around him.

Elle kept working on the download, trying to get this finished and get out of here before Judd concocted some other project that would keep them both working here until late into the night.

"There's no excuse for being this late. Shit, they could've thrown off our entire week's shooting schedule," he said, still pacing, his long shadow occasionally falling over Elle's corner, then receding.

As she worked she heard him talking on his cell—presumably leaving a message for Xavier Casting, his gruff voice restrained until he clicked off and bellowed, "Aw . . . don't tell me!"

Elle hunkered down to her task, trying to ignore him.

"Is this yours?" he asked.

She paused, turned to spare him a look, then froze. Freakin' frog fingers . . . she'd left her laptop on the PerfectPair.com site, the screen flashing hearts and flowers now. "Oh, *that.* I was bored," she said, quickly turning back to her work and hoping he'd drop it.

No such luck. "You can't be serious." He moved up behind her and she swore he was sucking the oxygen out of the little room with every big breath. "Would you really pay to meet some loser?"

"Now wait a minute." She swung round to face him. "Just because you haven't used a service like that doesn't mean that everyone who does is a loser. I happen to have a good friend who found her husband through a Web site like this." Actually, a friend of a friend—Lindsay's sister's friend—but he didn't need to know that.

"What's wrong with people today that they've abandoned the art of conversation, the personal exchange in the marketplace, polite civilities on the street? I said good morning to a guy who met my eye on the subway the other day, and do you know what he did? He gave up his seat. Got up and moved to the other end of the car, because my greeting made him that uncomfortable."

"You probably made him nervous," she said. "I know I'd be freaking if some two-hundred-pound man was eyeing my seat."

"One-eighty, and I was just being friendly." He grinned, a dimple emerging on one side of his face. "But his seat ended up going to a pregnant woman. There's a happy ending for you."

"Your point?"

"My point is that online dating is unnatural. Forget about cyberspace and hook up with someone from your world, your everyday life. Christ, you live in Manhattan! This island is crammed with people, half of them men."

"And a lot of them are very happy with each other," she said.

He shook his head, dismissing her tangent. "You know what I think? Women today are just too cool for their own good. If you're not meeting anyone, you're just not sending out the right signals, Elle."

"I'm not meeting anyone because I spend twelve hours a day working on a TV production team. Right now the sexiest thing I have going is the hot storylines of *Truth and Justice*, and that's just sad."

"No shit?" He winced. "Sorry to hear about that. But really, if you want to get with someone you gotta be open to it, Elle. In this random universe, you have to be ready for simpatico to strike: Talk to the guy in line at the coffee shop. Look someone in the eye on the subway. Share a cab with someone heading in your direction. Put yourself out there."

She turned back to the downloading files, rolling her eyes. "If that's not an invitation to be stalked . . ."

"See that? I suggest the simplest courtesies and already you're defensive."

"You don't have a clue what it's like to be a woman in New York City." She sagged in relief as the download completed. "And my work here is done." She shut down the computer and went to gather up her laptop.

"Listen to me. When you get in the cab now, talk up the driver. Don't be a snob. You just never know when you're going to connect with someone."

She clicked her laptop closed. "You're just plain crazy."

"And you're not following my instructions," he said, pointing an accusing finger at her.

Elle headed toward the stairs. "I'm off the clock, and I think I'll walk." Turning back, she winked. "That'll give me more of a chance to chat up vagrants and drug dealers lurking in doorways and alleys. Romance could be lurking just around the corner."

72

Lindsay

By the time I pulled myself together and boarded a train to Southampton Saturday morning, the weather was changing, clouds shifting, cooler air blowing in. As the train emerged from the East Side Tunnel, raindrops slanted across the window and the bluish gray sky on the horizon promised more of the same. Great. What was that expression Ma used to say? If I had any luck at all, it'd be bad luck. I pulled out a manuscript to edit—a light one, at two hundred pages—and settled in to make the ride productive.

Skies seemed brighter as I emerged from the train at Southampton a few hours later. I arrived at Elle's house to find Elle, Milo, Darcy, and Maisy splashing in the pool.

"You made it!" Elle called.

"Aunt Lindsay, come play Marco Polo!" Maisy climbed up the ladder and splatted over, water dripping from the pink bikini bottom drooping below her slender belly. Her curly blond hair sprang out in golden crinkles that framed a wide, expressive mouth.

Milo swam over to the side and shielded his eyes. "Hey, old friend."

"Old buddy, old pal." I smiled down at him. "How's tricks?"

"I can only tell you that this water feels fabulous," Milo said. "After the humidity we've been having, I couldn't wait to get out of Manhattan and peel off the sweat. Raj and I drove out last night. He's staying with friends but he'll join us for dinner." Raj was an aspiring actor who currently worked as a makeup artist on *Truth and Justice*, where he and Milo had met two years ago. Their first encounter had been a bit bloody, as Milo was dressing an unusual set—an S&M chamber where the victim had been held prisoner— where Raj was brought in to apply realistic bruises and bloody gashes to the body. A tube of fake blood was clogged, and when Raj tried to work it the plug popped and red gel splattered all over the set . . . and Milo's pants. "Sorry!" Horrified, Raj tried to rub out the stain, which only made it worse. Milo thought it was all very funny, and he asked Raj if he wouldn't mind going to lunch with a grip who looked like he was bleeding to death. Raj said he'd love lunch, as long as they stopped into the Gap for jeans on the way. "The show will pay for them, ducky, and besides, you could use something tapered to show off that ass." And they'd been together ever since.

I went over to a lounge chair beside Darcy, who seemed engrossed in a script. "Don't tell me that's the new Noah Storm comedy?"

Darcy grinned. *"Life After iPod."*

"Do you know if it's been cast yet?" I teased. "Who might have the female lead?"

"I can't believe any of this is happening to me," Darcy said. "I've never been so excited about learning lines before. I get to throw pies at the Union Square market, and there's a very funny scene where I emerge from the ocean in a business suit and drip my way down the road—I really shouldn't talk about it, but the role is packed with comedic possibilities."

"Need help memorizing them?" I slipped off my sandals and fell back in the chair. "I'll help you rehearse."

Darcy peered over her sunglasses. "But then I'd have to kill you. The script is top secret. But you know what you could do to help. Take that little Tootsie Pop over there and run her around on the beach for an hour or so. She's been bugging me to take her down to the ocean, but I'm afraid to tear myself away. Noah's starting rehearsals this week and I want to appear to be prepared, at least for the first week."

I was happy to divert Maisy for a while, and Elle decided to come along, complaining, "I get so darned lazy sitting by the pool. Sometimes you forget that the ocean is just down the road."

The air felt damp, and although the storm remained offshore the horizon was lined with clouds in bold shades of purple and blue, as if wells of ink had spilled at the edge of the sky. As Elle wrote Maisy's name in the smooth wet sand and Maisy searched for the perfect shell to dot the *i* with, I plunged my hands deep into my pockets and faced the salty, damp wind. That morning on the train I'd set aside the manuscript I'd been editing for a few minutes and started scribbling some notes. The ideas were just images now, almost a journal entry, but I knew that every book started with something simple—an image or word, a complex emotion or a simple longing.

The seed of my novel was in my hands; it was up to me to nurture it and find a way to let it grow.

We walked the length of Bikini Beach, passing a few joggers, clusters of children, and a few windswept sand castles. The offshore storm had driven away most swimmers but a few surfers were out, and I stopped for a few minutes to talk with Skeeter, whose eight-year-old son was skimming the shallows on a thin board.

The tide was going out, revealing low-lying jetties used to protect the shoreline. Maisy found them fascinating, especially the rocks covered with moss and seaweed. "That stone has a beard," she told me, inching forward.

"Careful," I warned. "The rocks are slippery. Pretty sharp, too."

"But I want to walk on them. I can do it. I have good balance."

"Stay away from them." Elle's eyes grew round with horror as she squeezed Maisy's hand and crouched beside her in the sand. "Those rocks are very dangerous. Someday when you're older I'll tell you the story of how I fell off them once."

A different time and place, but the images were still vivid in my mind. I wondered if Elle was haunted by that day.

Maisy's face brightened. "Tell me now."

I shook my head. Although Maisy was wise for her years, four was not really the appropriate age to absorb the vivid smack of a near-death experience.

"Give it a few years." Elle straightened and released Maisy's hand. "Look over there, by the edge of the dunes. See that tide pool? Why don't you go see if there are any starfish who floated in?"

"Sea stars. They're called sea stars!" Maisy corrected her, racing away.

"Do you ever have nightmares about that day?" I asked Elle. "Does it haunt you?"

"I don't think about the jetty, but I had to deal with the frustration that sent me over the edge," Elle said as she watched Maisy skirt the tide pool.

"Was the water cold?" I asked. "Or maybe you don't remember."

"It actually felt refreshing, cold but so soft. I remember it being so velvety, the way it surrounded me and sort of buoyed me up. The guy from the Coast Guard said I lucked out. Something about a storm system changing the currents. Lucky that I got swept toward the ocean instead of into the rocks of the jetty."

"That was one of the scariest things in my childhood," I said. "I remember talking to the police when you were missing. Every time an adult heard what happened, this look of horror crossed their face, and I knew what they were thinking, that you were gone. But I couldn't believe it. I couldn't believe any of it. I kept imagining you swimming out in the ocean, bobbing in the swells and sort of having fun."

"That part was wild, but not so fun. Like a swirling amusement park ride where you can't breathe. I figured I was going to drown, and I was so mad at Darcy that I thought drowning would be good, because I'd get her in tons of trouble." She sat down on the beach and rested her chin on her knees. "God, I was pretty goofy back then."

"You and Darcy were always on each other's backs, always competing."

"You guys were older and she was richer and so bratty about it. I always felt like she was winning and it killed me." Elle sighed. "When I went off those rocks, part of me wanted Darcy to fall in and drown with me. And at the same time, I wanted her to save me—pull me back at the last minute. I wanted her to reach out and be my friend, but that just wasn't happening."

I sat down beside Elle as a wave crashed nearby, sending a fine mist into the air. "Darcy was pretty brutal."

"Tell me about it. I'd pour a little cold water on her feet and she wouldn't speak to me for a week."

"In some ways, we were all a little bratty. But we got better. And Darcy . . ." I shook my head. "She's changed a lot. I would never have seen that one coming."

"You know, you should write all this down," Elle said. "I saw your laptop with your luggage. Are you writing again?"

I covered my hands with my face. "I'm just getting started, but I want to get back to it."

"So write about us. You're supposed to write about what you know. Write about the girls of Bikini Beach. You can use anything you want about me . . . the fucked-up parents, the exotic locales. I'll provide details if you want."

"I'd probably have to put my own spin on it," I said, "but thanks for the encouragement. You have an amazing story, Elle."

Elle turned to me and snapped her fingers. "And you're just the person to help me write a sexy Elle sales pitch for PerfectPair.com!"

"I'm not so sure about that. You know I don't believe in those Web sites."

"But I've seen your cover copy. You're as good as any Madison Avenue spin doctor. Please, write me up. Maybe it'll convince you to sign up yourself."

"That's not going to happen." I had no desire to put myself out there, like a kid vying to be chosen for a game of kickball. "I'll help you, but it's not for me."

"But don't you ever feel lonely?" Elle asked. "Don't you want someone to wake up with on a Sunday morning? The yin to your yang?"

"That sounds great." Bringing my knees to my chin, I hugged my legs. "But I don't see it happening for me."

"Come on!" Elle slapped the top of my bare foot. "You sound like you've taken a vow of chastity. Did ya sneak off and join a convent when I wasn't looking?"

This was uncomfortable territory for me. "You know, you try a run of celibacy and everyone tries to peg you in a category. There's a rumor going around at work that I'm a lesbian." I shook my head. "I guess it's really unfashionable to carry a torch for someone these days. I'm a dinosaur."

"Really?" Elle squinted. "Are you talking about that surfer guy?"

I swallowed. "Bear." It almost hurt to say his name. "I know, last I heard he'd married some surfer girl from Maui. It should be over . . . and it is. He's definitely moved on. I'm the one who can't let go." I thought of the way Darcy had once clung to her obsession with Kevin, how silly it all seemed . . . but this was different, wasn't it? I wasn't clinging to Bear for what he could do for me; I'd enjoyed being with him. Not that I was clinging much from thousands of miles away. Especially if the rumors of his marriage were true. But somehow, the memory of what we'd shared still burned bright for me, the essence of it lingering, strong enough to make any other relationships seem superfluous.

"Well, if that's what you want, get off your butt and go. Fly to Hawaii. Track down your man."

"If only it were that simple." Besides the fact that I'd never mess with a marriage, I recognized the true dilemma of my dream. I was nurturing a fire that had burned years ago, a love that was past tense. "I'm holding onto something that probably can't exist in this time and place. Look at me, Elle. I'm a relic from the past. A shell once occupied by two hermit crabs who found fleeting happiness."

"Don't just give up," Elle said. "You can't let him go."

"Don't I know it." I cupped a handful of sand and let it sift through my fingers. "But the sands shift. The tides keep pushing in and out. Time marches on."

And some of us are left behind, half buried in the sand.

That afternoon I drove home to see Ma and drop Maisy off for an afternoon of making fudge and playing in the garden. I pulled Elle's Jeep into a spot in front of the garage and took my time as Maisy ran into the house. But as I climbed out of the driver's seat, I heard something, a muffled laugh, on the other side of the shed.

Sensing something amiss, I crept to the edge of the snowball bush by the shed and pressed into its fat leaves with balls of lavender blooms. Goose bumps tingled on my arms as I took a look. There they were, Tara and Steve, making out behind the shed. I felt my jaw drop. He had Tara's arms pinned overhead so that her small breasts jutted out against her T-shirt as he kissed her neck, and Tara's eyes were closed . . .

A PG-13 moment.

I pulled back and paused, trying to process it all. Tara and Steve. Well, it wasn't a huge surprise, but why didn't Tara tell me? Why were they sneaking around?

Inside the kitchen, Ma turned to me and pouted. "Darlin', you look like you just saw a ghost."

"Just Tara and Steve, and let me tell you, I was shocked."

Mary Grace looked in on Maisy, who was watering plants in the dining room. "Not too much, pumpkin. That's good." She crossed back to the dishes. "So you've discovered our very own Romeo and Juliet?"

"How long has that been going on?" I asked. "Am I the only one who didn't know?"

"Of course not. Count yourself lucky for knowing now. It's been quite a while now. I'm not supposed to know, either, and so I pretend not to notice. I think it's very sweet, and they seem to enjoy each other quite a bit. Though I doubt that Tara's parents would approve. I think they still hold out hope that our Tara will meet and marry an upstanding African American man."

I felt a twinge of betrayal. I liked the idea of Tara and Steve, but Tara could have told me. I hated being on the outside. And though I wanted to approach Tara and clear the air, for now, I kept quiet about it. If Tara wasn't ready to come forth with this relationship, I could wait. It killed me, but I could wait.

73

Darcy

"Finding someone to go out with is sort of like walking through a ballroom full of balloons in stiletto heels and trying not to pop the balloons." Darcy sat at a table in a frosty cool rehearsal room with the principals of *Life After iPod*, three other actors including Bancroft Hughes and the director, Noah Storm. "Sometimes I feel like I've performed a ballet worthy of a standing ovation," she read on. "Other times . . . well, let's say I've popped more than my share of balloons."

"Let's stop there." Noah made a snapping motion with his hand. "Nice work, everyone. Let's break for lunch. We'll meet back here at two."

"I need a salad," someone said.

"I wouldn't mind Thai food." Marielle Griffin cocked her head and snapped her fingers. "A little chicken satay action, if you know what I mean."

Darcy laughed as she gathered her script. "I think the last time I had Thai, I went into labor."

"No way, sister." Marielle gasped. "You are way too young to have a kid."

"True, but she's stuck with me." From the corner of her eye Darcy noticed Noah zipping his portfolio and slipping out alone. "What's his story? He never comes to lunch with us."

"Is he painfully shy?" Bancroft slipped an arm over Darcy's shoulder, feeling very much like the suave husband he played in the film. "Socially maladjusted? Anorexic?"

"None of the above." Marielle tossed over her shoulder as she headed out the door. "I'll tell you Noah Storm's policy, because I worked with him twice before. That man just refuses to get personally involved with the people he works with. Smart policy, if you ask me." She turned back to flash a luscious dark grin at Darcy. "But then, I never was too smart."

That afternoon as the rehearsal continued, Darcy struggled to keep herself focused on the role of Nia. It was as if Marielle's words had cast a spell over Darcy, drawing her eyes to Noah, making her conscious of the electricity in his gray eyes, the glory of his rare smile, the proximity of his faded jean legs under the table. Where she'd felt intrigue and mild interest before, now she felt a challenge, a need to get past the line he'd drawn around himself, to penetrate the personal life of Noah Storm.

That first day she felt sure her interest would wane with time, that she was just fixating on the impossible. But day after day, with each reading, she found herself peering behind his black Chanel frames, daring to catch the spark in his eyes or soak up the energy in the aura that surrounded him. When the production moved to a rehearsal space she welcomed the chance to get physical with him, and she wasn't disappointed. Noah was always on his feet, almost on his toes, as if orchestrating the very vibrations among the actors. "I don't want to overthink this . . ." he would say, extending his arms toward the actors, as if embracing them but also pushing them off to freedom. Or "Don't anticipate the next line . . . stay in the moment." Or "It's just a line, not steeped with meaning. It's details, details."

"Lord, that man is intense," Marielle said one day as she and Darcy sat on the floor off to the side watching Noah rehearse a scene with Bancroft. "Good thing he's just directing a comedy. A drama and he'd make us all kill ourselves to get the severity of the mood right."

"Mmm." Darcy reserved comment, afraid that if she started talking about Noah her true desires would spill out, a flood of guilty pleasures and forbidden fantasies. Funny that such an average-looking guy could churn these thoughts in her mind, but something about those twilit hazel eyes and that unruly honey gold hair made her want to explore him and make the ultimate connection.

"Don't mmm me, girl. I've seen the way you look at him." Marielle tilted her head, a handful of baby dreads spilling over her face. "If I weren't a happily married woman, I might be thinking the same."

"It's all a moot point, since he's unattainable for me, at least while we're working together." Darcy leaned against the wall and sank down lower. "Not that I have time for a relationship, but it's been years since anyone really caught my eye. That line in the script, about how finding a man is like walking through a field of balloons on high heels? That's me. That's been my life for a while now."

"What about Ban?" Marielle said quietly. "You know, I think he likes you."

Darcy covered her face to suppress a snort. "Did he tell you that? One of those 'if Darcy likes me, then I might like her back' proposals?"

Marielle's face was lit by a smile. "No. But he's a hottie, isn't he?"

"Marielle . . ." Darcy planned to make a comment about junior-high scuttlebutt, but instead she burst into giggles.

Across the room, Noah seemed about to hiss at them, but he turned away when they grew quiet.

"We're in trouble now," Marielle said.

"Sorry, Marielle." Darcy had to bite back another series of giggles.

"Call me Mouse," Marielle said. "It's what all my friends call me."

"Okay." Darcy felt glad Mouse considered her a friend. "I'll bet there's a great story behind that name."

"Another time," Mouse warned. "We're in enough trouble already."

By the time shooting began, the cast of *Life After iPod* had bonded—a good thing, as they shared a single trailer, the two women in one room and the men, officially, in the other. The small, air-conditioned unit was mainly to protect Bancroft Hughes, the only star of the film, from being disturbed by fans and media, but Darcy was glad there was a place to escape the soaring temperatures, currently rising through the nineties. She was also grateful for the diversion her costars provided. Without them, she knew she'd spend every moment on the set watching Noah, analyzing the meaning of his body language, searching for some sterling mysteries in his pale gray eyes. She hated this obsessive behavior in herself, but she couldn't help it—the man was fascinating.

When they weren't needed on the set, Bancroft and his sidekick, Alton Leonard, liked to hang at the small table in the women's quarters, where they all sipped iced tea as they played cards or watched soap operas on the small TV. Tall and wiry with dark brown skin and an ability to bend his body in amazing ways, Alton played the comic foil to Ban's straight man, as well as the romantic interest for Mouse's character Nell. "I'd hang outside," Alton said, often going to the doorway and peering out on the street, "but you can't last in this heat for long. Whoever heard of filming in New York City in the dead of summer? That's just wrong."

"It's the perfect time," Ban answered, sorting his cards. "You don't get shut down by snow, and all the beautiful people leave the city for the local beaches or, God forbid, the icy tundra of the northeast." He folded his cards and slid an arm around Darcy's shoulders, a gesture that was becoming familiar since they'd fallen into an easy relationship. Although no words had been exchanged about it, Darcy sensed what Bancroft sought in her—a companion he enjoyed, a woman who would make it seem, from anyone on the outside looking in, that he was a heterosexual man. Since his rise to celebrity, rumors had circulated about Bancroft Hughes's sexual orientation, a matter of some dismay for female fans who'd fallen in love with him in his first romantic comedy, then fallen in love with him all over again when they saw his first drama the following season. Since the object of her desires and obsessions—Noah Storm—was definitely out of reach at the moment, Darcy didn't mind being Noah's cover girl, especially since she genuinely enjoyed his company.

"All right, gorgeous," Ban said, "show me your sevens."

"Go fish," she told him, pulling her cards out of view. "And no peeking. And when it's my turn to deal we are playing hearts. I'm sorry Maisy ever taught you her favorite games." Maisy came on set nearly every day, if only to spend a few hours with her mom. Mary Grace McCorkle was always around to supervise, and Noah said it was fine with him as long as Darcy was ready to shoot when they needed her.

Alton came back to the table, gathered up his cards, then went back to the door, cracking it into the blistering sunshine again.

"Would you sit, already?" Ban demanded.

"I'm just restless, cooped up in here." Alton started twitching, exaggerating until he was hunched over in a seizure. "Nerves, I guess."

"Cool your jets." Ban frowned at his cards. "Another week or two here in the city and we'll be heading out to the Hamptons to shoot the beach scene."

"Another week?" Alton pretended to be choking. "I'll be a ball of nerves by then."

"Let's get out of here." Darcy put her cards down and peered out the window. "There's a sidewalk café across the street. We'll ask the PAs to come get us there when they need us."

"Do we dare?" Alton gasped with exaggeration. "The esteemed Bancroft Hughes may be mobbed."

"Oh, shut up." Bancroft picked up a wide-brimmed khaki hat, part of his wardrobe, and pulled it low over one side. "No one will recognize me, disguised as myself."

No one even seemed to notice as they crossed the street and took seats at a small round table in the shade. Alton put up the table's green umbrella to provide even more cover from curious passersby. By the time their tall, frozen, nonalcoholic drinks arrived, they were laughing over Alton's story of how his girlfriend's family was trying to sneak onto the set to meet the famous Bancroft Hughes. "And I keep saying, hey, girl, I'll give you an autograph. What about me? I'm in the movie, too. Doesn't that count for something?"

"And they don't care?" Darcy asked, lifting a paper parasol from her drink.

"Nah! They just look at me with those evil eyes that say, move your black ass over, brother, and let me at the star man!"

Ban slung his arm around the back of Darcy's chair and gave a mock sigh. "Ah, it's so tedious, always being the top banana."

"Like you're really hurting." Alton cocked an eyebrow, giving

Ban a hard look. "No skin off your banana, if you know what I mean."

Darcy laughed so hard she dropped her paper umbrella to the ground. "I've got to save that for Maisy," she said, bending down to pick it up. As she reached under the table she noticed a new pair of sneakered feet edging toward them on the sidewalk as Alton complained. "Hey!"

Straightening abruptly, Darcy knocked into Ban, who slung his arm around her to keep her from bumping him in the chin. Pressed against his chest momentarily, she shot a look across the table, right into the lens of a monstrous black camera.

And that was how the face of Darcy Love, aspiring twenty-something actress, was photographed with star Bancroft Hughes and featured in more than a hundred nationally syndicated newspapers that week.

74

Tara

Almost there.

In one week, Tara would sit for the New York state bar exam and, hopefully, get this monkey off her back.

"Did you eat your Wheaties?" Steve had teased that morning when she took a study break to call him. "Sprint the last mile? Knock on wood and throw salt over your shoulder? You're in the home stretch."

"Easy, smart-ass. I'm trying to keep a level head about this."

"And when have you not been level and calm? Any more level and we'd have to light a firecracker under you to get a pulse."

"Hey! That's kind of mean."

"Oh, good. Now that I have your attention, are you going to be out east for Labor Day?"

"I don't know. I can't think that far ahead."

"Well, Ma's going to be at the house, and she mentioned something about you staying there, too. Like, that'd be okay. I think she's onto us, Mugsy."

Tara sighed. "I can't think about all that now. I'm just trying to hold it together until after the exam."

"You do that, Mugs, and I'll hold Ma off as long as you need. Though she's basically harmless."

"Unless she lets the word slip out."

"Well, there's that, and she does have a gift for conversation."

Steve had agreed not to "crack anything open" before the test, and Tara had returned to her work, reviewing the multistate section of the computerized law review course. She'd set her laptop up in her small bedroom on the fourth floor of the West Sixty-eighth Street brownstone—a small room, as most of the upstairs rooms were tight on space, their ceilings tilting under the dormers—but it afforded her a view of the street, and she'd always enjoyed watching traffic pass, keeping tabs on her own parents and brother and sister over the years.

A few hours later she stood up and stretched. The days to the exam were ticking down, and she opened her registration packet to see what she'd need to bring to the test. Her driver's license and birth certificate. She'd mentioned that to her mother, but Mom still hadn't extracted it from the strongbox in the closet containing family documents—the box Mama guarded so carefully, as if it contained jewels instead of yellowed contracts and certificates. Mama was out, she'd seen her head down the street around an hour ago from her fourth-story vantage point. Tara headed down to the den to pluck her birth certificate. She could run out and get a copy made while taking a break, and Mama wouldn't have to be bothered with it.

The precious box was kept inside a bench at the foot of her parents' queen-sized bed. The scarlet and gold brocaded seat lifted to reveal a metal box, fireproof, her mother used to say. Tara hoisted the metal box out of the bench and rested it on the thick Chinese rug on her parents' bedroom floor. The box was more densely packed than she remembered, containing expired passports for her parents, packets of collector's coins, the deed for the Manhattan brownstone, and even an old family Bible that she and her sister used to joke about as a "valued" inheritance. "Mom and Dad are leaving it to you," she'd tell her sister. "You're the oldest." And her sister Denise would respond, "But I'm sure you'll get it, since you're the baby." Underneath the Bible she found her sister's birth certificate, then a packet of old photographs that she set aside.

At last, Tara found her own birth certificate. She set it aside and started replacing the other papers. As she lifted the packet of photos, the yellowed envelope gaped open, the glue giving way, and a few small black-and-white photographs slipped out.

Tara smiled at the people in the photos, ladies dressed from head to toe in all their finery, including a smooth coat with velvet trim, a snaky mink stole, and a coat with military-style piping. But the crowning glory of their ensembles were the hats—bonnets embellished with arched feathers and fat berries and blossoms exploding with lush blooms. These ladies knew how to step out, and skimming the photos of their men in zoot suits and pinstripes, delis with vintage DRINK COCA-COLA! signs and the old facade of the BMT subway station, Tara imagined the wonderland New York must have been back then.

On closer examination she recognized her Grandma Mitzy in many of the photos—obviously in her younger days before her hair was streaked with white. Hard to believe those dark, shiny lips and slender hips belonged to her grandma, but then those laughing eyes were unmistakably Grandma Mitzy's.

"You were a very handsome lady," Tara said to the photo, recalling how this woman had hugged her so close, admiring her ears. "Like little shells. Wouldn't surprise me to find a baby pearl inside. Reminds me so much of my man Willy. Mmm!" And she'd pulled Tara to her ample breast, hugging the stuffing out of her. Grandma Mitzy was undoubtedly Tara's favorite, especially since she always took such pleasure in Tara. Though Tara never understood what Grandma meant by "my man Willy," since Grandpa was named Elwood Jamison. Once she asked her mother if Willy was a nickname for Elwood, but Mama just shushed her, told her to show respect.

As Tara went further in the stack, she noticed Grandma Mitzy on the arm of a white man in many of the shots—a beanpole of a man with medium dark hair, freckles, and a military uniform in some shots. Who was he?

The last few pictures made Tara's eyes bulge. Grandma Mitzy wore a wedding gown and veil, arm in arm with the skinny white soldier.

What? Who was this guy, some stand-in for Grandpa Woody?

As Tara leafed through the photos, she heard the familiar creak of the stairs. Someone was here, and she wasn't supposed to be meddling in these papers.

"Tara?" Serena Washington paused in the master bedroom doorway, hands on her hips. "What are you doing in here?" As her mother's stern gaze swept down over the floor, taking in the extent of the damage, Tara sensed her mother's composure unraveling. "Oh, no." Mama pressed her eyes closed. "Those are my private papers."

"With *my* birth certificate." Tara turned back to the photographs she'd fanned out on the floor. "Who is this man with Grandma Mitzy? The white soldier at her wedding."

Her mother let out a strangled breath. "His name was William Rockwell, and he was killed in the Korean War."

"That's sad, isn't it? I mean, if he was a friend of Grandma's?" From the way Mitzy smiled at him in one photograph, Tara sensed that her grandmother had cared a great deal for this man.

When there was no answer from her mother, Tara glanced up and saw wet streaks down her mother's cheeks. Tears. "Mama?" she stood up, approaching her cautiously. "Mama, what is it?"

"He was more than a friend. He was her first husband, her *Willy.*" Her voice cracked on his name.

A white man? Tara squinted, trying to focus on the facts despite the fact that the world seemed to be shifting. Shaky ground. "Grandma was married to a white man? But what about Grandpa Woody?"

"She married him later . . . after her Willy passed in the war."

"Oh." At least she understood what Grandma had meant about "my Willy." "So . . . this was a big family secret?"

"It's not something anyone likes to discuss. But obviously, my sisters know, and your father . . . I told your father, and he said it didn't matter that . . ." Sobbing, Mama pressed a hand to her mouth.

Tara touched her mother's arm gently. "Mama, what are you trying to tell me?"

"That man in the photos . . . don't you see? He was my father. Willy Rockwell was my father. That white man is your grandfather."

Tara had never cried on a subway train before, but today seemed to be a day for firsts . . . first glimpse of your grandfather's photos, first time your mother was honest with you about your genealogy . . .

The upside of crying on the downtown number three train was New York City passengers generally avoided eye contact, so Tara suspected few people noticed. Though when she felt her face crumple in a restrained sob, the gray-haired woman sitting by the door did tip her head in sympathy.

As the train raced downtown, she pulled a pair of wide oval sunglasses out of her bag and tried to sort through the pain. It didn't help that all this had been sprung on her during pre–bar exam mode, when she'd been trying to maintain a modicum of control over her life to maintain focus. The worst part was that she'd been so blindsided by her parents' subterfuge, by the way they'd pushed her so hard to embrace the black culture and ignore her pale skin tone, all the while knowing they were forcing her to live a lie.

Feeling like a zombie, she exited the train at Forty-second Street, emerged upon the blazing sign-fest of Times Square, and headed east, toward Bryant Park, where Lindsay had promised to meet her.

"Tara?" Lindsay waved from a park bench, looking cute in her A-line skirt with a silk tank—her work clothes. She screwed the top back on a bottle of iced tea as Tara joined her.

"Thanks for meeting me." Tara sat on the bench, too distraught to worry about sitting on pigeon droppings or someone's spilled soda. As she'd stumbled out of her parents' brownstone in a haze, Tara had started calling her friends from the alphabetical list in her cell phone. Darcy was on set with the movie and couldn't talk. She'd left a message for Elle, then finally, Lindsay had answered at Island Books. "Don't panic," she'd said. "I'm on my way out now. Meet me at Bryant Park, soon as you can get down here."

As she adjusted her sunglasses, Tara searched for a place to begin. "I'm so sorry to pull you from work, but—"

"Don't even think about it. I told the managing editor I had a medical emergency, and he's so squeamish I know he'll never ask me about the details." She circled her fingers around Tara's wrist. "What happened, honey?"

Tara told her everything, how she went looking for her birth certificate and found the photographs, how her mother walked in and confessed that this man, this Willy Rockwell, was her grandfather.

"And why did they keep it a secret all these years?" Lindsay asked.

"Embarrassment?" Tara shrugged. "My mother didn't quite admit it, but I think it made her feel separate from her half sisters, who had a different, darker-skinned father. You know, I've always noticed some tension among them, but I just chalked it off to my mother's stubbornness. I guess my instincts were right."

Lindsay's short A-line cut bobbed as she shook her head. "I can't believe your parents would do that to you. I mean, families keep a lot of things private, but to lie to you and then make you feel bad because you looked different from your aunts and cousins . . ."

"I wonder if Denise and Wayne know?" Tara's brother might not care so much; with chocolate brown skin like their father's, he'd never suffered the same identity crisis. But Denise would want to know. "I'm going to call Denise."

Just as she took out her cell phone, it beeped with a call. "Elle," Tara said, reading the caller ID. "Hey . . ."

"Got your message," Elle said breathlessly, "and I'm running, I tell you, fleeing a restaurant near the old meat market, where I just had yet another lunch date from hell. Meet me at my place in ten."

At Elle and Darcy's apartment in Hell's Kitchen, Lindsay ordered Chinese food and Tara called her older sister, who wasn't quite so interested in hearing about the family scandal. "We'll talk about it next time I see you, Ta," Denise said. "Right now, I've got to pick up Jordan from soccer camp and pull a dinner together for Curtis's clients."

"She makes it sound as if I overreacted," Tara said, closing her cell phone.

"She's in another world," Lindsay said as she handed Tara a bottle of water.

"No come, sit." Elle crimped her short red curls as she flopped onto a giant gold cushion in the living room. "Fill me in. You know how I hate to miss anything."

Tara felt better going through the story a second time; now that the initial shock of discovery was fading, the bald facts seemed clearer and easier to absorb, and the nugget of truth—the fact that her grandfather was white and she was a woman of mixed race—no longer seemed like such a scandal.

"Maybe I overreacted, but it just derailed me." Tara was curled in a ball on the corner of the burgundy chenille sofa.

"And you've been keeping such a low profile, hacking away at the bar review." Lindsay sat on the wide windowsill, her ankles crossed above tweed kitten heels.

"I'd be freaked," Elle said. "It's like someone pulling the floor out from under you." She punched the pillow and collapsed on it facedown. "I've been there. When I had to move back here, that feeling that there was no room for me in my own family, that they just couldn't fit me in anymore. And I didn't see it coming. I was totally blindsided."

"Blindsided, that's it," Tara said, recalling the sting of revelation. "There's the shock, and there's the realization that it's all been a lie, that my mother concocted this whole cultural identity that was a ruse."

"Yeah, the lies suck," Elle agreed. "I hate lies."

"But actually," Tara said thoughtfully, "this could be a blessing in disguise. I've always struggled with my cultural identity, always felt a little out of sorts, trying to be someone else. I guess it's a relief to know there's a reason my skin is pale, and it's not a bad thing. I'm not an anomaly anymore."

"Oh, honey . . ." Lindsay sat down beside her and squeezed her hand. "You never were."

"But sometimes I felt that way."

"You know," Lindsay said, "your grandmother was a social pioneer. Grandma Mitzy must have truly loved William to break the rules of social convention, fighting so many obstacles."

Tara took a deep breath as images swirled in her mind: her mother's tear-streaked face, Grandma Mitzy's ample-bosomed hugs and her Willy, the soldier in the photographs with the million-watt smile. "My Willy. She never stopped talking about him. I just didn't know who the hell she meant, and no one would fill me in."

"But now you know." Elle popped up suddenly. "There is a certain level of resolution in all this, don't you think?"

"Yes," Tara said definitively. "The truth is empowering."

"Hold that thought—it'll make a perfect fortune cookie," Elle said, jumping up as the doorbell rang. "That's our food."

Over lemon chicken and moo shoo pork, they talked about plans for the last weeks of summer. Tara hadn't let herself think that far ahead, and now, realizing that the bar would come and go, she entertained Elle's invitation to spend two uninterrupted weeks at Elle's place in the Hamptons.

"You deserve the break," Lindsay said, "and that house is magical. I've been working away in the attic this summer, and it's very conducive to writing. I feel a certain spirit there . . . I guess I feel free."

"I could use some of that," Tara said.

They were about to open their fortune cookies when the doorbell rang again. Lindsay went to answer it and returned with her brother Steve behind her, his necktie hanging from the open collar of his white dress shirt.

"Hey." His smile made her knees feel weak. "I heard what happened."

Tara shot a look at Lindsay, who shrugged. "So I called him. Who knew my bossy brother would ever be the perfect remedy?"

Steve opened his arms and Tara went to him, pressing her face to his chest as tears welled in her eyes and spilled onto his white shirt. His arms felt secure and solid around her, a safe place to be. So many secrets flying out of Pandora's box today.

"How did you know?" she asked Lindsay.

"Would finding your lingerie in the washing machine at the Brooklyn house be the tip-off?" Lindsay suggested.

"You didn't!" Tara laughed through her tears.

"Maybe not, but I figured it out. You two always did have that chemistry going."

"Yeah, but you always made it so hard, Linds," Steve said, stroking Tara's hair away from her face. "Every time I'd try to make my move, you were all over me, the pesky little sister, trying to get the details."

"That's so not true!" Lindsay shrieked, then laughed. "Okay, maybe it is."

Steve rubbed Tara's back, soothing between her shoulder blades. "I'm so sorry you had to go through this today. What can I say? Parents suck."

"Our mother is a saint!" Lindsay said.

"Yeah, yeah, St. Mary Grace, but Dad drank his way into an early grave." Steve rested his chin on the top of Tara's head, holding her close. "Maybe you were too young to remember, Linds, but I can't recall the old man without a can of beer in his hands. When he got sick the doctor told him to stop, but I don't think he knew how to cope without alcohol. He couldn't stop." Steve shrugged. "Shit happens. No family is perfect."

"I'll say!" Elle boosted herself onto the kitchen counter. "I've got a mother who's continually trying to lose herself in the desperate blight of some exotic land and a father who's trying to relive his second youth by sleeping with his students. No skeletons in our closet—my parents just put it all out there for everyone to see. So obvious."

Elle tried to make it sound comical, but Tara sensed the underlying pain she'd suffered, trying to make sense of her parents' behavior, trying to survive without the family support she needed.

"But we're the lucky ones," Tara said quietly. "Everyone has their issues. But we've got good friends to help us survive the scandals and heartbreaks."

"Words of wisdom, Grasshopper," Elle said as she cracked open a fortune cookie and flattened the slip of paper. " 'Your friends will help you survive.' " She grinned knowingly. "And your lucky numbers are 3, 7, 25, and 30!"

75

Elle

In the concrete jungle plentiful with descendants of the XY tribe, Elle was ready to stop issuing the tribal mating call and abandon the hunt. "I am getting onto PerfectPair.com and telling them to discontinue my account," Elle said. She had dialed up Lindsay to give her moral support as she dragged herself down the street toward a café holding a Perfect Pair "Event"—a speed-dating session, during which each hunter would have a mere ten minutes to make a love connection with potential prey before moving onto another ten-minute date. "If this doesn't work, I swear, I'm pulling the plug."

"Why are you even going to this?" Lindsay asked.

"Because I think, in principle, this procedure might work for me. My problem is that as soon as I meet someone, I *do* know in the first ten minutes whether there's chemistry there, whether the guy is worth pursuing. So, usually, ten minutes into the date, I'm done with him and ready to go home, change into my sweats, and dive into a pint of Ben and Jerry's in front of some *Friends* reruns."

The lunchtime speed-dating was moderated by Kyra "my on-line name is Hot_4U!" and she screened everyone who tried to get into the seating area of the café, checking their Perfect Pair member status and pointing to the rules sketched on the cafe's chalkboard:

* * *

NO REAL NAMES—GO BY YOUR ONLINE NAME.

NO FRATERNIZING AFTER THE FINAL BELL RINGS. IF YOU'RE IN-
TERESTED, CONTACT THE MEMBER THROUGH PERFECT PAIR.

PLEASE RESPECT THE TEN-MINUTE TIME LIMIT FOR EACH DATE.

SPEED DATING IS FOR MEMBERS ONLY.

Elle, or rather "CinderElle" was checked in and sent to a small
table for two and instructed to make a little nameplate for herself
with a piece of paper, since the gentlemen would do the "speeding"
from table to table. "We used to give the women name tags," Kyra
explained, "but then too many gals felt the men were talking to
their boobs."

As she settled in, Elle couldn't help but notice the bevy of bucks
gathered at the coffee bar, shimmying and nickering like horses at
the starting gate. Her overall impression was testosterone and a
few questionable hairdos. Oh, well. Five dates in fifty minutes. At
least it would be quick.

Bachelor number one . . .

PuppyLove wore a permanent scowl and a toupee that was so
poofy, Elle found it hard to tear her eyes away from the upward
swirl of dark brown fiber.

"Are you looking for someone to love?" he asked with a pitiful
expression.

"Well, actually, no," Elle began to respond, wanting to tell him
that she had abandoned silly romantic notions of finding a soul
mate or that one star-crossed lover in her path, that she was really
looking for a good male friend whom she could be a friend to and
share the Sunday crossword puzzle with and, well, of course, have
some fun with in bed.

"My quest, CinderElle, is to find a soul mate," he went on, interrupting her answer. "I have been pursuing her for many years
now, and we're talking about active pursuit. I'm a five-year veteran
with Perfect Pair, but I won't give up. Romantic fulfillment doesn't
come to quitters!" he railed with such passion, Elle had to check if
his wig stayed intact.

"Well, then I guess that explains Billy Joel and Christie," she
said with a grin.

PuppyLove squinted curiously. "Maybe. But as I was saying,
CinderElle, I've spent a long time searching, and, admittedly, I

don't feel that magic between you and me, but if you have any friends who might be interested . . ."

Ding! Next?

With the squarish jaw of a boxer and a toothpaste commercial smile, Vanilla Matt was immediately engaging.

"You look like my kind of girl, CinderElle," he said, checking her out from under lazy eyelids.

She flashed him a little smile, wondering if his "Vanilla name" came from his creamy skin and white-blond hair.

"Do you like to eat?" Vanilla Matt asked.

"Sure, and I'm not picky." Was this a dinner invitation? He was sort of cute. "I like Italian, Middle-eastern, Thai, Brazilian—"

"No, not food." He shot a naughty look over his shoulder and leaned over the table. "I mean, do you like to *eat.*" He shot his tongue out and licked his chops like a dog.

Next!

LowMoJo, the bass guitar player in a punk band, didn't have much to say, and Elle was hard-pressed to make conversation because she kept hearing Vanilla Matt behind her say, "Yeah, but do you like to *eat?*"

Ding!

The fourth contender, Apple Jack, seemed like a nice enough guy, a nurse, he said, but he'd been so smitten by someone else he just met that he kept turning back and calling out comments to the other girl, a big-jewelry type, with half a dozen links of fat bead around her neck, matched with big button earrings.

"Now, Apple Jack," Kyra called out, patrolling the aisles like a schoolteacher, "remember the rules."

"Sorry," he told Elle.

"That's okay," she told him, secretly envying that he'd made a connection.

Ding!

By number five, Elle had lost patience. "Listen"—she checked his name tag—"Wally O, I've got to be honest. You're probably Mr. Wonderful, but my tolerance for chitchat ran out about thirty minutes ago."

He laughed. "Tell me about it. I'd leave but I'm afraid Sr. Kyra will send me to the principal's office."

They laughed together, then he leaned back casually, making

Elle feel relaxed. "Okay, I'm not really here. Let's say I'm tossing the dice at the tables in Monte Carlo. I'm wearing a tux, and you look stunning in a Dior gown."

Actually, he was wearing a black Tommy Bahama brushed-silk shirt that hinted of tropical pleasures and dark tiki huts.

"Monte Carlo is overrated," Elle said, "but I do like the Dior gown."

"You've been there? I'm impressed. I've been anchored here for years. The family business. It's all fallen on my shoulders now, as my sisters want to be married with children."

"How many sisters do you have?"

"Seems like dozens—or maybe that's just the nieces and nephews."

A big family. Elle's heart swelled.

"And how about you?" he asked. "Where's your head right now, if you didn't have to be here?"

"East."

"The Atlantic? You mean Europe?"

"Eastern Long Island—the Hamptons," she said. "I've got a place there, and there's nothing like spending your summer on the beach."

"The salt air, sandpipers. The cool smack of a wave on your sunburn."

"You sound like a beach boy."

"Hyannis Port. My family has a place there."

Elle's eyes narrowed. Could it be? Was he from the famous clan? "It's a long drive from here."

He nodded. "You have to go by seaplane."

Ding!

Not to appear desperate, but Elle wanted to reach across the table and manacle his wrists.

"We're supposed to stop talking and scram," Wally O said, casting a look at the moderator. "But I feel like I could talk to you the rest of the afternoon." Watching cautiously for the speed-dating police, he pressed a business card into Elle's hand. "Let's cut through the Web site crap. Call me."

Elle clasped her hand over the card, a song in her heart thrumming happily as Wally O nodded again, then stepped into the line of people exiting the café.

A card . . . defying authority . . . she liked this guy.

And suddenly, though everyone was out the door and heading back to work, or, perhaps in Vanilla Matt's case, off to find quick "eats," Elle strolled out of the café with renewed hope.

She had Wally O's business card. At last, a solid prospect for Lindsay's Labor Day party.

As soon as Elle returned to the office, she set up her laptop and looked up Wally O's profile on PerfectPair.com. Lindsay's party wasn't until next week, but she just wanted to fill out some of the other details of this amazing man. Besides, she'd been assigned the odious task of removing old files from the cranky dinosaur of a computer in Judd Siegel's basement office, and she needed something to distract her from the smell of must and boredom.

Odd, but she didn't see him listed. She tried to check a few different ways, then called the number on the card. A recording told her the number was no longer in service.

"What do you think?" she asked Lindsay. "Is he a party crasher?"

"A Perfect Pair crasher!" Lindsay said with a giggle.

"Hey, it's not funny. He was the only guy there who was worth talking to."

"Probably because he totally fabricated his life. I mean, the whole Kennedy inference. Oh, Elle, I never did think that speed dating was a good idea. Just something about it, something I read . . ."

"I can't believe it, and I don't want to believe it." He'd been so real. He'd looked her in the eye and asked her to call him. "You know what? I'm going to call Perfect Pair and ask them to help me find him. After all, what am I paying them for?"

Just then Judd came down the stairs. "How's it going?" he asked, ignoring that she was on the phone.

She lifted her chin from the phone. "Slow but steady. There's a bunch of floppies with downloaded stuff on the table upstairs." Hopefully, that would get rid of him so that she could focus on more urgent matters, like finding Wally O.

"And you know what else?" she told Lindsay. "How the hell did he get past Killer Kyra?"

"I don't know, but how could a member of the Web site disappear like that?"

"Well, I am going to make him reappear. I've tracked down some rare, difficult items in my production career. A clapping walrus. A Model T Ford. I can find him. And then I'll invite him to your Labor Day party. How's that?"

Judd coughed from the other end of the room. *Oh, just go play with your old computer files*, she thought, willing him away.

"Elle, you've got to see this," Lindsay's voice sounded reluctant. "I just found something online about speed-dating event crashers. Serial speed daters . . . It says: 'men who appear at open dating events and portray themselves as the perfect match. One local impersonator has hit ten cafés in the past three months, usually claiming to be the descendant of British royalty or a Kennedy.' Hold on, I'm forwarding this article to you."

"Oh, no! What kind of loser goes around copping a ten-minute date?" Elle sank back in disappointment and embarrassment.

"A ten-minute man?" Lindsay joked.

"Oh, no . . ."

"Sorry, I don't mean to make fun of your predicament. Listen, I've got to run. Copy deadline beckons, but don't feel bad. I'm not going to have a date for the Hamptons party, either."

It was the law of converse good wishes that whenever someone told Elle not to feel bad, she felt worse. She flipped her phone closed and pulled her knees to her chest, and huddled on the crappy old desk chair, feeling crushed.

There was no Wally O Kennedy.

She didn't have a date for the party.

She would be there with her game smile on, that toothy grin of a desperate single woman. And after the party she would adopt a dozen cats and let the gray streak in her hair grow out—Spinster Elle.

"Is there a problem?" His voice interrupted her pity party.

She felt tears welling in her eyes, so she didn't turn to face him. "No."

"It's about this Web site thing, isn't it? The love match online?"

She shot a glance and noticed that he was standing by the PerfectPair.com screen on her laptop, which she'd left on. Dumb, Elle. Stupid, stupid. All these years she'd managed to stay under his radar, the perfect employee because she never had issues, never needed attention. And now she'd blown it all in one afternoon.

"Look," he said, "so the synthetic dating didn't work out for you."

"It's more than that," she said. "It's about my failure as a person to find a single person on this planet with whom I am compatible." Maybe her parents were right to send her thousands of miles away from them. She was hopeless.

"Whoa." She heard him edging closer behind her. "Aren't you being a little hard on yourself? I mean, you may have failed, but no one ever said that all that romance crap is a requirement for peaceful fulfillment on the planet."

"I'm not talking about romance, but you wouldn't understand. It's a girl thing." She couldn't believe they were talking about this. Judd was not an employer to notice that the office was on fire, let alone that an employee was having a problem.

"I heard you talking about the party. I can't help you out with the whole planetary compatibility thing, but I could be your date."

"What?" She rubbed the tears from her eyes and swung around to face him.

"I'll be your date for the Hamptons party. Haven't been out there in a while, and I think we're on hiatus that week."

"No." She knew he was joking, and it served her right for bringing her personal crises into the office. "Sorry. I'll figure this out. You just . . . go do whatever you were doing."

"Elle . . ." His baritone voice rocked her as he sat on the edge of the desk, nearly touching the huge, chunky old monitor. "I want to do this for you."

She shook her head, feeling tears well again at his generosity and pity. "No, you don't."

"A night in the Hamptons? What's not to like?"

She wiped her cheeks with her hands and stared up at him, awed by the sweet gesture and all the while wondering if they would be able to stop arguing long enough to look like a couple, just for a weekend.

76

Lindsay

"What made me think I could plan and pull off a party?" I was elbow deep in peanut butter cookie batter, as I'd promised Maisy I'd bake cookies for the party, then told Ma I'd do a double batch so there'd be enough to bring to the church picnic, since Father Healy was always reminding Ma how much he enjoyed the McCorkle secret recipe for chocolate chip cookies. "I hate parties. I'm a neurotic hostess. Why did I do this?"

"Because you wanted to bring together all the various worlds we dabble in," Elle answered, "all the publishing people you work with, the crew from Darcy's film, Maisy's friends and their parents. You wanted to give Steve and Tara our nod of approval in a comforting way. You wanted to heap gobs of pressure on my head to find a suitable match so that I am not, yet again, dateless and pathetic as another summer draws to a close."

"I'm doing all that?" Nodding, I dropped gobs of batter onto the baking sheet, then pressed each blob flat with a fork. "I'm a better person than I realized. I should get a medal or a Golden Globe or something. Besides . . ." I paused to shoo Elle's fingers from the bowl of batter. "You found a date, and he's freakin' gorgeous. You never told me Judd Siegel looked like Chris Noth."

"Don't let him hear you say that." Elle looked over her shoulder. "Believe me, Judd does not need any ego boosts. If his head gets any bigger he won't fit in that ridiculous little Miata."

"I heard that," a deep voice called from the hallway, and Judd appeared in the doorway, barechested and barefoot, dressed in black swim trunks. "And thanks about the Chris Noth thing, Lindsay. I worked with him on a Broadway show once, and people did mistake us for brothers."

Elle clasped her hands to her ears. "Get over yourself and let us finish up here. People are going to start arriving in an hour. Why don't you go get ready?"

He held out his arms. "I am ready. It's a pool party, isn't it?"

"Yeah, but you don't have to play the pool boy."

He came up to the counter and lifted a raw cookie from the baking sheet. "So I'll put on a shirt."

"That's it, hands off!" Elle ordered.

"You were stealing cookie dough," he said innocently.

"I live here. And . . . and . . ."

I bit my lip, enjoying the interesting chemistry between these two. I'd never seen Elle get so flustered around a guy before.

"Get a shirt," Elle instructed him, "and then you can come help us get the bar set up."

"Slavedriver," he muttered. "I'm glad you're not my boss at work."

Although he ducked out toward the pool, I still lowered my voice. "He really is a crack-up. Don't you like him?"

"Judd Siegel lives in another world—a place people like you and me do not inhabit. You can't imagine the high-powered studio execs, the multimillion dollar deals, and the celebs. He travels on the Concorde, and we're pedestrians. You can't mix two cultures like that. You can just stand outside and observe, that's it."

"Oh." I slid the last batch of cookies into the oven, wondering if Elle was overthinking this. "I just thought he was cute."

Three hours into the party, I passed a plate of cookies, tarts, and eclairs among the guests on the poolside lanai, reminding everyone that coffee and tea and cordials were on the table.

"I really shouldn't, but I have such a weakness for sweets," said Mouse, one of Darcy's costars from the movie. Mouse had driven out from Manhattan with her husband Kenny, a large, gregarious black man who owned two popular clubs in the city.

"Oh, go on, sugar," Kenny told her. "Since you started shooting you've been wearing yourself down into a little slip of a thing."

"I have, haven't I?" Mouse helped herself to a brownie and bit into one of my peanut butter cookies. "You have to e-mail me this recipe," she told me. "And I gotta thank you for this lovely evening. With Noah working us to the bone, we needed a little R and R."

"Did you hear that, Noah?" Alton said, waving at the director, who stood talking with Judd by the hedge. "Marielle's complaining again."

"That's no complaint; it's the truth," Marielle said.

"Mm-hmm." Alton nudged his girlfriend. "You taking notes, honey? Keeping a tally? 'Cause when the director starts editing the film, I don't want to be the one on the cutting-room floor. Mouse is the voice of discontent. She's the one!"

"He wouldn't have to cut you if you weren't such a camera hog!" Mouse teased.

Alton sighed. "Just go on and hide behind those brownies. I know what you're doing."

Everyone laughed, and I was glad that my friends from Island Books had fallen in quickly with Darcy's costars from the film. Jorge and his wife Rene, who usually left events after making an obligatory appearance, were still talking with Bancroft, Darcy, and Judd, having a heated discussion of books that had made successful and worthwhile films. Good indicators all around.

Except for Noah Storm, who did not seem to be having fun. His thick gold hair curled at his shoulders, his body a lean line in black T-shirt and jeans. Between the long hair and those squarish black Chanel glasses, he looked like an intellectual rock star, intense and dark but ready to explode to flashpoint on a moment's notice. I found the whole package intimidating, but I also felt a little sorry for him, standing there alone now that Judd had moved off to talk to some other guests.

I didn't want to scrape together lame conversation, but as host of the party it was my duty to deliver a good time, right? I had to give it a shot.

"Can I get you some coffee?" I offered Noah.

He held up a hand. "No, thanks. Caffeine."

I nodded, feeling the conversation dead end.

"I have to tell you, I usually don't do parties," he offered.

"Really?" Somehow, I wasn't surprised.

"Hate them. But this has been pleasant." He took a deep breath. "Do you ever smell the potatoes?"

I squinted. Darcy had said he was intense, but she hadn't mentioned borderline psychotic. "Excuse me?"

"The potatoes from the farm down the road? I've read that the Hamptons used to be covered by them—potato farms. At night, you could smell the starch in the air."

"My dad used to say that," I said, recalling my father's old mythology that if you didn't wash behind your ears, Long Island potatoes would grow there. I felt a twinge of nostalgia at the memory as I saw my mother on the other side of the pool, picking up discarded beer bottles and plates. "You don't have to clean up, Ma," I'd told her earlier. "You're a guest tonight." "Oh, you know me," Ma had said. "Got to keep busy."

"You can't capture smells on film," Noah said thoughtfully. "Sure, there's been Sniff-O-Rama, but really, in an organic way, it's an entire dimension that's missing for me in movies. When George Bailey rushes into his living room on Christmas Eve and you don't catch the smell of a fresh-cut pine tree. When Don Corleone peels the orange in *The Godfather*, the scent of citrus should cut through the air . . ." He took a deep breath. "It's a shame. Now if you could bottle the smell of the air tonight, sea salt and roses, barbecue and . . . and your perfume. That would be utopia."

Could he really pick up the tiny dab of Madam Jolie I'd pressed on the pressure point at the base of my throat this evening? Now I understood what Darcy had meant when she'd said that Noah felt things more intensely than the rest of us.

I turned to him, and he smiled, which suddenly made the complicated Noah seem surprisingly simple.

"I know," he admitted. "I need to chill."

I laughed. "I don't know. The heavy, artistic approach seems to be working for your career."

"Yeah, but it freaks people out," he said.

I laughed again, but realized he wasn't smiling anymore. Someone cranked up the music and Tara, wearing a crown of flowers in her hair, led Steve and Milo and Darcy and Ban around the pool in a ridiculous chain dance. It was a lavishly wild move for Tara, but since she'd finished taking the bar she had vowed to cut loose and relax for a while. Noah and I watched, as if waiting for a parade to pass.

"You know, Darcy thinks the world of you," Noah said. "That's why I'm here."

"Well, thanks. I guess."

"I meant that kindly. I respect your friendship, your family of friends."

"Then thanks, and I meant that sincerely."

"You want to dance," he said, a statement. "Don't let me hold you back."

"Dance with me," I said, taking his arm, a surprisingly muscular forearm for a guy who appeared gaunt.

"I can't do that to you. A geek from West Virginia trying to move with a modicum of grace and rhythm . . . it's not a pretty sight."

"Okay, you're off the hook. Until the next slow dance."

"Lindsay, I don't dance."

Just then the song ended and a slow ballad began. "What did I say? Perfect timing." I stepped toward him, feeling a surprising brush of electricity as our bodies came close. Placing his hands on my lower back, I lifted my arms to his broad shoulders and looked past his glasses to hazel eyes that registered mild panic. "Don't sweat it," I said encouragingly. "Just hold on to me and sway a little."

"I'll hold on. With my luck, we'll sway right into the pool."

Smiling, I held on tight and absorbed the surprising electricity connecting our bodies as we swayed under the lemony August moon.

77

Elle

The music of the party receded as Elle walked through the rose arbor to the far gate where a high stone wall lined a sandy lane. A decorative stone bench sat against the wall, and Elle kicked off her shoes, hitched herself up, and wiggled her butt onto the smooth stone surface, tucking her gauzy silk skirt under her legs.

She'd needed to get away from the party, needed some quiet time to figure out the questions weighing on her mind, and the old stone wall was her thinking spot, her place to come and meditate at night in range of the ocean's roar. As her feet dangled and the stars spread overhead, she wondered why Darcy seemed so strained lately. Was it the stress of doing the Storm film or was her "cover" relationship with Bancroft Hughes wearing thin? And she worried about Lindsay, working so hard on her manuscript. Didn't she feel the quiet desperation of being alone that rattled Elle? But Lindsay seemed so composed about it, so resigned, which made Elle wonder if there was something she was missing.

Then there was Tara. Would she be able to withstand her parents' disapproval of her relationship with Steve after she broke it to them?

And then, the big pickle: Judd Siegel.

A week ago he'd been simply a tyrannical boss; tonight everyone at the party thought he was her new boyfriend, and the problem with that was that it felt sort of good having him here, giving him a hard time about his superstar status, laughing with him, letting his hand touch her shoulder or gently press the curve of her back. The problem with having Judd as a temporary boyfriend was that it would hurt so much to let him go. She wanted to buy but the property was just a rental.

Noises stirred in the rose arbor, and she turned and saw him, his face a study of light and dark in the creamy moonlight, pale skin, dark hair and brows, and shadowed eyes. He climbed the bench behind her and flipped himself onto the wall with one smooth hop.

"Oh . . . it's you," she said despondently and hoped he hadn't caught her thinking out loud.

"You know, sometimes I just wish you could put aside how much you hate me and . . . you know, give me a shot. I know I come off as a big grouch sometimes, but overall, I'm not such a bad guy."

"I don't hate you." Elle leaned forward and pitched herself into the sandy lane. "It's just that I can't buy into the Judd Siegel, big-shot producer package."

He leaned forward and landed beside her. "You think I'm a big blowhard?"

"You're fucking brilliant, Judd, but you live in this other world, protected from daily annoyances by an extremely competent staff. Which I belong to. And you're up here"—she rose on the tips of her toes and reached up, waggling her fingers near the top of his head"—and I'm way down here, answering phones and wrangling the talent and putting out production fires. Not that I don't love my job, I do. But these two worlds, high and low, and there ain't no valley in between."

"Now that's just unfair." He pursed his lips, as if disappointed in her. "You'd discriminate against me because I'm a big-shot producer?"

"Not discrimination. I'm just steering clear of more power than I can balance."

"Ya think?" He tapped his chin. "By the way, is it true that you're a secret millionaire?"

"What?" She blinked. "Who told you that?"

"I still possess a few of my interviewing skills from the D.A.'s office. You told me you and your friends were renting this place, but no . . . it belongs to you, Elle. You bought it with your inheritance, isn't that right?" He took a step back and gave a ceremonial bow, then dropped to his knees and touched his forehead to the tops of her toes. "Salami, salami." He shot a look up at her. "Apparently, it's me who doesn't deserve to kiss your toes."

"Okay, now you're really pissing me off."

"And why's that? Because I'm trying to break through a wall? Making you uncomfortable, am I?" He grabbed her hand and gave a tug, and she came down to her knees, facing him. "After all those bozos you went through on that freakin' Web site, why can't you see me as boyfriend material?"

Elle hated to be put on the spot, especially when the answer was a shallow: "You're too unpredictable and impossible to control."

"Really? And you need the upper hand in a relationship? You need to be in charge?"

"That'd be great." But when she thought about it, she knew it would be boring to boss an entire relationship. "Actually, it wouldn't. I need some challenge."

He pointed to his chest. "I can be challenging."

"Ain't that the truth. But I need to feel safe." There, that was the heart of it. She thought of her parents, Genevieve and Jasper, of their perpetual movement around the globe, pulling up roots before any life could take hold. Elle would never know what had motivated their travels, but she would never forget that feeling of vulnerability each time she was dropped into a new home, registered in a new school. "That's my issue—what I never had growing up. I need to feel safe and loved. To know that I belong."

Judd sat back on his heels. "That's a tough one. No guarantees in life. Anything can happen, just like that." He snapped his fingers.

"True." They'd all been reminded of that the day the Twin Towers had fallen, the day New Yorkers feared they would never feel safe again. "But in a relationship, I think there can be a certain degree of safety, of comfort." She had that with her friends now, with Lindsay and Tara, Darcy and Milo.

"It's not something I think about. To me, comfort is a cold beer, a hot pizza, and a game with Boston College beating Penn State by a hefty margin."

"Sounds like a guy thing. You've got a lot of that going on."

"Yeah, but I could work on comfort." He leaned forward, almost nose to nose with her. "I might be able to learn about safe. You could teach me." His hands cupped her cheeks, forcing her to face him.

Admit it, just tell him you want him. But she couldn't let him in too easily; she had trouble letting go of the hard-ass facade. "Something tells me you'd be a rotten student," she said, knowing that she'd been trying to teach him all along, to civilize Judd Siegel in small ways . . . his beastly basement office, his shaggy hair . . . the mold on the ceiling. "You need a lot of work. But that doesn't stop a teacher from trying."

Still holding her face, he leaned down and pressed his lips to hers in a deep kiss. "I'll learn," he whispered. "I'll even stay for detention."

PART FIVE

Deal with It

Summer 2005

78

Tara

"Mirror hogs," Tara said, peering over the heads of her friends clustered around the vanity, trying to check her reflection in the mirror. From her bell-shaped pearl gray gown to her beaded pumps, she was every inch a bride. Getting married. Today.

Somebody stop the earth from spinning so fast.

With the deadline of Steve's job in Tokyo, the wedding had needed to be planned at light speed, with decisions made daily and a few compromises made.

But the most important decision had been made, and somehow the others fell into place, bringing twenty-nine-year-old Tara here to Lindsay's lemon-painted attic room dressed in her Vera Wang gown and made up and almost ready to walk down the aisle an hour before they needed to leave for the church. It gave her more time to soak up the joy swirling among her friends, her future mother-in-law, and Maisy, the six-year-old flower girl who couldn't get over the fact that she'd be strewing real rose petals down the aisle of the church. It would all be perfect, if her mother weren't waiting downstairs, holding back from the fun because Serena Washington wasn't comfortable being in the same room with her daughter.

"Do I have to pick up all the flower petals after the ceremony?" Maisy asked. "I might need a broom. Just a little one."

"Jumping the broom!" Tara blurted out, remembering the African American tradition at weddings. Her parents would be so disappointed that she forgot it . . .

"Got it covered," Lindsay called from the vanity. "Your sister Denise is bringing one, all decorated."

"But what about me and the flower petals?" Maisy persisted.

"You don't have to clean them up," her mother answered. "Someone in the church will take care of it. We'll be moving on to the reception." She searched for an outlet near the vanity, where Elle and Lindsay also vied for mirror space. "You know," Darcy said, holding pins in her mouth, "we could have rented a hotel suite for this."

"And what would be the fun in that?" Elle said as she dabbed sparkly red mousse into her hair. She was trying to blow-dry her usual ringlets into a softer, shaped cloud of hair that bobbed just above her shoulders.

"No fun, but plenty of electrical outlets and room service." Darcy was pinning Lindsay's brown hair atop her head so tufts fell in gentle curls, crimped by Lindsay's curling iron.

"I think I should pick up petals." Maisy's pale blue eyes went wide as she flopped onto the bed, the folds of her periwinkle satin skirt billowing around her thin legs. "We should save some. I need a wedding souvenir. Don't you, Aunt Tara?"

"Good point," Tara said. "Maybe you should collect a few after the service."

The service . . . the wedding. Tara never expected to have a day like this—a whopping celebration of her love and commitment to someone. She figured that if and when she got married, it would be a small ceremony that wouldn't stir up too much attention. After all, she and Steve had been living together in their Brooklyn brownstone for more than a year now. A month ago marriage was a distant probability. But first Steve got the job offer in Tokyo—a juicy package that would pay his and his wife's travel and living expenses—and then Mary Grace's latest prognosis turned shaky, and the timetable had been cranked up a notch. Fortunately, it all worked in well with Tara's career plans, as twenty months with the firm of Mengle, Kilroy, and Jameson was about twenty months too many. She had decided to drop out for a while and study to be a mediator—a negotiator of peaceful resolutions, she hoped—which she could do through online classes while in Japan.

"I still can't believe you guys talked me into having a big wedding," Tara said, sitting momentarily beside Maisy to slip off her satin pumps adorned with tiny beads—"magic slippers" Maisy called them when Darcy suggested she borrow them for the wedding. Now Tara was trying to avoid sitting for long, worried about putting a crease in her high-waisted gown, an elegant Vera Wang that they'd been able to buy off the rack since Tara was a size 8. But if she was going to stand, she'd have to keep her shoes off for now. "Steve and I are so low key, I worried this would be weird, but I'm liking it. Even my shoes look royal. And my feet!" She laughed as she wiggled her pedicured toes, frosted white polish with white gems on the toes. "I've never felt like a princess before, and oddly enough, I love it!"

"No one deserves it more," Mary Grace said. Lindsay's mother seemed frail, almost childlike in the overstuffed chair, a pillow behind her head so that she could save her energy for the ceremony and reception. "Besides, every girl should feel like a princess on her wedding day."

"Pampered and lucky," Tara said, lifting the skirt of her gown to flash Mary Grace a bit of leg adorned with a delicate blue lace garter her future mother-in-law had given her last week. Tara wasn't going to wear stockings or panty hose—too hot—but she wore the blue garter for good luck, part of the "Something old, something new, something borrowed, something blue," tradition. She had borrowed Darcy's shoes, her gown was new, and, as Mary Grace had said, "The garter is blue and it's certainly old—perhaps you can get a double whammy out of it." Enclosed in a tiny panel of the garter was a shiny copper penny from 1955, the year Mary Grace wed Lindsay's father, "My Tom," Mary Grace had said as Tara examined the penny. "Back then we always believed that it was good luck for a stranger to give you a penny on your wedding day. I got mine from a tourist lady visiting the Hamptons for the first time. She must have been quite amused by me and my friend Glenda, strolling into town in our house coats and rollers the day of the wedding. I didn't want to do it, but Glenda was convinced that we needed that penny, and I suspect she was right. It's brought me such luck over all these years, so many blessings. And I wish more of the same for you and Steven, Tara." They'd hugged, and despite the stiffness and pain pervading Mary Grace's body, she gave Tara a mighty squeeze. "Wooh!" Tara gasped. "You still got it, Mrs. Mick." And Steve's mother had laughed. "Oh, I don't know that I ever had it, dear."

When Tara showed Steve the garter, he was highly amused. "I remember my sisters taking it out of the box in Mom's closet and fighting over who'd get to wear it first," he said. "That thing was a valuable treasure in our house."

"The real treasure is your mother," Tara told him. "She makes me feel so special. Like she couldn't have dreamed up anyone better to be your wife."

"Yeah, well, that's no stretch." He slipped an arm around her waist and pulled her back against him. "Besides, Ma has always won my friends over. I'd be seeing someone in high school, a girl who was a little lukewarm about me, and I'd bring her around to the house and—bam!—Ma would win her over. Worked every time."

Tara laughed. "And look at me, doubly motivated. All I have to do is marry you and I get Mary Grace for a mother and Lindsay for a sister. What's not to like?"

"It's all part of the deluxe package I'm pleased to offer," he'd said, kissing her neck.

Looking from Mary Grace to her trio of friends primping in the mirror, Tara felt grateful that everything had come together so well, especially considering the lack of support from her own mother. Thank God for Lindsay, the wedding planner. Somehow she knew where to shop for gowns, flowers, caterers, and headpieces. Lindsay knew when to keep it simple and when to go for satin and beads. The woman had an instinct for weddings. "You are so good at this," Tara kept telling her. "Maybe you're next." To which Lindsay had winced. "Noah and I? I don't think so. Much as I love planning weddings, it's not in the cards for me." When Tara asked her why not, Lindsay couldn't answer. "You know I love Noah, but can you picture him in a little house in the suburbs driving our kids to school? I don't think so."

While Darcy searched her professional makeup kit for lip liner suitable for each woman's skin tone, Tara set Darcy's seed-pearled shoes on Lindsay's old desk, noticing the bulletin board still covered with postcards Lindsay had collected over the years.

"I can't believe you still have these up, Linds," Tara said.

"I'll never part with my postcards," Lindsay responded, as if horrified at the thought. There were nearly a dozen postcards chronicling Hamptons lifeguards starting in the 1980s and boasting GREETINGS FROM SOUTHAMPTON. Tara skimmed past the series, each featuring that year's fleet of muscled, tanned lifeguards, their buff torsos brimming over taut red swim trunks. Where were they now? Probably married with children. Writing software or selling cars. Everyone had to move on. Well, everyone except Serena Washington, who kept trying to recapture the days when she would snap and Tara would jump to follow her orders. Her mother refused to let go of her control over Tara, and as a result, Serena Washington now waited downstairs in the living room, one story apart from the loving atmosphere of wedding preparations, a world apart by choice.

"And you saved these postcards I sent from family vacations . . ." Those slow-paced beach weeks in Jamaica and Cancun. "Not to be outdone by postcards from Elle. There must be thirty of them. Sydney, London, Thailand, Rio . . ."

Elle and Maisy came over to check out the corkboard gallery.

"I've got everything," Lindsay said. "The ones Darcy sent from Europe. I never throw them away."

And there tucked between postcards from Jamaica and London was a photo of Tara, Lindsay, Steve, and his friend Skeeter, the four of them sitting around a Monopoly board, grinning as Skeeter tucked plastic red hotels into his nostrils. "Look at us . . . a bunch of goobers."

"That's real attractive." Elle pointed to Skeeter and shot a dubious look at Tara. "And you're marrying the guy fanning himself with Monopoly money? Of the two, I'd say he's the better choice."

79

Darcy

As Skeeter Fogarty toasted Tara and Steve, Darcy tried to keep her mind from wandering from the wedding festivities to the man seated across from her at the large round table for twelve.

Noah Storm. Dammit, everywhere she turned, he was there, like the ubiquitous, omnipresent facilitator of her artistic expression.

Not that she wasn't grateful for the huge boost he'd given her career. Critics had raved about Darcy's performance in *Life After iPod*, which had received an award at Sundance and was currently showing at the Tribeca Film Festival. They'd immediately shot a sequel with Bancroft, Alton, and Mouse. Noah had recently cast Darcy in an off-Broadway play that would begin rehearsing this month, and he'd hired Milo to do the set design—a huge opportunity for Milo, who'd been studying design at the New School for the past three years now. Noah Storm had been more than generous, and Darcy knew she had grown and prospered in the light of his capable talent. She hoped to continue working with him, learning from him.

Thanks to Noah, she'd also become something of a minor celebrity. Shots of Maisy and her walking the red carpet at premieres had appeared on all the TV mags, and Darcy had been fielding so many requests for interviews that she'd actually had to hire a publicist to manage them. The fact that she was a single mom pursuing an acting career alone seemed to endear her to the public, bringing interest from magazines as varied as *Ladies' Home Journal*, *People*, *Glamour*, *Rolling Stone*, and *Working Mother*. These days, whenever she and Maisy were waiting in line at the grocery store, her daughter would skip up to the checkout display to "find Mommy's cover," and inevitably, she did. Her friends were highly amused when they went to lunch and ladies stopped by the table to have their playbills autographed by Darcy. Sometimes, people would stare at her while she was walking down city streets or riding the subway wearing big round sunglasses and a floppy hat, and every day when she picked up Maisy at school there was the cluster of giggling fan moms, who pumped her for information on her latest project, her crazy schedule, her take on Noah or Bancroft or Mouse.

She owed Noah a huge debt. However, as she lifted her champagne flute, she wished for the millionth time that she didn't have to see him socially, that he weren't dating her best friend, that he didn't attend every momentous social gathering in her family of friends. Toasting the happy couple, Darcy sent up a silent toast: *And here's to moving Noah Storm out of sight and out of mind.*

Not that they'd had a disagreement or argument. On the contrary, they connected well artistically. Of all the directors Darcy had worked with, Noah was the best at communicating what he was looking for in a scene, the nuance of a scrap of dialogue or a single look. On set or in a rehearsal studio, they connected in a very personal, visceral way.

And that was the crux of the problem. Darcy's connection with him made it hard for her to retract, difficult to step back and remind herself that she was not entitled to a greater piece of Noah's life, that it would be wrong to reach for his hand or enjoy his embrace too much. Doubly wrong, because he was romantically involved with her best friend.

"Mommy, can we dance now?" Maisy held her hands high, ready for Darcy's embrace.

"Sure." Seeing the chance to escape Noah's entourage, Darcy lifted the light of her life off her feet and swirled her away from the table, toward the dance floor. Maisy was her date for the wedding, which was fine by Darcy, who'd drifted away from her public relationship with Bancroft Hughes after they'd finished filming the *iPod* sequel. Ban moved on to a pretty aspiring redheaded pop singer/actress and Darcy devoted the extra time to Maisy, taking her for walks in the park, watching her do her homework, baking cookies together, and reading her stories. Although Elle kept reminding her that the "girls of Bikini Beach" were pushing thirty, Darcy didn't feel the need to have a man in her life now. Between her work, which brought her juicy camaraderie and laughter, and her daughter, whose demands and capacity for love seemed endless, her days and her heart were full. When Mary Grace was diagnosed in February, Darcy was relieved to be available to both her daughter and Mary Grace, whose back pain had been slowing her down significantly.

"You can put me down," Maisy said, giggling. "Really, I'm not a baby anymore."

But still so light, so fragile. Darcy lowered Maisy to her feet and took her chubby hands. "Who gets to lead?"

"I do," Maisy said imperiously. "And please, don't step on my toes. I want this pedicure to last."

Darcy bit her lower lip. Like mother, like daughter.

80

Lindsay

As the band played the final song of the evening and Tara and Steve took their last turn on the dance floor, I felt the weight of disappointment pull me down onto a low retaining wall bordering the garden. I sat behind a potted palm wanting to cry for no reason in particular, just the vague letdown of having all the positive things in my life culminate in this evening. The wedding had provided so many juicy distractions. Deciding between roses and gardenias in Tara's headpiece had been a joyous task, though it had ended way too quickly, leaving me to face the train wreck that was my life.

Dealing with Noah and our lackluster relationship. Saying goodbye to Tara and Steve, who'd be too far for even a phone call at a reasonable time of day. And being there for Ma . . . I bit my lip to hold back the tears, not wanting to think about it.

Focus on Noah, and how to fix things with him. Hard to believe we'd been seeing each other for almost two years now and he still seemed to be a stranger at times, aloof and distracted and far more interested in scripts and films and rehearsals than he would ever be in me. It seemed that I'd suffered a thousand little heartbreaks, every time he missed a dinner date or cancelled plans because of work commitments—a last-minute rehearsal, a glitch in editing, a premiere he'd forgotten about. He'd missed my birthday gathering

at Tavern on the Green and sent me off to the Island Books
Christmas party without an escort. Mortifying. Upsetting.

But every time I planned my breakup speech, he'd boomerang
back, taking me for a latte in a quiet café to discuss story problems
in a script or stopping by my apartment with a bottle of wine and
gourmet takeout from Dean and DeLuca. In those moments, when
he actually looked across the table and seemed to see me, I felt
short bursts of hope that it might all work out, that I might weave
a relationship, albeit unconventional, with this man. Like brief
epiphanies, those moments seemed to light the way to our future
together . . . only to dim when Noah inevitably pulled away and
left me stranded once again.

What to do?

Ending the relationship was an obvious choice. But I did care
for him, very much, and I had to admit, the status of being Noah
Storm's girlfriend gave me a lift. It would be hard to let go. I was
rolling the Noah dilemma around in my mind for the thousandth
time when my brother shouted for me.

"Okay, Linds, this is it." Steve bounded over, the stiff collar of
his tux popped open, his black tie dangling. "Tara and I head back
to the city tomorrow, then the flight to Tokyo, so we figured we'd
better say good-bye now."

I glanced up at him, my lips pressed together to keep from crying. "Good-bye?"

His eyes narrowed as he took in my mood. "Hey, don't cry."

Which brought on the tears, stinging my eyes. I swiped them
away as he sat beside me, slinging an arm around my shoulders.

"We'll be back for Christmas. This is going to be a great adventure for us." He patted my back. "I gotta thank you for all the wedding stuff you did. Tara is, like, head in the clouds, and it's really
because of you."

"No problem," I said, my voice sounding as if I were swallowing
gravel. "It was fun."

"And I want you to know what a big relief it is to know you'll be
staying with Ma now. I can't tell you how much that eases my
mind."

I nodded. As the only single McCorkle child, it had fallen on
me to be our mother's caretaker. A labor of love, despite the bleak
outlook.

"I think it's going to help Ma, just having you around. She's going to beat this thing." Steve made a fist. "I have a good feeling about it."

"Steve, it's stage four pancreatic cancer," I said. What did he not get about the prognosis, which the family had discussed at length? It was the reason I was taking a leave of absence from Island Books. Ma wasn't even receiving treatment anymore, beyond pain meds and the drugs she'd agreed to take for a clinical trial. Hiding under a palm frond, I thought of the many walks I'd taken on the beach in the past few weeks, arm in arm with Ma, talking about all those end-of-life things that were important to our mother—her children, her extended family, her home. Knowing that her time on the planet was ending, Ma was working hard to sort through some things for herself.

Ma had even put a clause in her will about not selling the house on Rose Lane until at least a year after her death. "I'd like to keep the Hamptons house in the family," Ma had told me. "I know it's just a house, but so many wonderful things have happened there, and it's such a perfect place for the grandchildren."

"Let's not talk about the will, Ma," I said.

"But I want to get things in order." My mother paused near the foaming surf and shook my arm gently, her dark eyes all business. "It's my death, and I want to have a good one. Don't deny me that, lovey."

"I don't want to talk about it, okay?" I said. "It hurts too much."

"Then just listen," Ma told me. "Give an old lady her dying wish, and let me ramble on a bit."

So I understood Steve's need for denial; I just didn't have the luxury of hiding behind it anymore.

"I know what the doctors say," said Steve, "but I also know they're not always right. And Ma has an iron will; when she sets her mind on something, there's no stopping her."

Death and taxes. The old joke popped into my mind unbidden: What are the two things no human can escape?

I glanced at my brother, wondering if I should bring him back to earth with real information about Ma's condition. But he was staring off across the lanai, color high on his cheeks and a glimmer in his eyes as he watched his bride talk with some of the departing guests. Steve didn't want to hear the truth; he was in major denial.

Right now, he viewed the world through the rosy tint of newlywed optimism.

"And Ma's taking that trial drug, right?" Steve reminded me, proving that he had been paying attention to some of the facts. "The derivative of the Asian shrub? What if that's the miracle cure? Anything is possible, Linds."

"That's true," I said, leaving his hope intact.

We stood up and I grabbed him tight in a killer hug. "I'm going to miss you guys," I whispered, "but I'm so glad you found each other." Maybe he was right to stay positive and expect miracles. Hope springs eternal.

81

Tara

"Sounds like someone woke up on the wrong side of the broomstick," Steve said the morning after the wedding as Tara tossed small bottles of lotion and shampoo into her travel kit.

"Yeah, I'm cranky." She let out a small, strained laugh. "Not that it's your fault, but why did you agree to brunch at my parents' house the day after our wedding?"

"They offered to drive us to the airport, and your father said he wanted a proper good-bye." He balled up boxers and a T-shirt and tucked them into the corner of his duffel bag.

"Ugh." She zipped up her navy Louis Vuitton luggage and dropped it down from the bed with a thud. "I was hoping to get out of town without another confrontation."

"Out of town to Tokyo? Tara, we're flying halfway around the world. It's not like we can stop in next week for coffee. I think we can spare the 'rents a few minutes before we hightail it outta here."

Tara turned to glare at him, but the sight of her husband dressed in only faded jeans softened her anger. Not an inch of flab over his waistband, his tight, flat waist led up to rippled muscles and a light patch of hair.

"What are you staring at?" he asked.

"Thirty-three years old and you still got it."

Steve covered his nipples demurely. "I'm so embarrassed," he teased. "Did you marry me for my body?"

"No . . ." She stepped up to him and pressed her palms to his flat chest. "But it sure didn't hurt."

Thank the Lord for Steve; he made the meal with her parents tolerable, almost pleasant as he discussed sports with her father and ate enough of her mother's homemade biscuits to make Serena Washington's cheeks glow with pride. When everyone was finished eating, Tara's father arose from the table and beckoned his daughter.

"Come with me, sweetheart."

Shooting a look of regret to Steve, Tara found herself following her father up the back stairs to the small room lined with books. Her father's old maple desk sat at the center of the room, his "secret" stash of cigars in the top drawer, though these days he only nibbled on the ends and occasionally lit them in the garden for a few short puffs.

Laurence Washington went straight to the cigar drawer. "Sweetheart, I hate to see you leave this way, with you and your mother so at odds."

"I'm not thrilled either, Daddy." She lingered in the doorway, not wanting to enter the room and immerse herself in a conflict. "I'm struggling with it. She lied to me."

He held the cigar under his nose and sniffed. "And you can't forgive her for that?"

"As I said, I'm struggling with it."

"And you blame your mother." He turned away, a courtroom gesture that attracted attention to his next question. "Funny," he said, turning back to her. "I was in on it, too. I participated in the lie, and yet you don't blame me."

"Maybe I should." She stepped into the room, veering left toward a bookcase and running her fingers over the titles inscribed on the bindings. "But I don't feel that way. Look, Daddy, I don't want to argue the fine legalities. The secret was Mom's to create, and it hurt me, all the time I was growing up. I felt like a freak, and she tried to make me act like someone I'm not."

"We wanted you to have a cultural context, to feel like you belonged."

"Well, I didn't, okay?"

"Point taken," he said. "But may I point out, Tara, that we tried to do what was best for you and your brother and sister. We tried, honey, and maybe we took the wrong approach. It's something you'll want to think about for when you have children."

"I won't lie to them," Tara said slowly, not wanting to shut her father down. She didn't remember him ever opening up this much before.

"But when will you tell them that you're of mixed race? How old should they be? Of course, it will be more obvious with you and Steve as parents. Maybe you won't have the same problem."

"Steve and I haven't decided whether we're having kids yet," she said. "But if we do, we'll be honest with them. They'll know they're of mixed race. And we would probably get involved with some kind of support group, so that our children could spend time with other children of mixed race and know they're not alone in the world."

"You're smarter than we were," he said, leaning back onto the edge of his desk. "More socially aware. I shouldn't be surprised by that. You were always a headstrong, stubborn little girl. You know—" His voice cracked, his eyes shiny with tears. "I'm proud of you, honey. You're finding your way . . . your own way. I'm so proud."

He reached for her, and Tara hugged him tight. "We're going to miss you, honey," he said.

"We'll be back," she reminded him, feeling her throat thicken with emotion. This was the most affection she'd ever received from her father, aside from yesterday when he'd walked her down the aisle and kissed her under her tulle veil. "It's only for a year."

"God bless you, child," he whispered. "God bless."

There was the creak of footsteps in the hall, and then Serena Washington's voice. "Are we interrupting?" Mama's fake tone indicated she knew they were, but Tara just drew in a breath and turned to face her mother and husband, who smiled casually, fingertips tucked in his jeans pockets.

"I just realized we'll have to get going right after dessert," Mama said. "They still want you to check in two hours before an international flight."

Typical Mama, always on top of the rules. Studying her now, Tara noticed that the lines at the corners of her mouth had become permanent creases and the curve of her waist had disappeared, now well disguised by her double-breasted linen suit. She also noticed that her mother held a small velvet box in her slender fingers.

"We'd better stay on schedule," Tara said, casually, finding it hard to avert her gaze from the box, a rich royal velvet.

"Oh, and this." Her mother stepped forward and handed the velvet box to Tara. "I thought you might want it."

The blue velvet felt soft in her fingers. Inside was a heart-shaped locket, a beautiful silver sliver etched with old-fashioned flowers. "How pretty."

"I know it's not in style," Serena explained quickly, "and don't think you have to wear it, but it was your grandmother's. Grandma Mitzy. There are tiny pictures of her and Willy inside."

Pressing the tiny clasp, Tara popped the locket open to see the photos, old black and whites, with Willy in his soldier's cap. An old-fashioned locket. *When you close it, the people inside kiss*, Tara thought, remembering someone saying that when she was a kid. "This is wonderful." Tara put the velvet box on her father's desk so that she could put the necklace around her neck. Her mother helped her with the clasp.

"I love it," Tara said, reaching down to touch the heart nestled just above the cleavage revealed by her camisole top. "Thank you, Mama."

Serena waved her off. "It's nothing."

Tara caught her mother's eye, knowing this was as close as they'd probably come to a reconciliation. "No, Mama, it's very special." She reached for Mama's hand and gave it a squeeze. "It means a lot to me. It always will."

Mama drew in a deep breath, nodding. She knew. At last, she got it.

"Now," Tara said, gently checking the locket at her breast, "how about that dessert?"

82

Elle

"Good morning, sports fans. Looks like the Yankees are going to go all the way this year."

Elle awoke to Judd's gravelly voice, creases of sunlight through the blinds and the robust scent of warm coffee. "The season just started," she muttered, pushing back the covers and stretching. It was all part of their morning ritual, Judd waking her with a latte and telling her how the Jets did or that the Rangers dominated last night and Elle playing the skeptic.

"A-Rod hit two runs last night," Judd said.

"Damn Yankees," Elle joked. She sat up, propped up a pillow, and sipped the latte Judd had left on the nightstand beside her. "So good. Thank you, sweetie."

He rolled onto his side and placed his palm over her knee. "What's the plan for today?"

"I'm heading out to the Hamptons. I want to take Mary Grace some of that tea she likes, and I promised Lindsay I'd relieve her so she can take a break. Lindsay doesn't get to see Noah too often, especially since he's got the new show going in the city and she's got Mary Grace out there." Although Elle was happy to help out Lindsay, in truth she felt driven to sneak in as much time with Mary Grace as she could. Each week she brought out Mrs. Mick's favorite flowers or muffins or caramels or Irish teas and spent a day listening to her stories and trying to make her laugh. In the past few years Mary Grace had become a replacement for Elle's own distant mother, who clearly believed that her role of doctoring the masses was more important than raising one daughter. It was through Mrs. Mick's hospitality, giving Elle a home in the Hamptons that summer her parents gave her the boot, that Elle envisioned buying a house and sinking roots out there. The McCorkle house on Rose Lane had become a jumping-off place for so many people, strays and friends of Lindsay and Steve. Elle would always be grateful to Mary Grace for giving her a home when she needed it most.

"Did you have a chance to read those Falkowitz scripts yet?" he asked.

"Not yet, but I'm planning to dig in on the train." She yawned. "Unless you want to loan me your driver?"

"Let's see. I've got a lunch with Showtime today, but that's midtown . . ." Judd closed his eyes, going through his schedule. Although *Truth and Justice* was on hiatus, Elle was working with him on other ongoing projects, consulting on scripts and casting, working with writers, negotiating with agents. The work suited Elle's jack-of-all-trades personality, as did the long, unpredictable hours.

Still, the best part of her tenure on Judd Siegel Productions was her developing relationship with the executive producer. After a year of tumultuous dating Elle had leapt over the obstacle of those double doors on the first floor of Judd's brownstone with an invitation to the mysterious upstairs. To her delight, there were not skeletons or shrines, but a comfortable apartment, including a den lined with bookshelves, a claw-foot bathtub, and a granite-counter kitchen with Vulcan stove and cappuccino machine. Elle had forged past the barriers and consequently she'd come to enjoy the daily patterns of her relationship with Judd, from lattes in bed to the full-time driver to the comfort of having a burly, argumentative man around 24/7.

"You can have my driver," Judd said, "but you'll need to send him back. I've got a meeting at Silver Cup tomorrow." He squeezed her knee. "Are you staying out in the Hamptons?"

"Probably through the weekend. Mary Grace is having trouble getting around. I want to be there to help."

He nodded. "I'll meet you out there Friday night?"

She smiled. "That'd be perfect."

"You okay?" he asked, his dark eyes full of concern.

She sighed. "Yeah. No. I don't know." Judd had heard various tales of her special relationship with Mary Grace McCorkle, her surrogate mother.

"Sounds like she's going," he said quietly.

"Why are you saying this?"

"Because I hate to see you blindsided." Judd had been through a similar loss a few years ago when his father died.

Swallowing back a swell of emotion, Elle nodded. "Lindsay has been in touch with a hospice. They're starting to send someone out, a few times a week."

He nodded, his eyes steady. "It's going to happen. I'm sorry, sweetheart."

Elle just nodded as a tear rolled down her cheek.

"Wheels! You got wheels?" Elle sat down in the wheelchair on the McCorkles' screened-in porch and propelled herself through the door. "Woo-hoo!" she screamed as she went flying down the newly installed ramp, a little too fast for comfort.

"I knew you'd be jealous," Mary Grace said from the porch divan, where she was sitting with Milo. "Get your own, Elle, and I'll race you."

Lindsay appeared in the doorway, looking smart in black linen pants and a burgundy camisole top that matched the highlights in her dark hair. "The rationale behind the wheelchair is to help Mom save energy by limiting her walking around town and down to the beach. With the chair, she can still get out and go where she wants." Lindsay said. "As far as I remember, Dr. Garber didn't mention anything about races."

"Fiddlesticks!" her mother crowed. "What does an oncologist know about having fun?"

"Good point," Elle said, running the wheelchair back up the ramp.

"*And* . . ." Lindsay pressed her hands to her chest in a dramatic pause. "I have good news. Great news. That was my agent on the phone."

Milo's eyes grew round as his glasses lifted. "I didn't know you had an agent."

"I found Debra through Island Books. She represents a few mystery writers, some romance writers, some serious novelists. And, to make a long story short, she said the story speaks to her and she's going to auction it off next month!" Lindsay raised her arms and did a brief happy dance.

"That's great!" Milo jumped up and gave her a hug.

"You worked on that manuscript for so long." Elle shared her excitement, remembering the days that Lindsay had holed up in the fourth-story room, reappearing only to replenish her supply of Diet Cokes. "That's the story of us, isn't it?"

"Inspired by us," Lindsay agreed, "with some creative license."

"I hope the names were changed to protect the innocent," Milo said.

"I think you're safe," Lindsay teased. "I made you bald."

"Why'd you want to do that?" Milo rubbed his bristly brown hair as if in need of reassurance.

83

Lindsay

Later that day, after Milo and I shared a train ride into the city and walked uptown to the theater district, I sat in the shadowy seats of the small theater on West Forty-fourth, replaying the bright afternoon in my head—probably the best day I'd had since the wedding. I hadn't realized the dark cloud I'd been living under, being Ma's caretaker and giving up work, until it lifted, letting a ray of light through. Elle brewed a pot of Irish tea for Ma and placed the Zabar's muffins she'd brought onto a tray while I made a pitcher of lemonade. When the tea was ready, Milo wheeled Mary Grace out to a shadow spot in her garden, where white and purple clematis climbed gracefully up the stone wall of the garage. We sat around the old stone table and talked about possibilities . . .

How much money would my book bring in if it sold? What wild, impulsive purchase would I make, at least with part of the money? Would I want to quit my job at Island Books to write other novels?

"I'm so proud," Ma said, putting her teacup down with a satisfied clink. "I'm beaming with pride. Can you tell?"

"I just thought you overdid your blush this morning," Milo said as he swiped a chunk of blueberry muffin.

"My daughter, the author." Mary Grace shifted in the wheelchair, adjusting a pillow behind her back. "I'm just dying to read your book, Lindsay. How soon can I get a copy?"

"It'll be a while, if it sells," I said. "Depending on when the publisher schedules it . . . a good rule of thumb is that it takes around nine months from manuscript to printed book, like a baby."

"So I'll be getting one more grandchild." My mother smiled. "That's delightful. But I can't wait nine months."

"I'll print out a copy of the manuscript," I promised.

"This is great news." Mary Grace rubbed her hands together greedily. "I suppose it's compensation for the fact that you girls are holding out with your single lives, refusing to bring me real grandchildren."

"Ma!" I gasped, and Elle let out a snorting laugh.

"You never put on the pressure for me to get married before," I said. "Don't start now."

"I'd love to get married," Elle said. "Judd and I have talked about it, but he's not into it. He figures we've got a good thing going, why ruin it."

"Men," Mary Grace scowled. "Pardon me, Milo, but I just can't understand their reluctance to commit to marriage these days."

"I'm with you, Mary Grace," Milo said. "I've been coercing my partner Raj to make things legal, register at City Hall, but he's very resistant, says he'd feel trapped by making a legal commitment."

"You guys should press on for what you want," I said, wanting to set the record straight. "But for me, marriage isn't going to happen anytime soon. Noah and I just don't have that kind of relationship. His first priority is his work. It consumes him, and when he's in the middle of a show or film, there's very little left of him at the end of the day." I thought of all the things he'd missed or cancelled in the past year. "He couldn't even make my birthday celebration because they were shooting that day. That's not the kind of relationship I want to sign on to for a lifetime commitment." Taking a sip of lemonade, I realized the others were watching me. "What?"

"You must have some interest in Noah," her mother pointed out. "You go into the city to see him, even if it's just to watch him rehearse the actors."

But I go to the city to escape, to take a break, to hide in the dark theater . . . I wasn't sure how much of that was true, but I didn't want to hurt Ma by suggesting that I was using Noah as an escape from her. "I don't think people should get married unless it's a perfect match," I said. "Not to sound too idealistic, because I know we're all human and flawed, but for two people to make it, there's got to be that undying attraction. A chemistry. A spark."

"And you don't have that with Noah?" Milo asked gently.

"If we do, it's fleeting." I shrugged. "I'm not complaining, it's just that I don't want to pretend that our relationship is something it's not."

"A wise bit of insight," my mother said. "You're so much more aware than I was at your age."

Now, sitting in the shadows of the tenth row of the theater, I had to wonder about the future of this relationship, especially when my boyfriend could become so consumed in his work that he didn't take time to acknowledge my presence in the theater. Not that it bothered me for the first hour or so as I watched him block a scene with Darcy and Ban and a dour woman named Helen who was playing Ban's mother in the play. Helen was straight man to Ban's comic cut-ups, and Darcy was the one who reacted with laughter and giggles, so amused that she managed to draw Noah into the comedy of it all, until he was laughing, too.

I studied them, as if observing a science experiment, a chemical reaction of foaming, colorful liquid in test tubes. When was the last time I'd seen Noah laugh? Not at his apartment, not while we were having dinner at our small table in the back of Joe Allen. And certainly not in bed, where he brought such sharp intensity to our love life that I often felt as if I were trying to play an edgy, dramatic part and failing miserably.

Where do I fit in this picture? How do I fit in Noah's life? Am I just orbiting the periphery? I wasn't sure of the answer, but somehow the questions took a lower priority as my mind went back to the phone call from my agent about the manuscript. An auction. I couldn't have asked for better news. It was a huge lift, a gift during this worst summer of my life.

As Noah started to wrap the rehearsal, I went to the edge of the stage to wait for him. "Linds . . . hey. I saw you out there." He leaned down and touched the top of my head, as if patting a bunny. "I know we were supposed to do dinner, but something came up at the last minute. The guys financing the show want to meet, and you know what that means . . ."

"You can't say no," I said, surprised that I didn't feel more dis-appointed. "I understand."

"Come to dinner with Maisy and me!" Darcy insisted. "I promised I'd take her to Mars 2112, that underground restaurant decorated like the red planet. You take a ride in a spaceship to get there."

I laughed, a little uncomfortable about the invitation. "Sorry, but I don't have twenty-five light-years to spare!" It bothered me that Darcy hadn't been out much to see my mother. When she did make it out with Maisy, it was Elle who brought Maisy over to spend time with Grandma Mick. I understood Darcy's tendency to withdraw when things became painful, but to tune out Ma . . . it was just wrong. "I should see if Milo wants to do something."

"Let me warn you, he's usually submerged in the workshop till late. After midnight. Come on," Darcy said persuasively, "we'll have fun, and Maisy will be thrilled if you come along."

"Do they serve liquor?" I asked, not wanting to shut my friend down completely. When Darcy nodded, I gave a thumbs-up. "Then let's climb aboard."

As I headed back to Darcy's dressing room, it occurred to me that I hadn't had a chance to tell Noah about my book. And oddly enough, it didn't seem to matter.

84

Darcy

"Well, this is one way to force us to put blood, sweat, and tears into our parts," Ban groused as he stood at the edge of the living-room set, sweating under the stage lights.

"I don't see any blood," Helen commented astutely.

Ban pointed two fingers at his own face. "Look closely in my bloodshot eyes."

"Isn't August an unlucky time to open a show?" Darcy asked.

"Very unlucky when your audience is going to melt," Helen said. An older actress with a bulldog face and a gravelly voice, Helen Mertz was the queen of deadpan.

"People, please." Noah raised his hands, his shirtsleeves rolled up to reveal forearms sprinkled with golden hairs. "The air-conditioning is being fixed. I would cancel rehearsal, but we need to be here this afternoon for the photographers. Previews start next week and we have to have promotional photos."

"Isn't July an unlucky month for previews?" Ban asked.

Noah folded his arms and actually smiled. "Let's try to survive this with our humor intact. I've got to run. Let's meet back here at two."

After he left, Darcy, Helen, and Ban collapsed onto the set furniture, too hot to move. "I'm going to have lunch someplace crisp and cool," Helen said. "Just as soon as I have the energy to breathe again."

Darcy planned to sneak home and enjoy a salad in front of the blasting air conditioner. "I'm heading home, if anyone wants to join me."

"How far?" Helen asked.

"Four or five blocks."

"Too far. I'll never make it," Helen said.

"I'd come along," Ban said, "however, I'm afraid we can't be seen together anymore. Now that I'm arm candy for the illustrious Nicole De Young, the press would have a field day finding me at your place."

Darcy giggled. "How is the Diva De Young? Last time I saw a picture of her, she was looking a bit gaunt."

"Are you talking about her eating disorder?" Ban clamped a hand over his mouth. "I don't know a thing. You didn't hear it from me."

"Tell us, Ban," said Helen. "Does she ever eat? Have you witnessed the Divine Nicole consuming sustenance?"

"Only sesame seeds and cranberry juice. Unsweetened, of course." He grinned. "I don't know what all the fuss is about. So the woman is thin."

"She's a negative role model for young women and impressionable girls," Helen barked. "And need I mention that people have died of that disease? Really, Ban, anorexia is no joke." She closed her script and rose from the couch dramatically. "And with that, I am going to get a sandwich. A very large, overstuffed club sandwich. A goddamned Dagwood!"

"Well," Ban sighed as Helen disappeared into the wings. "Just the two of us. You know, sometimes I regret ending our little thing."

"We had some fun," Darcy agreed, closing her eyes, "but it was hard for me to keep up with your publicity schedule. Besides, I've given up my party-girl days. I'm almost middle-aged."

"Horrors! Don't you ever let me catch you saying that again." He stretched his legs, crossing them at the ankle. "I miss you, my dear, but I don't mind losing you to a better man."

"Really?" Darcy opened one eye. "And who might that be?"

"You don't have to be coy with me. I've seen the way you look at Noah, the way your lovely face lights up when he enters a room."

Both eyes shot open. "You have?" She didn't think it was obvious. She didn't know anyone could tell . . .

"So when are you going to make your move? Go after him? Here's my personal footnote on Noah Storm: a brilliant director, but won't have a clue how you feel about him until you script it all out for him."

Darcy took a deep breath, realizing it was no use denying her attraction for Noah. "That's one script I won't be performing. I could never do that to my friend." Especially considering everything Lindsay was going through now, taking care of Mrs. Mick. Darcy had heard that they'd called in a hospice worker, but the burden of care was still primarily on Lindsay's shoulders.

"You're not doing your friend Lindsay any favors, love," Bancroft said. "I've seen the way Noah looks at you, too. You have this gift for making him laugh. No one else can lighten that sad sack up."

Darcy wiped beads of sweat from under her eyes. Could it be true? Did Noah really respond to her that way . . . romantically?

"Isn't it wrong to leave your friend embroiled with a man who doesn't love her, just because you're afraid to rattle everyone's cages?" For emphasis, he gave her the trademark Bancroft squint.

"Don't give me that lazy-eyed look," she said. "You don't know that about Noah. It's not like he's confided in you."

"Noah doesn't confide in anyone. A secretive bastard, that one."

"Okay, then. You just can't go meddling in other people's relationships, Ban. You can't know what's going on from the outside."

"Half the time you can't know what's going on from the inside, but that's never stopped me from conjecture. And based on my astute observations, I say your friend is not happy with our esteemed director. She and Noah are a rather unhappy couple. If I were you, I'd ask her if she wants out. You have the power to set it all on track, my dear."

"But I don't," Darcy said, wishing he were right, wishing that Lindsay really did want out of the relationship and that Noah really was attracted to Darcy. But as Ban said, it was all conjecture.

That afternoon, standing under the hot stage lights waiting for the photographer to get the lighting right, Darcy felt her skin covered with a fine sheen of sweat and guilt. How could she do this to her best friend? What demented part of her brain had decided to fall for Lindsay's guy? And if Bancroft could see the attraction, surely other people were aware of it.

She was just a rotten person.

Although it was not part of his usual duties, Milo was operating the lights up in the booth, and Noah was working with him to determine which lights could go dark to reduce the heat in the building. Noah lingered at the fringes of their scene, popping into view to smooth the collar of Ban's shirt or the angle of one of the actor's arms.

He moved behind Darcy and she held her breath as he placed a hand under her chin. So intimate, so invasive. It nearly brought tears to her eyes as he gently tilted her face higher. "Can you keep the chin high and look down—remember, an air of superiority."

"Got it," she said, going for imperious even as she fought hard to contain the response that flared to his touch. She longed to grab his hand, press his palm to her cheek, and kiss the soft skin of the tender pressure point on his wrist.

Did he feel the same attraction? The same spark? She tried to read a message in his eyes, but the pale gray glint of intelligence and energy remained—the intelligence of Noah's eyes, as flat as a mirror yet distant as the view through a telescope.

There were no answers in his eyes, no answers for the dilemma she found herself in, falling in love with her friend's lover. And Darcy was left in an awkward pose in an extremely stuffy, humid theater feeling bereft of hope . . . and incredibly guilty.

85

Elle

In the offices of *Truth and Justice*, production was in full swing, and Judd barely broke stride as he walked by Elle's cubicle, barking about the scuba scene in next week's script.

"We have two options," Elle told him without looking up from the budget spreadsheet on her monitor. "We can find actors who have scuba licenses, or hire scuba divers who can deliver a few lines."

"A scene in the East River!" he bellowed, circling the wall to step into her cubicle. "Who wrote this crap?"

Elle smiled. "It's your script, boss. And not a bad one. Anyway, I'm leaning toward the latter. Especially since, as I understand it, anyone going into the East River is advised to have their shots updated. Licensed divers would be prepared for that."

"Point two, and more urgent," he went on, "I understand the scene slated for this afternoon requires a stuntman, and our usual guy is out sick—"

"I know, I know. A dark-haired man to jump from one rooftop to another. I've got Jose Sanchez from Spectacular Stunts. I told him to be on set by one so he can get fitted for wardrobe."

Judd cupped her shoulders and massaged gently. "Good job, honey."

"Able to leap tall buildings in a single bound, that's me." She looked up at him. "And maybe you should watch the massages and endearments here in the office." Not that she really cared, but two assistant directors shared the cubicle beside hers, and some of the production assistants were meeting with the associate producer in the conference room on the other side of the glass wall. "You don't want the other producers to be jealous, do you?"

With a sexy glint in his eye, he trailed one finger down along her bare neck, dipping toward the cleft between her breasts. "To hell with them." He pressed his lips to her neck, whispering, "I'm not in love with them."

"So why don't we make it official, then?" Elle reached up and cupped his burly cheek. "Marry me, big guy. I got a house at the beach and we can have a happily-ever-after under a rose-covered trellis."

"Not that again." He pulled away and spun her desk chair so that she faced him. "What, have you been sneaking peaks at bridal magazines again? Believe me, happily ever after has nothing to do with signing your life away on a marriage certificate. How does that song go? Some inkstain dried upon a line . . ."

"You are so sarcastic."

"That's me, baby."

"Well, it hurts me when you put down the notion of being committed to me."

"It's not about you, Elle, it's about someone else's institution. Their rules. We don't need that. We know we're committed to each other."

Elle knew she was his one and only. Between the time they spent at his place and the long hours in the office, on set, or on location, she was cognizant of every aspect of Judd's day and night. The commitment was there. So why did he always balk at making it real?

"Then why not make it official?" she asked. "This is the society we live in, Judd, and when it comes to you, marriage is a rule I'd like to follow. I want to marry you and make it real. I want a home that we share, not shuffling between our two apartments. And yes, I want kids and all the challenges and heartaches they would bring us. I want to share that with you, Judd. Why is it so wrong?"

"Because I've been down that road, Elle." His dark eyes were soulful, bitterly dark. "It doesn't work for me. Marriage was really bad for my personality. A lethal match."

From her discussions with Judd, she'd learned how deeply he'd been hurt by the failure of his marriage. She'd also learned that it wasn't the convention of "marriage" that made the relationship fail. Even Judd had admitted, "We were just young and stupid. She was all enamored that I was a Hollywood script writer, and I was all about her long, long legs."

Elle reached for Judd's hand, peering intently in his eyes. "It won't be that way with us . . ."

"Says you."

"Judd, our relationship is completely different from your marriage, you've said so yourself."

"Yup. And our relationship has worked out well *because* it's so loose, because we're not married."

"That's not true," she objected.

He spun her around so that she faced her desk again. "Discussion ended. Back to work."

"We'll talk about it another time," she said firmly.

"Don't waste your time or mine," he said in that gruff executive producer voice he usually reserved for tough negotiations. "It's a done deal, honey."

Elle refused to give him the satisfaction of looking up as he walked away. She didn't want him to know that this time his gruff executive producer tone had cut right through her, and she didn't want him to see the disappointment that rocked her to the core.

86

Lindsay

The beginning of August brought a significant change at the McCorkle house on Rose Lane—daily visits from a hospice worker named Calida and the arrival of a huge clanking metal hospital bed on the screened-in porch. Although I had argued that the porch was going to get rainy at times, Ma would not hear of being sequestered in the living room. "If I'm to be stuck in one room, let it be a place where I can hear the birds in the morning and the waves breaking at night." I had wanted to argue that the fall and winter months would be bitterly cold out on the porch, but Calida, the soft-spoken hospice worker with bushy eyebrows and graying temples, had advised me, in a kind but firm way, not to worry about the cold months. Although it took me a moment, I got the under-lying message: the hospital bed would be gone by then.

So it was on the screened-porch that I sat in the warm days of August, reading my manuscript to my mother, who now grew tired so quickly that reading had become too much of a strain. At first, reading the prologue aloud, I had burned with embarrassment, stumbling over my own words. But as I progressed in the manu-script, I found an easy rhythm and a command of my own voice, as if I were reading an animated picture book to a child.

Ma seemed to enjoy it, as evidenced when she laughed at the jokes. "Oof! I never expected a comedy."

"Probably the Irish in me, I can't let anything go without a smirk," I said. "Besides, with a title like *Greetings from Bikini Beach*, I couldn't get too heavy."

One August day I was reading to Ma when she got a call saying that Elle would be right over.

"I thought you were back in production," I said.

"I'm sick," Elle said. "I can't go back to the office."

"Is it contagious?" After all, Ma's immunities were compromised in this weakened state.

"Is a broken heart contagious?" Elle snapped, lacking her usual cheerfulness. "I'll explain when I get there. You just get ready for a day out. I'll spell you with Mary Grace."

Realizing that I hadn't showered this morning—and probably hadn't shaved my legs in the last week—I jumped into the shower, moving quickly to make myself city worthy. Funny, how being homebound was making me lose my desire to get out. "It's depression," Calida, the hospice worker, had told me. "The best way you can take care of your mother right now is to take care of yourself. Give yourself some breaks." But how could I do that when my siblings were a hundred miles away, wrapped up in their own families, the kids' baseball games, their houses and jobs? Their incredibly important lives. Right now I hated them . . . even Steve, who'd gone off to Tokyo thinking Ma would miraculously recover. What a fool.

Elle arrived with a tale of woe to add to my misery. "I just don't know what to do about Judd. Every time I bring up marriage, he turns into an ogre. Yesterday, in the office, it got a little ugly." As Elle talked she put a muffin in a bowl and cut it into small pieces for Mary Grace. "I went home to my own apartment—alone—last night in a funk. When I woke up this morning, for the first time, I felt uncomfortable going to the office, knowing Judd would be there."

"And you've always loved your job," Mary Grace said. "Such a shame that this would spoil it for you."

"Yeah, well my mistake to get involved with the boss." Elle shook herself out of the blue mood and thrust her hands into the air. "So I'm on sick leave, and I came out here to see you guys."

"How much sick leave do you get?" Ma asked.

Elle shrugged. "Who knows? I never used it before." She dug into her shopping bag, lifted out an Estee Lauder makeup kit in a lavender bag with silver piping, and handed it to me. "This is for you. Saw it when I cut through Macy's and thought you should have it. You don't get enough time to shop these days, sweetie."

"Thank you," I said, stunned as I sorted through the beautiful lipsticks, sparkly as candy sticks, and powdered eye shadows in cool palettes of green, brown, and mauve. "I don't even remember the last time I wore makeup," I confessed. What a hermit I'd become lately.

"You're very welcome. Why don't you try some of that stuff on, then hightail it out to the train station? I'll bet Noah will be glad to see you."

Noah . . . the artistic genius, brilliant director, lousy boyfriend who was always too busy to call.

"Go on, darling," her mother said. "No reason to stay cooped up here with me. Get your fanny on that train."

"Okay." I tucked the makeup kit under my arm and headed inside. "Just give me a few minutes to make myself beautiful." Passing through the kitchen, I added, "Actually, better make that a few days."

Emerging from Penn Station into the sunlight of an August day, I felt like a zombie of my former self, moving through the familiar streets of Manhattan that somehow no longer belonged to me. Walking toward the theater I passed Joe Allen, the restaurant where Noah and I had spent hours discussing scripts and story. Down another street was the subway stop for the number one train, which I used to ride to Island Books. And ahead loomed a square blue sign for my bank, such a familiar stop, back when I had a life here in the city.

No one questioned me as I passed through the stage door of the old theater. The props mistress gave me a nod as I moved through the wings, finding my way to the middle seats of the cool theater suffused in amber light. The cast and crew of Noah's shows had gotten used to seeing me wait on the fringes, like Noah's personal fan club.

I sank into a chair in the middle of the theater, wondering if it was worth interrupting Noah to let him know I was here for an unexpected visit. He stood at the foot of the stage, running a scene with Bancroft and Darcy, the three of them laughing over some mistake that Ban kept making that struck them as funny. Since the actors were not miked, I could only catch bits and pieces of their conversation. Feeling like an outsider, I had just sunk down into my seat when someone tapped my shoulder—Milo, sporting a wide grin.

"Hey, Linds. Does Noah know you're here?"

"It's a surprise visit. Elle showed up to stay with Ma at the last minute."

"Come on up to the booth to keep me company. I'm working on the light board until they hire a proper lighting designer."

Feeling like I was sneaking off to an adventure, I followed him through a door in the back of the theater to a catwalk that led to the lighting booth, a small box perched high at the rear of the theater, barely big enough for two people.

"It's a good thing neither of us has a weight problem," I said, tucking myself behind the console of red lights, switches, and levers. "But it is cozy up here. A real bird's-eye view."

Onstage, Darcy doubled over, giggling about something I had missed.

"It's not that funny," Bancroft said, laughing despite himself.

"They're punchy today, aren't they?" I commented.

"Rehearsals have been going well," Milo said. "Noah seems happy with the way things are shaping up, don't you think?"

"I wouldn't know." I ran my fingertips over the edge of the light board, feeling like a spectator of my own life. "He always pulls away when he's working on something. Spins himself into a cocoon."

"One of those artistic types," Milo said, half joking.

"Sort of. But lately I feel very far away from him, as if he's working in a foreign country and phoning in every few weeks. I don't know. Maybe it's because I'm stuck out in the Hamptons with Ma and he's stuck here with the show."

"Maybe," Milo agreed, his voice slowing tentatively. "Or maybe there's something else to it. Did you ever consider that Noah might be interested in someone else?"

I tensed, stabbed by the hint of bad news. "I can't imagine Noah fooling around," I said evenly. "He doesn't have time for another girlfriend, and I can't see Noah cheating on me. He's just not that type."

"Not cheating, exactly," Milo said, his eyes straight ahead on the stage, where Bancroft exited and Noah jumped onto the apron, motioning Darcy closer. Apparently Noah was blocking her soliloquy, directing her to possible marks downstage left.

I shifted my sandaled feet uncomfortably. "Milo, what are you trying to say?"

"Um . . ." Milo pressed his lips together, frowning as he followed Darcy with a spotlight. "Have you ever thought that your boyfriend might be in love with someone else?"

I looked from him to the stage, spotlight on Darcy and Noah. He had one hand behind her back, the other pressed to her sternum in a gesture so intimate it stole my breath away. He was probably instructing her on projecting or feeling the scene with her heart or letting the energy flow up along her spine—business as usual, but in a most personal way.

"Oh, God." I pressed a fist to my mouth, unable to turn away from the new source of pain. The glaring discovery was so apparent, so obvious that I felt a slight sting of foolishness at the thought of all the people who'd been watching it happen for months. "I feel so stupid." I turned to Milo. "How long has it been going on?"

"It hasn't. You know Noah wouldn't cheat on you—you said it yourself. And Darcy is your friend." He shook his head, his eyes glimmering, dots from the light board reflected in his glasses. "She wouldn't do anything to hurt you. I'm fairly sure no one has acted on this attraction, out of love and respect for you."

"Me? Oh, great. Now I'm the one keeping two star-crossed lovers apart." I turned back to the stage, feeling the corner of my mouth twitch as a sob came on. My froggy face, I called it. "I'm screwing up everyone because I want to have a boyfriend," I blurted out.

Milo shrugged. "Nobody can blame you. Noah's a hot property."

"Not a very good boyfriend," I said, my voice catching with a sob. My defenses were down. I was tired, and my mother was dying, and I missed my job and my Manhattan life.

But I couldn't let all that cloud my judgment. Noah and I had been going through the paces for a while now; a loveless relationship based on convenience, social status, and probably some pity on his part.

"I've been such a moron."

"No, you haven't." Milo put a hand on my shoulder. "You've been forging ahead, fighting your own battles miles away from all this . . . this dynamic that seems to have a life of its own."

Down on the stage, Darcy's golden hair fell over one shoulder as she lifted her head to face Noah. He moved closer to her—close, but not touching. Such intensity, their eyes locked on each other.

I felt the sting of jealousy. Something *was* going on between them! *Look! Look!* I wanted to shriek at Milo. *They're in love—they've got chemistry—and Noah and I always struggled to find common ground.* "It's not fair," I said aloud.

"It never is, kiddo."

I ended my relationship with Noah that very day. Not surprisingly, he didn't seem too distressed but expressed his concern for me. "You're going through so much right now, I know I haven't been a great source of support," he said. "I'm sorry, but though I don't show it, I do worry about you. Don't slip away, Lindsay."

"I'll be fine," I told him with more confidence than I felt. "I've got good friends." I wasn't sure that I could count Darcy among them at the moment, but I didn't want to go through all the sordid details with Noah. Chances were, he wasn't even aware of his own feelings for Darcy; though Noah was a master at interpreting other pieces, he was clueless when it came to reading the indicators and feelings in his own life.

I returned to the Hamptons that evening, fighting my way among the rush-hour throngs of passengers. Ma was asleep when I crept into the house, but Elle was in the living room, watching syndicated reruns of *Truth and Justice*.

"I can barely stand it," Elle said sadly, her legs folded like a pretzel on the Chinese rug. "What am I going to do? I love my job, but I can't keep working on that show with *him* in the same office. The whole damn show has his thumbprint on it, but I can't turn it off."

I picked up the remote and turned to the Cartoon Network, where *Courage the Cowardly Dog* moaned for mercy. "I broke up with Noah today."

Elle winced. "Oh, honey . . . what happened?"

I opened a bottle of wine and spilled my troubles to my friend.

"Now let me get this straight," Elle said, cupping her wineglass to her chest. "You're giving Noah to Darcy?"

"I'm conceding graciously," I said.

"And you're not pissed?" Elle's green eyes went wide. "She stole your man, girl!"

"He was never mine in the first place. Noah and I never had the rapport he seems to have with Darcy."

"And you're not mad at her?" Elle shook her head. "Are you depressed, or just incredibly mature?"

"I'm not mad . . . well, maybe a little," I admitted. "But I think this was just one of those things that snowballed out of control. That's the thing about love. It bites you in the ass when you least expect it." It had been years since I had known how it felt to be in love . . . the sudden laughter, the spark of attraction, the resoundingly familiar echo of Bear's face. I'd memorized that face. A good thing, as the memory was the only trace of the only real love of my life.

"Yup." Elle tipped the bottle into my wineglass. "Love certainly does bite."

"Yeah," I said, "and when it doesn't bite, well, that bites, too." When the bottle was dry, we turned on the monitor connected to the porch, filed up the dark stairs, and fell into the two single beds in my old attic room.

As I spiraled into a dream, I breathed deeply in relief. Single again. At least there was a modicum of peace in closure.

87

Elle

The next day Elle stayed in her pajamas until noon, when Lindsay suggested a game of Scrabble on the porch with Mrs. Mick.

"Perfect!" Elle said, recalling the many summer days when they'd taken over the porch, staging Scrabble tournaments and Monopoly marathons. What better way to plod through the "I've just lost my guy" blues?

Mary Grace was kicking their butts, having just scored an extra fifty points by using all seven letters for the word *monkeys*. She replaced her tiles, then stared above their heads at the side yard. "Good Lord!" Mary Grace gasped. "I swear to God, the undertaker's come for me early."

"Ma, are you hallucinating now," Lindsay said, her head tilted over the Scrabble board, "or just trying to distract me from finding a way to use the triple word space?"

Elle scrambled to the door in her pink Joe Boxer shorts and red T-shirt, amazed to see a black limousine parking in the driveway. As the driver's side door opened, she recognized Judd's driver. "Judd's limo," she said aloud. "Shit!" She hated being caught, even though she wasn't really doing anything that wrong.

Lindsay padded to the screen door in bare feet and swung her denim hip against it as she leaned out. "Hi, Judd," she called, adding for those inside the room, "it's about time."

Judd unfolded himself from the limousine, looking taller in the McCorkles' side yard. "Is she in there?"

With a squeal, Elle ducked behind Lindsay. "Tell him no!" she giggled, pressing her face to the back of Lindsay's T-shirt.

She didn't hear an answer, but she suspected that her friend gave her up, as Judd's shoes scraped up the steps. A moment later, his booming voice filled the room.

"Cute, Elle. Here, I think you've been mugged or something and you're out here playing Scrabble in your pj's?"

Elle straightened, determined not to be bullied by him. "How the hell did you find me here?" she asked, her hands balled in fists on her narrow hips.

"You forget, I was a lawyer first, a district attorney second. I know a few things about investigation, missy."

Missy? Elle wanted to laugh. Was that the tough language he used to use when interrogating the really bad guys?

"When you weren't at your apartment, where you were *supposed to be sick,*" Judd glared at her for emphasis, "I called Darcy."

"She doesn't know I'm here."

"She figured you came out east. I talked her into auditioning for the new pilot, then got my driver to bring me out here. When there was no answer at your place, I knew I'd have to shake down the neighborhood." He swung around to face Mary Grace. "Sorry to intrude, Mrs. McCorkle."

With the help of the hand mirror and comb, Mary Grace had quickly plumped her short curls into an acceptable hairdo. "Not a problem, Judd. You just go on and take care of business and don't mind me. I'd skedaddle but I'm not very mobile these days."

And this confrontation was very likely one of the juiciest Mary Grace had been privy to for the past six months, Elle thought as she watched Judd turn on the charm. The smooth operator.

"I wouldn't dream of putting you out," Judd said, pressing a hand to his chest in a dramatic gesture of sincerity. His left hand clutched a brown paper bag, soggy on the bottom.

"What is that?" Elle asked, wrinkling her nose at the bag.

He held it up. "This, my dear, is chicken matzo-ball soup, Jewish penicillin for a young lady who called in *sick.*" He frowned down at the bag. "Must be cold by now. Would've tasted great, if you were *sick* at home in your apartment. Where *sick* people are supposed to be."

"I'll take that off your hands." Lindsay grabbed the bag and disappeared into the kitchen.

"Sick people who don't even bother to call in sick the second day," Judd went on. "For all I know, you could have passed out in the shower or fallen down the stairs."

"I don't have stairs in my apartment," Elle pointed out, her anger giving way to amusement over Judd's histrionics. To think that he'd actually blown off his schedule to drive all the way out here . . . well, that meant something.

"As your boss, I'm appalled by your unprofessional behavior," Judd said gruffly, folding his arms. Behind him, Mary Grace's eyes went wide and she wagged a knowing finger at Elle. "You're taking advantage of the sick-leave policy," Judd added.

"The first time I ever used it in more than two years," Elle argued, determined not to cave in.

"And as your boyfriend, I'm really pissed. You could've called."

"I left a message with your assistant," Elle said. "Besides, you could've called me, if you really cared."

"I came all the way out here with chicken soup!"

"A day later." She folded her arms and turned away from him. "Do you even know what made me sick? The reason I couldn't drag myself in to work yesterday?"

He pulled in a deep breath, then sighed. "The argument? What do you want, an apology?"

"No. Not good enough." She spun around to face him. "I want to know that you're committed to our relationship, Judd. I want to make it official and start a family."

He sank down onto a chair at the foot of the hospital bed. "I'd like a family," he said quietly. "But you know how I struggle with the marriage deal." He shot a look up at Mary Grace, explaining, "The old ball and chain."

"If you'll pardon my two cents, some of us get very used to having that other person attached," Mary Grace said. "I miss my old ball and chain."

"I'm just not sure." Judd shook his head. "Don't know if I can do it."

"Well, I know that I'm not going to settle for anything less," Elle said, feeling her hands ball into fists again. He could be so frustrating. If she didn't love him, she'd kill him. "What *do* you know, Judd?"

He pointed toward the door. "I know that I'm not getting into that limo without you. I know that I miss having you at work, poking your nose into my business and bothering me on the set."

"I do *not* bother you."

"I know that my brownstone feels like an empty museum without you there." He reached into his pocket and held up a shiny gold key dangling from a ring. "I had this made for you so that you could move your stuff in. Make it your home, too."

Elle felt her knees soften at the mention of home. It was her weak spot, the need to build a nest and feather it for a family. She stared at the shiny key, saying, "What does this really mean?"

"That I want you in my life," he said. "That I want to wake up with you in the morning and go to sleep with you at night."

"Sounds like the old ball and chain to me," Mary Grace said cheerfully.

Elle took the key ring from him, slid it on her ring finger and jiggled her hand. "It's a little big," she complained. "Not to be pushy, but I'd like a solitaire diamond. Tiffany's would do."

"You are pushy."

"Yeah, I am, and I'm not going to settle here, Judd. I want to marry you. I want to be married to you, and I'm not ashamed to say it. I've got a spectacular rose arbor at that house down the road. Would you give me a chance to use it?"

"It does make for lovely photos," Mary Grace chimed in.

"I wish I had your confidence," he said. "Look, can we live together for a while first?"

"A few months?" she said.

"I was thinking years," he admitted.

"How about a one-year trial period?" Mrs. Mick suggested. "Like a purchase with a one-year warranty. A lease with an option to buy. I got that on my last car, and I was quite pleased with it."

Elle looked up into Judd's dark eyes and said, "I'll take it," as he nodded. She threw her arms around him in a hug that lifted her off her bare feet. Judd, her big bull of a man. She loved him way too much to settle for anything less than forever.

"Lovely," Mary Grace said, pushing away the table with the Scrabble board. "With that resolved, it's lunchtime, and I hear we have some delicious chicken soup. Any takers?"

88

Lindsay

For me, the month of August came to be measured by progress in reading my manuscript to Ma. Forty pages was a good day, sixty sensational. Twenty had to suffice on a day when Ma needed pain meds, an increasing event now that the tumor had grown. "It's very likely the tumor has created a blockage in the bowels," said Willow, a pear-shaped rented nurse who seemed to match her name with her wooden clogs and wiry gold hair down to her waist. "That's going to be causing you a lot of pain. Dr. Garber says I can increase your pain medication, if you like."

"Day by day," Ma had answered, pressing her eyes closed as Willow helped her shift positions in the bed. There was to be no more surgery, no talk of stents or chemotherapy. Even the drug trial was over for Mary Grace McCorkle. "I want to go with dignity, at home," she told anyone who cared to listen. "I'll not linger on, a bag of bones in some cold hospital." I understood my mother's decision and, though I respected it, watching the inevitable unfold wasn't easy.

By the third week in August, we were a mere fifty pages from the end of my manuscript. I went to bed that night with a promise to read more in the morning, and Ma flipped from Jay to Dave and back, looking for some comic relief in the night. "Are you okay, Ma?" I asked the question I seemed to repeat a million times a day.

"Are you okay? Are you hot? Are you cold? Do you need juice? Are you hungry? Do you need the bedpan?"

"I'm fine, dear," Ma said, pushing a smile. "You sleep well."

But up in the dark attic, I fell into a deep sleep that led to a nightmare I couldn't escape. Despite the dream's surreal quality, its choppy sense of reality, I was unable to pull myself out of it, unable to run fast enough from the towering tidal wave that loomed over me, unable to dig fast enough in the mound of sand that had covered the people on the beach.

I bolted up with a screech, unable to shake the image of the impossible mound of sand despite the watery moonlight of my bedroom. My brain seemed to throb in my head as I threw back the covers and padded downstairs to the porch, where black-and-white images of soldiers in WWII tanks flashed on the television. Ma's eyes were closed, her breathing steady. I clicked off the television and turned to leave.

"You can leave it on," my mother said. "I was just resting my eyes."

It was an old family joke, something my grandfather had started when he fell asleep reading the newspaper on lazy Sunday afternoons. "Just resting my eyes . . ."

"I had a bad dream," I admitted, my hands still trembling. "A whopping nightmare."

"Come here, lovey." Ma curled to one side of the bed and patted the mattress beside her.

"It was awful," I said, lowering myself to the crisp white sheets of the hospital bed.

"What happened in the dream?" Ma asked, running her hand over my arm soothingly.

"I dreamed there was a huge, towering tidal wave coming. You and I were on the beach together, and we just stood there, frozen in a panic as this monster wave arched over us. People were screaming, and I got toppled by the water. And when the wave receded, there was just this mound of sand beside me, and I knew you were under there, and I just kept digging, but . . . but . . ."

"Shh." Ma stroked my hair, pressing my face into the white sheets as I sobbed. "It was just a dream."

"I was in such a panic," I said, remembering the sensation of tearing into the sand with my bare fingers. The panic and fear, the helplessness.

"It's okay, lovey. Let your problems fall away, sand through your fingers."

My mother had used the sifting sand metaphor many times before, but tonight it brought back the horror of the dream again, the digging and scraping to unearth her. In the dream I needed to save my mother from death, and yet my conscious mind reminded me that her last days were inevitably near.

"Ma?" I swiped at my tears and lifted my head. Ma's skin was pale, with dark half moons under watery brown eyes that once had burned with such energy. "Are you scared?"

"What would I be afraid of? An end to the pain? Eternal rest? An all-expense-paid trip to heaven?" Mary Grace drew in a tired breath. "I'm so exhausted, weary to the bone, any kind of rest would be a blessing. I've had a good life, Lindsay. Thank the Lord, I'm not leaving anyone in the lurch if I exit the planet soon. I wouldn't mind doing more, but my body is simply not cooperating, so I guess that will all have to be saved for my sequel in heaven."

Ma made it all sound so lyrical, like an old Irish poem.

"Do we need to have a night nurse for you?" I asked, latching onto the only tangible thing I could control. "Is the pain getting worse?"

"The nights are long, but I don't want to go all loopy with the drugs. It's tolerable for now. But since we're both not likely to find sleep anytime soon, why don't you read some more for me? If you don't mind. When you read it to me, I find it's an effective diversion. A lovely distraction."

"How's that for a cover quote . . ." I slid out of bed and pressed the shoulder of my T-shirt to my damp eyes. "Critics call it 'a lovely distraction!' "

"I'm no critic," Ma chirped. "I'm your mother, and I've always known you'd be a writer some day. I'm very proud, lovey."

"Thanks, Ma." Trying not to blush, I took a deep breath as I removed the rubber band from the manuscript and flipped ahead. Just two and a half chapters left. We might just finish, after all.

89

Darcy

When the phone beeped just before four in the morning, Darcy knew.

With a sick feeling twisting her stomach, she sat up in bed with her eyes closed and felt her way to the receiver, hoping to catch it before Maisy was awakened. "Hello?"

"She's gone," Elle said in a warbly voice.

"Oh." Darcy's voice fell in the dark stillness of her bedroom. She pushed her pillow against the headboard and crossed her legs. "We all knew it was coming, but somehow it's still a shock, isn't it?"

"It's true." Elle seemed hesitant. "Darcy, I know your show just opened, but you gotta find a way to get out here. The wake's going to be at the house. The funeral at the Catholic church in Southampton."

"Of course I'll get there," Darcy said, alarmed that Elle would think otherwise. It was the third week in August, and it would be hell getting away from the show, with so many sold-out nights, but some things just stopped you in your tracks. "Why wouldn't I be there?"

"Oh, you know . . ." Elle said vaguely.

Darcy wondered if Elle was thinking of the distance that had grown between Darcy and Lindsay of late, the separation Darcy had nurtured out of guilt over Noah. Damn him! Darcy had vowed never to let a man get in the way of her relationship with a friend, and somehow, without even trying, Noah had pushed her and Lindsay apart.

"How's Lindsay holding up?" Darcy asked.

"It's hard for her," Elle said quietly. "It's a big loss, but also a relief. Nobody wanted to see Mary Grace in that much pain."

"She did so much for her mom," Darcy said, thinking of the last time she'd seen Mary Grace, just weeks ago when she'd been able to walk and laugh and cajole Maisy. Somehow the conversation had gotten to the ingredients of a good marriage, and Darcy had asked Mrs. Mick how she'd made her marriage work for twenty-plus years. "Was it your good cooking that kept Mr. Mick in the game? Those yummy Irish meatballs?" Darcy had asked. But Mary Grace shook her head. "When we got hitched, I couldn't even boil an egg! That's how pathetic I was in the kitchen." "So what was the secret to keeping it all together?" Darcy had asked her. After giving it some thought, Lindsay's mom had answered, "It's all about kindness. Be kind to others, that's all. Oh . . . and I should add, never wear blue eye shadow."

How long ago had that been? Just two or three months. And though the doctors had warned that pancreatic cancer often moved swiftly, Darcy hadn't really believed them. Perhaps the only one who really got it was Mary Grace herself, brave, bold Mrs. Mick.

"Can you tell Noah?" Elle asked, bringing Darcy back to her dark bedroom. "Lindsay doesn't want to talk to him, but I think he should know, don't you?"

Darcy turned on her bedside lamp and drew away from the circle of yellow light. "I don't get why she doesn't want to tell him. Did they have a fight?"

Elle was silent, then she blurted out, "You don't know? They broke up, weeks ago. Didn't he tell you?"

"Well, no. We don't talk usually about personal stuff." Darcy wasn't surprised that Noah hadn't mentioned anything, but what about Lindsay? Wasn't this something worth telling your best friend?

"Wait a minute! That's a royal waste of time," Elle said. "So you two haven't . . . I don't believe this."

"You two, who two?" Darcy asked as Maisy plodded into her room like a wraith in a flowered nightgown. She dove onto the bed and pressed her face into Darcy's thigh. "No, I haven't talked to

Lindsay for at least a week, but she never mentioned this. What happened?"

Elle groaned. "I can't really go through it now—I've got these phone calls to make about Mary Grace."

"And I've got Maisy here now."

"We'll talk later," Elle said. "But you'll tell Noah, right?"

"I'll tell him," Darcy said, clicking off the phone with a feeling of dread. She didn't mind telling Noah; the difficult one would be Maisy. Six years old and she'd now lost the only person who'd ever been a grandparent to her. Darcy felt a tear sting her eyes and she found herself wishing she could spare her daughter this pain.

"Mommy?" Maisy moaned without lifting her head. "Who was that?"

"It was Aunt Elle about Grandma Mick." *Your only grandparent*, Darcy thought. *A gift to both of us.*

Maisy lifted her head. "Did she die?"

Darcy nodded, then pulled her tearful child into her arms. *Please, let me be half the mother that Mary Grace was*, she prayed. Darcy could only hope that some of the older woman's generosity and kindness and goodness had rubbed off on her.

90

Lindsay

I stood on the threshold of the porch door, signing the truck driver's voucher. The man and his crew had loaded our rented hospital bed into their truck, and now the screened porch of the Southampton house looked hollow and empty, like the gaping hole in my heart. "You'll heal in time," my mother had promised before she went. "We all do. Adapt or die—it's our only choice."

I'm just getting a little sick of adapting to disappointment, I thought as I tore off my receipt and handed the mover his clipboard and a tip. "Thank you," I said, glad to have yet another onerous task off my list.

When I turned away from the door, Tara was already on the porch, sweeping sand and dust bunnies into a pile. She and Steve had arrived two nights ago and were still struggling with the time change. "You know, Linds, you're brave to have the wake here at the house. In a few hours you're going to have more than a hundred people streaming through here."

"That was what Ma wanted," I said, sliding one of the porch chairs out of its corner so Tara could sweep. "All the grandchildren and neighbors and friends. A good old Irish wake, she called it. She didn't want her grandchildren creeped out by having to go into a funeral home with bodies lying about in coffins. Ma always believed you've got to feed the grieving, and a little drink doesn't hurt, either."

"Looks like there'll be plenty of both," Tara said, brushing the debris into a dustpan. "Your neighbor Nancy recruited all her friends to cook, and the Red Hatters are coming with desserts, I hear."

"Which just leaves booze." I hugged myself. I had volunteered my brothers from upstate. "Think the brothers can handle it?"

"The McCorkle brothers?" Tara tossed her head. "They know their way around a bar. It'll be fine."

As Tara dumped the dust into the kitchen trash, I found the woven India print mat in the closet and lugged it out. "This will help fill the space on the porch," I said.

"And we can open up the table and push it toward the center of the room," Tara said as Steve joined us, his hair wet and fresh from the shower.

"Help us with this stuff, will ya, sweetie?" Tara asked, and he hoisted the heavy mat onto one shoulder.

As we worked, Tara asked about my book. "I'm glad it happened while Mary Grace was still alive to see it," Tara said. "But I have to tell you, it makes me nervous to think that my life is going to be on display for the world. I still hate the way my father plays to cameras."

"I'll get you a copy of the galleys to read," I said. "Trust me, I didn't give up anything personal," I added, hoping it wasn't a lie. Had I gone over the line? Had I revealed any personal secrets of Tara's? At the moment, my brain felt too compressed to recall my own story.

"Did Mom get to read it?" Steve asked.

"Her eyesight was going, so I read it to her," I said. "We finished two days before she died, and let me tell you, I was reading fast in the end. Calida, the hospice worker, had warned us that Ma was going into systemic failure. I wanted to finish before she slipped out of consciousness."

"That's speed-reading for you," Steve said, with a laugh.

I laughed along, but my giggles quickly turned to sobs. "I just wanted to finish," I said, recalling my mother's approving smile as I sat at her bedside reading.

"Aw, Linds . . ." Tara touched my back gently, and Steve swept me up into a bear hug.

"It's okay to cry," he said. "You did it all. You did everything for her in the end, and we're all grateful for that."

I let myself cry on his shoulder, thinking that the tears would subside one of these days, that it would be time to move on with my life, a thought that truly terrified me. I wanted to tell Tara and Steve that I'd just lost my mother and my boyfriend and maybe my job, and I wasn't really sure how to start rebuilding my life.

Instead, I could only manage, "I'm going to miss her."

With a rigorous crying jag behind me, I felt ready to face the mourners two hours later with a glaze of peace and good humor. I bounded down the stairs, surprised to find Darcy Love helping my brother Tim McCorkle set up a drinks table in the dining room.

It was difficult to look at Darcy, her skin gleaming and blond hair sparkling as if she had glitter in her genetics. Even in a black tank dress, she looked stunning. Gorgeous as always, while I had given up trying to cover up the red blotches that always appeared around my eyes when I cried.

"Hey, you." Darcy stepped up to the stairs and waited as I slowed at the landing. "I was hoping we'd have a chance to talk before the masses arrive."

"Looks like the first wave is here," I said, scanning the downstairs. "That's just the McCorkle family, though I think our numbers rival a small army. I'm trying to avoid my sister-in-law Ashley, who seems to think we pulled a Kevorkian on Ma."

Darcy rolled her eyes. "There's one in every family."

"I think she's in the kitchen." I nodded toward the front door. "Let's get out of here before they make us serve ziti or hand out mass cards."

Outside, we wound around the house and found a shady spot in the garden near the shed. The old stone table held half a crate of impatiens, their stalks leggy and yellow, bending to withering pink buds. "Ma never finished with these," I said haltingly.

Turning toward the shed, Darcy disappeared and returned with a pair of potter's gloves, empty pails, and two spades. "There's some potting soil in the shed. Here, I'll be lefty," she said, tossing me the right glove.

"So, Martha Stewart, besides repotting impatiens, what's on your mind?" I asked.

"I know this might sound self-centered," Darcy began.

"Who, you? Self-centered?" I gasped with mock surprise.

"However," Darcy continued, "I keep thinking back to that summer when my life was falling apart. I mean, my parents are still alive and healthy, but my father was going off to jail and my mother went off to a younger man and a very different life that didn't include me. And we were losing the beach house. And the Visa card. And all the status. There wasn't enough money to finish college, my boyfriend was marching off to fight fires, and then I found out I was pregnant. Remember how I cried in my salad?"

I shook a plant loose from its plastic container, recalling those days well. "You were so freaked about your father's reaction to the pregnancy," I said. "And remember what Tara said? 'The man's in the big house for fraud; do you think morality is actually high on his list?' "

Darcy smiled, a dimple showing on one side. "I was such a mess. But you guys pulled me out of it. You gave me a place to live. Your mom helped me so much with Maisy. Elle loaned me the money to finish school. And then she bought the damned Love Mansion and turned it into our summer spa." Darcy swiped a strand of hair out of her eyes as she pressed a flower into its new pot. "You guys saved my life. And I know this is different for you, but I want you to know I'm here to help, in any way."

"I think I know that." Slowly, I tapped the spade against the table to remove some dried dirt. "But I have to admit, I was pissed at you for a while." I caught Darcy's eye. "The Noah thing."

Darcy shook her head. "I am so sorry." When I waved her off, Darcy lunged forward and grabbed my arm with a soiled glove. "I mean it. I never went after him. Whatever developed between us, it just happened. Sort of work related."

"I felt so stupid when I had it pointed out to me. I didn't see what was going on before my own eyes."

"But nothing was going on," Darcy insisted, slamming a spade against the stone table. "And I was guilt ridden just because of what I was thinking about him."

With a deep breath, I looked down at the spade in Darcy's hand. "I think you've knocked that one clean, Darce."

She let the spade drop onto the table. "Are you still mad?"

"Nah. I went from mad to jealous to just a little envious of what you guys have going on. There's real chemistry between you," I said.

"I know what you're saying, but I'm not sure Noah feels that way." Darcy stripped off the garden glove. "He hasn't made a move. I didn't even know you guys broke up until Elle told me the other night."

"Are you crazy? He's totally into you. I've seen it myself."

"Well, he's holding back pretty well."

I potted the last plant and swept soil from the table with my gloved hand. "Maybe he's waiting a respectable amount of time after the breakup with your friend." I burst out laughing. "What's a good cool-down period? A year? Two?"

Darcy snorted. "Go on, laugh! The pathetic part is, that I'd wait that long for Noah." She pressed a hand to her forehead. "I should be embarrassed to admit that, but somehow I'm not. It's just that there's this connection between us." She shrugged. "It works. Like your morning latte or yoga three times a week. You just know what works for you. Have you ever felt that way about someone?"

"Aaargh, a million years ago, back in the stone ages, in the days when you really were self-centered." Conjuring memories of Bear, my surfer guy, I fell back on a bench and motioned Darcy beside me. "You've changed a lot, Darcy. I think Maisy made you grow up fast."

"We've all changed," Darcy said, sitting beside me. We leaned against each other, our heads touching. "You know, I used to think my life would come together perfectly when I met the right guy. Big mistake. I didn't realize that life sort of assembles itself in bits and pieces, in stages. And it's my friends who really did the assembling. The romance thing—that relationship can only happen when you've pulled yourself together. And who helps you do that? Your friends."

"Maybe that was why things didn't work out for Bear and me," I said, my mind still stuck on his image, that broken-tooth smile, dimples, flashing blue eyes. "I still think about Bear, you know. He was the one who worked for me, my morning latte."

"What's he up to? Is he still surfing?"

"Living in Hawaii. Married. Probably has a boatload of little hula dancers by now."

"The bastard."

I leaned forward to look at my friend. "Promise me that you

won't let Noah slip through your fingers. It would be really pathetic for both of us to end up as old maids."

Darcy smacked her shoulder. "Nobody says old maid anymore. We're independent women of the new millennium."

"Promise me," I said sternly, relieved that Darce and I had cleared the air.

"Okay."

"And now, I hate to say it, but I'd better get inside to meet and greet," I said reluctantly.

"Yup." Darcy stood up, tugging me by the arm. "Come on, old maid, time to wake the dead."

Overall, it was a fairly good party, or so I thought as I squeezed into the kitchen. Attendance was huge, with people overflowing from the house into the yard and gardens, food from the neighborhood ladies was delicious, and the grandchildren set up a table in the attic where they began to sort through Grandma Mick's old photos to make a collage for everyone to see at the funeral mass.

I tried to be a good hostess, despite my awkward track record. At one point Nancy handed me a plate and ordered me to load it up and eat before I withered away to nothing.

"Like that'll ever happen," I muttered as I sampled Mrs. Giorgetti's lasagna and Nancy's sesame pork roast from the buffet table. I was about to take my first bite when the image hit me like a flash.

There he was, standing in my living room, three-dimensional and in vivid color.

"Bear?"

I dropped a piece of Mrs. Washington's cornflake-fried chicken back onto the plate and tore out of the dining room to where Bear, Steve, and Skeeter were talking beside the old stone fireplace.

"Lindsay." Bear put his beer on the mantel and turned to me with open arms, and suddenly the face I'd memorized so long ago was a reality before me.

"Bear!" I hugged him but quickly pushed out of his arms to make sure it was really him, not some trickster in a mask or body double Steve and Skeeter had brought in to put me over the edge. "What are you doing here?"

"What do you mean?" He lowered his head, that familiar flicker in his blue eyes. "I came for you, Linds. When Steve called, I knew I had to get back here."

Emotion welled up inside me at a crazy rate. I wanted to know everything at once, then realized this was not what it seemed. Bear had gotten married. He lived in Hawaii. "How've you been?" I said, trying to bring my excitement down a notch. "How's your wife? Is she here?"

"Theresa?" Bear touched the top button of his tropical print shirt. "She's not here. Actually, she's not my wife anymore. It didn't work out."

"Oh?" I gushed with hope. "Sorry," I lied, trying to sound more sympathetic.

"Didn't Steve tell you?" Bear asked.

"No!" I slugged my brother in the arm. "He omitted a few updates. Like the fact that you were on your way." I punched him again.

"Ow, enough already." Steve stepped away from me, rubbing his upper arm. "What am I, a voice-mail service? You two figure it out." And he and Skeeter went off to get some food at the buffet table.

Once I had Bear all to myself, the two of us engaged in a rapid-fire game of fill-in-the-past-eight-years, why-don't-ya? Later that night, as I lay in bed, I tried to remember our conversation word for word, but could only bring back the most eye-opening segments.

"Hawaii . . ." I gushed. "It must be beautiful."

"I fell in love with those islands. Of course, I made the classic mainlander's mistake of thinking that I could live in paradise. My wife and I spent a year living with her parents in a one-room shack in Hana, this little one-shop town on the backside of the Haleakala Crater. The beach was magic, but the house was a dump. It's the way a lot of islanders live in Maui. The dream just doesn't match up with the reality."

"But you're still surfing in tournaments?"

"Got my last one next week, then I'm done. When things fell apart with Theresa I moved back to Kahului, Maui's main city. But after the competition next week, I'm packing up and moving back to New York. Going back to school for my MBA so I can get a real job."

"You're going to school?"

"Don't look so shocked. I got my bachelor's degree in Hawaii. I can read and write, Linds." He cocked his head, curiously. "I have a mind, Linds. Are you saying you just loved me for my body?"

"No, but . . . well, what do you want to do with all that education? I mean, workwise?"

He explained that he'd be consulting with the sporting goods company Steve worked for. "They'd like to hire me full time for their water sports division, but I need to have the graduate degree first."

"So you'd be working with Steve?" I asked, sensing that many conversations had transpired between my brother and Bear. When I got a chance, I was going to strangle my brother. "That's great. I know he missed you. We all did." *I can't even say how much*, I wanted to add.

"I never stopped thinking about you, Lindsay. I'd start to do stupid things and I'd hear your voice, a blast of sanity, saying, 'Oh, come on, you big jackass.' "

"That must've pissed off your wife."

"It was a short-lived marriage. My fault," he said. "I never gave it my all."

I had heard some of the early, predivorce details from Steve, but I wanted to hear everything all over again from Bear, in his own words. "I can't believe you're here." I poked at the shoulder of his suit jacket. "And real. Solid."

"Hey." He rubbed his shoulder. "I gotta say, after all these years, in all my wildest fantasies, that was not how I imagined you'd touch me."

"Well, give me time!" I laughed out loud, a rich, gutsy laugh that I thought I'd lost. "That's probably inappropriate for a wake." I pressed my hands to my mouth. "I'm sorry. I've never thrown a funeral before and I think the stress is getting to me."

Bear grinned—a wide smile that revealed two perfect front teeth. I had loved him when they were chipped; now, I felt my knees go weak at the sight of that grin.

"Oh, God, this is crazy," I said aloud. "You're older, more mature. We both are. You're not the guy who left here eight years ago." *The guy I fell in love with . . .*

"I sure hope not," he said, wincing. "I'd like to think I figured a few things out in that time. You know, mellowed and matured." He tilted his head to the side, studying me carefully. "And you've changed, too, squirt."

"There's less of me."

"Not just that. The outside package is similar, but inside . . . more intricacies. And still that same big heart. You always did feel the weight of the world, and you were never afraid to knuckle down and take on some pain if it meant helping out a friend. You were like the anchor for all of us. You're the one holding the rope so that dozens of stir-crazy boats don't trail off into the abyss."

"Really?" It was not the way I saw myself, especially not since I'd gone "underground" to take care of Ma, but it wasn't a terrible role. The anchor. A person to come home to.

And this time, this anchor was going to reel Bear in.

91

Tara

As she picked up some paper plates that had scattered in the wind, Tara had her intended target in her sites—one Ashley Sinay McCorkle, first-class bitch and troublemaker, hell-bent on raising a stink over the way Mary Grace had died. Ashley had been going around trashing Lindsay to anyone who would listen. A bad move.

In her work as a mediator, Tara patiently let people air their grievances. Today, however, Ashley had stepped over the line, and Tara was not going to stand for bad behavior. Time to sanction Miss Ashley.

"I'm telling you, I think someone should be investigating this," Ashley was telling two of the neighbor ladies, who seemed uncomfortable with the conversation as they removed trays of spinach tarts from the oven. "I talked to that hospice lady and she told me that my mother-in-law was never given an IV. No fluids, no feeding tube. It's downright inhumane, that's what it is."

Tara remembered that Lindsay had never taken a shine to Ashley, though she didn't recall why. Now, after five minutes of hearing the woman whine, it was all coming back to Tara. "Ashley," Tara stashed the paper plates and stepped into the fray, "can you just take a chill pill on this thing?"

"So I'm supposed to sit back while someone murders my husband's mother?" Ashley said, her tone rising to a shrill pitch.

"Pipe down, there," Elle said, coming in from the screened porch with Darcy. "No one was murdered."

Darcy shook her head in dismay. "And this is not the most appropriate conversation for this day. This is supposed to be a celebration of Mrs. Mick's life, not a bitch session."

"I'm just stating facts," Ashley said, her beautiful pale eyes afire with fury. "Mary Grace was cut off from food and water in the last two days, and that's what killed her."

"First of all," Elle stepped forward, into Ashley's line of vision. Having spent a good deal of time with Mary Grace, she was the most informed on her medical condition. "I saw you talking with Calida, and she didn't really say that Mrs. Mick was cut off. Didn't she mention Mary Grace's living will, and her own end-of-life plan? Her wishes? Didn't I hear her mention that Mary Grace might not have even survived the procedure required to insert the feeding tube?"

"When someone is sick, they don't always make sense," Ashley said. "You can't kill them just because it's part of their final wishes."

"Ach!" Elle slapped her forehead. "Do the letters D.N.R. mean anything to you?"

"I know the difference between right and wrong," Ashley said, folding her arms across her chest. A closed gesture, Tara had learned in her study of negotiation.

"Do you know that Mary Grace was diagnosed with stage four pancreatic cancer?" Elle went on. "Do you know she was receiving palliative treatment for pain? Do you know any of the facts?"

Ashley's eyes closed to slivers as she scowled at Elle. "Who the hell are you, anyway? You're not even in this family."

"That's it." Having lost patience, Tara snapped her finger at the offensive little twit. "Her name is Elle DuBois, and she's more a part of the McCorkle family than you will ever be, especially if you go on dredging up what's done and questioning Mrs. Mick's own requests for her life and death. Let me ask you, have you reviewed a copy of the will? Are you aware that she had a living will that designated Lindsay as her medical care proxy?"

"I don't care about the legal details," Ashley said. "This is a moral issue."

"Okay, Miss Morality," Elle said, having recovered her bearings. "If you're the great moral gauge, tell me, where were you when Mrs. Mick needed a ride to a doctor's appointment? Were you here when she needed someone to wheel her down to the beach? How about when she wanted lunch or someone to read her the newspaper? Where were you?"

Ashley lifted her chin defiantly. "Just because I couldn't be here doesn't mean I don't care. I have two children to raise."

"They're teenagers!" Tara said. "You could've hooked them up with Easy Mac and spent an afternoon down here, if you really wanted to."

"You're not going to make me feel guilty because I wasn't here," Ashley said. "You're just ganging up on me."

"And you're beating up on our friend," Darcy interjected. "Lindsay's been through a lot these past few months, and we're not going to let you make it worse."

"So let it go," Tara said.

"But I—"

"You heard her, drop it," Elle added.

"Am I not entitled to my opinion?" Ashley asked, lifting her pretty chin pompously.

"Sure you are," Tara said. "Just don't be sharing it with anyone else."

Just then Lindsay bolted into the kitchen, her cheeks bright pink. "Oh, my God, did you guys know Bear is here?" She pointed out to the living room, bouncing up and down like an Olympic track runner before the race.

"I thought that guy looked familiar," Elle said.

Tara smiled. At last, the reunion Lindsay had been waiting for. "Steve was supposed to tell you he was coming. With everything going on, I guess he forgot."

Lindsay did a little happy dance, then paused and stepped back when she noticed Ashley. "You look like you've just seen a ghost."

"More like the Hamptons mafia," Ashley muttered. But when Lindsay waited for her to explain, Ashley just clamped her mouth shut, grabbed a tray of spinach puffs, and marched out into the dining room.

"What got into her?" Lindsay asked. "I've been avoiding her all day, but now she seems to be derailed from her campaign."

Elle put an arm around Lindsay's shoulders as Tara and Darcy looked on, trying not to snicker. "Let's just say your friends took care of business," Elle said with a mischievous wink.

92

Darcy

Although Darcy had never been inside Noah's apartment, she had seen the address often enough on production schedules to commit it to memory.

West Sixty-fifth, just off Columbus.

Lindsay had once mentioned that Noah's apartment was surprisingly comfortable, with a view of the Lincoln Center Plaza and "very livable" furniture inside. Although Darcy hadn't been able to reach Noah by phone, the stage manager at the theater had told her Noah had taken the night off, so she took the subway, the number one train straight from Penn Station to West Sixty-sixth, counting on him being at home.

Her hunch paid off, and he buzzed her up.

Her quick impression of the apartment was that it was cozy but disheveled, the tables and floors littered with newspapers and magazines, crumpled receipts and paper coffee cups. Noah's honey gold hair was wild, as if he'd been raking his fingers through it, searching for answers that didn't exist.

"Darcy . . ." His eyes burned bright and round without his usual glasses. He scratched the stubble under his chin, as if trying to deflect her interest. "I thought you were out in the Hamptons."

"I thought *you'd* be in the Hamptons," she said pointedly.

He frowned. "I couldn't do it," he said, turning away.

"Don't tell me, let me say it. You aren't planning to go to Mary Grace's funeral."

He went to the window, staring out at the lights of the city. "How did you know?" he said, then, "I forget, you know me so well."

"Yes, I do. You're the reason I came back to Manhattan tonight." She moved to the window behind him. She didn't touch him—it seemed wrong to go there now—but she remained a presence, his conscience, his connection to the rest of the world. Below them Lincoln Center was alive with color and light and opera patrons skirting past the fountain shimmering in the center of the plaza. When she was a kid her class had attended an opera at the Met, there in the center building with its colorful modern art, sweeping staircase, and majestic chandelier. Although she'd been prepped with the story of the *Marriage of Figaro*, Darcy remembered feeling somewhat lost, in need of a translator to get her through certain sections. *What are they saying? What does it mean?* She'd felt consumed with the emotion and yet lost at the same time.

She imagined that was how Noah felt every day, passionate and yet oddly disconnected. "You need to go to the funeral tomorrow, Noah. It's the right thing to do, for Lindsay, and for you."

"I know, it seems uncaring, but I just can't face her, knowing the pain she must be feeling . . . and that I've probably contributed to it."

"Don't flatter yourself," Darcy said, only half joking. "Your share of the pain is just a smidge at this point. But by being there, you can help, Noah. You can't ignore her now."

"I'm not ignoring her. I've sent my condolences, and really, why would she want a stiff like me at her Ma's funeral?"

"Because you're her friend."

He cut her a look, as if she'd shocked him. "Actually, idiot that I am, that never occurred to me."

"Well, you are. Forgetting about the dating and relationship stuff, Lindsay cares about you, and I know you want the best for her. You need to be there."

He raked his fingers through his hair with a sigh. "I do. You're right, I do. How did I make such a mess of this? I was a terrible partner for Lindsay, and now I'm sealing the deal by acting like a royal ass."

"Just be there tomorrow," Darcy said. "You're a brilliant director, Noah, but right now, you're in need of some life direction. Let me help you."

He lifted his eyes hesitantly. "Ever directed before?"

"No, but I'm very bossy, and I love to give orders."

"Perfect," he said. "Although you may not want to be seen with a schmuck like me. People talk, you know, and the media swarms around a rising celebrity like you. I'd hate for you to lose your chances with someone else. Someone better."

"Finding someone to go out with is sort of like walking through a ballroom full of balloons in stiletto heels and trying not to pop the balloons." The words flowed so easily, it took her a moment to realize that they were not her own, but a line from one of Noah's scripts.

"Brilliantly stated," he said, his eyes glimmering with a hint of amusement.

"Yes, isn't it?" She tipped her head to the side and smiled, allowing the full rush of emotion for Noah to sweep through her. It was okay to like him now; okay to love him. "And you know what? I think I've finally gotten across that ballroom without popping a single balloon."

He nodded, his hazel eyes awash with understanding and a touch of intrigue. "I'll see you tomorrow, then," he said. "I'll be the one wearing black."

She let herself laugh as she walked to the door. "Aren't you always?"

93

Lindsay

"Crematorium . . . where did that word come from?" I asked my brother Steve as we walked up the drive of the graveyard. "It sounds like a place where they churn butter. Or maybe a factory where they make creamy bisques and chowders. Not a good name for the kiln where they fire up—"

"Enough, Linds," Steve interrupted. "Some of us don't have rock-hard stomachs for this stuff. I still cross myself when a hearse drives by, and I find graveyards extremely creepy."

"You big baby, it's not a graveyard, it's a crematorium," I reminded him, although Green River's complex actually contained both funeral plots and cremation facility. It seemed a little weird to actually leave my mother's body here, but Ma had chosen cremation, not wanting to take up all that land and have a place her children felt obliged to visit. Some of the McCorkle offspring had reacted in horror in the family meeting when the question was raised as to where the ashes would go, with Steve shaking his head like a twisted bobblehead and Tim insisting that cremation was unnatural. But still . . . Ma's wishes were being carried out, and here we were, filing into the stately brick building with molded cornices known as the crematorium.

It was a balmy, rainy day, one of those East Coast summer days with humidity that grabs you by the collar and squeezes. I was feeling a little better now that the mass was over and we'd made it to the last stop in the funeral proceedings. So far I'd shed a few healthy tears but had resisted breaking into heaving sobs—my goal for the day.

The funeral director, a precise but flavorless man named Doug who wore a tasteful black suit, assembled the family outside the door, explaining that friends were already gathered inside. As he passed out a long-stemmed rose to each woman, he instructed that she place it on the coffin as she walked by. *A little creepy*, I thought. *Ma would have wanted us to keep them.* I could hear her remarking, "What's the use in burning a perfectly lovely live flower?"

At last, Doug let the family file into the single vaulted room, where youthful voices rose, singing a capella. I blinked. We hadn't paid for a choir.

I turned and saw a youth choir, dressed in deep royal blue robes, each kid's eyes fixed on the director, who rolled his head and swayed passionately in time with the music.

Who had brought them here?

Noah caught my eye, his lips straightening to a frown. An apology? Commiseration. And then, uncharacteristically, he winked at me encouragingly.

I felt the corner of my mouth wiggle up to a smile, but somehow tears stung my eyes as he breached the separation between family and friends to join me.

"The Harlem youth choir," he whispered, "courtesy of Storm Productions. I hope you don't mind, but I know your ma would have detested another tedious batch of gladioli and carnations."

"A children's choir . . . Ma would have loved them," I said, squeezing his wrist as my vision clouded with tears and the children began to sing a four-part choral arrangement. "May the road rise to meet you, may the wind be always at your back . . ." I recognized the song, an old Irish blessing. Ma had a plaque with the words over her stove.

"Thank you," I said quietly.

He hugged me with one arm, the embrace of a friend. I considered it a good omen, a sign that we'd both moved on and could now meet on new terms. "By the way," I whispered in his ear, "I hear that Darcy needs a ride back to the city when this is over."

Noah turned to me with a questioning look, but I just pretended to be focused on the minister, who was reading a prayer from his book. As the final ceremony went on, I stared at the coffin, the simplest pine box the funeral home offered—again, Ma's request. This was the end. I felt glad that I'd been able to be with my mother in her last days, but now, as Father Healy closed his prayer book and the funeral director was motioning the women to step forward and leave their roses on the casket, it felt wrong to leave Ma here, so cold. It was my turn to pay respects, and I stepped forward and pulled a silken petal from the rose. "Bye, Ma," I whispered, dropping the petal onto the smooth pine.

A piece of the rose, a piece of my heart.

I touched the smooth wood, reluctant to turn away despite the old Irish lore that admonishes mourners to turn away and never look back. I could almost hear Ma saying it with that air of superstition: "Turn away, turn away." But I couldn't bear to turn away, afraid of letting go, fearful of what would come next.

I felt frozen to the spot when someone touched my shoulder, not the cold hand of the funeral director, but a warm, familiar touch.

I turned and saw Darcy's open face, her blue eyes shiny with tears. "It's time, Linds."

Behind Darcy stood Steve and Tara, Elle, Milo, and Bear, their faces soft with grief. They stood arm in arm, my family of friends. As Darcy took me by the arm and brought me into the fold, I felt the heaviness slide from my heart like a thawing clump of snow falling from the roof. These people were my friends, my future. As they embraced me, I imagined that Ma was an angel watching over all of us, nodding and smiling.

When we stepped outside the building, the gray sky was spitting rain, a slow assault that promised to increase as the black clouds on the horizon rolled closer.

"It figures it would have to rain on the day of your mother's funeral," Elle said, popping open a black umbrella with *Truth and Justice* stenciled in gold. "Come under, I'll share," she said, motioning her friends closer.

Tara and Maisy ducked under, but I turned my face up to the splattering drops, not really caring if I got wet at this point. Rain, I could handle.

"I know why it's raining," Maisy said, her eyes wide. "Grandma Mick is watering the gardens from heaven."

"They must have some big-ass watering cans up there," Elle bellowed.

"Okay, does everyone know who they're riding with?" Steve asked. "There's extra room in the limo. Oh, and you need a cab!" he said, snapping his fingers at Bear.

"I hate to cut out now," Bear said, his suit jacket slung over his shoulder like a politician as he touched my shoulder, "but I have to head out to the airport and I wanted to say good-bye."

Elle grabbed Maisy's hand and tugged her back. "Onward and upward. We'll meet you at the restaurant, Linds."

With a perfunctory wave to my friends I followed Bear over to the overhang of the building. "You'd better come closer," he said, pulling me out of the rain. "It's starting to pour."

I reached for the crisp, rolled-up sleeves of his shirt. His arms were still strong, still the moderate heft of biceps there as I squeezed down over his elbow to his lean forearms. "I still can't believe you made it to the funeral," I said. "And that you're leaving already."

"I'm glad I did." His hands rested gently on my hip bones, as if they'd had a familiar place there for years. There was still so much to say, so many blanks to fill. Eight years—was it possible to back-fill a gap like that?

"Are you really coming back?" I asked. "I feel like you're this phantom passing through our lives. Casper the Friendly Ghost, the remake."

He laughed. "God, I've missed that sick sense of humor. Of course I'm coming back. I've laid my money down at Pace. Classes start in two weeks. Linds, I dread this flight. I don't want to go back today, but I'm committed to this last tournament, and I can't let my sponsors down. They've been good to me."

"You're a stand-up guy." We were leaning into each other, our lower bodies touching with savory sexual suggestion, and I wondered at the inappropriateness of wanting to throw my old boyfriend down and go at it in front of the crematorium. Well, at least I knew Ma wouldn't mind—as long as the grandchildren were spared the bawdy details. Trying to act as if I didn't care, I focused on a distant spot over his shoulder, the group of Red Hatters taking cover under a gazebo, talking to my sister-in-law Ashley, who was probably bitching about her personal stake in the estate. "Are you going to call me when you get back?"

"Don't play the casual thing with me," he said, pinching my chin and steering my face toward his until he caught my gaze. "There's still something between us, and I'm not going to let it go."

"Well, it's about time," I said, laughing aloud. "Eight years it took you, Bear."

"We both did a lot during that time," he said. "Maybe we were meant to learn other things from other people before we could be together."

"Maybe," I agreed reluctantly, though it was all a bit too Zen for me.

"I'll call you when I land in Maui, if you're going to be up late." Bear slid his hands around to my back, massaging between the shoulder blades. I breathed in the humid air, wanting to melt on the spot. "Hey, maybe you can pick me up at the airport?" he said. "That way, we'll be sure to connect."

"I could probably do that. Let me check my calendar," I said, wondering what I'd do to fill the yawning emptiness of the next few weeks. Rekindle my editorial job at Island Books. Close up the Southampton house for the winter. Vacuum the cobwebs from my Manhattan life. Start writing my next book. Throw fairy dust on Noah and Darcy. "Yeah, I guess I can squeeze you in."

He smiled, his newly capped teeth like two delicious Chiclets, so irresistible I had to lean forward and kiss this man I loved. Mourners and crematorium and ministers be damned . . . this time he was not going to slip through my fingers.

Epilogue

Southampton, Summer 2006

"So you're telling me that one of the characters in this book is actually Darcy Love?" My new fan Esther picks up a fat, lemony book from the stack and shakes it, as if expecting Darcy to let out a little "Peep!" from inside.

"Well, sort of," I answer, thinking how I just spent ten minutes explaining to Esther how *Greetings from Bikini Beach* was inspired by nuggets of truth from my life and character traits of my friends. I told her about rearranging and changing events, pinning in a plot. I told her that the character of Angelique was inspired by Darcy. But all she seemed to hear was that it was a book about Darcy Love.

"Is she here?" Esther's brows shoot up as she opens her eyes wide, fleecing the crowd. "I don't see her, dear. Oh, how disappointing for you. To be friends with a celebrity like Darcy Love and then she doesn't show up for your party."

"Tell me about it, Esther," I let slip. The whole party was Darcy's idea—her treat, actually—and could she make it? Well, okay, there was that film festival in Cannes, across the pond, but they do that every year. "You know, that's not the worst of it." I tap the shiny cover of the book with my fingernail. "I've got a bunch of friends featured in this story, and do you think any of them made it to this party? Not a one."

She gasps, as if sucking soup between her teeth. "Oh, bubbelah, I feel for you."

I fold my arms over my bulky middle, the new resting place for crumbs, folded hands, and tears, which seem to gush so easily these days. Hormones! TV commercials are the worst. A happy family at McDonald's or a whimpering puppy getting his kibble—these are all suddenly reason to blubber like an idiot. In fact, I feel the slight sting right now, heightened by Esther's gushing sympathy.

"Excuse me," Bear says in a robust voice. "I didn't mean to interrupt, but . . . were you going to buy that?" he asks Esther.

"I'll take three," Esther says, opening the first copy to the title page for me to sign. "Autograph this one to me, dear. The others, I'll give to my girlfriends. They could use a good kick in the fanny."

I sign away as Bear places a hand on my shoulder and leans close. "Your brother and Tara are here. I sent them to get drinks, seeing as it's their first time out without the baby."

As I nod I see them crossing the lawn, Tara's gauzy cinnamon orange skirt blowing around her slender legs as she smiles up at my brother. "We weren't planning to have kids, certainly not so soon," Tara confided to me when they'd returned from Tokyo six months ago. "This little baby, well, sort of an oops, but now that it's happened, we're really happy. It's like this big decision that's been weighing on our future sort of sprang itself loose. Decision made." Two weeks ago, my niece Rachel came into the world with alert hazel eyes and a walloping yelp. At last, I got to use my childbirth-coaching skills, reminding Tara to breathe and helping her stay on her feet and walk through the contractions until she was properly dilated. "Better you than me," Steve kept telling me. That unenlightened brother of mine.

After we exchange hugs and Tara and Steve make the appropriate fuss about my book, Esther emerges from the fringes. "Which one are you in the book, dear?"

Tara cocks an eyebrow at me. "I would be the reluctant friend who shies away from publicity because her father has a high-profile career in the limelight," she tells Esther. "Basically, I'm the one who doesn't want to be in the book."

Esther laughs. "Delightful. So, which one is that? I want names, dear. Details."

"That would be Dinah, the voice of jurisprudence," I answer. "Believe me, you'll recognize her when you read the book."

Then Milo and Raj join us, regaling us with tales of the backups on the Long Island Expressway, which is typical weekend traffic, but for some reason it's always the topic of conversation in the Hamptons.

My new best friend Esther is spinning a tale for Milo about her belly-dancing lessons when Elle hoots from behind me, and she's jumping up and down under the blue and white striped awning of her house, waving like a madwoman trying to park a jumbo jet. She kicks off her shoes and runs across the lawn. Behind her, Judd walks with dignity, pausing to pick up her discarded high-heeled sandals.

"The LIE is a parking lot!" Elle shrieks.

"So we heard," Bear says, squeezing my shoulder.

Elle bounds over and pulls us all into hugs, curtsying before Esther as if she'd just been crowned queen of the Hamptons. Then she makes a show of embracing the huge stack of books in front of me. "You're buying a copy, sweetie. I see TV potential here," she tells Judd, who graciously accepts the book and shakes my hand and warmly congratulates me for my success. "I've been tooling around with writing since high school, but I've never gotten anything published," he tells me. "Congratulations."

"Well, I've never had a script go on air," I respond. "That's gotta be a thrill, too."

He nods. "The first time, I guess it was." He flips through the book, the pages turning rapidly. "Elle tells me she's in here. At last—" He kisses my book. "The manual. Does it explain why she jumps on my back and calls me monkey chum?"

"I'm afraid that's not in the book," I say. "I could reveal the origins of that behavior, but then I'd have to kill you."

"Just my luck," Judd mutters, grinning.

"I told you they'd come," Bear whispers in my ear, and I want to hug him and flick his ear for always being right. The baby kicks inside me, reminding me to be nice to her daddy, and I feel that secret thrill to know that the tiny amazing life growing inside me is the result of our love.

"Didn't I tell you your new book was a great excuse for a party?" a familiar voice calls from behind me.

Enter Darcy Love, a slender, sparkling blonde, growing impossibly more beautiful each day as she approaches thirty. But I no longer hold that against her, and she kisses Bear's cheek, then beams a smile at me.

"You made it!" I reach up for her and we hug, not one of those kiss-kiss air-blow things, but a real bone-crusher.

"How's it going, little mommy?" She rubs my back as she looks down at my tummy fondly. "Maisy can't wait to babysit."

"Where is she?" I ask.

"I sent her down to the beach. We saw those girls playing in the surf and I figured she'd find them more interesting than the old farts up here."

I follow her gaze down to the beach where Maisy walks the path through the dunes, her blond hair blowing in the wind off the ocean, her thumbs hooked in the pockets of her denim skirt in that way-cool gesture of a kid trying to make an impression.

"Is Noah here?" I ask.

"He had to stay on at Cannes, but he sends regards." She bites her lower lip and folds her arms across her chest, flickering the fingers of her left hand, where a diamond catches the sunlight and explodes with refraction.

"Darcy!" I grab her hand, my mouth dropping open over the glimmering pear-shaped stone. "When did this happen?"

"Just yesterday," she says, a little breathlessly. "I've been dying to tell you guys, but I kept my cell phone off so I could save it for today."

"I'm thrilled for you!" I say, and I mean it.

"Congratulations, Darcy," Bear tells her. "You two seem to make each other very happy."

"Spoken from the voice of experience," Darcy says. "Did I ever thank you for coming back and saving my friend Lindsay here from herself? She tends to get way too analytical when you're not around."

Bear puts a hand on my shoulder. "It's a tough job, but somebody's gotta do it."

"Stop it, you two, and let Darcy show off her ring." We call the others over, and they flip over the news. Milo shares his blue sapphire "commitment ring" from Raj, and Esther asks Darcy if she ↄn have an "exclusive" on the engagement news.

"Well, sure," Darcy says, patting the bony woman's shoulder. "I'd love that."

After Esther puts her empty glass down and runs to the house to phone it in, Darcy asks, "Do I know that woman?"

"That's Esther, writer of the Beach Buzz column, and she's partied with the best of them. One of the original Hamptons party girls," I tell her. "She once attended a gala event right here, when your parents were hosting."

"Really?" Darcy looks toward the house. "Party on, Esther."

The conversation turns to weddings, since there now seem to be a few in our future. Judd and Elle are planning a New Year's Eve event at Tavern on the Green, a winter wedding, where guests can ride through Central Park in hansom cabs and share stories by the big old fireplaces.

Darcy and Noah haven't had much time to plan, but they're leaning toward a summer ceremony in the Hamptons. "Somehow, that just feels so right."

Bear and I aren't quite as organized. "I'm thinking about a double whammy," Bear tells our friends. "We've found a priest willing to do a wedding and baptism all on one morning. That way we can maximize everyone's time and throw one hell of a party."

What he isn't saying is that we're waiting for his first marriage to be annulled so that we can have a Catholic ceremony.

Another secret that our friends don't know is that we went to city hall in Brooklyn around seven months ago and said our vows before a judge. It was Bear's insistence that brought us there, his worry that something might happen to him and the baby and I would be left without his insurance and benefits. Smitten by the fact that he wanted to take care of us, I was happy to sneak off to my own wedding, saying "I do" during my lunch hour and between Bear's final exams. Somehow the secret quality adds an element of danger and romance.

"Is that a cat fight?" Bear asks, pointing his chin toward the beach.

Everyone scrambles toward the bluff for a better vantage point of the beach, where one of the girls is running with a bucket, tossing bursts of cold water onto the others. Girls scramble off the blanket, sand flying as they flee.

One girl stands up to the water fiend, hands on her denim-clad hips. I recognize Maisy, jabbing a finger toward the girl with the bucket, who promptly slaps water onto Maisy's feet.

"Meeoow!" Steve screeches.

"Girls are so vicious with each other," Judd says. "I'm glad I'm a guy."

Elle pushes his shoulder. "Yeah, me, too."

"They're just playing," says Tara, the mediator.

"They couldn't be worse than we were," I say.

Darcy purses her lips, then leans back with a wicked grin. "Give them time."